Zephyr's Flight

The Dragons' War–Book 1

By Ray Strong

if
Impulse Fiction

Zephyr's Flight
The Dragons' War–Book 1

Ray Strong

Published by Impulse Fiction, Pleasanton, CA

Cover Illustration:
Donna Harriman Murillo and S. C. L. Benini

.

ISBN: 978-0-9863599-4-1
Library of Congress Control Number: 2025909357
LCCN Imprint Name: Impulse Fiction, Pleasanton, CA

Dedicated to:
Marina, Yuri, Veronica, and Elizabeth

My brightest stars are you.

Other Books by Ray Strong

The Dragons' War	*Available On*
1 Zephyr's Flight	May 12, 2025
2 The Wounded Sky	June 16, 2025
3 The Book of Chaos	August 11, 2025
4 Aeterna's Wings	October 2025
5 Angel of Death	December 2025
6 The Storm Queen	February 2026
7 The Empress's Winter	May 2026

Hope's War	*Available*
1 Home: Interstellar	Amazon Now
2 Pandora's Razor	Amazon Now

Contents

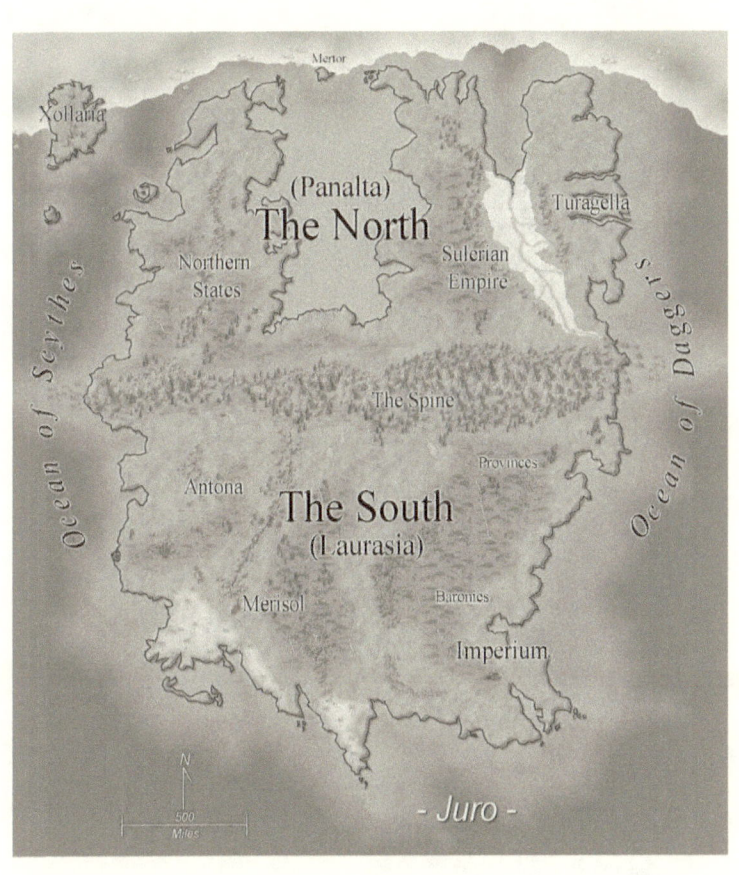

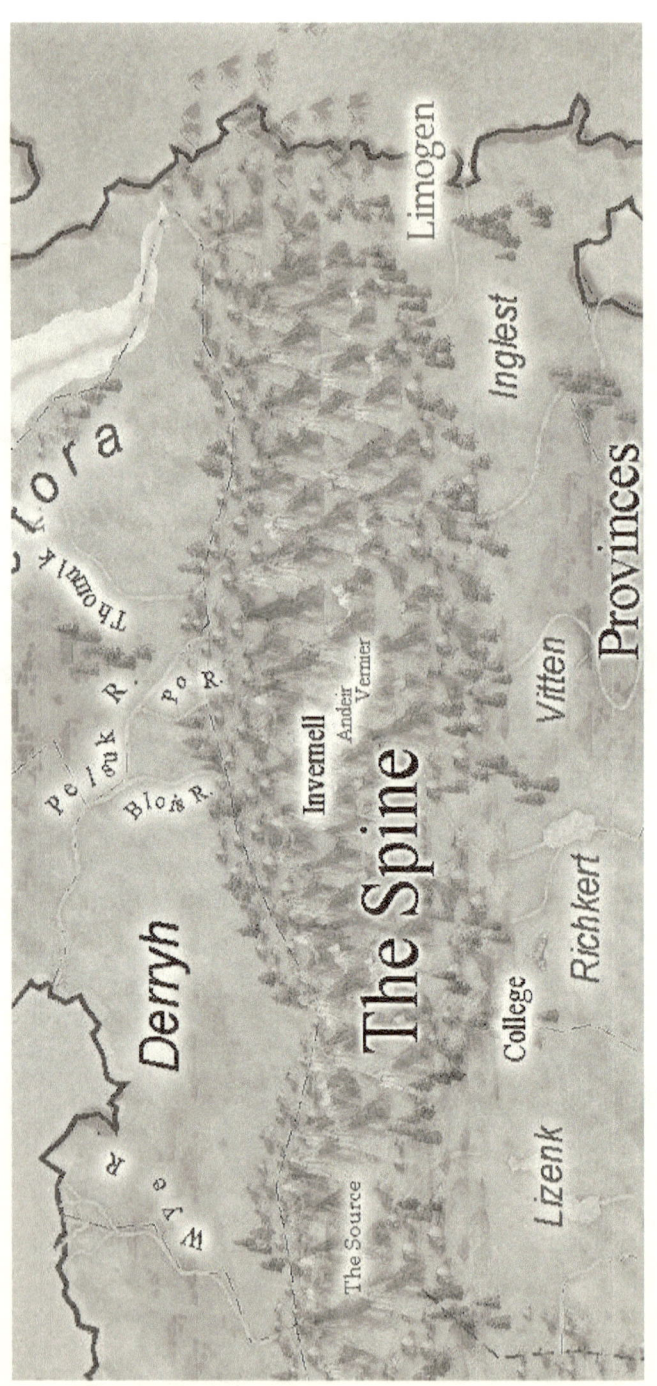

From "The Singer's Oath"

There was History before history,
When Juro wore our civilization like a crown,
And women flew like birds.
A time when we knew the ages of the stars,
Before we forgot who we were . . .

Now we know nothing of this History but myths and
fairy tales.
But ignorance of it does not mean we can escape it.

"The Singer's Oath," v.2/s.4

Chapter 1
The Oracle Comes

A thousand years after the Wandering, 10-year-old Astria Sannfjaer learned her world would end.

The news came with the rattle of grax skulls and chicken bones that called Astria to the split door of her tiny cottage with her sketchbook. There, along the cobbled path to the village center, came a cart pulled by donkeys whose eyes were painted with the heavy brows of hawks. And Astria sketched them in charcoal.

On the cart rode the Oracle of the Seers in a linen toga, her gray hair braided and curled across her shoulders and waist like a dragon's tail. Around her neck hung a chain of wooden blocks with runes of sacred mysteries cut into them. Along her wrinkled arms, tattoos of spells and curses protected her from evil and influence.

From long willow branches at the back of the wagon fluttered paper kites fashioned after the dragons that soared above in the late afternoon sun. With her arms outstretched, Astria imagined she rode one.

In the Oracle's wake drifted scents of sandalwood and the dark capes of Seers. From among them came a girl perhaps a year younger than Astria, with a kerchief covering her eyes. At the split door of the little cottage, the girl held out a doll of straw with a skirt of wheat spikes the color of Astria's hair.

With nothing else to offer, Astria removed her favorite woven hair tie and placed it in the girl's hand to trade for the doll. The girl rubbed her fingers along the tie, grinned, and gave Astria the doll. She placed her palm on Astria's cheek and reached into her own pocket to offer a handful of wicker trinkets.

"Please," the girl said.

Astria's father joined her and took a wicker mandala from the collection. "Thank you. That's all we need."

A Seer dragged the girl back to a procession of adults and children with beaded hair, their ghostlike faces covered in chalky clay. Bones of small animals and colorful feathers dangled from sticks lodged in their belts.

"Who are they, Papa?"

"Druims," Jorie said. "They're Seers who venerate the dragons."

Astria's mother, Skye, leaned over and dropped her voice. "They say they're witches."

"They haven't been to Invernell for years," Jorie said.

"Why do they come now?" Astria asked.

Jorie smiled. "Let's find out." He gave each of them a stick of fragrant stenifer and hibiscus. After lighting them, he opened the lower door, took their hands, and joined the villagers who followed the Druims.

At her father's side, Astria walked in sunbeams as villagers nodded with respect for him, a Rider of dragons.

Past small, thatch-roofed cottages of stone and wood, the procession of Farmers in coveralls, craftspeople with leather aprons, and women in pinafores marched to finger drums and pan flutes. Along their path, Seers and acolytes brushed leaves from the shrines and trimmed the overgrowth around the rune stones. As they passed, the shutters of craft halls and taverns slammed closed, hoping to avoid an evil eye from the Oracle.

The procession stopped at a stage beneath a red canopy of stenifer branches. There, acolytes in sackcloth sprinkled incense into a firepit from which blue smoke swirled. In turn, the Seers and Druims filed past, leaned over to inhale the smoke, and took places by the stage. To one side, the musicians sat cross-legged. Opposite them, Seers led the Oracle to a chair adorned with flowers.

The dry leaves of fall crackled underfoot as the audience arrived and made way for Jorie near the front. From the edge of the stage, Astria's friend, Yana, waved for her to come.

Astria turned to Skye. "Mama?"

"Go, hon," Skye said.

Behind the stage, children donned capes of green and red to match the trees or deep brown with fox ears. Like five others, Yana wore a colorful outfit with long sleeves and a grotesque, horned mask.

"Hurry," Yana said and handed Astria a similar costume of even brighter colors. "Our dragoness is sick. Put this on."

"They look like dragon colors," Astria said as she slipped on the costume.

"That's the idea. And yours is the female, Aeterna."

"What do I do?"

"Wait here," Yana said. "When I wave to you, enter and flap your arms." With a thumbs-up to an acolyte, the flutes stopped, and when the rhythm changed to a heartbeat, the Oracle spoke.

"Welcome to a time beyond remembering, when everything under Helios was born," the Oracle said.

On cue stage right, a child held high a bright yellow circle the size of his head, while other children in dragon costumes followed Yana onto the stage, their long sleeves fluttering like wings.

"Dragons are the children of the Worm," the Oracle began, "born at the Source when time began. From their birthplace deep within the highest peaks of the Spine, they flew over Juro to instill order for Goddess Fairma. Dragons are elementals, at one with the rocks and the sky. We know them by their actions, for actions do not lie.

"Dragons were the first. And after they tamed the Worm of the World, other plants and animals appeared: forests of pine and stenifer, butterflies and flitterbies, wolves and graxes, and after them, humans."

The other children joined onstage, each portraying a tree or prancing about like animals.

The Oracle continued. "Among them, dragons live in a state of grace, at peace with all life on Juro, except man. From the seasons to the cycles of the three moons, the dragons keep Juro in balance and everything as it should be. Under their protection, all life prospers. But that will not be forever."

One at a time, the boy holding the yellow circle of Helios eclipsed it with other disks representing the three moons—one larger than Helios and gray; another smaller and white; and the third smaller yet and red. As the rhythm of the finger drums slowed, a black lace curtain fell across the stage, casting the actors in a dull red. The children dressed as trees wilted, and Yana and the dragons lay down to sleep. Around them, acolytes in black robes jabbed spears at the animals as the clouds hid the sun.

"Chaos will come to threaten all life on Juro, and dragons must rise to defend it," the Oracle warned.

"But they cannot defeat the Darkness that brings the End Times without Aeterna."

Yana waved to Astria, who fluttered among the cowering animals and sleeping dragons. In the audience, Skye and Jorie smiled.

The Oracle said, "Together with Aeterna, the dragons will defeat the Darkness so Juro can live in harmony once more."

The dragon actors rose and pushed the spear carriers offstage. And as they tore down the dark lace, the trees and animals came back to life, and a gust fluttered their costumes.

High above the stage, dragons circled. When they hummed, Astria's eyes rolled back. Her jaw went slack, and she stood with her arms wide. The stage and actors faded from her awareness and the fall day disappeared.

In a vision, she flew with the dragons above, chasing the sun west to the horizon through orange-and-yellow clouds, thrilled with the freedom of flight.

River of White asks Young Sun of my fate,
And Moon asks Old Sun if I am the last,
But Sun does not answer our questions.

The setting sun turned the sky red, and she swooped low over the glaciers. Blood stained the pristine snow as men in heavy furs screamed like animals and hacked at one another with axes. As she circled lower, the shadow of her wings swept over them, and she roared, but they did not stop.

"Blood," Astria whispered onstage. As the audience and the Oracle stared at her, the winged costume slipped from her shoulders, and she fell to her knees.

Through grumbling Farmers, Jorie and Skye ran to her.

"Asti?" Skye said and took her hand, but her daughter only moaned and trembled. "Astria!"

Jorie picked Astria up and hugged her tight.

"I'm cold, Papa," Astria said, shivering in his arms as they hurried away.

In a clearing a half-mile past the cottages and craft shops, where Lake Norven discharged into the Blois River, Skye spread a picnic blanket.

"You saw the glaciers?" Jorie asked as he built a fire.

Astria sat and hugged her knees, watching the sun drop behind the high cliffs surrounding Invernell Valley.

"When the dragons hummed," she said. "What does it mean?"

Jorie shook his head. "Nothing good. We don't use weapons like that anymore."

"It felt old, Papa. Like the memories of someone long . . . gone." She shivered again.

"Dragons live much longer than people do," Skye said and handed her chestnuts from a basket.

"Much older than any dragons we know," Astria said as she scored the nuts for roasting, but stopped and turned to Jorie.

"Papa, will the Darkness come?"

"The Oracle sees further ahead than we can," Jorie said.

Her mother scoffed. "No one knows the future, hon. What we care about is a good harvest and food on the table."

"What if we can wake Aeterna and stop the Darkness before it comes?"

"You'll have to find her first," her father said.

After placing the chestnuts around the fire, Astria lay back and watched the dragons fly west and smiled. One was her father's dragon: Klokbror, her first friend, the first mountain she climbed, the first island she circumnavigated, and the first to sing with her. And even at hundreds of feet, his wings hid the moons.

"Where do they go, Papa?"

He looked up. "To find a vantage for the sunset. It's still daylight where they fly."

Astria sat up straight. "Teach me to ride, Papa. And I can fly with you."

"Tell her," Skye said.

Jorie shook his head. "We'll begin when—"

"They won't let her."

"They won't be able to stop her," he said with his jaw set. "We'll begin as soon as I return."

Astria frowned and threw a pebble to splash into the river. "Where will you go?"

He sat by her side and tipped his head to the glaciers of the Spine. "North."

"Do people live there in the Wild where Klokbror hunts?"

"No. It's too hard to live outside the valley," he said and put his arm around her. "But that's where the wonders lie. To the west are the glaciers and the crystal spires that rise from them. Beyond lies the Source where dragons go to die."

His eyes gleamed as he spoke, and Astria captured his face in her sketchbook.

"Wise kings live farther to the west and evil ones to the south. And to the far north live fierce barbarians who will make a necklace from your ears."

From her vision, images of ferocious men in animal skins came to life in the fire, and she jumped when her father pinched her ear. He pointed east where the brightest stars of the winter constellations gleamed through the twilight.

"To the east, the Worm of the World, whose spine forms our mountains, dives into the Ocean of Daggers and leaves his back-plates in a sea of islands." Jorie held out the silver-gray half coin that hung from a cord around his neck. "And that's where I found this."

Astria touched the intricate reliefs that sparkled in the firelight. "What do the runes mean?"

"I'm not sure," he said and held the coin near her nose. "But if you look close, this might be the sun and these plants." His smile disappeared. "The Seers believe it has something to do with the failing harvests."

Astria dropped her gaze. "I don't want you to go, Papa."

He glanced at Skye. "I must. But I'll be back soon." His words did not cheer her, and with a finger, he turned her head back to him. "When I come home, you'll ride."

Above the peaks, two moons set, and the stars glittered as bright as candles. Jorie pointed to the sky.

"See the star above the constellation Nidhogg, the dragon? That's your wishing star."

She whispered, "How do you know?"

"Because our stars are fixed there next to yours," he said and hugged her again. "Olim willing, you will ride. And when you do, the world will never be the same."

"How, Papa?"

"Together, we'll explore the world from coast to coast and meet kings and emperors. And everywhere we go, everything we touch will change." His eyes glinted as he pinched her nose. "But first, you'll need a dragon."

Chapter 2
Dragons

As the ghosts of three moons crossed the sky, Astria dangled her legs over the riverbank and hummed to the murmur of the rapids. At the iron scent of blood, she stopped humming and sat motionless.

"Come where I can see you," she said, patting the grass by her side.

Next to her right leg, a claw the length of her forearm dug deep into the thawing soil. Even so, she did not turn. A mottled, blue-and-green jaw followed, then a glint from a fang that could tear her in half. Above her, a melon-sized eye changed from milky brown to pearl. Seven times her length, the monster lay by her side with his head on his front paws, mussing her hair with a puff.

This was not Klokbror, for he disappeared with her father on their last journey five years back. Every week after, Astria came back here to their picnic spot by the river and prayed to Fairma for his safe return.

But Jorie did not return.

Turning a page in her sketchbook, she ran her fingers across her sketch of him. And whenever she looked at his portrait, echoes came of his laughter and infectious joy—the joy that vanished from her life.

Though a stranger, the dragon's eyes sparkled as Astria scratched between his broken horns and kissed him on the nose. She leaned against his shoulder and hummed again, her back buzzing with the vibrations of his harmony. And as they hummed, a vision came to her of the sunset behind the high glaciers and the season's first thunderheads.

"Welcome, Vandrare," she whispered, although dragons could not understand human words. "So what brings you, Wanderer?"

The dragon inspected her as she combed the hairs on his neck with her fingers and watched them knit together like bird feathers. She gazed at him with hope, but he turned away, and she sighed.

Astria resumed her drawing and singing to the river, hearing only Vandrare's harmony until the click of rocks interrupted, and she turned back to the clearing. There, her father's friend, Efrin, pounded a stick into the dirt within an arc of sundial-stones. Sun-bleached leathers marked him as a Rider of dragons like her father.

Near him lay a young dragon she recognized by the jigsaw of earthy browns and greens: Agnarr, Efrin's partner. Nose to tail, she guessed him to be about thirty feet long, average for a dragon.

"Hello, sir," she said and rose to gather twigs and kindling to make a fire.

"No *sirs* here, Astria," he said and brushed the ash from the firepit. "Waiting for Skye?"

"Yes," she said as a branch tore another stitch from the pocket of her tattered pinafore. "Mama's at the Clanough." *Again.*

Her frown melted into a smile as a rabbit munched its way to the edge of the clearing. But from the corner of her eye, she caught Vandrare staring at it, too, his eyes turning pink and his lip exposing a fang. She stepped into his line of sight with her arms folded, glared at him, and shook her head. He moved to look around her, but she blocked his view again, and the dragon laid his head down. When she did not move, he sighed and turned his head away, but glanced back at her.

The rabbit hopped back into the forest, and Astria delivered her twigs and moss to the firepit where Efrin watched her and Vandrare.

"What?" she asked as she built a pyramid of twigs over the tinder.

"He's curious, not hungry," Efrin said. "Dragons don't hunt in the valley."

Astria turned to Vandrare, who peered back from under a heavy brow. "Sure."

"If he wanted a snack, you couldn't stop him," Efrin said and lit the fire with a strike of stones.

"Your dragon is tired."

A smile creased the tattoos around his temple, softening the aspect of his eyes from those of an eagle to a dove, and he chuckled. "You might say I'm *his*, for all the rein I have on him."

"I'll be a Rider, too, someday."

"Another dreamer. How old are you now?"

"Fifteen summers, sir. Why is that a dream? *You* ride."

"Have you found a dragon yet?"

She shook her head. "How will I know if they want to partner? Papa said he didn't know."

Efrin shrugged. "They seem to find you." A furrow creased his brow, and the eagles returned. "There are fewer now. When it's your time to choose, there may be no strays left to partner with."

"Why do they leave?"

"No one understands the dragons or why they wander," he said. "The Seers only mumble about the long winters." He leaned toward her. "Riding isn't as exciting as the tales we tell. It's a tough life—"

"For a girl," she said with a pout.

"Nonsense. Riders don't care if you're a girl. We need your skill. You need to know the geography better than the palm of your hand, be quick with a bow, and shoot true from a saddle. You'll spend hours scouring the peaks to keep the Quarajii scouts below the cliffs. That's why the Council expects a parent to train new Riders."

"My father is a Rider."

"Aye, but he's not here to train you." Efrin cupped her cheek with his big hand, and with a thumb, traced a pattern around her eye. "You'll need to be very clever to earn semaphores like his and mine," he said, tapping his fingers on the tattoos at his temple. "You'll have to convince the Council as well, and they're not your friends."

"My mother's on the Council."

"Skye is only one of twelve."

"Then how am I to—"

A blend of goose honk and elk cry interrupted, and Astria's ears tingled. Efrin stood with a hand on his sword hilt and scanned the sky, but he did not draw.

Over the crowns of pine trees flew a dragon with a broken brow horn, and with a gust, he landed next to Agnarr and Vandrare. From the new dragon, a fat young Rider dismounted and loosened the belt that constrained his riding gear. Behind him, his dragon panted, his head resting on his paws.

"Ho, Efrin," the new Rider said. "Flight Leader says you're to patrol the Northern Cliffs at five."

Efrin took his hand from the sword and glanced at the shadow on the sundial stones. "Then you're late." He pointed to a blood-rimmed slice in the Rider's thigh. "What happened, Huld?"

Huld twisted to inspect the rip in his leather britches. "Graxes. The North Pass through Kreer's Gorge. A pack surrounded a caravan and killed the lead horse. A few of 'em jumped me, and my dumb friend here came a bit late to the fray."

Astria jabbed the embers at Huld's insult to his own dragon and imagined the tattoos at his temples in the shape of snakes.

Efrin raised an eyebrow. "You don't seem grateful he saved your life."

Huld glared. "Like I said, he came late."

Efrin stood, and Agnarr stood with him. "Any sign of scouts?"

"No," Huld said. "I don't know why we keep up this routine. The Quarajii raiders haven't been a problem since the Northmen cut off the river valleys. My boy here is too dumb to recognize them, anyway."

Astria fumed. "He's smarter than you are. He doesn't think like you do."

Efrin smiled, but Huld crossed his arms and said, "And you know so much about them, smarty pants."

"I know Belastad disagrees with you."

Huld put his hands on his hips. "Is that right, Imp?"

Imp! "And you're too fat for him to carry," she said, immediately pursing her lips.

He glared at her. "And he won't carry your little arse, *ever*."

She jumped to her feet and matched his glare. "I will ride just like you."

"Yeah?" he said, aiming a finger at the mountains. "And what're you gonna do out there if a barbarian steals your nose for a souvenir?" He reached out to pinch her nose, but she pulled away.

Efrin stepped between them and faced the Rider. "That's enough."

Huld leaned around Efrin. "My kids will ride before you do 'cause your father won't be here to train you."

Speechless, she planted her fists on her hips, but tears glistened in the corners of her eyes.

"You don't have kids, Huld," Efrin said.

"Well, when I have one, he's still gonna ride before she does," he said and wagged a finger at her.

Efrin gripped Huld's shoulders and turned him away. "I said that's enough. Go. See to your wound. I'll scout the pass."

"But she—"

Efrin pushed him back. "Go. Now. Belastad will appreciate shelter before the rain starts."

Huld turned and whistled for his dragon. "Come, boy," he said, but Belastad only whistled back, turned away, and laid his head on his paws.

Efrin chuckled, and Astria stifled a laugh.

"Kid of an Elder, huh," Huld said as he walked to his dragon.

When Belastad and Huld flew away, Efrin returned to the fire, sat, and rubbed his knees. "Pay him no mind, girl."

Astria sat by him, her fists clenched in her lap and her lips pinched together as tears gathered. She caught his glance and knew what he would say: what everyone said after her father disappeared.

He laid his hand on hers. "We all miss Jorie, girl."

It hurt less now, but still hurt, and a tear squeezed out with a blink. "Thank you, sir."

"He's a good man, and I'm proud to call him friend."

She nodded, thankful he did not speak in the past tense as others did.

"Don't be hard on Huld. He's part of the same fraternity of brothers and sisters as your father."

"What did he mean about barbarians and the Northern Cliff?"

"It's our geography. Barbarians from the north are slowed by the hard climb and are easy to spot."

"Did you and my father fight them?"

Efrin smiled. "My grandfather was the last to fight one. We only see scouts and stragglers now, and a dragon is enough to warn them away. The big troubles to the north and south were hundreds of years ago. To the south, Vernier protects the valleys from the Imperium, and we patrol the Northern Cliffs to protect against the barbarians."

"Why?"

He added a branch to the fire. "The Imperator and the barbarians both promise slavery and death."

Astria set her jaw and added another stick. "We resist, and I will, too."

"Good girl," he said and stood. "Well, I'm off to patrol. Your mother knows you're here?"

"Yes, sir."

"If the storm breaks, head home. Remember, the spring rains began last night beyond the falls, and the water will rise with the snowmelt. Stay upland and don't hang about."

"Yes, sir."

"And don't wander into the Wild, or a grax may nip off your ears."

When Agnarr disappeared over the trees, she returned to the bank near Vandrare. Too far away for thunder, lightning arced over the glaciers, and the tart air of the approaching storm tickled her nose. The moons came to life and shone through the storm clouds that swallowed the snowy mountain peaks and smothered the glaciers.

But Skye did not come.

The fire burned down, and Astria folded the corner of her sketchbook page. Above, lightning flashed, and thunder echoed within the walls of the valley, and she leaned against the dragon for warmth.

But still her mother did not come.

With Vandrare by her side, Astria sang softly to the River.

> *"Beside the fire, mama sits smiling,*
> *watching the chestnuts roast,*
> *Hearing your stories of princes and fools*
> *Near a magical coast.*
> *We need you, Papa, to bring back our smiles,*
> *And ..."*

She closed her eyes as a tear traced her cheek.

> *"And help me befriend a dragon."*

She raised her eyes to her wishing star. "Please Papa, come home."

He lives, the river whispered.

"I know," she replied and tossed a pebble into the water.

A cry drifted above the whisper of the river. Beside her, the big dragon raised his head and turned his ears toward the sound. Between thunderclaps, the cry came again, but he made no move.

Curious, Astria stood and began following the wail upriver toward the falls. The cry became louder, but so did the river. One hundred yards upstream, she peered over the bank, and in a flash of lightning, found the cause.

At the bottom of the ravine, an ordinary, mottled brown-and-green dragon, only as long as she was tall, gazed up at her and squeaked. He held his right paw up, drawing her attention to an hourglass-shaped wound on his foreleg. Rising water trapped him on a small beach. Scour marks on each bank of the narrow cut left him no safe place to hide as the river rose higher.

"Fly!" she shouted, miming her words with her arms. The little dragon flapped his wings and jumped with powerful back legs, but could not escape.

"Can't fly?" she asked, but he cocked his head and stared at her.

Too small or too hungry.

No vines or tree roots protruded from the bank below, and claw marks marred the sandy soil.

And he can't climb out.

Far from the village center, the river would swamp the little beach before she might bring help. Without escape, the river would carry him through the Notch at the exit of the valley and over the waterfall to crash on the boulders hundreds of feet below.

Near the bank, she searched for something the little dragon might use to climb out of danger, but the forest held nothing she could carry. The darkening sky made her search harder, and she tripped over a thick vine buried under the leaves. With a rock, she chopped the vine until it broke free and then dragged it back to the river.

When she returned, the little one squawked and limped along the beach, his eyes glistening.

"Be right there," she called as the rain began.

She tied the vine to an exposed tree root, threw it over the edge, and peeked over. Below, the little dragon tugged on it but could not grip the wet vine with his claws. After the third failure, he lifted his eyes to her and honked.

With her back to the river, she wrapped the vine around her waist and placed her feet on the cliff edge. She leaned back and let the vine play out of one hand until she was nearly horizontal. Then she stepped off the edge. Letting out more vine, she placed each foot with care on the loose soil and gravel and lowered herself down.

I can do this, she told herself, but halfway down, she slipped on a layer of clay. Her body twisted, the wet vine slid through her hand, and she fell to the beach flat on her back, the breath knocked from her lungs.

Past blinking stars, a sparkling little eye gazed at her before the world turned dark.

Frigid water splashed on Astria's neck and woke her, and the drum of a hard rain beat in her ears. But when she opened her eyes, it was dark. As she rose on her elbows, a wing fell away, exposing her to the rain, the night, and a splitting headache.

The little dragon gazed at her with melon-green eyes, and when he honked, his breath warmed her.

"Zephyr?" she asked. She put a hand on his cheek, and his eyes sparkled. "Well, how're we going to get out of here?"

She frowned after surveying the shrinking beach. The river now flowed higher and angrier—not a whisper, but a roar of freezing cold glacier melt. The vine that betrayed her had blown out of reach.

"Help!" she yelled again and again until her voice was hoarse. As she waited for an answer, icy water swirled around their feet, driving them beneath the undercut bank.

A lightning flash exposed Vandrare, who sat across the ravine, unmoving, his eyelids half-shut.

"Help us!" she called and waved her arms.

The big dragon opened his eyes and stared directly at her. His stare pinned her feet to the rocky shore, and her arms stopped and fell to her sides.

Promise me, she heard in Vandrare's honk.

She glanced at Zephyr, who looked up at her with sparkling eyes. *Anything.*

Without breaking his stare, Vandrare honked, but his wings spanned too wide for the narrow gorge for him to reach them. Instead, he threw his head back and roared. Beneath him, the eroding bank collapsed, and he flew away.

The slide pushed the rising water to her side, forcing them deeper under the bank. Astria hugged her knees, and the little dragon snuggled under her arm, but flinched when his wounded leg rubbed hers.

"We can't give up," she said as water splashed over her toes. "Mama will get too sad." *But what can we do?*

In a break in the thunder, a faint call reached her over the rush of wind and rapids: her mother's voice.

"Astria!"

"Mama!" she called back.

Skye called again, but from farther away.

She'll walk away unless she hears me.

Wading into the river, she tried to shout again with her ruined voice. Desperate, she plunged her hand into the icy water for pebbles and threw them over the edge. When the torrent rose too high, she dug rocks from the bank and lofted them until she could lift her arms no longer.

Out of ideas, she kicked the river with her numbed feet and then quenched her raw fingers in the freezing water to ease the pain. The little dragon squeaked in distress, and in the gloom, Vandrare honked again.

A shadow appeared at the edge of the bank. "Asti?"

Astria waded into the frigid water and waved. "Mama!"

"Can you climb?" Skye shouted over the roar of rapids and the crash of thunder.

The little dragon sidled up to Astria, and she put a hand on his head.

"I won't go without him," Astria said.

Skye waved and disappeared.

Cold and wet, Astria returned to the shelter of the overhang and bit her fingernails. Eddies lapped at her feet, and she could sit no longer, so she stood with her arms crossed and the warm little dragon curled around her feet.

An eternity later, one end of a dead tree with broken limbs slid down the bank and lodged in the rocks. Astria gripped a branch intending to climb with the heavy little dragon on her back, but he managed to get his back legs on the lower branches and leaped to the bank ahead of her. At the top, he peered down at her and bleated.

"Up you come," Skye shouted.

Rushing water pushed harder on the dead tree, so only Astria's weight kept it moored. With her mother holding the tree steady at the top with both hands, Astria began to climb.

A flash of lightning lit a surge of water heading toward her, and Skye shouted, "Hurry!"

The rising water chased Astria up the tree. When she put a hand on the bank, her weight left the tree, and the torrent pushed the base from its moorings. As she fell, she gripped the overhanging grass, but it ripped away, and the torrent swept her away into the freezing water.

Surging rapids spun and pounded Astria on the rocky river bottom, and in the blackness, she could not regain her bearings. As her air ran out, panic gripped her.

Lightning flickered, and Astria swam toward it, breaking through the water's surface. She gasped for air, but another surge dragged her under. Battling for the surface again, she gulped water and never got enough air in her lungs to cough.

Finally, the water calmed, the rain ebbed to a drizzle, and Sister Moon, Elein, burned a hole in the clouds. Exhausted from fighting the frigid water, Astria rode the current to catch her breath.

But breathing would not be enough. Unless she found shore, the river would carry her through the Notch and over the falls.

Astria swam for shore, but each time she neared, an eddy pulled her back into the churning river. She reached for debris to support her, but branches and brush caught in the whitewater scratched her face and sank when she gripped them.

With the last of her strength, Astria swam for a floating log. The log bucked and cracked her in the ribs, and before she regained her breath, the river shot her over a cascade and under the water. Again, the beacon of Elein led her to the surface.

For a few moments, Astria floated on her back. She prayed, but before she finished, an eddy spun her and banged her head against a rock, and the river disappeared in a sea of stars.

She was warm now and without pain as she snuggled into the arms of her father and mother.

Teach me to ride, Papa—

Wake! Astria heard in Vandrare's roar.

Her vision cleared, and forty feet above the rapids, she flew, untouched by the raindrops that hung in midair around her.

Below, a young girl's body drifted face down in the narrow river, her skirt tangled in twigs and branches. The ravine widened, and when the body slowed, the dragon swooped low, grasped the girl in his claws, and flew her to a meadow. He gently laid the girl on the grass and sat beside her, his wing shielding her from the rain. Around them, Zephyr limped and hopped and then stopped to nuzzle her.

Skye ran to the girl and held her, weeping.

Let the girl live, Astria thought. *She did nothing wrong.*

The big dragon raised his head as though observing her flying above them. He honked, but Astria heard, *keep your promise.*

The next instant, she fell to the ground and into the girl's body. With a gasp, she opened her eyes, coughed twice, and threw up water.

"Oh Fairma! Thank you!" Skye cried and hugged her tight.

Awake now, Astria shivered in her mother's arms as Zephyr snuggled beside her. Vandrare dropped the back of his wing to the ground to shield them from the cold draft and laid his head alongside to warm them with his breath.

Brother Moon, Fures, rose, and a red fog drifted from the damp grass as Skye rocked back and forth with Astria in her arms.

"You scared me," Skye said and helped Astria sit up. Together, they leaned against Vandrare, who kept an eye on Astria.

Skye moved a lock of hair that lay over the wound on the girl's forehead. "Are you all right?"

Astria winced at the touch. *Keep your promise, he said. But what exactly did I promise?*

"Honey?" Skye said and put a hand on her daughter's cheek.

Was it a dream? Astria glanced at Zephyr and Vandrare and then remembered her answer.

Anything. And what does that mean?

"Asti!"

Astria nodded, unconcerned by her injuries. But in trying to say, "I'm all right," she forced out a honk. The dragons honked back, and she giggled.

Skye closed her eyes and hugged Astria closer. "We need honey for your throat. You sound like a dragon," she said as Astria snuggled under her arm. "I didn't find you at the meeting ground."

Pointing to the little one, Astria said in a gravelly rasp, "Zephyr cried out, and I had to help him."

Skye brushed her hand over Astria's hair to squeeze out the water. "How do you know his name?"

Astria shrugged as Zephyr sat by her side, laid his chin on her thigh, and gazed at her. *Can you be my partner?* she thought and scratched between his eyes.

A furrow crossed her mother's brow. "Well, I think we should call him Trouble. I followed the big fellow's honks to find you."

"Vandrare saved me, Mama."

"He pulled you from the river."

"I saw," Astria said.

Her mother cocked her head and frowned. "I thought . . ." Unable to finish, she squinted, and tears fell again.

"I woke when he honked," Astria said. She shivered, and her mother pulled her closer still.

Skye smiled at Vandrare and stroked his brow. "Thank you." His eyes sparkled, and she turned to her daughter. "Time to go home, sweetie."

Astria stood but wobbled and leaned a hand against the dragon. She took her mother's arm, and they headed home, followed close behind by Zephyr.

Halfway home, moonlight from Elein and Fures blinked through dissolving clouds, and Astria raised her eyes to the sky.

Thank you Elein for showing me the way.

The moonlight also shone on little Zephyr, who limped by Astria's side.

"I'm going to ride, Mama," she said and smiled at him.

"I don't think I want semaphores marring your pretty face."

"Really, Mama."

Skye frowned. "Your father disappeared in service to the Riders, and I don't want that happening to you." She closed her eyes, and a tear escaped. "I can't lose you both."

"I might help find him," Astria whispered, but Skye did not answer. "The day Papa left, you said 'they' won't let me ride. What did you mean?"

"The Council may not let you choose the path of a Rider."

"The dragons decide who rides them."

"But the valley can only support a few Riders. The Council decides who, and some of them are afraid."

"Afraid of what?"

"You have an affinity with the dragons, and—"

"Why would that scare people?"

"Dragons are powerful, dear, and we don't understand them. Many fear what dragons might do if they're led by bad people."

"But dragons never hurt us," Astria said and slowed for Zephyr to catch up.

Skye tilted her head and studied her daughter. "Some people don't trust dragons the way we do and fear them in numbers. And some of those frightened people are on the Council."

At their little cottage, Astria sat outside with Zephyr until Skye returned with an ointment and wet cloth.

"I don't know if this will work with dragons, but Philina swears by it," Skye said. "Wash the wound first and spread this on."

Astria treated the little dragon, and his eyes sparkled. Skye stroked the bridge of his nose, and his eyes changed from dark green to opalescent.

"We've not seen a little one like you for ages. But still, you need to go now," Skye said.

Skye turned to enter their cottage, and Zephyr took a step to follow. When she stopped, he sat and gazed up at her.

"Shoo, now," Skye said with a wave of her hand, and the little dragon lowered his head and backed into the woods.

Astria stood at the door and looked into the night. "I made a promise to help the dragons, Mama."

"And how will you do that? Dragons are the most powerful beings on Juro."

"I don't know," Astria said, smiling as little Zephyr rustled the bushes at the woods' edge.

Maybe just one?

The clouds opened and her wishing star appeared. She saved her wishes for what mattered most and wished again for her father's safe return so they could fly together.

The silhouette of a dragon crossed Elein, and Astria whispered to the night. "What if Zephyr could fly?"

Indeed, the trees replied, and hidden between them, the eyes of the little dragon glinted in the moonlight.

Chapter 3
Partners

A week after her ordeal with Zephyr, Astria sat in a clearing in the peach orchard amid the scents of honey and hyacinth. Her cracked ribs ached no more, and the wounds shrunk to scabs. All was forgotten.

Except for the dragon.

Zephyr followed her everywhere, including to the orchard, their spring classroom where Yana—in her best spring dress—hung the scrolls of runes and maps of their world from the trees. And in front of the twenty-eight children stood their teacher, Vinga.

"Many of you have been practicing your trade," Vinga said. "But for those of you undecided, head to the faire today and stop by each of the animals and craft displays. The Vederlofte is a few months away in the fall. You may not get the trade you wish, but it's better to declare your interest early."

But Astria lost interest and flipped to a page in her sketchbook where she imagined ways to help Zephyr fly, carried aloft by older dragons or jumping off a cliff. And she hummed softly as she sketched Agnarr carrying him on his back.

A girl in front of her put her hands over her ears. Another said, "Shush. That's annoying."

To Astria's side, Fynn, the new boy from a valley without dragons, smiled at her. She blushed and smiled back, but returned to her drawings and hummed softly.

A low harmony drifted from within the grove, and Astria turned to face six-inch fangs that glinted below melon-green eyes. He was small for a dragon, not quite two yards of mottled fur marred by an hourglass scar on his foreleg. A whack of his tail on a tree shook the overhanging branches, raining peach petals on the students.

Fynn gasped, leaning back with wide eyes as the beast raised a paw to expose a claw, the merest touch of which might kill him if he made a wrong move.

With eyes glaring pomegranate red, the dragon stood on his hind legs, opened his wings, and inhaled deeply.

"He's gonna fry you," Yana said. "Run!"

Fynn stood to shield the smaller children from incineration, closed his eyes, and cringed.

The beast brought his fangs to within inches of Fynn's face and knocked him onto his butt—not with flames, but with a blast of fishy breath.

Zephyr chuffed a few times, Yana doubled over with laughter, and Astria and the students laughed with them—all except Fynn, red-faced but unscorched.

"Psst," Astria whispered. "Dragons only breathe fire in stories. Everyone knows that."

Vinga folded her arms across her chest. "Thank you, uh . . ."

"His name is Zephyr," Astria said.

The teacher waved her hand as if to brush him back into the trees. "Thank you, Zephyr. You're excused."

The little dragon purred, his eyes opalescent. Humming a harmony to Astria's song, he backed into the peach trees and hid under a bough.

Astria ignored Vinga and gazed at Zephyr. *If he could fly, he'd not be here.*

She put her chin on her palm. *Oh, but if he could fly!*

A bell rang in the commons, and the children rose to leave. As the others left, Astria hung back while Yana waited at the edge of the trees.

Vinga frowned. "Your dragon doesn't belong here."

"He's not mine," Astria said. "Can I ask a question?"

"About your geography project?" Vinga asked as she collected the chalk tablets and scrolls.

Astria dropped her gaze. "No.

"Well, it's late. You'll need to finish before school is out, or I'll have to set you back."

"Yes, ma'am."

"And you'll miss the graduation party."

"I promise to finish."

"What's your question?"

"Do you know about dragons?"

"They're rather hard to know, dear. But I gather I know as much as anyone but the Druims." She smiled. "Zephyr seems quite attached to you."

Astria nodded. "When he's bored or hungry or sad, he finds me."

"What's your question, dear?"

"When do dragons learn to fly?"

"And why is this of interest?"

Astria pursed her lips and turned away.

"I can keep your secrets."

"I want to become a Rider."

"May I?" Vinga asked and held out her hand. Into it, Astria put her sketchbook. The teacher flipped through the pages and stopped at the portrait of Jorie on Klokbror's back.

Vinga smiled. "What did you use for the reds?"

"Ochre."

"I thought you might choose the practical arts." Vinga sat and returned the sketchbook. "If a Rider is your choice, it'll be a hard path."

"I know—training."

Vinga pursed her lips, and a crease appeared between her eyes. "You asked when dragons learn to fly. Nowhere in our oral history is there a dragon that didn't fly."

"Even when they're little? My mother said there hasn't been a dragon so small here for a long time."

"Even so, he could fly."

Astria's brow furrowed. "Will he die?" she asked, but kept her real question quiet: *And if he does, will that break my promise to the dragons, and end my life as well?*

"Dragons are a mystery, dear," Vinga said. "And keep their secrets. But you know that even if he flies, he may not partner with you or your friends."

Astria twisted her lips. "I know. Is there an elixir or something that can help him?"

"The Seers have potions for people, not dragons. They have one that will help you not care."

Astria shook her head. "But I want to care."

Vinga smiled, and the wrinkles at the corners of her eyes softened. "Perhaps, in time he, will fly."

"How much time?"

Vinga stood. "That's dragon business, child, and not ours," she said and tied the scrolls and tablets together with a belt.

Keep your promise, echoed in Astria's head. "Well, it's my business now."

"Then the Seers might help. But don't expect an answer you can understand."

"Thank you," Astria said and turned to go, but Vinga stopped her. "And don't forget your geography project."

"Yes, ma'am," Astria said as she backed away.

At the edge of the clearing, Yana took Astria's arm, and they headed to the faire. "What did she say?"

"She said to ask the Seers. What about La'a?"

"My mother's with Getmordare guarding the caravans and won't be back until tonight."

Astria shook her head. "Then help me find the Seers, so you won't have to wait for me."

"I'm not waiting for you. Just don't get mad if I find a partner before you do."

Astria bit her cheek as Zephyr joined them. *And what'll I do if he never flies?*

***

In the late afternoon, strangers filled the fairgrounds near Lake Norven. Some traveled a week through the mountain passes for trade and entertainment, and others came to represent their valley at the gathering of clan councils—the Clanough.

Above them, a pair of dragons cavorted and squawked at each other. Without saddles and with the blue-and-white underbellies of all dragons, Astria could not tell if they were wild or partnered with Riders.

Unable to fly with his fellows, Zephyr walked at Astria's side, heedless of the scowls of Farmers. When the crowds became too thick, he followed in Astria's wake, but still the villagers stumbled over him.

At the faire's edge, Chairman Kendrick's dragon, Krigsmanen, napped as a dozen children climbed on his back pretending to ride. Every so often, the dragon half-opened an eyelid, twitched a muscle or shook a horn to knock them off, and then went back to sleep.

"And what are you doing here?" Yana asked the big dragon who replied with a side-eye. "The other dragons are all on duty."

"Kendrick is at the Clannough with my mother," Astria said and pointed to a tent that could hold scores of people. She patted Krigsmanen on the shoulder and kneeled beside Zephyr.

"Crowds aren't for you," she said, and Zephyr's eyes sparkled as she scratched between his eyes. "I think you should stay here with Krigsmanen."

Zephyr cocked his head, and his eyes returned to melon-green as he sat and turned away.

"He's too big for people," Yana said. "And too small for a dragon."

Astria frowned at Zephyr, but Yana dragged her away.

"Farming's not for me," Yana said as they passed the livestock pens. "I'll be a Rider." But Yana's interests were not the animals or the dragons. "Don't look. I think we're being watched."

Unable to resist, Astria raised her head and spotted two boys grinning from across the goat pens.

"What're they smiling at?"

"Us, of course."

Astria rolled her eyes and took Yana's sleeve. "Our goal is the Seers."

At the booths, the mountain clans displayed their finest crafts: glazed pottery from Vernier, rare metal tools from Andeir, and engraved weapons, all useful but too beautiful to use. But the finest were inlaid wooden furniture made here in Invernell, home valley of the master crafters of wood.

Wedged between craft goods hung household items and intricate embroidery. On a table lay scarves, folded into rose petals and dyed in the vibrant reds and blues of pigments unknown in Invernell.

Yana stopped at a table where vials and jars stood, each marked with the rune for love. As Astria tapped her foot, Yana sniffed a vial of love potion and leaned over to her.

"They've followed us," Yana said and tipped her head to the two boys.

"We're too young. C'mon. Our future as Riders awaits."

"I have a summer on you," Yana said with a wink and dragged her to a table of perfumes.

Astria crossed her arms. "Someone else picks our mates, and the Council approves or not. That's how they breed sheep."

"Better we pick before they pick for us." Yana put down the small bottle and smiled. "I will pick someone brave and handsome, and—"

"Focus," Astria said as she pulled Yana toward the footraces. At the finish line, Fynn and Jenks Kohout crossed in the middle of the pack, and Jenks waved to Yana.

Yana beamed at Jenks. "And I think I've picked."

Astria returned Fynn's grin with a reserved smile. *I've not.*

One boy who followed them approached, and Astria blushed at his attention. Fynn caught the look and shouldered him hard. The boy complained, and Fynn spun on him, pushing him to the ground. The boy's friend joined the fray, and Jenks tried to separate them. A few moments later, a Farmer intervened and set them on different paths.

"What was that about?" Astria asked, but Fynn scowled in silence.

Yana took Jenks's arm. "Come. We're heading to the Seers."

"Why?"

"To learn if our goal to ride is just a fantasy."

"I'll ride," Jenks said. "I have no doubt."

"Well, we do," Astria said. "Come."

The sky grew dark as the setting sun cast the valley floor and fairgrounds in shadow. There, far from the crowds, alone at the edge of the clearing, a single tent hung from the adjoining trees. To both sides, torches shone on the black flag of the Seers, and long sticks wavered as dragon-shaped kites fought for their place on the wind.

"There," Astria said and took Yana's arm, who in turn took Jenks and Fynn and dragged them to the tent. At the door of the tent hung a pennant marked with a rune for Jeluuk of the Nembs, goddess of *what is yet to come.*

Jenks resisted Yana's pull. "A fortune teller? I don't believe anyone knows the future."

Astria stepped inside and waved for them to follow. "Remember, it's bad luck to ask a direct question."

Astria furrowed her brow as she entered. Until now, her mission seemed clear. *But if I might truly know my future, what will I ask? Will Zephyr fly? Will he be my partner, or must I find another? Was my promise to the dragons a trade for my life? Will my father return? Is he . . . dead? Which question will it be?*

She wrinkled her nose at the thick incense that obscured the runes on fabric draped between the tent poles. And as her eyes adjusted to the dark, hanging talismans and weasel skulls emerged in the corners.

Yana jumped into Jenks's arms at the sight of a grax on its hind legs ready to lunge at her with teeth bared and claws out.

Jenks laughed. "It's stuffed, girl."

Across a firepit where coals glowed dusty orange sat a Seer in a toga with a red sash. Beside her, a girl-child wove bracelets without looking at her work. Around her wrist in the same pattern lay the hair tie Astria once traded for a wicker doll.

"Why do you come?" the Seer asked and waved to a bench opposite the firepit.

Astria looked to her friends. "To learn of our future with the dragons."

The Seer examined each of them. "Jeluuk has left your lives as the clay in spring, to be molded by the hands of Jerdani, goddess of *what is coming to be*. To tell your future now may fix it forever. Are you sure you want to do this?"

"Yes," they said at the same time.

"Put your palms out."

The Seer closed one eye to examine their palms and then raised her eyebrows. "It's often better to hope than to know."

"It's hope we need," Astria said.

The Seer nodded, dipped her fingers into a bowl of powder, and sprinkled it over the firepit. The powder twinkled in the lamplight as it drifted down and sparked when it touched the coals. And from them, swirled blue smoke with the woody tang of myrrh.

Astria's head spun as the firepit grew to cover the floor and the runes danced on the fabrics.

The Seer snapped her fingers and said, "Ask."

When Astria looked up, the girl-child faced her with closed eyes.

"Ask," the Seer said again.

"Where will the wild dragons be?" Jenks asked, his voice distant and muted.

"No one knows why they do what they do," the Seer replied.

Jenks narrowed his eyes. "But you know."

The Seer closed her eyes. "They follow the seasons to the Source."

"Will they return?"

"Only when you understand why they left," the Seer said and turned to Yana.

Yana blushed and whispered, "Is love in my future?"

The Seer glanced at Jenks and smiled. "Certainly."

"Soon?" Yana asked.

"You hold the answer to that question." The Seer turned to Fynn. "Do you have a question about your future?"

"Will we become Riders?" Fynn asked.

Yana frowned and punched him in the arm.

Creases appeared between the Seer's eyes. "Is this your heart's desire?"

They nodded, and the Seer closed her eyes. When they opened again, she faced each and flinched when she came to Astria.

The Seer sighed and looked to Yana, Fynn, and Jenks. "You three will ride, but only because of the little one."

"The little one?" Astria asked. "Zephyr? Will he fly?"

The Seer stiffened, and her eyes glistened. "Only when you know why he does not."

"And what of my promise?" Astria asked.

The Seer winced and stood. "I can say no more. Come, Angelica," she said, after which the blind girl-child picked up her cane and took the Seer's hand.

Outside the tent, Astria sat cross-legged on the ground, the chatter of her friends drowned out by the fog in her head and the roar of her inner voice. Above her, the moons shone bright in the sky, and she turned to the valley rim.

The Seer was in pain. Why?

"What did you promise?" Yana asked and sat at her side. "Was it important?"

"Only to me," Astria said.

"So, Zephyr will fly when you know why he cannot. The smartest people in the valleys don't know the answer to that question."

Astria kept her gaze on the glaciers. "Then it's up to us."

The moons rose as Astria considered what she might do, but no answers came until above her, a dragon and Rider raced past: Efrin and Agnarr.

"The Riders return," she said and took Yana's arm.

In the clearing by the lake, the dragons landed. Efrin and La'a landed first, followed by two more pairs with stretchers strung between them. The six dragons represented most types: with and without crests and frills, horns of various lengths, colors solid and mottled. All had protruding fangs, mouths like wolverines, and eyes like feral cats, and none of them were pretty.

When they landed, the dragons honked and pawed the ground.

"They're worried," Astria said, and Yana raised an eyebrow.

In blood-stained riding leathers, Efrin ran to them and clasped Jenks's shoulder.

"Run to the Clanough," Efrin said as he walked backward to Agnarr. "Tell Flight Leader Lothen and Chairman Kendrick the Andeir caravan was attacked. Tell them I'll rally the squadrons. And bring Philina and the healers. Hurry now!" he shouted as Jenks ran across the fairgrounds.

On his way to the dragons, Efrin stopped to speak to La'a, who had a bloody bandage on her arm. When he left, La'a waved to Astria and her friends.

"Help me with the wounded, kids," La'a said.

They followed La'a, where the Riders were unstrapping stretchers from the harness. Astria and Yana picked up the ends of one stretcher that carried an older man whose bloodless face shone in the moonlight. La'a led them to a merchant's tent and pushed the goods aside.

"What happened?" Astria asked.

"Later," La'a said as she lit lamps and hung them from the tent poles. She gave Astria a cloth to stanch the bleeding and then loosened a belt around the man's thigh. Blood squirted from the leg wound, and she tightened the belt again.

"Hurry, Philina," La'a mumbled and opened the patient's shirt.

Astria caught her breath at the clean slice across the man's belly and the open wound that exposed is innards. With wide eyes, she leaned away, but kept her hand on the compress.

Fynn and a Rider brought in a young man, who groaned with pain.

"There, Jerrick," La'a said, pointing to an empty space where Jerrick and Fynn put the young man.

"Best save your aid for the boy here," Jerrick said.

Jenks returned with Elder Philina and the healers, who nudged Astria and Yana aside to treat the wounded. Kendrick followed with the Seer and Angelica, who waved sticks of smoldering sage and chanted incantations.

A crowd of villagers formed outside the tent, and from them, a woman elbowed her way to the wounded young man. "Oh Tegbert! No!"

La'a took the woman's shoulders and pulled her away. "We'll take care of him."

The woman shook off La'a's hands and kneeled by the boy's side but glared back at La'a. "And where were you, brave Rider? You're supposed to protect us. And now my poor boy lies dying on your watch."

"We warned them not to take the North Pass," La'a said.

The woman stood with her hands on her hips. "You steal food from our mouths and then blame us, the victims," she said and swung a fist.

La'a dodged and blended with the missed strike as others grabbed the woman's arms.

"Where were you when my family risked their lives to feed you!" she shouted as villagers stepped between them.

"I'm sure she didn't mean that," Philina said.

"I'm sure she did," La'a said. "Get ready. Other wounded are coming by wagon."

Philina turned to Astria and her friends. "Run along now children. And thank you."

La'a hustled the children outside, but Kendrick stopped her.

"How did this happen?" he asked.

"A grax pack attacked a caravan along the North Pass from Andeir," she said and pointed to the older man. "That one led them along the trail, and the lead wagon found the graxes gnawing on him. When they tried to retrieve him, the pack attacked."

A healer pulled a sheet over the face of the man with the stomach wound and went to Kendrick. "The blade wound would have killed him even without the graxes."

Kendrick nodded and took the healer aside.

"Let's look at that arm," Philina said and led La'a to a stool outside the tent. As she loosened the bandage, Yana winced at the fresh blood dripping from the ragged tear in her mother's arm.

La'a took Yana's hand. "You've seen what can happen and why we do this. Do you still want to ride?"

"Yes, Mama."

"You'll still need a dragon," La'a said.

"That's why we're here." Astria said. "We were waiting for you." She glanced over to Zephyr, who squawked and honked as the dragons returned and landed.

"Zephyr can't fly," Astria said. "And I want to know when he will."

"They're a mystery, dear," La'a said. "But I bet you've heard that before."

Now what?

"Then how will we ride?" Yana asked.

From a pouch at her belt, Philina took a dab of ointment, spread it on La'a's wound, and bound it again.

"You'll need to bond with strays," La'a said.

Philina tied the bandage and stepped back to admire her work. "Leave that on for a day and see me tomorrow."

"Thank you," La'a said and tried to hug her.

Philina pushed her away. "None of that now."

A woman in a Miller's apron approached and took Fynn by the shoulder. "This is no place for you."

"We were looking for stray dragons, Mama," Fynn said.

"I have an eye on them, Jedaile," La'a said.

Jedaile held up Fynn's bloody sleeve. "Really?"

Philina turned to her. "They helped care for the wounded."

Jerrick walked up, wiping the blood from his stained leathers. "They're fine here, Jedaile. Don't worry."

"You look no better than the victims."

He smiled and opened his arms wide. "At a time when the Riders protected the valley from harm, I flew among them."

Jedaile frowned at the dragons who gathered and the others landing. "And the dragon . . ."

"Dragons would never hurt us," Astria said.

Jedaile put a hand on her hip. "Says a child. You might ask why they haven't already. Why do they hang around, anyway?" she asked and took Fynn's collar. "Come, Fynn. Now."

"Let me escort you home," Jerrick said with a slight bow from the waist.

"And I should trust our lot to you?"

"I insist."

A momentary glint lit Jedaile's eyes. "If you insist, then. Come, Fynn."

Astria turned back to Zephyr, who stayed with the dragons as Efrin landed with another squadron of Riders.

Skye hurried up to them, nodded to La'a, and raised her brow at the sight of Astria's bloody pinafore.

"There you are," Skye said. "Are you alright, dear?"

Astria took her hand. "It's not my blood, Mama."

A wagon rolled up next to the healers, and Riders ran to unload the wounded. Among them, Kendrick waved to Skye.

"I need to go, hon," Skye said and backed away. "Can Asti stay with you?" she asked La'a.

"Of course," La'a said and led Astria and Yana to the cobbled path. "Time for bed, girls."

"Zephyr wants to help," Astria said.

"He can't fly, dear. By the way, Vinga tells me your geography project is late. She can hold you back and stop you from being a Rider."

Yana inspected her shoes, but Astria smiled and said, "I have an idea."

That night in her dreams, Astria ran from the graxes that attacked helpless men and horses on the North Pass. In the shadows along the edge of the trail, a shadow thrust a sword at a merchant, the man whose stretcher she carried earlier that night.

The merchant fell to his knees as guts and blood spilled from the wound. And as he fell, helpless children huddled in fear as the graxes circled them.

"No!" Astria shouted and lurched upright in a cold sweat.

Yana sat up with her. "What is it?"

Astria described her nightmare. "You saw the wound."

Yana nodded. "The healer said a blade made it."

"People don't kill one another here. So who held the blade?"

Chapter 4
The Oracle Returns

The next morning, Astria rushed to the door as the rhythm of finger drums called them to the Oracle's performance.

"Come," Astria said to Yana. "Let's ask the Oracle if she knows how to help Zephyr."

"Or where the wild ones have gone."

Villagers crowded the field when they arrived near the end of the play. Within them, Angelica sat with one hand on the Seer and her other on Zephyr's front paw. At the sight of Astria, he sidled up closer to the girl-child to make space for Astria, Yana, and La'a.

As the acolytes reenacted the familiar play, Astria kept her eyes on the dragons that circled high above. When the dragons began to hum, an echo came of men in furs fighting on the glaciers under a blood-red sky, her vision the day her father left. The Seer turned to her, and Astria fought not to be swept away again.

When the play ended, the cast sat at the edge of the stage. The Oracle limped to the firepit, breathed the blue smoke, and sat with the Druims and the cast to each side.

The Seer stood. "Does anyone have questions for the Oracle?"

Half the audience raised their hands, but a Farmer stood.

"Why are the harvests poor?" he asked.

"Something comes," the Oracle replied. "Something we cannot avoid."

"What do the dragons say?" asked another.

"No one understands the dragons. But I sense Aeterna comes."

The Druims gasped, and the audience buzzed.

Near Astria, a Miller scoffed. "And the Darkness with her? What nonsense is this?"

The Oracle stood and raised her voice. "Dragons are the claws of Juro, elementals like wind and fire, the most powerful force on Juro. Aeterna comes because Juro is challenged."

The Miller waved his arm and sat again. "Bah, you Seers always say the end of the world is just around the corner."

The Oracle raised her voice and wagged her finger. "We warned you of the long winters, and you did not heed us!"

"Why fear Aeterna?" asked La'a. "She's good and loves humans."

"Aeterna loves humans because she *is* love," the Oracle said. "And like all dragons, she expresses her emotions through her actions and rips away the shroud of Darkness so we may prosper. It's not Aeterna we fear. But if Juro is challenged, what will happen to puny creatures like us? Without dragons to stop the Darkness, the End Times will come, and humans will become beasts again."

Anxious rumblings rose from the audience and drowned out La'a.

A Potter stood up. "You said dragons are at peace with everything on Juro except men. What do you mean?"

"Men lie, and dragons do not understand lies. Once, a human lied to the dragons and led them against humans."

"The Speaker?" the Potter asked. The Oracle nodded.

"What's a Speaker?" Astria asked, but the Oracle did not answer.

With closed eyes, Angelica turned to her. "It's not a what, but a who. The Nembs told us that a Rider once spoke to dragons and used them to enslave the world. To prevent it from happening again, Fairma took from us the ability to communicate with the dragons."

Astria shook her head. "If we can't communicate, how can a Speaker arise again?"

"Because humans are clever."

"Did the Speaker begin the Imperium that enslaved us?" Astria asked.

"Myths are never so clear," Angelica said.

"Did the Speaker bring the Chaos?" shouted a Farmer. "The Darkness?"

"Or is one merely a reflection of the other?" the Oracle replied.

Astria frowned. *She answered a question with a question. And what's the answer?*

As the Oracle spoke, the blue smoke drifted toward Astria, and the audience disappeared in the fog, leaving only the Seers and the Oracle. An echo returned of Astria's vision the day her father left.

"Men with spears fighting on the glaciers," she whispered, barely aware as she spoke.

Angelica turned to her with milky-white eyes and gripped Astria's hand. "Tell me what you see."

"An old dream when a dragon sang to me." Astria said no more, fearing they would call her mad. "Is the Darkness our past or our future?"

"Maybe both," Angelica said. "Perhaps it is what dragons fear."

"Does the Speaker bring the Chaos?"

"Myth upon myth? The Oracle does not know, and dragons cannot speak for themselves."

At Angelica's side, the Seer sat straight and stared past them into the night. "Long ago, when the race of humans was born, Jurdi of the Nembs, goddess of *what once was*, whispered her secrets to the Seers and gave them the torch of knowledge. But the flame has dimmed over time. The Oracle now sees the light only through the smoke."

The Seer stood and took the blind girl's arm. "Come, Angelica."

"But you are Seers," Yana said. "If you don't know, who does?"

"No one sees the future clearly," Angelica said as the Seer tugged her away.

"Does that mean the wild dragons won't return?" Astria asked.

A reflection caught her eye, and she turned to the Oracle's steady gaze. Though others spoke to her, the Oracle's eyes bored into Astria.

"That will depend on you," the Oracle said.

The spell broken, Astria woke to the eyes of the audience watching her. She blushed at the attention and scratched between Zephyr's sparkling eyes as he leaned on her leg.

But oppressed by the frowns and furtive glances, she stood and took Yana's hand. "Come. We have a project to finish."

And while the villagers and acolytes spoke to her, the Oracle looked back at Astria and raised a hand in blessing.

***

Two days later, Vinga knocked at the door of Astria's home. There by the fire, Skye repaired Jorie's spare leather harness.

"What brings you, Teacher?" Skye said and patted the stool at her side.

Vinga frowned and entered. "I worry for your daughter."

"Why, dear?"

"She's inattentive in class and spends all her time with her sketchbook," Vinga said as she sat by her side. "And that silly dragon pesters her constantly."

Skye stopped stitching. "She does seem childish, but I know she's learning."

Vinga frowned again. "I'm not so sure. She skipped school yesterday and today."

A deep crease appeared in Skye's brow.

"Britta saw her collecting flowers, of all things, and she hasn't submitted her geography project. This is the last day of school before the planting. Without knowledge of our mountains, she can't navigate to the neighboring valleys."

Skye parked the needle in a stitch and put her project to the side. "She hasn't declared to be a Rider."

"Yes, but she and that little dragon have a . . . special relationship. At the Vederlo—"

"Zephyr is too small."

"Yes, but—"

"Skye, come!" called Efrin from the doorway, wearing a grin that spanned his entire face. "Come! You need to see this. Vinga, you, too."

"Is this about Astria?" Skye asked.

"Just come," Efrin said.

Along the cobblestone path, Efrin led them through the village to the Manor House, where they plunged into a crowd. Through it, Skye followed Efrin as he elbowed his way inside the building to the north wall, past windows flung open to the sun.

Spring blossoms covered the long plank wall—blue hyacinths surrounding a field of ivy. Through the middle ran a wide stripe of gray-and-white poppies, splitting the green in two. Sprinkled through, tiny red, yellow, and blue petals stood out like wildflowers in a meadow.

And Astria stood in front of it with Yana and Fynn.

"What is this?" Vinga asked.

"It's our geography project," Astria said.

Vinga frowned. "Is this a prank?"

"Come."

Astria took a chair in one hand, and Vinga's hand in the other, and led her to the middle of the room. When Vinga stood on the chair and looked over the scores of heads, she stared, mouth open.

On the wall hung a map of the known world in flower petals. The map displayed all the villages of the mountains and the large countries to the north and south.

Villagers jostled the chair to get closer, and Astria held Vinga's hand.

"Is this us here in Invernell?" one asked, pointing to a small bluebell by the eastern edge of the white camellias.

"Winterthur and Vernier are here," Fynn said, pointing to two nearby flower petals.

"My cousin lives in Vernier," Yana added.

Above the white poppies of the Spine lay a field of green, and Astria pointed to it. "And Derryh to the north."

Vinga stared at the map and nodded. "And the Imperium to the south of the Spine."

"From where our ancestors escaped," Astria said, "Slaves and princes all."

Vinga smiled. "And the islands to the far south where we once ruled the seas."

A young boy stared with wide eyes and a frown at the big smear of red belladonna above Derryh, poised to bleed south into the mountains: Turagella, home of the barbarian Hordes of their nightmares, the Quarajii.

"Is Tur really so close?" he asked.

"Yes, child," Vinga replied, and the smiles vanished from the children.

Lothen stepped forward, and with a finger, pointed to the Spine just north of their valley. "And the Riders patrol the northern cliffs to protect us."

Philina pushed her way through the crowd. "Don't fear, child. It's not a real map." She fluttered a hand toward the wall. "See here? The northern oceans are free of ice and should be blue, not white. And the mountains are mostly green, not covered with snow. Take no mind of this foolishness."

The boy's mother grabbed him and gave Astria a disapproving glare. "Don't fret, Kel. The Qu can't enter the mountains."

"But what if they do?" he asked.

"If they do, the Riders will dispatch them."

"But what if . . ." The boy's voice faded into the crowd as his mother dragged him away by the arm.

***

At the edge of the map, Fynn leaned over to Astria. "Maybe we shouldn't have used red for Tur. No one wants a reminder of how close the Hordes live."

Yana pulled Astria close. "So, what did the Oracle say yesterday?"

"You didn't hear?"

Yana shook her head.

"No one heard," Fynn said.

How could I? "Another riddle to match the Seer's," Astria said.

"With no clue how to solve them," Yana said.

"Nice work," Vinga said as she approached with Skye and La'a. "Those are my old scrolls?"

"Yes," Astria said. "Did we pass?"

When Vinga nodded, Yana whooped and hugged Astria and Fynn. Then she took La'a's hand and dragged her away. "I'll see you at the party."

"What're you wearing?" Astria called after her.

Yana glanced at the door where Jenks waited, then turned back to Astria and grinned. "Something cute."

At Astria's side, Vinga shook her head in wonder and pointed to a sky-blue carnation on the continent's west coast. "Asti, what's this?"

"I don't know," Astria said. "But something should be there."

"Why, dear?"

"Something pretty belongs there."

Vinga took Skye's arm and smiled. "Your little girl dreams of the big world outside our little valley."

Skye nodded. "It appears you're a better teacher than you thought."

"Much better. She's added places I've not taught them about."

Villagers elbowed their way up to the wall and pointed out neighboring valleys where their relatives lived and exotic lands known only from stories. As they did, Astria wandered the sprawling Manor House, her fingers tracing the hand-carved columns that told the story of her people's flight from slavery hundreds of years before. Once seafaring warriors from the far south, the Imperator conquered and enslaved them, but could not hold them.

The carvings came to life for her in shadows cast by the afternoon sun, and she imagined herself one of the refugees who first found their valley, terrified their sanctuary was also home to the mythical beasts that could destroy them all: dragons.

As she dreamed, she hummed in harmony to a melody emanating from the walls. She whistled, and a moment later, Zephyr stuck his head around the Manor House door, and she waved him inside. He came to her, maneuvering carefully between the people.

When she pointed to a dragon in the oldest of the woodcuts, his eyes sparkled.

"These are your ancestors who made their home here. Born of the strongest and the wisest, born to greatness, you are," she said and smiled at him. "Do you already know?"

He could not answer, and she sat by his side and scratched between his eyes.

"Born to greatness, yet you can't fly," she said, but Zephyr simply gazed at her.

Astria glanced back to the thinning crowd where Skye talked with Flight Leader Lothen. He put a hand on her arm, but she brushed it away and leaned forward with her fists on her hips. After a few words, she marched toward Astria.

In the distance, a drummer marched the sun to set, and Skye grabbed Astria's hand.

"What was that about?" Astria asked.

"Time for your party," Skye said and dragged Astria out the door.

On the way to the party, they walked past craft shops and guildhalls jutting from cliffs and cottages facing the village trails, each with torches to light their way. As she passed, Astria ran her hands along the intricately carved doorways as she had in the Manor House.

"Who made these beautiful carvings?" Astria asked.

Skye's pace slowed, and she relaxed her grip. "These are older than your grandfather."

"What do they mean?"

"They chronicle the craft or family that works within. They're our history, like the Manor House woodcuts, the masterworks of our artisans. But these are personal. No one has time to carve like this anymore."

"Why not?"

"We're too worried about food."

***

Lanterns filled the clearing with light when Astria arrived, and in the middle, Yana danced with Jenks in a promenade for couples. It was spring, and Astria could no more stop herself from dancing than she could stop her heart from beating. So when Fynn offered his hand, she curtsied and joined him.

The next dances were from the neighboring valleys and left the locals laughing at their own clumsiness. Other boys approached to dance with Astria, but Fynn warned them away with a scowl, and she was having too much fun to care.

When the dances of Invernell finished, Yana and Jenks slipped away. More couples left the clearing as two of the three moons rose, and the music changed to ballads. One was a song of homecoming from a faraway land called Mimm, and Astria turned to the stage.

The singer wore a dress from Andeir, but the song came not from the mountain clans. A boy nearing four summers sat cross-legged near her, under the watchful eye of a gray-haired man.

Astria stopped, mesmerized by the beautiful voice, and hummed in harmony as dragons circled lower above them.

"Over the hill where he left me,
For a war that saved us from harm,
With love in his heart he returns,
And I open my heart and my arms.

"He walks not so fair on crutches,
The scar on his cheek so malign,
But he's home with the heart he left with,
And I welcome him home with mine.

"But my legs can't run to meet him,
And my cold lips can't kiss his cheek.
All I can do is nourish my grave
And greet him with blooms on the hill."

When the song ended, Astria frowned and took a step from the dance floor. Fynn misunderstood her intent and tugged her toward the shadows. But instead, she dragged him to the stage.

"Excuse me, ma'am," Astria said. "The dragons like your song. Where did you learn it?"

The woman smiled for an instant. "From a witch. At least, that's what her murderers called her. And what are you called?"

"Astria Sannfjaer."

"Mine's Merythe. Do you sing?"

Astria raised her head to the darkening sky as, one by one, the dragons flew away. "I only sing with the dragons now."

Merythe smiled and sat beside the boy. "And that's good enough for them, yes?" She patted a place by her side.

Astria sat while Fynn tapped his foot. "Did the witch live in Andeir?" Astria asked.

"Oh no. She lived in the provinces."

"No one here has ever traveled so far south."

A wistfulness crossed Merythe's face. "I followed my love there after the Elders exiled him."

Astria narrowed her eyes. "Through the Wild?"

Merythe nodded. "It was summer, and we were in love, heedless of peril and predators." She pulled up the hem of her dress to expose a long, ugly scar on her leg. "Neither of us knew how to avoid the graxes and still feed ourselves. And even in the summer, the nights are cold."

"How did you survive?"

"We nearly didn't. My teacher found us and nursed us back to health." Merythe gazed into the night. "My love was ever so much fun but no end of trouble," she said but then blushed. Her entire body seemed to sigh. "When he discovered I was with child, he left me."

Merythe told her story with the rhythm of a poem as the boy snuggled into her side.

"When I gave birth to Garath, my teacher served as midwife. She trained me to sing to comfort him. I only needed to promise never to sing near a village."

"And your song?"

"That was hers," Merythe said. "She taught me about singing and performing. She also taught me about the corrupt Imperator in the south and Suleria and Turagella up north."

Astria shuddered, and her ears twitched. "Where the Quarajii barbarians live."

"And the fiercer Turajii. She said she learned at a college."

"What's that?" Astria asked.

"I really don't know. She said they trained her voice there and taught her many things."

Fynn sat next to Astria, but she paid him no mind. "Where is it?"

"The foothills south of the mountains and west." Merythe raised her eyebrows. "But don't go there. All their gods have left them, and the people are vicious and selfish."

"Did she come back with you?"

Merythe glanced away. "She bewitched a lord but spurned him, and it drove him mad. At least, that's what the villagers claimed. They came to silence her and . . . murdered her."

She pointed to her collar and a small pin on which was stamped a line through two concentric circles.

"Before she died, she gave me this and said it would help me find my way." She sighed again. "After she died, I searched for the college, hoping they might take us in. For weeks, I searched but never found it."

"Did a dragon bring you back home?"

"No. They never fly south of the Spine. It was our good fortune my father found us. We were starving, but still I fought him to continue my search." Her eyes lost focus, and she smiled as if she glimpsed heaven. "I loved her like my mother and dreamed of the future she painted for us."

A glimmer of torch light reflected from a tear, but then she hugged her son. "But I love my Garath more, and the South is no place to raise a child."

Merythe stood. "Well, my boy must be off to bed now." She said her goodbyes to the band and leaned over to Astria. "You said the dragons liked my song. I rather think they liked your harmony."

Astria furrowed her brow. *Why?*

As she watched Merythe and family walk away, Fynn put an arm around her and drew her close.

Her body warmed to his touch, and she blushed. But in a heartbeat, she knew what he wanted and pushed him away.

"No, Fynn. I want to dance and have fun."

He pulled her back. "Yana and Jenks are having fun—"

She brushed off his arm. "That's not what I mean."

"We're old enough—"

An image came of Merythe bearing her child alone, her lover gone. *I'm not ready for that.*

"No," she said, breaking his grip before hurrying from the party.

Astria found Zephyr by the river and sat on the bank next to him. She scratched his brow ridge, and his eyes sparkled in the moonlight.

"Why don't I like him?" she asked, and Zephyr turned his head to her voice. "Fynn, I mean. But I do like him. Just not the way he likes me. Will I grow to want that? Should I apologize? Should he?"

She leaned against the dragon and sighed. "I'm a woman now, and this is not only about him and me. If I'm not a Rider, will I still have a choice of mate? Will the Council pick him for me? But what'll happen if I say no?"

It was all too confusing, and Zephyr had no answers for her.

At a distant honk, Astria caught the silhouettes of dragons against the dim red light of Fures as they circled the valley rim. When they honked again, Zephyr rose and left.

"Hey, I'm not done talking!" she called after him. But Zephyr did not stop, and she followed.

A half-hour walk upriver, past the water wheels that powered the mill and wood lathes, brought her to the valley edge. After a slow climb by rock and vines in the half light of a moon, she neared the rim. Just below the sheer face of the final climb, lay a bramble-covered area the size of the Manor House with a panoramic view of the valley. From it rose a whiff of rotting vegetation and liquor. After a rustle and flutter of dragons, she lifted herself to the ledge.

Through brush and brambles, she found a circle of rocks that enclosed a pile of red berries with green leaves where old dragons munched. She had never seen dragons so old, with paper-thin wings and bony frames, and she bit her lip at the strength and grandeur gone from them. As they ate, life returned to their eyes, they took off, and they flew west.

Astria sighed and felt the tears rise as she turned to leave, but a twig snapped, and she froze.

Through the bush across the clearing came Zephyr, his head low. He sniffed the pile and stirred it with a paw, then lay down and stared at it with his head over his paws and sighed.

He needs this, or he wouldn't be here. But there's none left. He's stronger than the old ones and could take what he wanted. But he waited for them to finish.

Will he die without it, and will I die with him?

With a blink, the tears fell unbidden. She opened her mouth to sing and ease his sorrow, but stopped. *Maybe I shame him with my presence?*

The moons glinted in the eyes of an old dragon perched on the cliff top: Vandrare.

Again, you do nothing? she thought. But as he stared at her, his rebuke came in a glance: *And what of your promise?*

With tears clouding her vision, she crept back down the cliffside. At the bottom, she sat and tugged her knees to her chest.

If Zephyr felt a small part of my desire to fly, he would be hurting. Will he feel that pain over the hundreds of years he has yet to live? Will he never know the sky? Will he become feeble and old without ever being able to fly and never go home to the Source? And what will he do if the other dragons leave him here alone?

***

"Did you have fun?" Skye asked as Astria slammed the cottage door behind her.

Astria nodded and drifted to the mantel holding her father's keepsakes. She ran her fingers over them for luck: a wooden box with a sparkling ivory inlay and a small cone covered in shiny metal. Next to them lay her sketchbook with the drawing of him showing the finely wrought coin hanging on a cord around his neck.

Astria brushed her hand across her father's face. "My drawing is old."

"You can always draw a new one," her mother said and set a quick supper of mutton and bread. When Astria sat at the table, Skye turned a chair around and sat opposite her.

"The Vederlofte will come at Summer's end," Skye said. "And you'll need to offer your service to the clan to trade for the efforts of others. If you wait too long, they'll choose for you."

Astria stopped eating and stared at her plate with a hand clenched tight under the table. "I don't care."

"You like to draw. The Potters have an apprenticeship open."

She rolled her eyes. "There's no sunset on a pot."

"You might add one."

Pausing mid-bite, Astria considered her mother's idea, but then curled her lip.

A soft frown crossed Skye's face. "You still wish to become a Rider."

The words stung, and Astria pursed her lips. "Really, Mama, how can I without Papa to speak for me?"

"It's not like your life depends on it."

Astria looked away. *Maybe it does.*

"What else would you choose?"

Astria's eyes darted among the corners of the cottage. *I want nothing else. How can I help the dragons if I can't fly? How can I find Papa and understand the dream we had together?* Everything she wanted depended on her becoming a Rider. She had no other goal, no other future, but that path was impossible.

"Time's running out, dear. Think about it."

"Sure," Astria said to please her but forgot in the next instant. After finishing the last morsel, she laid her head upon her arm and sighed.

"What's the matter, sweetie?"

"Mama, Zephyr still can't fly."

"Even a little?"

"Nope. His wings haven't grown to his size. I think he needs some berries. I found a circle of rocks near the valley rim—"

"People didn't build it," Skye said. "There's no reason to go up there."

"Well, I saw dragons bring some plants to the old ones. Red berries with green leaves."

"Hmm. Do they smell?"

"Like liquor."

Skye nodded. "Daemonberries."

Astria's face brightened. "You know of it?"

"Yes. The Seers say the dragon's fly west to the Source when they get old. Maybe that's their last meal before returning home."

If Zephyr flies to the Source, is my promise lifted? Or is it broken and my life at risk?

Astria shook her head. "Why don't we grow it here?"

"It withers and doesn't bear fruit in the valleys."

"I think Zephyr needs it, and he's not strong enough to search outside the valley like the others. Is that why dragons only live in the mountains?"

Skye raised an eyebrow. "That's an interesting idea. Maybe he needs more of it."

"But he'll die, Mama."

"I think he'll just stay small."

"He wants to soar with the others, and he's sad all the time."

"How do you know he's sad?" Skye asked.

Astria shrugged and pursed her lips.

"I don't think we should intervene," Skye said. "It's their way."

Astria frowned at her mother and stormed out.

At their spot by the river, Astria found Zephyr and lay by his side.

"What are we gonna do now? If you can't fly, I'll . . ." She couldn't say it aloud. *I'll have to find a new dragon.*

She threw a pebble into the river and watched the reflection of three moons dance in the ripples.

Could I really do that? She turned her head and looked into his sparkling eyes. *Could I fly free and watch you languishing on the ground?*

"No, I wouldn't do that to you," she said with a shake of her head and sighed. "Mama says it's just the dragons' way and I should leave you be." Standing straight, she threw another pebble into the river.

"Well, it's not my way," she said, and with her jaw set, left to find Yana and Fynn.

Chapter 5
The Berry Patch

The next afternoon, loaded with a bundle of shovels and a tray of sprouts from the daemonberry pile, the three friends headed for a plot of land near Lake Norven. As they passed the peach orchard, Farmers eyed them, and one hurried away.

"If more dragons come to Invernell, we *all* can ride," Yana said and moved the shovel to her other shoulder.

"Maybe just you," Astria said. "Your mother will train you."

Yana grinned and pointed a thumb at Fynn, who carried a tray of daemonberry sprouts the dragons left behind. "His mother and Jerrick are dating."

"He's a good guy," Fynn said.

"And a Rider who can speak for you," Yana said.

Astria's hopelessness returned, and she dropped her gaze.

"They're not married yet," Fynn said and turned to Astria. "Don't worry. You'll get someone to train you, or we'll train you ourselves."

"When you're a Rider, what'll you do with your free time?" Yana asked.

Astria turned to face them and walked backward. "Explore."

Fynn opened his eyes wide. "You want to leave Invernell?"

"I want to see where the sun sets and rises," Astria said. "I want to see the Ocean of Daggers to the east."

She dropped the bundle of tools at the plot she scouted earlier that morning, a plot with good sun and water from the lake: an ideal place to grow anything. In the ground, she marked a two-by-two grid with each square five feet wide and made another by its side. Nearby under the shade of an oak tree, she marked two more. When the plots were marked out, she opened her sketchpad.

"To start, we have four combinations to test, sun or shade, and compost or manure," Astria said.

"Sure," Yana said and added compost to one square.

Upset by the proximity of humans, a jay jumped to a nearby branch and scolded them.

"Shush," Astria said. "We won't bother your nest."

Fynn frowned and picked up a berry sprout. "Why do you want to see the ocean? You already know where it is."

"That was a map. I want to *go* there."

"Why?"

"To feel it." She spun on her toes with her arms outstretched. "To taste it. To see what it looks like."

"It looks like here," Fynn said under his breath while planting the little sprout.

"No, it doesn't."

"Is this about finding your father?" Yana asked.

"If I can. Only a dragon can cover the terrain."

"Are you sure Zephyr will fly?"

"No," Astria said. "But dragons name one another after real things. Kendrick's dragon, Krigsmanen, has a red streak like Brother Moon, and Agnarr's fur is the color of wheat chaff. So why would they name Zephyr for the wind if he'll never fly?" She shook her head. "Even if Zephyr doesn't grow big enough to carry me, I want him to fly with the other dragons. They ditched him, and the valley folk treat him like a tree across a trail."

"In the way?" Fynn asked.

She glanced at the dirt. "Yeah. Like me."

"Why do you think that? The Vederlofte?"

"My mother mentioned it again."

"Finding a job's not a problem," Yana said. "They always need someone to turn the compost heap."

"If they choose for me, I may never ride," Astria said.

Yana dug the shovel into a new furrow. "I'm sure this will—"

"What are you doing here?" asked a large woman as she entered the clearing with four burly Farmers in coveralls.

"Good afternoon, Elder Britta," Yana said.

Astria smiled. "We aim to grow daemonberries using—"

"What did your mother say about growing things here?" Britta asked.

Astria narrowed her eyes. "I didn't ask."

Britta matched Astria's narrow gaze. "Did you get permission from an Elder?"

"No," Astria said and raised an eyebrow. "Do we need it?"

Britta looked down at them with disdain. "Yes, you do. Anything that might affect the food crops needs to be approved by the Far-... by the Council."

"But it's only a little plot," Astria said.

"Anything. No matter how small."

"Fine. Then after we have this first batch in."

"No, before you begin."

Astria put a fist on her hip. "Why does—"

"Defiance means exile," a Farmer said and stepped forward.

Britta held the Farmer back. "Now, now, no need for threats. The Council will decide this. Come, children."

"No one told us—" Astria began.

Yana stepped in front of her. "After you, ma'am."

Astria and her friends followed Britta to the Council Room in the Manor House and pointed to chairs facing a long table. When they sat, Fynn fidgeted, and Yana pursed her lips. But Astria studied the woodcuts of their ancestors throwing off the shackles of slavery and heading north to the Spine.

Still in their working clothes, the Elders on the Council of Twelve filed in and sat at the long table, and Astria mirrored their narrow eyes and knitted brows.

Each Elder represented a role vital to their valley. In the middle of the table, Chairman Kendrick sat and drummed his fingers. The Mediator, Skye, sat alongside him, and midwife Philina sat opposite. Next to them, Flight Leader Lothen spoke for the Riders, Vinga represented the teachers, and Britta the Farmers. Urquil, the most senior, napped in his chair at one end. Apart from the table sat the Seer, with Angelica sitting cross-legged on the floor beside her.

As the last entered, each wearing shop aprons with pockets filled with tools, Astria leaned over to Yana.

"Who are they?" Astria asked.

"First is Terach, who speaks for the Craftsmasters," Yana said. "The short pair are Radlig and Malik, who represent the cabinetmakers and potters. Elsete from the builders is the tall lady." A fat man with a bloody apron entered. "And the last is Kleb from—"

"The butchers," Astria said.

When Kleb found his place, Kendrick stood and said, "Britta, this is your meeting. Proceed."

"These youngsters have decided on their own to grow daemonberries," Britta said. "The Farmers banned that crop hundreds of years ago."

"Daemonberries aren't a crop, Britta. Surely you could have worked this out without . . ."

"I'm sorry to interrupt your busy schedule," Britta said with a sharp edge to her voice. "But the Farmers petitioned me to speak for them, and—"

Kendrick raised his hand. "All right, you speak for the Farmers. Who on the Council speaks for you, Yana?"

After a long silence, Skye stood. "I'll speak for them."

"Britta, state your request, please," Kendrick said with a wave of his hand.

"Long ago, Farmers tried to grow daemonberries in the valleys," Britta said, glancing at the Farmers as they drifted in and took seats behind Astria. "They failed, but they learned the leaves make the rams crazy and the ewes infertile. To grow this now is a waste of energy and dangerous to our food supply. The Farmers request the council reconfirm the decision to ban daemonberries in the valley and find more productive labor for our children." She held her hands out, palms up, and sat.

"Skye?" Kendrick said.

"Yana, you're the eldest, can you tell us your plan?" Skye asked.

Yana turned to Astria. "Well, it's just to plant . . . We—"

Astria stood. "We aim to bring more dragons to Invernell."

The Farmers behind her grumbled.

"By growing the berries?" Skye asked.

Astria smiled and stepped toward the table. "Yes, we think the dragons need it—"

The Seer interrupted. "Dragons need nothing from humans."

"Astria, how do you know this?" Flight Leader Lothen asked.

"Well . . . I saw old dragons at a pile of berries at the valley rim, and—"

"So this is conjecture?" Lothen asked.

Astria glanced at the floor. "Well . . . I guess."

"Why would we risk our food and wool on a guess?" Britta asked.

Kendrick raised a hand. "What do you propose, Astria?"

"We aim to try different fertilizers to see which is more—"

"We tried all the fertilizers," Britta said.

"Each one alone may not be enough, but together—" Astria held up her sketchbook and flipped to the page with the first combinations. "This is a method to keep track."

Britta slapped her hand on the table. "Who are you to presume you can achieve what our ancestors could not?"

"It's just an idea to—"

"It seems all this has been tried before and failed, Astria," Lothen said.

Skye gave him the side-eye and turned to Britta. "Did the Farmers pass down what they did? Perhaps the children could try something new."

"It matters not," Britta said. "We cannot allow the berries in the valley, or we risk our livestock.

"Tell them about my missing chickens," a farmer called out.

"There are hogs and chickens gone missing, and your little dragon has to hunt in the valley."

Astria frowned. "I'd blame the foxes for that. Zephyr wouldn't touch our food, and he doesn't need it. There are plenty of wild rabbits in the valley."

"One subject at a time," Kendrick said.

"But it's about the dragons," Britta countered.

Skye shook her head. "No, it's about the daemonberries."

Britta fumed. "Even if they do grow the berries, we can't support more Riders with the resources we have."

"That's not your decision alone," Kendrick said.

Astria rallied at the unexpected support and leaned over the table. "Even without new Riders, dragons keep the graxes away."

Vinga nodded. "Perhaps with more dragons, the Farmers can farm outside the valley's rim without fear."

Murmurs of assent came from behind Astria.

But Britta's eyes narrowed. "The risk is too great. More dragons will drag in foreign weeds that can hurt our food supply."

"That's silly," Astria said. "Traders drag stuff with them from everywhere."

Britta glared at her. "Silly? Who are you to say it won't matter? It's harder now with shorter growing seasons. We don't want to make it any harder."

"Anything more?" Kendrick asked, and Astria shook her head. "All in favor of Britta's request to not allow daemonberries in the valley?"

The Elders raised their hands: seven to five supporting the Farmers, with Chairman Kendrick on Astria's side and the Seer ineligible to vote.

As she passed them on the way out, Astria felt the Farmers' hidden sneers, and Efrin's words came to her: "They're not your friends."

But Astria set her jaw.

That afternoon as they cleaned up their plot, Yana threw a plant onto the pile for disposal and glanced at the rim of the valley.

"Are you thinking of finding a stray in the Wild?" Astria asked.

A sigh escaped Yana's lips. "If I have to."

"You won't survive exile for long," Fynn said.

"Not exile! I don't have to live there, just visit. But don't tell my folks. Papa says the Wild is unfit for a young lady."

"So you're a lady now?" Fynn joked, and Yana swung her shovel at him.

"You're not afraid of Quarajii scouts?" Astria said with a playful smile.

Yana brushed the back of her hand across her forehead. "Oh no! Enslaved by barbarians." She dropped to her knees with her wrists crossed. "Forced to marry a fierce—though handsome—warlord! What will become of me?"

"Jenks would rescue you," Fynn said.

Yana blushed and sat in the dirt, frowning. "He's partnered with Orkvanin, and they're off training half the day." Her voice softened. "What'll you do, Astria?"

Astria sighed. "My mother wants me to be a Potter."

Fynn stifled a chuckle, and Yana frowned at him. "*Your* future looks so bright?"

"Mama wants me to be a Farmer. And so I am."

"You haven't grown anything yet," Yana said and threw a dirt clod at a tree. "With our luck, we may all end up turning the compost heap."

As Astria stared at the plot, a beam from the setting sun lit their patch for a moment, and she crossed her arms. "Will you let your dreams die to appease some frightened old people?"

"So what'll we do?" Fynn asked. "We only have a few months before the Vederlofte."

"If we clear a patch by the rim, they'll never find it . . ."

***

Through the summer, Astria and her friends snuck out every night to their hidden grove with Zephyr to protect the shoots. And every night they took a different path to the plot, aware that the Farmers might follow them to assure compliance with the Council's edict.

But each batch of plants withered and died. Now they hoped the fourth batch would succeed. Just in case, Astria brought a new trial mixture. But the sight of more dead plants stopped them.

Yana kicked a dead plant and threw it on the disposal pile. "We've tried everything."

Fynn set the tray of sprouts on the ground. "Why do we expect to succeed when all the clans failed before?"

"One more try. Please. I have another fertilizer," Astria said.

"What is it?" Fynn asked.

"Guano," Astria said, and her friends pinched their noses at the same time.

"Bird poop?"

"We've not tried it yet."

He wrinkled his nose and reached for the bag. "So really, this is our plan? I mean, it's not like this is gonna work, right?"

"One more time?" she pleaded, and her friends nodded.

***

A fortnight later, Skye entered Astria's secret garden. "No fruit yet?"

Astria dropped her trowel and jumped to her feet. "Does the Council know? Did they send you? Did you tell them?"

"No, no, and of course not," Skye said as she set down a basket.

Astria sat again and marked an *X* in her sketchbook to record the combination for her most recent failure. At her side, Zephyr peered at her shriveled plants and then lifted his head. She followed his gaze high above, where other dragons circled.

"Fynn and Yana quit," Astria said.

"Discouraged?" Skye spread a cloth and set it with a lunch of sausage, bread, and fruits.

Astria crushed a clod with her hands. "They say they have other things to do."

"The grain will ripen soon, and the harvest will begin. The frost will follow."

"And Zephyr will hop around like a cripple for another year." *And I'll be stuck here with no future,* she thought and bit into a peach. "I'm close, Mama. This batch lasted longer than any of the others."

"Summer is nearly over," Skye said as she made sandwiches. "You'll need to stop soon and help with the harvest. The Vederlofte follows soon after." Unable to crack Astria's disappointment, Skye handed her a sandwich.

Astria took a bite and then threw a dead plant on the pile.

"If you succeed here, your friends may partner with dragons and leave you."

"I know. This is about Zephyr now, Mama. He needs my help." She threw a clod into the brush. "I shouldn't have to ask the Council's permission to do what's right."

"I understand your irritation. But you can't count on the cooperation of others unless they agree."

"I'm fine without their cooperation."

"We depend on Farmers for the food you're eating and need to respect their opinions."

Astria bit into the bread made from grain grown by the Farmers and lost her appetite. "Maybe *you* do."

"Maybe I *must*."

Astria put a hand on her hip. "And what if *I* don't?"

"Growing our food is their responsibility, and the harvests are failing. We don't want them blaming you for starvation."

"Did they say that?" Astria asked after her last bite.

"No, but I know them. If they catch you continuing your experiments, they ... They control our rations, hon. And my job. And your job to come."

Astria recognized the threat, stood, and paced. "I can't give up, Mama," she said.

"Well, then hurry and keep it secret before they demand retribution," Skye said and kissed her on the forehead. "Come home for dinner, dear. Efrin brought iceberries for us."

As her mother walked away, Astria picked up another dead plant and threw it into the trees. Beside her, Zephyr snuffed and gazed at her with big, green eyes.

He knows what this means: another summer stuck on the ground. She turned away, unable to face him, and kicked the dirt.

"I can't help you. I'm just a kid and don't know how to do anything."

He nudged his head into her side and hummed, inviting her to sing. But she wouldn't, and his attention became another burden, irritating her even more. She needed to be alone, away from him.

The dragon followed her when she walked away and chased her when she broke into a run. He tracked her until they reached a cliff he could not scale or jump.

Through a secret way too narrow for him, Astria passed through the Valley rim. From under a waterfall that hid the exit, she ran into the Wild.

When his honks subsided, she stopped in a clearing, threw her sketchbook against a tree, and kicked a bramble that retaliated by scratching her ankle. At the foot of a chalk cliff grew a tiny bush, and she kicked that, too. But the bush hid a rock, and she stubbed her toes. Holding her throbbing foot and hopping on the other, she lost her balance and fell.

Realizing where she was, she jumped back to her feet.

The Wild. Home of the graxes.

Astria looked around for spoor and sniffed for the rancid smell of grax and sensed neither. *The smell of dragons must be strong near the valley.* She bent over to rub her smarting toes, and the little bush came into focus. It was small, with green leaves and red buds ready to fruit. *Daemonberry?* To confirm her hunch, she put a broken leaf to her tongue and raised an eyebrow at the sharp bite of thyme and fermented grain.

"Where in Hel did you come from?" she said and limped around the clearing to find no other bushes like it.

Returning to the little bush, she sat and rubbed her toes. It was not even a mouthful for a dragon and not enough to harvest. But it had achieved something she had not: buds that would fruit.

"All right, what's here that we haven't tried?" she asked the plant as she dug up the roots. "Shallow. Then your food comes from the surface soil. So what's close by?"

She surveyed the area. Above her, the white cliffs shielded the plant from the wind.

"Chalk," she whispered. *The same material as the eggshells I grind up for my drawings. But I tried that as an additive.*

She retrieved her sketchbook and flipped back to when she had used chalk before.

"But I missed some combinations," she said as she scanned the matrix and frowned. "There's too many gaps to try them all myself." She shook her head. "I still need help."

On her return through the secret passage, Zephyr met her with opalescent eyes.

Astria flipped through her sketchbook to the page where Zephyr flew through rose-colored clouds and held it in front of him.

"Come on, you. They can't keep us cooped up here anymore," she said with a smile and ran to find Yana and Fynn.

Chapter 6
Riders

The Tops, the highest points on the valley wall, were visible from everywhere on the valley floor. Split by the Blois River, the lofty pillars of the East Top and West Top formed the Notch at the exit of Invernell Valley. At the base of the Tops, the Blois narrowed and poured through the Notch into waterfalls on the north side.

Children first scaled the valley rim here, and lovers watched the moons rise. From there, they viewed the orchards to the south, Lake Norven, and the beauty of their valley. Past the glaciers to the west, the peaks of the Spine glittered in the distance. And beyond the horizon lay the Source, where legends told them dragons hatched and returned to die

In the late afternoon a month after discovering the successful fertilizer blend, Astria rested her cheek on a cliff face of cold stone. A hundred feet below her, at the trailhead to the West Top, Zephyr hopped and chittered in distress. She would not fall so far; the nearest ledge was only fifty feet below her, but that was far enough to crush her skull.

Securing a foothold on the cliff, Astria stretched out her hand. "Three points of contact" was their safety rule, but there were no secure holds within her reach, and she paused her climb.

She took the hard way up, pushing Efrin's training. Her friends had taken an easier way eight feet to her right, with notches chiseled into the stone. But she could not traverse that distance safely.

So close, yet so far.

As she wiped her free hand on her jerkin, a cramp pinched her calf. When she took the weight off her toes, her foot slipped, adding to the stress on her aching fingers.

A chickadee landed sideways on a branch a few feet to her right, cocked his head at her, and chirped.

"Thanks," she said and grabbed the branch. But when she pulled on it, she dislodged it from a vertical crack, raining dirt and pebbles on Zephyr below.

Astria felt for the crack, about two inches wide, but did not find a grip. Then she jammed her hand deeper into the fissure and wedged her hand open. But when she tried to support her weight, her hand slipped and tore the skin from her knuckles.

Now what? I can't see where to grip if I reverse my climb. And every second I wait, I'll tire even more.

After licking the scrapes, she jammed her hand back into the crevice, and ignoring the pain, wedged her thumb under her palm, secure enough to support her weight for the next move. Without a foothold, she forced her foot sideways into the crack and twisted it until it held her weight. Moving her left hand and foot to the crack, she reached out with her right hand again. She felt a larger crack and wedged her entire hand horizontally into it and made a fist. Then she wedged her right foot and left hand into the new crack.

Just as she moved her left foot, her right foot slipped, and with her legs dangling, all her weight pulled on her fists wedged into the crack. If she relaxed either fist, the fall would cripple her, so she tightened her fists until her nails bit into her palms.

Zephyr honked from below.

Will he break my fall? Maybe not.

With closed eyes, she found the crack with her foot by feel, crammed it in tighter, and followed with the left foot. The next reach was to the simple route, and when she wedged both hands and feet in the carved notches, she let out her breath and leaned her cheek against the cold rock.

A short climb later, Yana and Fynn met her at the ledge with outstretched hands.

"Slow poke," Yana said as she gave her a hand up.

Astria twisted her mouth in a frown. "I almost fell."

"Serves you right."

After backing away from the edge, Astria laid back and licked her skinned knuckles as her friends sat by her side and gazed at the valley.

Below them near Lake Norven, Riders tended the new daemonberry plots using Astria's soil supplement. And above the valley rim, dragons soared up the thermals and circled.

"New dragons keep coming," Fynn said.

"You can't see them all from the ground," Yana said with a smile. "Which ones will be ours?"

"So can we stop worrying about the Council punishing us?" Fynn asked.

"Yes," Astria said. "My mother says the wild dragons came before the farmers heard what we were doing. The Traders and Craftsmasters want more dragons to keep the graxes away. And they voted to plant more rather than punish us."

"We'll see," Yana said.

"When we're Riders, we'll never have to make this climb again," Fynn said.

Astria sat up again and poked him in the shoulder. "*If* we're Riders."

Evening shadows from the peaks crept across the tilled fields of the valley and over the Manor House and village where lights flickered from homes and craft shops.

As the sun neared the peaks of the Spine, a chill wind drifted past. Sweaty from the daylong climb, Astria shivered and stood. "Come on, lazybones."

At a run, they followed Astria and chased the sun along the winding trail to the summit. During stops along the way, they practiced with bow and arrow on well-worn targets. At other stops, they fought straw dummies with hardwood spears and practiced tethering themselves to saddles to not fall off in flight.

When they reached the summit of the West Top, the setting sun touched the peaks of the mountains. Shadows covered the valley to the rim and pinpoints of light shone from the homes built on the cliffs. Another chill breeze blew, and they retired to a shelf just below the summit protected from the weather by an overhanging rock.

"The snow will come soon," Fynn said.

"And the jenalei with it," Yana said and brought firewood stacked by the entrance.

Astria smiled at the image of translucent blossoms that alternated with edelweiss and snow to keep the cliff tops white year-round. The blooms brought tiny wheezits that wren-size flitterbies gobbled up.

With her kit of flint and iron, Astria lit the fire as dragons, both familiar and new, clustered near a pond at the far rim beside the Blois, before it fell into the valley. When the sun reached the peaks, the dragons took off and perched on a ridge facing west. And over a meager dinner of smoked mutton and oats, Astria and her friends gazed at the setting sun with the dragons.

"What are they doing?" Fynn asked.

"They come to watch the sunset over the Source," Astria said.

"How do you know?" Yana asked, but Astria shrugged.

"The new ones don't seem interested in partnering," Fynn said.

"They're not used to us," Astria said. "Give them time. And we're not in shape yet. Efrin wants us to repeat this every week."

He frowned and threw a pebble over the edge. "If dragons are the most powerful beings on Juro, they don't need us. So why would they befriend us?"

"I think because they know we're the only animals as smart as they are," Astria said.

"What'll you do when you can ride, Fynn?" Yana asked.

"Hunt. Tusks from mountain boar trade well in Vernier and Winterthur." He glanced at Astria. "There's a ring that—"

"I just want to fly free," Yana said. "What about you, Astria?"

"I don't want to think about it."

"Why?"

Astria stared west as the sun touched the tip of the far mountains, changing the clouds from white to yellow. "Zephyr may never fly."

"He has plenty of daemonberries and is growing now."

"But he still can't fly."

"*If* you could ride him, where would you go?"

"Well . . . north, I guess."

"Why?" Then Yana understood. "How do you know your father is there?"

Astria dropped her gaze, afraid of what her friends would think. "The dragons . . ."

"They told you?"

"No, nothing like that. But sometimes I get feelings or pictures when we sing."

"Like what?"

"Like the Ocean of Daggers tastes salty. And it's winter all the time farther west."

Fynn turned to the row of dragons perched nearby. "If we could talk to them the same as you, we—"

"But I don't. My father thought they speak using harmonics. Like they talk in pictures and color."

Fynn raised an eyebrow. "I don't understand."

"Well, a word to us is a sequence of changing sounds, one after another. Dragons make lots of sounds at the same time."

When the last slice of sun dipped below the farthest peaks, a cool breeze picked up, and Fynn added wood to the fire. "You can sing. Why can't you do that?"

"We can only voice one note and a harmonic, and I can't even do that. My father said dragons can sing twenty or more notes at once. And we can't hear the high and low tones, much less produce them."

"How do they learn?" Yana asked.

"They're born to pictures the way we're born to melody."

"Do you see their pictures? Is that why you sing together?"

"No, I—"

Yana took Astria's hand. "My mama says some Farmers fear you're the Speaker to Dragons."

Astria narrowed her eyes. "That old myth? Why do they think that? Because I sing to them?"

"No," Yana said with a smile. "Because they listen."

"Nonsense," Astria said and poked the fire. "Dragons have their own motives. We just don't know what they are. That confuses some and scares others."

Fynn sat next to her. "Why don't you sing for the rest of us?"

"Yana knows why. It's because I don't sound very good."

Her friend blushed but said nothing.

"Then why sing?"

"It sounds different to me. And dragons like it."

"Sing for me," Fynn said, and Astria sang softly.

> *"When winds come ashore*
> *   And ships land no more,*
> *I'll . . ."*

Astria's voice trailed off after Flynn cringed and his eye twitched as if he had bit into a lemon. He raised his hand.

"I understand," he said. "But the dragon's like it?"

Astria nodded.

"It's like they're listening," Yana said. "Like they want something from you."

My promise? Astria gazed at the distant glaciers. Then she puffed out her chest and stretched out her arms. "I command the dragons." She dropped her pitch to the deepest tone she could reach. "Fly, my minions!"

The dragons, stray and partnered both, turned their heads and gazed at her.

Yana furrowed her brow. "Don't make fun of me. I didn't start the rumor."

"Sorry. It's a silly idea. They're not a flock of geese. They won't follow one another, or me."

The conversation died, and Astria caught a glance between her friends.

Sister Moon rose, and Yana rolled over to sleep, leaving Astria and Fynn at the fire. Astria laid her hand on Fynn's arm and broke the silence.

"It's all right. I know."

He blushed. "Know what?"

"That your mother and Jerrick will marry. He'll be able to speak for you to be a Rider."

He frowned and dropped his gaze. "I wanted to tell you myself."

"My mother's on the Council, and no one there can keep a secret." She turned her head away. "I guess I'll be the only one turning the compost heap."

He put his arm around Astria's shoulder and smiled. "Don't give up. We'll always be here to help you. We're inseparable, us four. Nothing can keep us apart."

She patted his hand again and leaned into his hug. "Jenks isn't here, Fynn."

"Ah . . ."

"I'm fine, really. I'm just so happy for you, both of you. You'll be Riders, and—"

"Only if the Elders agree." He pointed a thumb to the dragons on the cliffs. "And if we can find partners within the rabble."

"I'm sure you will. Now, if you two are going to ride, we'll need to train more often. How about midweek?"

"Sure. Just you and me?" From behind his back, he took a small bouquet of wildflowers.

Astria accepted them, not knowing what to say. Then he took her hand, his other arm still on her shoulders.

"What do you mean?"

He closed his eyes and pulled her in for a kiss, and she let him. But his lips were cold and dry without the magic she hoped for. Her body did not react, and she pushed him away.

"Fynn, I—"

"I know you like me, Astria."

"Of course I like you."

"I hoped we might . . . become more than friends."

"We're still kids," she said.

"Not so much anymore."

"Well, I am."

"Yana and Jenks are spending more time alone."

Astria smiled. "Her mother flies above to check on them."

"And some of our friends are promised."

"Fynn, I'm sorry, but I'm not ready for that."

"What about . . . more time together?"

She stood and fidgeted. "You and Yana will start training soon and won't have any time left for me."

"I can make time."

She sat again and took his hand. "Fynn, I need a friend now, someone to talk to and confide in and complain to. I need to tell someone what the dragons—"

"I can be that, too."

Astria sighed and stared at her hands. "I can't say no to you."

"Then don't." Again, he leaned toward her for another kiss, but she pulled away, and he frowned.

"You don't understand," she said. "If I say no, you'll stay away, and I don't want that. I need you, but I need you to be my friend."

"But—"

"I'm sorry, Fynn. I can't be what you want."

She stood again and went to sit by the ledge with the dragons. Above her, Mother Moon rose to join her daughter, painting the valley below in charcoal and chalk.

Behind her, Fynn threw the flowers into the brush and stomped away.

Soon they'll be too busy for me. Zephyr can't fly, I can't ride, and now I'll lose my friends.

That they loved her did not make it hurt any less.

And what will become of me?

Brother Moon rose, and her wishing star appeared.

"Please bring Papa home," she whispered. "I don't know what to do now." *How can a star understand how much I need him? How much Mama needs him?*

She began another wish to become a Rider but hesitated. *How can I still wish for something that will never happen?* she thought but wished it anyway. "And please help Zephyr fly."

When the fire burned to embers behind her, Astria shivered and leaned into a wild dragon who sat near her. From the Tops, the daemonberry plots glistened in the moonlight, and Astria sighed.

"Have I kept my promise?" she asked the dragon, but he only cocked his head and turned back to the moons.

She began to hum Merythe's melody, and he hummed in harmony. And when she closed her eyes, the colors of the sky filled her. A vision of her father and Klokbror came, but when her tears fell, the dragon stopped humming and put his head in her lap.

***

Three weeks later, at the annual Vederlofte, her friends' choices were clear, but Astria's was not.

The fresh daemonberry plots attracted scores of wild dragons. And from them, Yana and Fynn befriended Trunghanger and Omattlig. Zephyr grew bigger and stronger each day but still could not fly. And when her friends' dragons flew above, Zephyr followed on the ground until they sped away.

Outside the Manor House, surrounded by other teens, Astria shared a bench with Yana while Fynn paced. Around them, friends and relatives gathered to celebrate the path chosen—or assigned.

"Zephyr's wings are growing now," Yana said to Astria. "Go ahead. Tell them your choice. What can they do? They won't exile you."

"Would they?" Fynn asked.

Her friends became quiet.

"My mother's an Elder," Astria said. "I don't know what they'd do to her."

Yana pointed to a little wheezit perched on a jenalei flower. "It's like the parable of the little wheezits," she said. "They're industrious and never stop gathering pollen for their families. They can't stop being what they're meant to be, and you're meant to be a Rider, Astria."

"Did they describe the initiation?" Astria asked.

"No. Only to report to the beach at dawn. My mother and Jerrick put together a party for us before then. You're invited, of course."

From the door, Efrin waved. "Yana, Fynn. They're calling for you."

They rose, and Yana took Astria's hand. "You have to, Asti. The fortune teller told us."

Astria smiled. "The fortune has already come true whether or not I ride."

As they entered the Manor House, out of sight of the three friends, a flitterbie swooped down to the jenalei flower, pounced on the wheezit, and munched.

Inside the Manor House crowded guild masters, initiates, and parents. At the table sat the Elders of the Council of Twelve in their ornate robes of office. But today, Craftsmaster Terach ran the proceedings.

Amid the four-score attending, Yana and Fynn sat on two empty cushions on the floor in the front row. Uninvited and with nowhere to sit, Astria found a place near the door to stand.

The affair disappointed her: all business, without ceremony or celebration. Terach called the names and heard the roles desired. After a brief discussion, the Council approved the career or assigned a new one. The Elders appeared bored and distracted, with most choices negotiated beforehand. To her, it was less exciting than the fish market.

After Kendrick's beautiful daughter, Furnia, chose to be a furniture maker came time for Yana and Fynn.

Terach raised his hand to quiet the crowd. "Yana Mirim, step forward, please."

Yana jumped to her feet.

"What service to you offer the clan, young lady."

"Rider, sir, if'n that's all right."

"And your dragon?"

"Trunghanger, sir."

"We're grateful to you for the new dragons in our valley," he said, which sparked grumbles from the Farmers. "Yana, who speaks for you?"

La'a stood. "I, Rider La'a, speak for her."

"Thank you," Terach said and turned to Elder Britta. She nodded, and he turned back to Yana. "As you promise to help the clan, the clan promises to help you. The Council accepts your offer."

Yana whooped and raised her fist, but then blushed. "Sorry."

"Fynn Selcast, step forward, please," Terach said.

As the Council repeated the ritual for Fynn, Astria fidgeted and scanned the faces of the Elders.

Will they exile me? Mama will stop them, but what would it cost her? I really don't know these people or what they're willing to do. How far will Britta push her grudge against me? Vinga will support me . . .

Really? Why? Just because I'm her student? No. Because it's the right thing to do, and—.

Terach interrupted her thoughts. "... Fynn, as you promise to help the clan, the clan promises to help you. The Council accepts your offer."

Fynn grinned and hugged his parents.

Terach spoke again. "That concludes the Vederlofte. If there is no further business—"

Astria raised her hand and stepped forward. "Sir, I'd like to offer my service."

Skye pursed her lips and glanced at the Elders.

"Yes, Astria Sannfjaer. We didn't get advance notice, or we would've invited you earlier. What contribution do you promise?

"I offer to be a Rider, sir."

The crowd hushed, and the Farmers grumbled. Skye's lips formed a *no*.

Lothen leaned forward and spoke with firmness. "The dragons are spoken for, Astria."

"One isn't."

"You speak of the flightless one?"

"Yes, sir. Zephyr."

"I'm sorry, dear. If he can't fly, you can't ride, and your offer is of no value."

"I hope with more daemonberries, his wings will continue to grow, and he'll fly, sir."

"If he becomes healthy, the Council will decide who rides."

"Who speaks for you?" Terach asked.

"My father will return to train me," Astria said. "We just need to wait for him."

They gazed on her with pity, and Astria turned to Skye, who blushed in silence and closed her eyes.

"It matters not if Skye says yay or nay," Terach said. "Your mother's not a Rider and can't train you."

Efrin stood. "I'll train her."

"That's generous, Rider, but you're not her parent, and you have other duties. I'm sorry, Astria, but—"

"Zephyr won't let anyone else ride him," Astria said.

Lothen's deep voice interrupted. "If no one else can ride him, then he's unsuitable as a partner, and you must contribute by another means."

Furrows etched Terach's brow. "Do you have another service to offer, Astria?"

Her eyes narrowed. "No, sir. I aim to ride."

"That's not to be. We hoped you'd choose a different role. We have a craft for you, and—"

Astria's eyes glistened. "As a Potter? Tell me you can't find someone else to make pots."

Skye put her hand to her mouth.

Terach scowled. "Some want to be Potters just as much as you want to ride and get as much pleasure from working with their hands as Riders get from the sky."

"I'll be more valuable to you as a Rider," Astria said.

Britta smirked. "Of what use will you be if your pet can't fly?"

"He's not my pet!"

Fynn stood. "This isn't fair. You acknowledged our help in bringing dragons back to the valley. But Astria showed us all how."

Britta spoke with a honied tone. "Perhaps you will trade your choice for hers?"

Fynn did not understand the warning and opened his mouth, but his parents pulled him back to his seat.

Yana stepped forward and shook off La'a's hand. "I will."

Lothen raised his hand. "You can't trade your training, Yana." He turned to Astria. "We're aware of your discoveries and grateful for—"

Astria glared at him. "I don't need your gratitude. I need your consent."

"Astria, please," Skye said.

Red-faced, Lothen began again. "The daemonberries you grew for us—"

In tears now, Astria stomped her foot. "I didn't grow them for you! I grew them for Zephyr and my friends because you would deny them just like me."

Lothen's face turned hard. "Still, you need a family member to speak for you and train you, and you don't have one."

Efrin raised his hand, but Kendrick shook his head.

"This concludes our business," Terach said. "The Vederlofte is over."

Astria stood motionless as the chamber cleared and Fynn's and Yana's parents dragged them away. Efrin stood by her but left when Skye hugged her.

"I'm sorry the Council refused your offer, dear," Vinga said and leaned against the table opposite her.

"They don't understand dragons," Astria said and slouched into a chair. "How can the Council decide what happens between us?"

"It's not about the dragons. It's about feeding you. In the South, the Imperator dictated what we did and what our rewards were. Our ancestors had the hardest work and the least reward. Now we have the Council who helps to decide our occupations, and—"

"What's the difference if I am a slave to a tyrant or slave to our clan?" Astria asked and raised her hands in the air. "I still have no choice."

Skye sat next to her. "Your enemy isn't the Council. It's the long winters that force us to ration our food."

Astria shook her head. "It wasn't the weather that said I couldn't be a Rider or grow daemonberries." She paced like a lion in a cage. "What if what I want is valuable to them, but they don't want it?"

"You would deny them their choice, as they deny you yours?"

Astria raised her arms again. "No. But am I to live only doing what they value? What about what *I* want? What about my value to *myself*? Does that mean nothing?"

Vinga knitted her brow. "I won't defend our way of life to you."

"You're my teacher. Teach me."

"It's better than slavery."

Astria crossed her arms and paced. "In what way? If we need a master to tell us what to do, then we still think like slaves."

Anger flashed across Vinga's face, but instead of striking back, she stood and brushed her fingers along the carved columns and woodcuts hanging on the walls.

"My grandmother told me it was easy here when we first came," Vinga said. "Blessed with pleasant weather and plentiful resources. But the elderly die in winter now, and many are afraid."

"Then why not free us to discover how best to succeed rather than the Council muddling it out? I'm sure the Council would improve our lives *if* they knew how. But they don't."

"Well . . . I . . ." stammered Vinga.

Astria paced again. "If I give up my dreams, would they let me be a Farmer? I'd be outside with the dragons. I've shown them I can grow things."

Skye shook her head. "They don't trust you."

"What about my idea to plant in the fall?

"They won't listen. They're afraid, and—"

"Of what?"

"Some fear you're the Speaker to Dragons," Skye said.

"That nonsense? This rumor is a brand everyone sees but me." Astria threw her hands in the air. "I have no power over dragons!"

"Not yet," Skye said. "But they're different around you. There's something more—"

"I've heard enough," Astria said and stormed out.

At the riverbank, Efrin found Astria throwing pebbles into the water while Zephyr watched.

"I'm sorry, Astria," he said and sat next to her, evoking a blink from the dragon.

She put her hand on his. "Thank you for offering to train me, but why do I need it? If we needed training to ride, there would never have been the first Rider."

He smiled. "True. Training isn't about riding. It's about being safe and coordinating with others in the air. We patrol separately but fight as one, so we must work together."

Astria pouted with her chin on her hands. "I asked if they'd let me be a Farmer."

He sighed. "Could you really accept such a choice?"

"What else can I do?" she said, throwing another stone into the water.

"Don't ask again. Some on the Council aim to break your spirit. To break you to the yoke." He gazed out to the valley rim. "Please ... don't be upset with your mother."

"Why not? Those are her friends. And her Council."

"That she fights with constantly. She loves you and doesn't want you in danger. With Jorie missing, all her concern is for you."

"I'll be fine. My friends will ride. Why not me?"

"The Council is pressuring her."

"She told me. They think I'll bring the dragons down on them."

"That's not it," he said. "But I understand their fear. If you've ever seen a dragon hunt, you'd—"

"What about Lothen? Does he lead them against me?"

"The Council is pressuring your mother," Efrin said. "They want me to speak for you—"

"You did."

"Speak for you as your father. They want Skye and me to wed. They threatened her."

"Oh," Astria said and dropped her gaze. "You love my mother?"

"Yes."

Astria opened her mouth to protest, but Efrin raised his hand. "But I won't ask while your father is missing."

She looked him in the eye. "I will ride."

He nodded. "She can't lose you, too, and she wants you safe."

"Thank you." She kissed him on the cheek, stood, and ran home.

Astria found Skye at their cottage.

"Mama, I'm sorry. I didn't know about your fight with the Council."

"Efrin told you?" Skye asked and sat at the little table.

Astria nodded, sitting down next to her.

"Efrin is a fine man and thinks the world of you."

"I know how he feels about you, Mama, but you can't. Papa's still alive. Why don't they believe us?"

"You believe, and I hope, but no one else does. And they won't credit us with sanity if we believe something they don't. They've moved on and are annoyed we haven't."

"You wouldn't."

Skye narrowed her eyes. "They withheld Riders to search for your father." Her lip twitched, and her hands formed into fists. "The moment they threat—... the moment they mentioned it, I refused and offered to resign."

"Would they let me ride if you two marry?"

"Perhaps. But if I marry again, it will break your father's agreement with the Clanough. I'd lose my position, and we'd be at their mercy."

"They want me to pressure you? And all I need to do is forget Papa?" Her dreams of flying through the clouds and searching for her father crashed against reality. "But I won't. It's not right to put this on me."

"I know, dear. That's why I didn't mention it. If we follow their rules, it'll be harder for them to refuse you."

Astria crossed her arms and paced. "They're bastards."

"Not all of them. Kendrick is your biggest ally. And Vinga. The others are afraid. Lothen envies your rapport with the dragons." She sighed. "This is their compromise. They think Efrin can keep you from turning bad."

"To tame me? He said some want to 'break me to the yoke.' Is that what he meant?"

Skye nodded. "Your father defied the Council and went right to the Clanough to be named Explorer. Some are bitter and don't want that again."

"Can the Clanough name me a Rider?"

"No, dear. Only the Council assigns the Riders, but the Clanough can change the assignments."

"Can you ask?"

Skye shook her head. "It would be defiance. They planned to punish your father until the Clanough agreed to hold the faire here every year."

Astria sat next to Skye again. "And all we have to do is give up Papa."

Skye took Astria's hand. "But we won't."

Astria leaned into her. "This isn't fair."

Her mother put her arms around her. "No, it's not."

***

Three weeks after the Vederlofte, white jenalei bloomed in the fresh snow as Astria turned the compost. The odor of rot rose with the steam, and she sniffed to determine how much straw or water to add.

With each turn, Zephyr's nose twitched. In mere weeks, Zephyr had grown to four times Astria's size, and his crest grown so it might protect a Rider from the wind.

Neglected by her friends who trained during every free moment, Astria occupied herself with her art and Zephyr. Though the river did not whisper to her anymore, an echo sometimes came when she sang with him.

And there at the compost heap, the Seer and the blind acolyte came to her.

"May we visit with you?" Angelica asked.

Astria nodded but continued to work.

"The dragons miss your songs."

"I've been busy."

"The little one grows strong with the berries and his wings to match his size."

"But still he doesn't fly," Astria said.

"You made a promise to the dragons."

"How did you know?" Astria asked, put down her shovel, and sat between the dragon and Angelica. "I promised to help them, but I don't know how. I can't ask them, and they can't tell me."

"He loves you."

Zephyr gazed up at Astria with sparkling eyes.

"He's my only friend now. But I don't know how to help him."

"You already have," the blind girl-child said.

"Then is my promise fulfilled? And I can move on?"

"Move on? Do you care for him less now?"

"No, but he may never fly."

Angelica pursed her lips. "I see. And because he can't help you become a Rider, your concern for him has ended?"

Astria dropped her gaze and blushed at Angelica's judgment. "No, I—"

"What did they grant for your promise?" Angelica asked.

"I was drowning, and I lived."

Angelica took Astria's hand. "Your life is not over."

"Am I bound to them for life?"

Angelica turned her head to the mountains of the Spine. "Your promise is about you, not them. Be true to what you believe you promised. Keep your promises to yourself, or you imperil your soul."

"What do you mean?"

The old Seer spoke: "Do not be afraid of death of the body, for Fairma reserves a place in Folkshome for the virtuous. Be afraid of the death of your soul and living your life in regret and shame after betraying that promise. That is Hel. Be true to yourself."

As the Seers rose to leave, Astria watched the sky with Zephyr by her side. And when the sun reached the rim of the valley, they left for home, unaware of the

Farmers who frowned at the idle hands and the job undone.

***

The next day after work, Astria hoped to capture a dramatic sunset from the wide stone shelf at the trailhead to the West Top. With her, she brought chalks of red-orange and yellow, the same colors she used for blossoms in summer. But the overcast sky bleached the color from the valley.

She needed only a few dark lines to distinguish treetops and craft shops from snow. A few more marked footpaths heading to the village center like rivulets merging into a stream. The reflected sky turned the Blois River's deep blue into shades of gray, echoing the monochrome woodcuts on the Manor House walls.

"Welcome," she said as Zephyr sat beside her, nuzzling his head under the arm of her wool coat to invite a scratch. With early winter, his coloring had lightened to shades of tan and gray that blended into evergreen and stone.

Today, he fussed, unable to settle down and sit quietly by her side. His muscles twitched, and he repeatedly rose to stretch and flap his wings and sat again. She leaned against him to quiet him. After taking a bite of her sandwich, she held it over her head, where his fang snagged a tiny corner.

Zephyr squawked when Omattlig swooped overhead. Lonely for her friend, Astria waved as Fynn landed and smiled as he approached.

She shared her sandwich, and he offered a gourd of tea.

"How's your training?" she asked.

"Hard. My arrows haven't hit a target yet from the saddle. Even when Omattlig is on the ground."

"And Yana?"

"Trunghanger is fast, so Lothen is thinking about making her a herald like Jenks. And your duties?" he asked.

"You get used to it," she replied but sensed his impatience.

"Are you happy?" Fynn asked.

Astria shrugged. "I'm settled. For now."

He brightened. "Without being able to ride?"

"Not in that."

His discomfort returned. "If you can't be a Rider, perhaps you and I—"

"You think I won't ride?"

"Come now, Zephyr is grown but still can't fly. And what would you do if he could fly?"

"Ride him, if he lets me."

Fynn frowned. "But the Council didn't accept your offer to be a Rider."

"What could they do but accept us?"

"We see no path for you to—"

"'We?'"

"Skye. Everyone."

"My mother, huh? And you?"

He shook his head, and with every heartbeat, he seemed farther away.

She was alone now, without support from anyone. Even if they loved her, they did not understand, and she could never explain her desire and her promise.

"This is the path I choose," she said.

"You're making your life harder. Perhaps if we—"

He's going to ask me again, but I'm not ready for that. "You have another path for me, a path that's easier."

"The Seers say the gods burden us if we deny our fates, Asti."

She frowned. "And you speak for them? Really? Was it your *fate* that we struggled to grow the daemonberries so Omattlig would partner with you?"

"My fate was to be your friend, and perhaps it's yours to give up this—"

"It's not my *fate* you speak of. It's the role you want me to play."

"I only want you to be hap—"

"I hear you've been spending lots of time with Furnia," Astria said. "Doesn't she make you happy?"

He made a fist.

"Are you going to hit me now?"

He relaxed his grip. "Never," he said gently.

"I know what you want, Fynn. I don't want to hurt you, but I can't agree. Maybe later . . . when I am older."

He thrust out his jaw. "That may be too late."

She put a hand on her hip. "Too late for what?"

But Fynn walked away and mounted Omattlig.

"If you truly love me, it will never be too late," she whispered as he flew away.

Am I right to ask him to wait? Is he my only choice? Is compliance my only path?

Fynn shattered her peace, and she could not draw anymore. *Is he right? Am I just stubborn?*

"He doesn't matter. I will ride."

Zephyr nuzzled Astria's side to soothe her, but it was not enough. She needed distance.

A better view of the glaciers lay above her, and the climb would take her along the same route she took so often with her friends, but never in the cold.

The initial ascent was easy, but her fingers stiffened from contact with the cold rock. Before she reached the shelf, the steady spray of snowmelt soaked her coat and weighed her down. Continuing her climb was too risky, and she descended.

No one spotted for her now, forcing her to find her footing by touch alone. Her descent was slow, and the rock wall, now wet, fell into shadow and became treacherous with frost. Below her, Zephyr honked excitedly.

Stupid! She misjudged the mountains, and that could be fatal.

If I fall, who will care? Zephyr, my friends, and my mother. Life will go on. Mama will miss me. But what of my promise?

Astria shook her head to clear her mood. But as she searched for her next foothold, her support foot slipped on the frost. Her stiff fingers now carried all her weight. She found a better foothold, but when she put her weight on it, a hand slipped. Scrabbling frantically for a better handhold, she broke her nails on the rock. Her other hand slipped, and she fell backwards.

In an instant, her life as a cripple flashed before her eyes. But she stretched out her arms and smiled.

But first, I will fly!

Wind rushed around her, and she expected the hard impact on the rocks below.

Instead, her coat stiffened at the shoulders, and around her whirled the *pop* and *whoosh* of dragon wings. Zephyr caught her in his claws and now carried her back to the shelf.

Astonished, she forgot that only moments ago she expected to die. When he let her go, Astria opened her arms to hug him, but he knocked her to the ground, hopped on four legs, and scurried around the wide shelf like a chicken. With each hop, he stayed aloft for a few wingbeats, but then fell to the ground again.

She laughed and rose, ducking his wings and dodging as she tried to hug him. She chased him, and his eyes changed from green to sparkling silver and back again. After failing to fly, he paced along the edge of the shelf, gazing at the valley floor hundreds of feet below, and then at the sky.

"You can't," she said.

He turned to her and cocked his head, but a moment later he turned back to the cliff and opened his wings.

"Wait!" she shouted and ran to him. But before she reached him, he jumped off the shelf and disappeared.

"Zephyr!" she cried and ran to peer over the edge, expecting a crash site. Instead, a rush of air knocked her back on her butt as he raced past her straight up into the sky. High above, he darted with the erratic flight of a mayfly rather than the graceful glide of a dragon.

Astria smiled and stood with her arms outstretched, turning as he turned and twisting as he rolled. He dove, and she cringed when he pulled up just before hitting the cottages.

Agnarr appeared, and Zephyr copied his maneuvers and the steady rhythm of his wingbeats. The older dragons joined, and together, they flew in formation, banking and rolling as a single, graceful dragon. Younger and more agile than they, every so often, Zephyr spun or looped.

Astria sat cross-legged and smiled with tears rolling down her cheeks as the dragons flew past and honked— honks that to her meant, "Thank you."

His world is unbounded now, no longer constrained to the valley walls

She lost her smile and sighed.

I'm the valley's only captive now.

Just before sunset, Zephyr landed nearby. And when she ran to him, he kneeled in the dragon's offer for her to ride.

"We know them by their actions, for actions do not lie," the Oracle said. And he knows me by what I did for him.

"You came back for me," Astria said and hugged him.

Her heart drummed in her ears as she tied her hair up in a ponytail, and without saddle or bridle, she mounted in front of his wings. Under his watchful eye, she secured herself with her calves hooked under his wings, and her fists gripped his neck hair, trusting him with her safety.

She leaned forward, anticipating his takeoff, but stopped and frowned. *The Council. They didn't approve of my offer to ride.*

But Zephyr's eyes sparkled, and she smiled again. "What can they do to me now?"

When she patted his neck, the dragon hopped off the cliff and dove for the ground, leaving her breath behind in a gasp.

Following the slope of the mountain, he leveled off and buzzed the treetops. At the opposite cliff wall, he followed the thermals up above the rim and straight into the sky, leaving the scents of pine and wood smoke behind. And she never caught the breath she had left on the cliff.

At the top of the rise, her weight left his back, and her stomach met her throat before he rolled to fly level. He slowed, and she ached to sit up and stretch her arms wide as she did in her daydreams.

With her on his back, he flew with the grace of a crane between the clouds, as smooth as the wind. Flying was as natural for him as breathing, and the strength in his shoulders and chest coursed through her thighs.

He was her dragon now—*her* dragon—*her* partner. And she was his, for on the most momentous day of his life—the day he was finally free of the valley and free to see the world—he chose to be with her. And never did she care so much for anyone or anything as she did him.

It was cold there in the sky. She could not sit up, and she could not sing in the wind.

It wasn't like she had imagined. It was better!

Elated, she ignored the icy wind that bit through her coat. The tears on her cheeks she carried from the valley floor dried in the wind, and the new ones froze on her cheeks.

Together, they soared above the valley walls. The horizon encircled her, and she knew at once where she and her map of flowers came to life.

That way north lies Suleria. There, to the south, the Imperium. Vernier and Andeir lie to the southeast, just over those peaks. And somewhere far to the west, along the Spine of the Worm, beyond the edge of the world, lies the sanctuary of the dragons: the Source.

And here in the heavens, I'm home.

This was her father's home, too, and she wished he and Klokbror were here to fly with them, to share what they could never explain in words.

Her dragon lowered a wing and spiraled down to Lake Norven, losing elevation with each circuit. Skimming the surface, his wingtips raised ripples on the water with every beat. From the lake's exit, he raced downstream to the Notch where the Blois River split the Tops in two. Through them, he flipped and dove again and followed the waterfall down to the chasm below. Astria reached her hand into the water, and falling at the same speed, the drops did not wet her hand.

Before they crashed onto the rocks, Zephyr turned and opened his wings. Six times her weight pressed on her back and drove down onto shoulders turned to iron as he recovered from the dive. Through a mist so thick it dampened her heavy coat they sped, and when the mist cleared, he glided through the Blois River's narrow canyons.

He soared again to carry her through the layers of clouds that shrouded the valley, first the reds and oranges that set the glaciers ablaze, and above them to hazy yellow clouds. Above them all the sun still shone, while far below them, torches blinked in the shadows of the Spine through breaks in the cloud cover.

As the clouds changed from rose to dusty gray a thousand feet above the peaks, she found peace, at one with the sky and the night. When the setting sun left them in shade, moonlight from Lon and Elein lit the valley.

In the clear air above the smoky valley rim, she was closer to the stars than to home. Within them, she found the constellation Nidhogg and her wishing star. "Thank you," she said and hugged Zephyr tighter.

She belonged here, and she would have nothing less.

"Olim willing, you will ride," her father had said. "And when you do, the world will never be the same."

She smiled. *And he was right.*

When Astria's shivering became too severe, Zephyr landed near her home. Her cheeks burned from the wind, and her toes and fingertips stung with frostbite.

Filled with joy, she did not notice people watching through windows and doors ajar, and she ran inside to find Skye wiping tears from puffy eyes.

"Mama! Zephyr can fly!"

"I know, dear. They—"

"He saved me. I would've fallen if he hadn't flown to catch me. Tell the Council!"

Skye did not smile. "Britta saw you ride."

Uh-oh. "And?"

"They spoke to me. They didn't accept your choice."

Astria crossed her arms and cocked her head. "Too late. Zephyr made *his* choice."

With her thumb, Skye brushed her daughter's wind-burned cheeks. "They say you defied them, and they can't risk that. Resources are too scarce, and people are resources."

Astria winced at the touch. "I didn't steal him from a Rider. They should think of this as a bonus."

"Not if they must support you. They meant you to do other things, and now you won't be there."

"Efrin will train me."

"They won't let him."

"I won't give up Zephyr."

Skye found a salve and painted her daughter's cheeks. "They've already decided."

Astria knocked her mother's hand away. "They need to know he saved—"

"It doesn't matter. Exile was—"

Her mother's warnings and those of the Council finally struck her. "Exile? I did nothing wrong, and . . ." Astria's voice trailed off as she sat. "They can't do this, can they?"

"They can make sure citizens of the valley don't share with you. Including me."

"What if you marry Efrin?"

"It's too late for that," Skye said. "But they are grateful for the daemonberries, and for that reason, they didn't exile you. That was Kendrick's compromise."

Astria let out a long sigh of relief.

"But they declared you a Rogue and a visitor in Invernell. They won't provide you with the goods of the valley except in trade."

"They cast me out? I can't sleep in my own bed? How can they do this? What value can I bring if I ride but am not a Rider? What about Explorer?"

Skye smiled gently. "Your father's role was unique and not for a child, dear. If you hunt and share your catch, they'll welcome you. But not as a Rider."

"I can hunt and be welcome?"

Skye nodded. "Only to trade."

"What did this cost you?"

"It matters not. I can't lose you, too."

A knock interrupted them, and Astria opened the door to find Yana with tears in her eyes, nailing a parchment to the doorframe.

"The Council of Twelve declares Astria Sannfjaer a Rogue," Yana read. "We cast you out with no home in Invernell, and our citizens turn their backs on you. You can take no part in our lives nor any measure of our goods unless by fair trade." She paused to wipe tears from her eyes. "After sunrise tomorrow, you will be allowed only in public places to trade and as a temporary guest."

She turned to those gathering behind her. "Citizens of Invernell, heed this proclamation or risk being cast out as she is."

"Did Lothen pick you for this duty?" Skye asked. Yana dropped her gaze, but Skye understood. "Bastard."

"I'll never abandon you," Yana whispered and left.

Their neighbors hugged Skye and offered their condolences before returning home. A few glared at Astria, but no words passed between them.

The crowd dispersed, and Skye took Astria back inside to the corner by the fireplace where she sat so many days. There, she lifted a cloth to expose her husband's old saddle, repaired and polished. And on the fender, she had tooled Astria's initials.

"It's dangerous to ride without a saddle."

Astria ran to hug her mother and wept. "Thank you!"

"You'll need a jacket . . . and goggles," Skye said and held her.

But Astria could not stop thinking of the graxes and wolves.

It won't be enough.

Chapter 7
The Wild

The chill night wind rattled the shutters and whistled through cracks in the walls of their little cottage as Astria tapped her fingers on her thigh. On her bed before her lay the essentials she had assembled for the Wild: heavy coat, waterproof tarp, bow and arrows, blankets, pots for cooking and boiling water, bone knives, cord for snares, and rope.

She frowned and crossed her arms to quiet her hands. *My life depends on what I choose.*

But no one ever lived in the Wild to tell her what skills or supplies were essential, and Astria regretted not asking Merythe how she and her beau survived

"How's this, Mama?" she asked and pointed to the array of survival gear.

Skye bit the thread from the knot that sewed quilts into a sleeping bag, rolled it up, and tied it. From her dress, she took a small pouch and handed it to Astria.

"The Seer grows ginger and peppermint indoors," Skye said. "And I made a kit for you."

"Why?"

"You're not used to the rhythm of Zephyr's wingbeats or the turbulence in flight, and you may get nauseous," Skye said as she packed dried foods. "That should last until you can visit to barter. There's always a demand for venison and furs to trade at the Manor House."

In the twilight before sunrise, they finished packing the supplies and left the cottage to strap the packs onto Zephyr.

"What will it take for me to be invited back?" Astria asked.

"There aren't any rules for this, hon. It's up to the Council. But it can't be worse than for a stranger."

"Which is?"

"Well, you need to be useful with a proven skill."

"A hunter?"

"I don't think so. We're mostly Craftsmasters and Farmers in the valley. You'd need to prove you're loyal and obedient to the Council."

Not likely. "What if I can ride Zephyr and help the Riders?"

Skye frowned. "You'd need to communicate with others in the air, and that requires training."

"Which is unlikely with Lothen. But if I achieve all that, how long must I stay Rogue?"

"I'll ask them, but it can't be more than two years."

That hit her hard and she sat. *Two years? I'll be dead by then.* But she stayed silent, not wanting to frighten her mother or burden her.

"Stay south and west, and close to the valley," Skye said and pursed her lips.

Astria tied the bags behind the saddle. "Once I get settled in, I might search for Papa."

"I suggest you wait before thinking so far ahead. Focus on surviving."

Surviving. Mama fears for me.

Skye hugged her and looked her square in the face. "There's only one of you, and I need you in one piece. Hear me? And don't go north."

"Why not?"

Efrin ran up to them. "I just heard. Are you ready for your big adventure?" he asked, checking the saddlebags and bindings. As he worked, other villagers gawked in silence. "Lothen warned Fynn and Yana not to see you off. They told me to wish you luck."

"I'll need more than luck."

He turned away from the crowd and spoke quietly. "Don't be afraid. You can do this. Winter's coming, and you'll need to learn fast. There'll be no time for idle hands. Your major task is to get ahead of the food problem. Every night before you sleep, do something to prepare for the next day."

"Does Agnarr help you hunt?" Astria asked.

Efrin shook his head. "You're on your own for food. Dragons aren't like us. They don't share their catch, and they scare the game away. If you've seen them eat, you'll know why the animals fear them. And I don't recommend you watch, either."

"Can he spot other game from the air?"

"We tried, but they're gone by the time I get there on foot. But keep Zephyr close to ward off predators. The graxes are mostly to the northeast. But don't tempt them by leaving food around."

Efrin tied an extra bota of water to the saddle. "You'll be spending lots of energy tracking game and lugging things around, so you need lots of water. If you get dehydrated, fly back."

"How will I know?"

"Dark pee, dizziness, dry skin. And stay away from the jenalei tea unless you boil it off. It'll dehydrate you. But never let that happen. It should be easier when the snow comes. But only take snow from the surface or from the tree leaves. And don't take any chances. Any mistake can be fatal, so you must be very, very careful."

Efrin glanced at the eastern horizon and frowned. "I'm sorry I canna go with you to pick out a campsite. Lothen has his eyes on us." He leaned close and whispered, "But I'll see you as soon as I can. All set now."

Dawn broke on the Tops, and Zephyr twitched.

"Go with Fairma," Skye said and hugged her.

Astria held the hug. "I'll be OK, mama," she said but could not keep the tone of question from her voice. She mounted Zephyr, and as she flew away, she turned back to see Skye with her face buried in Efrin's chest.

She was free of the Council's rules now, flying with her dragon and excited for the chance to explore like her father. But everything she knew told her the Wild was not safe, and she wanted to hide.

From the air, Astria found a suitable campsite by the edge of a glade, large enough for Zephyr to land, and a short hike uphill from a creek.

As she unpacked, an eight-point buck wandered into camp followed by a doe, both unafraid of the dragon that could devour them. As the buck grazed on brush at the edge of the clearing, the doe approached Zephyr and sniffed.

"Seems she thinks you're cousins," Astria said and sat with her legs crossed. "What do you think?"

Without moving his head, Zephyr curled a lip to expose a fang. The doe backed up and scampered to the buck that watched them, curious but unafraid.

"You've never seen people?" Astria asked. "Or only gentle ones? Did you come from the north? Did you see my papa?"

The buck turned away, and with no forage in the campsite, he sauntered away, followed by the doe.

Graxes wouldn't be as gentle as Zephyr, she thought, *but graxes won't come near a dragon.*

When the deer left, Zephyr took off to hunt for his dinner, and Astria made her camp.

Over the next few hours, Astria erected a lean-to and gathered wood for a fire. After a cold lunch, she secured her food bag high in a tree branch. She notched the tree with her bone knife to mark her first day in the Wild and sat to tie slip knots for snares she would set the next day while scouting for game. The work kept her busy and her fears at bay.

Dusk came as she struggled to make a fire with flint and iron, and she finished another cold meal before the flames steadied. Night brought a chill, and with fingers too stiff to continue tying snares, she sat closer to the fire. Exhausted and drowsy from lack of sleep, she squinted into the shadows outside the circle of firelight.

At the edge of the woods, pairs of red and blue eyes blinked, and she wrinkled her nose as a rancid smell drifted past. She froze. Fire might keep the wolves away, but graxes were not afraid of the flames.

She jumped to her feet and drew her knife.

Why are they here if Zephyr is nearby?

The answer came in an instant. *They wouldn't know—he rested here only here a few minutes without time to leave his scent. I should have gone with him.*

As more eyes joined in the underbrush, Astria backed into a tree, holding her bone knife in front of her.

Brother Moon beamed through the trees to light her campsite, and one pair of eyes cautiously stepped into the clearing, its head scanning both sides. The beast was half her height, twice the size of the stuffed model in the fortune teller's tent, almost unrecognizable under thick cords of muscle on its back and gangly forelegs.

This isn't supposed to happen! Zephyr is supposed to be here.

Her heart pounded in her ears, and her legs shook to run.

Unchallenged, more graxes followed their leader and spread out. One little knife would not stop them.

The leader stared as it stalked forward, its oily fur tinged red in Fures's light and drool glinting from long fangs. But a momentary glance to its right tipped her: the grax in front was a distraction.

She turned to her left with the knife out and slashed the grax that lunged from behind the tree. Before it attacked again, she jumped for the first branch of the tree. The grax leaped to follow her, but its small hind legs gave it no height, and she kicked it in the snout when it snapped at her. After a quick climb, she reached the second branch and felt safe. Other graxes tried to climb, but their forelegs proved unsuited for it.

But they were persistent and hungry.

One grax climbed over the others and made it to the first branch and snapped at her. She stepped farther out on the branch to avoid it, but her weight made the branch droop. The graxes did not have to reach her. All it had to do was force her to the end of the limb where she would either fall, or the branch would bend with her weight and the pack would get her. She kicked away the swipe of his claws, but with each step, the branch drooped more.

I should have gone with Zephyr, she thought again. *And that was the fatal mistake Efrin warned about.*

As the grax stood on his hind legs to bite her ankles, a sudden gust of wind distracted it, and hot blood splashed her face, blinding her.

She could not see but heard the crunch of breaking bones and the shrieks of wounded graxes. And when she wiped the blood from her face, Zephyr stood alone in the clearing, eyes red and licking blood from his muzzle.

She jumped from the tree, and as she ran to him, his eyes sparkled.

"Next time, a little earlier," she said and hugged him.

After Zephyr's snack, the forest was quiet. Safety returned with her dragon, and she sang to him. As she sang, she thought of what could have happened—and what might happen whenever her protector was gone. Exhausted, she finally slept.

***

The next morning, a blinding sun and the sound of tearing cloth nagged until Astria woke. Zephyr was gone again, and in the clearing lay her food bag, torn open and strewn across her campsite. In the middle of the mess sat two bear cubs, one gobbling down her food and the other pawing through flour and dry goods, spreading them around in the dirt.

"Hey!" she yelled and waved her hands. But when the mother bear at the edge of the clearing stood on her hind legs and roared, Astria stopped.

"What beautiful children you have," Astria said in a soothing voice and backed up slowly with her arms wide. "I'm sorry if I scared them. Take what you need." *As if I have a choice.*

When the mother went back on all fours, Astria lowered her hands and sidestepped up the hill as the bears tore up the rest of her campsite.

At home, she never missed a meal. But now she sat helpless as breakfast, lunch, and dinner disappeared.

And the means to make more lay broken and scattered in the dirt.

Her ordeal just became much harder. *I might die without that food.*

A half-hour later, Zephyr returned and honked, and the bears woofed back. Unmolested, they ambled away, and her dragon curled up at the edge of the camp and gazed at her.

Late again.

"You might have made an effort to stop them, you know," she said as she came down from the hill to the ruined campsite. "I can't get new provisions until I bring something back to trade."

But Zephyr just cocked his head.

As she picked through her stuff for remnants—a basket without a handle, a torn blanket, and broken utensils—Zephyr came to her and put his head in her hand for a scratch.

She sat with him, and tears welled up, but she fought them back. *Tears won't help me.*

With nothing left to eat, she packed her weapons and snares, and headed out to hunt.

In widening circles, Astria spiraled out from her campsite, searching for tracks and spoor of game. As she walked, she gathered cones from the many pine trees and acorns from the few oaks that grew this high in the mountains. At each sign of a rabbit or fox runway, she set a snare: a simple noose to entrap them as they ran through or over it. But days might pass before she caught anything, and she would need to come every day to check and set new snares.

Throughout the day, Zephyr followed or flew overhead, and when he peed within sight, Astria filled her game bag with the moist dirt. On return to her campsite, she sprinkled the dirt around the edges of the clearing to ward off the graxes who had not suffered the slaughter of the prior night.

At sunset, a doe with a shredded ear appeared, and Astria smiled. It was beautiful, and she hesitated. Before she nocked an arrow, Zephyr's shadow passed, and the doe scampered away.

That night, Zephyr did not return from dinner, and she spent the evening worrying about the graxes and laying pine cones around the fire to roast through the night. Then she put the acorns in a pot of water to skim off the infested floaters and left the rest soaking in a wicker basket to soften the shells. While she waited, she held her knife ready, flinching at the calls of the night owls and howls of wolves.

Zephyr's absence made the predators brave, and with little of his scent downwind, or his body upwind, they approached the edge of the trees where she had sprinkled the dirt. These were not the red eyes of graxes, but the reflected firelight from the eyes of wolves, and she kept the flames high until her firewood ran down.

Near dawn, Zephyr returned, and she cuddled up to him and slept.

***

Her growling stomach woke Astria late next morning, and she searched for food. The pine cones had opened with the fire's heat, and she worked them to retrieve the nuts. But after shelling them, only a handful were edible. She also shelled the acorns with a rock and put the meat in a porous basket and left it in the creek to leach out the tannins.

Her stomach rumbled—she was hungry for the first time in her life, really hungry, and she chewed her cheek. This was a new kind of hunger, and it gnawed at her.

It was early winter, and nearly half of the short day was gone. The only berries she could find were from jenalei, and she downed a few mouthfuls. As she left to check her snares, she was energized and confident that her luck had turned and the day would be hers. But she forgot Efrin's warning to boil the alcohol off the jenalei, and a few minutes from camp, the world spun. Unsteady on her feet, she sat with her back against a stenifer tree, but as she waited out the dizziness, she fell asleep.

The sun reached the peaks, leaving her in shadow, and she woke to an icy breeze and a stabbing headache. She jumped to her feet and hurried to check her snares but found all untouched or broken by larger game that skittered away before she could shoot.

As the afternoon waned, the split-oval hoofprints of wild boar shimmered in a mud puddle. Astria nocked an arrow and followed the tracks to a thicket. In a clearing beyond, a male boar rooted with his head buried in the dirt. Around him skittered a female and three piglets with striped coloring. Astria leaned against a tree as the male raised his head to expose white tusks curled to a half circle. He grunted and wiggled his nose to sniff the air, and Astria leaned back out of sight. He grunted, and again she spied him rooting.

Astria drew her bowstring back and aimed, her mouth watering with the taste of bacon and ham and—

Without a sound, Zephyr swooped down and grabbed the boar and sow in his claws while the piglets squealed and ran. Zephyr bit the male in half and whipped his head around, showering Astria in hot blood and gore while she stood frozen.

After wiping the blood from her face, she found Zephyr staring at her with red eyes and bloody fangs as he munched on the sow.

She raised her hands and backed away. "All right, big guy."

The blood that dripped from her made her stomach growl with hunger but was bait for the graxes. At a nearby stream, she washed off the gore. The icy water chilled her hands and face, and without a towel to dry them, the wind chilled them more, and she shivered.

When she finished, the sun had set, and she lost her way in the dark. Zephyr came to her whistle, and she followed his honks back to her campsite, a dead fire, and no food.

Zephyr landed, his muzzle still covered in blood.

"Efrin didn't say you were such sloppy eaters," she said and pointed to a spot on his mouth where a hoof hung from his lips. He glanced down, slurped it up, and wiped the blood from his lips with his tongue.

With fingers stiff from the cold, she lit the fire and let it grow as she checked the acorns. The acorn water still ran brown with tannin, so she returned the basket to the creek. Then she tied snares until she ran out of cord, not knowing how else to prepare for the next day. With her stomach growling, she regretted sparing the beautiful doe.

***

Zephyr stayed that night and kept her safe, but hunger cramps kept her up all night, and she woke groggy.

The acorn water ran clear, and after she set the nutmeat by the fire to roast, left her camp to hunt. She checked her snares with her bow out and arrow nocked, but her arrows missed her prey to break on the rocky ground until only a few arrows remained.

When she returned to her camp, she found the acorn meat burned. After removing the char, all she had left from the handfuls of acorns, was a nutty paste that fit in a soupspoon.

On the day they left Invernell, she had thought herself an equal partner with Zephyr. But this was his world, not hers, and he was the natural hunter with better eyes and weapons than hers. She was not competent to manage hunting and gathering while keeping herself fed, warm, and rested. Without hunting, she would have nothing to bring back to trade for new arrows and supplies.

That's why the valley does so much better, with each doing what they're trained for and skilled at. All I have is me, and I'm not skilled at anything.

Without skills, she would die, but what could she do?

Ready to give up, she threw a wormy acorn into the fire for each Elder on the Council except her mother.

I'll die here before I kneel to them. I'll never give them the satisfaction of begging to rejoin the citizens.

But her cramping stomach argued otherwise.

At noon the next day, a small rabbit struggled in a snare, and Astria fell to her knees in tears.

It was beautiful and helpless. And she killed it.

Back at her campsite, she lit a fire. And while it grew, she gutted the rabbit, skinned it, and put it on a stick to roast.

At home, her mother would stew the rabbit with potatoes and leeks, but her mouth watered every time the wind blew the scent her way, and as soon as she thought it cooked through, she bit into it.

As the juice dribbled down her chin, she did not notice it was tough and burned. Nothing ever tasted so good, and in a few minutes, it was gone.

When she finished, she was still hungry but not famished. With the sharp edge of hunger dulled by the rabbit, she could think again. It was so much work for so little, but now she might have a real chance to survive.

I'll get better. And when I do, I'll cure the hides to make a coat and mittens.

With closed eyes, she prayed to Fairma and laid her hand on the little fur pelt. "Thank you for my life."

***

Three days later, after the villagers had left the Manor House, Kendrick answered a knock on the door. There stood Astria with a dirty face, shivering from the cold. Without a word, she entered and laid three uncured rabbit pelts on the trading counter while steadying herself on the edge.

"That's a meal and your choice of arrows or flour," he said, but she did not reply. "Take a seat by the fire. I'll bring you something to eat."

With her shoulders hunched over, she sat by the fire with her coat on. A minute later, Kendrick set a meal of double portions and cider on the table in front of her.

"Don't eat too fast," he said, "or you won't keep it down."

As he turned to go, she grabbed his sleeve. "Please don't tell my mother and friends I'm here."

"Of course. I need to close up now. When you're finished, you can clean up in the kitchen. There's hot water on the hearth."

She only half-listened to his birthday wishes as she dug into the lamb stew; plain food, barely tasted, but the best meal she had ever eaten. The cider was sweet and filled her nose with cinnamon. And in a minute, it was gone.

The feast was her sixteenth birthday celebration, and she prayed she would see another.

When Kendrick returned, he found Astria curled up next to the fireplace out of sight in the shadow of the mantel. He put a blanket over her and a pillow under her head. And into her game bag, he put a small sack of cornmeal and a quiver of arrows.

The next morning as Kendrick opened, he found a spool of cord missing. Astria was gone, and where she had slept was the sack of cornmeal.

***

With her stomach cramping and her mouth watering, Astria sat on her haunches and rocked side to side as she turned the spit over a fire. The tiny rabbit on it was her only meal in two days since trading with Kendrick.

I should've taken the cornmeal, but I wasn't hungry then and could afford my pride. She reached for her quiver and counted the few arrows left, snapped the arrowheads off the broken shafts, and threw the shafts into the brush. *And I'm wasting arrows in desperation.*

She stared at the rabbit, too tired to be angry, and listened to her growling stomach. Her entire world narrowed to allow no thought but her next meal.

The flap of dragon wings drew her eyes up as Agnarr glided down, and she jumped up and ran to him. A frown crossed Efrin's face at the dark circles under her eyes and sallow skin, but he quickly recovered a big smile. He dismounted, and she offered her hand in welcome, but he hugged her instead.

"I'm having lunch," she said, her eyes glistening. "Please join me." She took his hand and led him to the fire, where they sat.

"I've eaten," he said but softened as the shame on her face. "Just a bite, then."

Without plates, she put the largest piece on a catalpa leaf and gave it to him.

"Too much, dear," he said and switched portions with her.

She ate slowly to hide her hunger. "Are you spying for my mother?"

"No, but she worries about you. I've flown by to see how you fare."

Then you couldn't see me faring poorly. "What of my friends?"

"Yana and Fynn ask about you, but Lothen keeps them busy. They think this is a grand adventure for you."

"Do they?" she asked and frowned.

The tiny rabbit was quickly finished, and Efrin offered her a drink from his bota. To her surprise, it was mead, and stronger than the jenalei berries.

"Did Kendrick send you?" she asked.

"I'm here on another mission. Your training."

"I thought Lothen said you couldn't?"

"The Council cannot take what's mine to give, and this is my time." He winked. "And they won't know. You need to learn to signal other Riders and their dragons. Dragons all seem to learn from one another, so this is for you. Let's see, and weapons training, and—"

"Do you know about hunting?" she asked.

"A little. We can start there if you like."

"Yes, please."

After she showed him her simple noose snare, he nodded and went to Agnarr's saddlebags for cord. He took her to a new rabbit run and demonstrated how to make a spring snare. Then he showed her how to tell poisonous hemlock from wild carrots and picked some for bait. Throughout the afternoon together, they made snares, and he showed her the edible roots to gather in winter.

With her preparations complete and her stomach full, she stopped on a hillock overlooking a valley and sat. Below her, fall had painted the elm and maple in shades of yellow and red as the stenifer turned again to green for the winter.

"It's beautiful here in the Wild."

Efrin sat by her side. "Yes, it is. And those at home never see it from the ground or the air."

When the shadows of the trees grew long, Efrin turned his head to the sky.

"Have you watched the sunsets with Zephyr yet?" he asked.

"No. And when would I have time for that?"

He stood and waved her to follow. "Now."

She frowned and panicked at each of the many things she must do that night to reduce her risk of dying.

"Whatever you need to do, we can do together when we return," he said. "Come."

She rose. "What do I bring?"

"Only your attention."

After mounting, Agnarr and Zephyr flew them to a cloud of dragons who circled a prominent ridge with an unobstructed view west over the glaciers. As the clouds above changed from white to yellow, their dragons landed with the others and immediately honked and hummed to each other. And with bright eyes, Zephyr attended to the honks as if each held a fascinating story.

When the sun touched the horizon, the dragons all quieted and turned west. Time slowed as they watched the clouds above change from yellow to orange and red. And when the last of the sun disappeared, the dragons took off and soared.

After a glance at Astria, Zephyr followed Agnarr and the others.

"They'll be back for us," Efrin said. "And can find your camp in the dark."

"Where do they go?"

"To chase the sun. It's still visible way up there."

"Why do they do this?"

"I don't know. But Agnarr stops to view the sunset on many nights, with or without me."

Dusk came with a chill wind and their dragons returned. On the way back, Agnarr stopped to gather branches for the fire and Zephyr copied him, saving her hours of work. Back at her camp, she built the fire quickly and lit it.

"Are you showing off?" Efrin asked.

Astria smiled. "Yes."

"My treat for dinner," he said, and from a saddlebag took bread, smoked meat, and a bota of grape juice.

After dinner, he retrieved a long, square stick and a bag from his kit. At the fire, he opened the bag and took out woodworking tools.

"Stand, please," he said.

When she did, he placed the stick in front of her and made a mark at eye level. He cut it at the mark and handed it to her.

"Next lesson: This will be your constant companion. It'll be in your hands anytime you don't have a weapon in it. Most people aren't frightened by it because they've never seen it in skilled hands."

She gripped it. "It's too heavy and hurts when I hold it."

"It's oak and heavy to build your muscles." He sat her down and gave her a hand plane. "It's your job to round it and make it easy to wield." He made a pass with the plane to blunt one edge.

"How small?"

With a calm voice like her father's, Efrin guided her hands on the plane to round the edges, thin it for her grip, and taper both ends to two-thirds of the middle. In a kit, he left for her stones to smooth it and a jar of flaxseed oil to seal it from the weather.

"How will I know when I'm done?"

Efrin leaned back and stared at the fire. "You'll feel it in your hands."

"Do you believe I'm this Speaker person?" she asked as she worked the stick.

"You'd know better than I," he said and threw a pine branch into the fire to make it sparkle. "Ask Agnarr to come to you."

She turned to Agnarr, who gazed at them from the edge of the trees. "Agnarr, come to me."

The big dragon glanced at her and rolled his eyes before closing them again.

"Agnarr?" she asked, but the dragon did not respond.

Efrin threw another stick into the fire. "That's all the proof I need."

"What about the other Riders?"

"They see the same behavior as I do. Even if the dragons understand you, if they don't do what you want, you're not to be feared."

"What about Lothen? He knows dragons. He can't believe it, either."

"I don't think so."

"Then why's he so against me becoming a Rider?"

"It's complicated."

"Uncomplicate it. I'm out here alone and . . ." She closed her eyes and took a deep breath to quench the tears. *Don't whine. He's doing what he can, and I'm not his burden to carry.*

"This is really hard," she said. "Winter will be here soon, and I'm worried about living through it. Someone should tell me why."

He sighed. "Lothen placates the superstitious Farmers, so the Council doesn't cut our rations. And the Farmers fear the rise of a Speaker."

"Why?"

"Harvests are getting poorer, which is the Farmer's responsibility. And they're being criticized for ignoring the Oracle's warnings. Myths are a useful refuge to avoid blame when they can't solve our problems. They need to put a face on it and hide their pettiness within the Council rulings."

"And I'm that face."

"Yes. The Druims fan their passions, and the Farmers can't resist."

She turned the stick to plane another edge. "I saw my mother arguing with Lothen. Is there something else between them?"

"That's her story to tell. Did she mention she wanted to be a Rider, too?"

Astria sat up straight. "No."

"Jorie and Skye rode Klokbror together when they were kids. When they became teens and too heavy, she partnered with Lusmiddag—"

Astria smiled. "Really? She never told me."

"Perhaps it brings back sad memories. Within a year, he sprained a wing and flew west."

Oh, crap! What would happen if Zephyr sprained a wing while we're in the Wild with the grax and he could not hunt? I can't hunt enough to feed him.

"How often do dragon's sprain their wings?" she asked.

"It's rare, I wouldn't—"

"What caused it?"

"We don't know," he said. "You have enough to worry about without Zephyr too."

"He flew west to the Source?"

"Only the dragons know. It broke your mother's heart, and she blamed herself, though she hadn't been the cause."

"So the Farmers fear dragons, the Riders partner with them, the Seers respect them, and the Druims worship them."

"And the Council uses us all."

"You make them sound callous."

He shook his head. "Not callous. Especially not your mother and Kendrick. But when they're wrong, it's on us. There's no recourse for us and no consequence for them, so they remain mired in the same old thinking."

Astria worked the wood in silence, and when the third moon topped the trees, Efrin stood.

"Time to go," he said and walked to Agnarr. She followed and he turned to her. "I'll be back in—"

Astria jumped into his arms and hugged him tight with her cheek on his chest and squinted to stop the tears.

Efrin hugged her back. "You've faced this boldly and with courage. Face each day with the same commitment. Don't quit."

She nodded. *If I quit, I die.*

When Astria eased her hug, Efrin stepped away and mounted Agnarr. "I'll be back in a week to continue your training."

Agnarr rose above the trees and headed home. Where he once sat lay a small bundle of cornmeal, cord, and a quiver of arrows. At the bottom was a small flower pressed between parchments—one her mother had saved from the map of flowers. A daemonberry plant in a canvas bag tied with a cord could only be from Yana and Fynn. She set her gifts in a protected corner of the lean-to and returned to the fire.

Under the three moons, Astria worked the stick, searching for its imperfections with her hands as fresh snow fell around her. When she grew tired, she closed her eyes and prayed.

"Thank you, Fairma, for friends like these."

***

When the door to their little cottage opened, Skye gasped and smiled like Astria had not seen since her father went missing.

"Come in, come in, hon," Skye said.

"I'm snowed in, and they say I can stay the day," Astria said as she knocked the snow from her boots. "And you are the person I want to see most."

"What a perfect thing to say," Skye said and helped her hang up her coat. Then she put her hands on Astria's cheeks. "Now let me look at you." She frowned at the dark circles under Astria's eyes, kissed her on the forehead, and hugged her. "Are you eating enough?"

"Yes." *Not since I left.*

"Sit, sit," Skye said with tears in the corners of her eyes. She went to the pantry for plates and smoked meat. "Tell me all about your adventures."

As Skye set the table, Astria told her mother only the things that would not worry her. Skye sat opposite, and with moist eyes and gentle smile, watched her eat.

After a month in the Wild's clean air, Astria smiled at the scents that made their small cottage home: the linen and soap of her mother, the leather and dragon of her father, and the smell of mutton and onion infused in the walls.

The tension in Astria's shoulders eased as she finished eating, for here, she was safe. Nothing could harm her within these walls and the rim of the Valley. She leaned back in her chair and put her feet up on another.

"I've been lonely here without you," Skye said and took her daughter's hand.

"Me too. Any word from the Council on when I can come back?"

"No decision. But another year, I think. Meanwhile, I've contacted Vernier and Andeir and found those who will speak well of you."

"But won't speak *for* me," Astria said. "And I want to be a Rider. Efrin said you once wanted that, too."

Skye flinched. "Lusmiddag's crest was blue like Jorie's Klokbror," she said with a weak smile. "Your father and I shared the dream of exploring and were constant companions until my dragon sprained his wing."

"It wasn't your fault."

"Maybe not. But I didn't fly that day, and he didn't return to me. I found him by the lake and nursed him until he could fly again. But he couldn't carry me, and a few months later, he flew west."

"Is that why you didn't want me to ride?"

Skye folded her hands in her lap and dropped her gaze. "Maybe partly, hon. I just hoped for a quiet, happy life for you."

"Did Efrin tell you he's training me?" Astria asked and took a slice of apple bread for dessert.

"Shh, that's between us and Kendrick."

"He knows?"

"Only him and Vinga."

"Lothen again?"

Skye nodded.

"Efrin told me that Lothen allies with Britta and the Farmers against me."

"Our food and defense. They are hard to argue against."

"Why? I saw you arguing with him. More than once."

"An old feud," Skye said. "I'm sorry you're wrapped up in it."

"I think it's more than that. Does he love you?"

Skye smiled gently. "He, Efrin, your father, and I were childhood friends."

"Really?"

"Lothen and I were promised by our parents, but I wouldn't commit to him. When I became eighteen, I chose Jorie."

"Is he taking that out on me?"

Skye glanced away. "I thought he understood, and we stayed friends. They became Riders, but your father was never serious. When Lothen became Flight Leader, he was hard on your father. And when the Clanough named Jorie Explorer, it meant he wasn't under Lothen's thumb which angered him."

"Why?"

"We'd never had that, never had someone not engaged in resources or defense before. And the Farmers were livid. To appease them, the Clanough now meets here in Invernell."

"Why did they make Papa Explorer?"

"That was before my time on the Council and the Clanough. Your father told them of his coin fragment, that it was important to the dragons and might explain why the growing seasons are getting shorter. But when he went missing, the Council seemed relieved, like they didn't really want to know why, if they couldn't do anything about it."

"Does Lothen still love you?"

Skye narrowed her eyes. "I think he'd be content to control me."

"Some men are like that."

"You mean Fynn?" Skye asked.

Astria nodded.

"I don't think that boy knows what he wants, except not to lose what he thinks is his."

"Is that why Lothen ended the search for Papa?"

"The Council chose not to believe that."

"What do *you* think?"

"I think that question is lost in the past, dear."

"So is Papa," Astria said.

*****

Weeks passed and the snow deepened, but the worst of winter was yet to come. Astria moved her lean-to beneath the shelter of a stenifer tree's wide branches, and at night, Zephyr closed off the exposed side with his body.

With Efrin's help, her hunting and trapping skills improved until her endless fear of surviving ebbed slightly.

During his visits, Efrin taught her the hand signs and calls dragons responded to. With Agnarr, Efrin coached Zephyr to match the speed of Astria's prey to improve her success with the bow. And Efrin explained why she needed to follow rather than lead a still target when shooting in full flight. On the ground, he trained her with the staff and edged weapons. And at night, he taught her how to navigate by the moons and the stars.

While Efrin trained Astria on the ground, Agnarr trained Zephyr in the air how to change his wing profile to control stall and glide: to soar effortlessly like the condors or swoop soundlessly like an owl. All the while, they chattered nonstop, and occasionally, when they honked, Zephyr glanced back at her.

Astria sensed it was about her, and she smiled. "I think Agnarr is entrusting Zephyr with the dragons' secrets."

"Pay attention," Efrin said, standing with his staff in both hands and one end on the ground.

She took her stance next to him and slowed her breathing. Quieting her mind, she let the chittering wheezits and rustling stenifer leaves drift in and out of her consciousness.

She did not need to think during the pattern: step and thrust from the waist, spin with the staff with both hands for the longest reach, drop to one knee, and sweep an inch above the ground. A melody came to her, its timing irregular to match the rhythms of the moves. She hummed, remembering the harmonies Zephyr would add, and a vision came.

The images were clear as a blue sky: the sun rising at the edge of a vast sea, soaring high above the glaciers, and the sun setting through layers of clouds. Elation filled her, and her feet left the ground as if she flew.

The crack of staff on staff and the sting of its vibration broke her reverie. She opened her eyes to her staff, blocked by Efrin's an inch from his head.

"Your mind wanders," he said. "These are weapons."

She blushed, and in the clearing, Zephyr and Agnarr faced her with sparkling eyes. Storm clouds rose over the glaciers, and Efrin's brow furrowed.

"Sit, Asti," he said. "I'm sorry, but I may not visit for a while. Winter is here and brings special concerns. The grax get hungry and the caravans need the Riders' protection. And winters have become deeper and longer, and challenge us who ride. It's colder up high, and the wind in flight will chill you faster than you realize. Your breath will freeze on your face, and your goggles will frost. So don't start taking long rides. Even the trip home can be dangerous."

He turned to the glaciers and the approaching storm. "Most of your game doesn't hibernate but may be harder to find. The graxes haven't come back?"

She shook her head.

"Good. But the wolves will see you as competition." He sighed and glanced at the storm clouds again. "If Philina were here, she'd tell you to gather the poplar leaves before they're all gone and use them in a tea if you're feeling ill."

She nodded and pointed to a line of herbs and leaves hanging in the shade of the stenifer tree. "Mama told me. I've started drying some."

"Good. I'll fly by, so if you're in trouble, mark an *X* in the clearing with branches or anything you can find, and I'll stop by."

Their parting was brief, but Efrin held his hug longer than usual. And as he flew away, she imagined what could force her to leave a signal in the clearing, and her confidence that she might survive was shaken.

If he's worried, then I should be even more so.

***

Unstoppable coughs and stabs of headache woke Astria to squint into a featureless, gray sky. Two nights after Efrin's visit, she returned late, shivering after scouting for game on Zephyr. Without the sun to wake her, she overslept and now rose in clothing damp with sweat.

On shaky legs, she dressed slowly to ease the pain in her head, and then walked to the creek and cracked the ice for fresh water. At the edge of the clearing, she coughed again. Without the sun, the snow merged with the gray sky, the world spun, and she fell to her knees. Her forehead burned in her palm, and she cooled it with a handful of snow. It felt good but did not ease her dizziness, and she threw up.

I'm sick, she realized, and all the horrors of what might happen to her if she could not defend herself overwhelmed her.

She stumbled to her lean-to for ginger to ease her stomach and grabbed a handful of poplar leaves. After relighting the fire from the coals, she brewed a tea. Sitting cross-legged, she stirred it, and her pounding head seemed to rotate with the spoon until she closed her eyes to ease the nausea. When brewed, she poured a cup of the tea, cooled it with a dash of snow, and drank slowly, rocking with the cup in her hands to warm her.

From beside her, she grabbed the rabbit fur wrap she had stitched together over countless hours, the start of her winter coat. Even so, the cold bit through, and she shivered.

Fresh snow fell as she cut frozen pieces of rabbit meat, added it to the pot for a stew, and stirred it until her shivering became too severe. Taking a step toward the lean-to for more clothing, she fell again.

I won't make it like this.

After grabbing a blanket, she rose and stumbled toward the trees. There, she gathered stenifer boughs to make into an X in the clearing to signal for Efrin. But the snow covered each bough as fast as she laid it down. While shaking the snow off, the world spun.

It did not matter now what dangers confronted her; she could not help herself. Her knees gave out, and she collapsed.

Curled up on the ground, Astria shivered alone in the snowfall and kept her eyes closed to stop the world from spinning. As if she watched from the air, scenes came from her childhood.

***

Behind her home, under the watchful eyes of her father, 6-year-old Astria lay on Klokbror's broad back and sang softly.

> *"When winds come ashore*
> *And ships land no more,*
> *I'll wait on the Isle of Gilmora . . ."*

Klokbror took the song and carried it without words, along with jumbles of images with the smell of salt air and an ocean breeze blowing her hair. Around her tiny voice, the dragon filled the soundscape like a chorus.

As she sang, she scooted up behind his crest to shield herself from the imaginary wind. When the song ended, she sat up and pointed to her left to a beach lapped by ocean waves.

"There it is, the Ocean of Daggers," Astria said and climbed down his muscular shoulder. "Let's have a swim!"

Alongside her, 7-year-old Yana slid off Getmordare's back. "The sand is hot in the sun."

Astria wiggled her bare feet in the sandy soil. "And tickles my toes," she said, and her pinafore changed to riding leathers like Yana's.

Klokbror changed to Zephyr, and she mounted to fly to the Manor House, where her mother and father waited by the door. Inside, her friends surrounded a banquet table topped with meats, fruits, and desserts. At one end, Merythe sang a village song, and Astria danced with her friends. With her tummy full, she was safe, and nothing could hurt her.

But even with her eyes closed, the world spun, and a red cast fell over the banquet as if Fures alone shone on them. The walls opened to the ice flows of the glaciers stained red with the blood of men in furs hacking at one another.

As she neared the fighting, the barbarians' faces resolved. And at the center of the carnage, she recognized one—herself. As men rushed to slash her, the sun glinted off an axe aimed at her skull and blinded her.

**

Astria swung her arms to ward off the axes, opened her eyes to the bright sliver of sunlight that woke her, and blinked at Zephyr's silhouette. When she tapped his nose, he opened an eye that sparkled at the sight of her. She smiled back, and he lifted the wing that protected her from the cold and snow. He shook it, and two days of snow fell away.

Woozy, she stood and wavered.

Not sick. Weak.

She sat and ate a mouthful of snow and then rubbed the rest on her face as she checked her campsite. Layers of snow buried the X of boughs, her signal to Efrin.

"Will I tell him the signal failed? No. No one could save me from this, but he'll blame himself. You must be hungry now, too," she said to Zephyr and pushed him away. "Shoo. I'll be fine. Go get lunch."

How long have I been sick? The notches in the tree that marked her time in the Wild could not tell her, and the shadows only implied it was midday. More storm clouds passed overhead, and she set her jaw. *Every moment I sit here feeling bad is an opportunity lost. I survived for another day. What more can I expect out here?*

What was I doing before I got sick? The banquet from her dream popped into her head, and her stomach grumbled. *Food? Poplar leaves?*

The meat she had hung to dry was gone, the pelts torn and chewed on, worthless to trade.

If predators did that but left me unmolested, then Zephyr *stayed here to protect me.*

"Thank you, Fairma," she said and smiled at Zephyr's retreating silhouette. "And thank you, partner."

The pot with the rabbit and poplar leaves had frozen over, marred by the tiny claws of raccoons. Her stomach growled as she cleared her firepit down to the dead coals. After adding aspen bark and dried moss, she used her kit to start a new fire. Once warmed, she dipped the spoon into the broth. The rabbit meat fell from the bone, and the broth warmed her, more satisfying than the banquet in her dream.

She knew her sickness came because of exhaustion. *Don't work yourself down so far, eat more and more often. But I'm already working my hardest to do that.* And unless she had more food, she would tire and might not rise again.

"Time to check the snares," she said and gathered her bow, staff, bone knife, and twine. She took no time to recover—the next storm would not wait for her, and she was hungry.

***

During an afternoon in deep winter, Astria trudged through the deep snow of the desolate forest and climbed the icy rim of a mountain valley. The bow around her shoulders was her distance weapon, and the bone knife in its sheath was for close-in work. Like her coat, fur covered her cap and mittens, and lined her boots.

At the ridge, she sat on her haunches and surveyed the valley below. Only gray trails and hints of green from the fir and spruce trees peeked through the snow-covered valley. The river that cut through it rushed down the narrow channel between the ice-covered shore and flowed beneath the frozen central lake.

She would not hunt there. Wild game would be thin in the valley, too shy for the lights in the cottages and the bustle of workshops.

The smoke captured by the rim drifted up to Astria with scents of varnish from the workshops and stews on the fires. Together, they brought memories of comfort and a full belly.

Lanterns on the trails and the commons lit the way to the Manor House, with all its windows lit bright. It was the annual winter party there, the Feast of Dorin, and she brought gifts of small fur bags tied with sinew that held her favorite treats: cooked chestnuts gathered over many hours while she hunted.

But I cannot deliver them.

She stayed in the cold, imagining Fynn and Yana flying to her and inviting her to the feast. There, surrounded by people she loved, they would welcome her in the warmth of the fire.

But they did not invite me.

Astria opened one of the little bags and ate while she watched as if she were there with them at the celebration. Having nothing to trade at the Manor House, she was not welcome. They might all be strangers rather than her friends.

Why haven't they come to visit me?

She knew all the reasons: Their commanders said no. They were watched. A visit might jeopardize them becoming Riders. They could not venture safely in the Wild. Though explanations came quickly, it still hurt that they did not come.

Would that be enough to stop me? No. But that attitude is why I'm out here alone.

When shadows covered the valley, the hunter looked west as she did every night to watch the sunset. But storm clouds hid the glaciers and the sun. A gust of cold air announced the coming storm, and a dragon landed by her side.

"Let's go, before the snow falls again," Astria said to her dragon, and without another word, she mounted and returned to her camp.

***

Two days later, a figure in a long cloak with a high fur collar stood at the edge of Astria's camp. A large bundle lay at the Rider's side and, on top of it, a short sword. Next to Zephyr at the edge of the clearing lay another dragon—Trunghanger.

"Yana?"

Her friend turned, and they hugged as Yana babbled on about the valley and events. But Astria barely listened, caring only for her friend's cheerful face.

"Did you sneak away?" Astria asked.

"I'm supposed to be off with my mother. I've passed my first signaling tests last week, and Lothen is not watching me so closely." She dropped her gaze. "That was our first Dorin party apart, and we missed you."

Astria nodded. "Can you stay for dinner? I have rabbit and acorns, and . . ." It would decimate her stores, but she would do anything to have her friend stay longer.

"Save your food, hon. I brought dinner from the Dorin feast."

Yana untied the bundle at her side and laid out two meals from the annual party. She handed Astria a tenderloin of wild boar, which she lay next to the fire, and opened a bowl of a cold beet salad with onions. Astria's mouth watered at the richness of the spread as she set a jar of mashed yams to warm next to the boar.

From her kit, Yana held out two crocks. "Vinga said to eat this."

"What is it?" Astria asked, opened it, and smiled at the aroma of cinnamon and cloves.

"Spiced apples," she said. "Turns out the old bat can really cook. There're two more here for you. She said to eat it every day until the wild fruit ripens."

"Why?"

"She says that without fruit you may get sick."

"Like how?"

"Well, you feel exhausted and sad, and your joints ache—"

"That's all the time," Astria said and dipped a finger into the crock.

While the food warmed at the fire, Yana brought out another bundle. "I come bearing gifts," she said and handed a small box to Astria. "This one's from your mother."

"Does Lothen know?"

Yana's face grew hard. "I don't think he can stop us." She shrugged. "I'll just say I came to trade."

"Did you see my mother at the party?"

"She wouldn't come without you."

Inside the box, Astria found fishhooks, line, needles, and thread of various sizes to sew everything from linen to leather. *Of course I need them, but how did mama know? Efrin.*

"This is from Efrin," Yana said and handed her a freshly oiled canvas tarp, large enough to enclose the other sides of her lean-to.

Speechless, Astria ran her hands over the tarp as Yana untied a wicker basket from Trunghanger's saddle. Spanning the length of her arms, it narrowed at one end.

"Kendrick says to put the small end facing upstream and check every day for fish trapped inside."

Astria inspected it and blinked back the tears, for woven within the wicker were bowstrings, and inside lay a quiver of arrows.

Yana handed Astria a small jar. "This is from my mother. It's a balm that Philina makes. Mama says to use it on any open wound or scrape to help it heal."

Her friend smiled and put her palm on Astria's cheeks to wipe away the tears. "And this is from me. You need something bright and happy out here."

She handed Astria a flint knife the length of her hand with a bone hilt wrapped in red-and-yellow cord. She ran her thumb across the edge that could cut a blade of grass lengthwise, so much sharper than her bone knife and so much more dangerous—a weapon rather than a tool.

"And these're from Fynn," Yana said and gave her a small package tied with string. Inside were little ceramic bells. "He said you can use them to warn of predators."

Astria glanced at Trunghanger and Zephyr. *Two dragons would be even better.* She turned to her friend and bit her lip. *And two sets of hands would make survival easier. Don't leave, my dear friend. I need you.* She surveyed her primitive campsite. *But I have nothing here that would entice you to stay. And if I ask, Lothen will end your dreams.*

The clear ring of the priceless little bells cheered her, and she held them next to her heart.

"They're pretty," she said and rose. "I have something for you all." She ran to the lean-to for the small packages of nuts, her fondest memories of picnics with her mother and father. "I know the trees in the valley are spare of nuts in the winter, and I . . ."

But she could not continue. Her gifts were nothing like the lifesaving gifts her friends gave her.

Yana hugged her. "Our gifts took less from us than yours took from you, which makes your gifts even more precious. And all we wish for is your safe return."

Yana served dinner on polished wood plates, and they ate with new forks she brought. Astria wolfed down her food but caught Yana's worried gaze and slowed.

"Things hard as a hunter?" Yana asked.

Astria did not want to complain, but it spilled out. "Game is scarce this time of year, and the snow buries my snares."

"But you can ride."

"Not far. It's so cold up there, and I need to hug Zephyr to stay warm."

"But you *ride*," Yana said with a smile.

Astria returned the smile. Her friend was right. She dreamed of being an official Rider, but she would never give up Zephyr to return to Invernell as a Potter. *Without Zephyr, I wouldn't have lived this long.*

"I understand why we never hear from Exiles and Rogues again," Astria said.

"It's freezing cold in the valley, too. And we have less game."

With Yana's response, Astria knew her friend did not understand how hard it was outside the valley. But she nodded anyway and dropped her gaze.

"But you have each other."

With dinner over, Yana took Astria's hand. "There's more," she said and reached into a saddlebag to remove a flask and a small package of syrup candies. "Kendrick won't miss these."

As the sun crossed the sky, Yana told stories of home, and Astria relaxed for the first time in months.

"What of my mother?"

"She worries for you constantly and has thrown herself more into the work of the Council. Britta refused your idea to try planting in the early winter, so Skye is experimenting with the home gardeners." Yana laughed. "Lothen tried to use the Riders to scout for offenders, but the dragons wouldn't help." Her voice dropped. "The Oracle came again and talked more of the Darkness."

Astria added a stick to the fire. "Can the Darkness be worse than this?"

Yana laughed and raised her cup to Astria. "If the Darkness comes, I'll join you here."

Why wait? she thought but could not ask. Instead, she glanced at the little bells. "Fynn hasn't come to visit."

Yana blushed. "You want him to?"

"Of course. He's my friend." Astria dropped her gaze. "Or was."

"He's afraid of being caught. He hasn't passed his signaling tests, and his parents are not as understanding as mine."

"And that's all?"

Yana stared at the fire. "He went to the Dorin celebration with Furnia. She really seems to care for him, and Kendrick can be influential in making sure he's promoted to Rider."

Astria's heart sank. "Is he just using her?"

"I don't think so. At least, not knowingly."

"And Jenks?"

Yana smiled and leaned back. "All that I'd hoped him to be and more. We can ride together now and watch the sunsets from the clouds."

Astria nodded. "You're going to marry?"

She sat up straight. "Of course! We only need to decide when."

A chill breeze came as the sun dipped below the tops of the trees, leaving the clearing in shadow. Together they brought the dishes and utensils to the stream, took sand from the bank, and broke the ice for water to clean them. And when clean, Astria asked where to put them.

"These are for you, too," Yana said. "To entertain your next guests."

Astria blushed. "Thank you." *And until then I'll eat with my hands.*

Yana kissed her on the cheek. "I have to meet my mother at the Tops before sunset so we can go home together."

Stay with me. Please, Astria thought, but again, would not ask.

Without bidding, Yana put Astria's meager gifts into her saddlebag. "I'll see they get these, hon," she said and hugged her but then held her at arm's length. "Do you still want to be a Rider?"

Astria pursed her lips and nodded. "To do my part."

Yana's eyes glistened. "They cast you out. Why would you help them?"

"Because what they have, what you have, is better than this."

"Better than freedom?"

Astria shook her head. "You help one another, and that makes life easier."

Yana gave her a side-eye. "I might prefer it here."

"No, you wouldn't." *But it would be so much easier if you stayed.*

After Yana left, it was colder than before she arrived, and Astria's heart was the reason.

Until now, she held some hope that a strong, young man would defy all the rules, defeat all her enemies, and destroy the barriers that kept them apart. That a man would curse the gods and change the course of rivers to come save her and build a life with her. And only now, after it was not possible, did she realize it was what she had hoped.

It was romantic, but the Wild had no place for romance.

Who but Fynn would come for me? But he has not come.

"Maybe I don't love you the way Mama and Papa love each other, Fynn. But if you had come to me, I would love you as I've never loved before and respected your courage and your sacrifice. I'm sorry, if that was my test for you, and I didn't know.

"I'd hoped to love you in time. But you went to Furnia."

And hope died, for the Wild had no place for hope, either.

***

Icy cold on her neck shocked Astria as she clawed her way to the surface of the river, searching for the light.

Her hand found a grip, and she pulled a tarp away to blinding sunlight, waking her from the dream of drowning. When her eyes adjusted to the light, she surveyed the wreckage of her camp.

The stenifer tree had shielded her and Zephyr from the worst of the flurries and howling winds, but two tarps supported by branches were not rugged enough for a three-day blizzard. The late-winter sun melted the snow that weighed on the branches and slid off to collapse her lean-to. Now a thick blanket of white covered everything she hadn't stuffed under the tarp.

Unaffected by cold, Zephyr watched through the open gap of the lean-to, but otherwise did not help as she dug out her supplies.

"Damn," she said as she swept snow from a drift with a branch. If she were not tired and hungry, the day would be beautiful. But three months of winter and struggling to survive had killed her fantasies of riding.

After clearing her camp of snow and rehanging the tarps, she refreshed her bedding of pine boughs to keep her off the cold dirt. Then after the last bite of jerky, she crawled out to check her snares.

With each step, the new snow deepened until Zephyr picked her up and dropped her back at the camp. There, she rebuilt the fire and emptied snow from her boots while Zephyr left to find his breakfast.

From the tree, she cut flexible branches using the serrated spine of her flint knife. Heating one branch to soften it, she bent it in the shape of a teardrop. With strips of leather, she tied its ends together and made cross braces and a toe loop. Bushy branches woven between the strips served to support her weight. She repeated the steps to make a twin, and after tying them to the toes of her boots, she could now walk on the snow's surface. But the morning was spent, and hunger ate at her again.

For a snack, she split open a jenalei pod to free the raw wheat and oats. From the leaves, she made a tea over the remains of the fire. The heat boiled off most of the alcohol and left the sweet flavors of peach and bay leaf. Energized by the tea, she tied the snowshoes to her boots and left her camp.

As she searched for her snares, the sun shone bright in a blue sky, but the blizzard that grounded Zephyr might return.

None of her snares or flags appeared above the snow, which also buried the tracks of game. She needed better traps but did not have enough to trade for them. So trapping meant another day to set new snares, and that would put her at risk if the snows came again. She would need to hunt now or beg for dinner when she returned to Invernell.

If the weather stays clear. If Zephyr can still fly. If, if . . .

Near the edge of a spruce grove appeared the prints of a snow fox. Too beautiful to kill, she would not track it. Rabbit tracks crossed those of the fox, but she declined again: hunting a rabbit on the run would exhaust her few arrows. When Zephyr hovered above, she signaled him to leave and not scare the game.

Astria followed fresh deer tracks to a wide ravine hidden in shadow by the surrounding trees. With bow out and an arrow nocked, she followed the tracks inside. The ravine grew darker as it narrowed, and she crouched and squinted to see the tracks in the snow. But when stones clattered from the canyon wall, it was too late.

A weight slammed into her back and pushed her face first into the snow. Knives sliced through the shoulders of her coat, and a vise gripped her neck through her thick parka. Whatever it was would kill her, but the snow stifled her screams.

With her shoulders pinned, she could not reach her knife. Instead, she untied her coat, rolled, and sloughed it off, twisting back on her attacker.

She turned to face a mountain lion about her size. Left with only the hide of its prey in its jaws, the lion jumped away and crouched nearby.

Astria drew her knife and made herself as large as she could, yelling and waving her arms, but without her winter coat, she appeared small. Instead of attacking her, the cautious lion jumped to the rocks, seeking advantage from higher ground.

Above them, Zephyr honked, and the cat crouched and hissed at him with fangs bared. While her dragon distracted the lion, Astria turned and ran for the exit.

But Zephyr could not reach into the narrow ravine, and, safe from the dragon, the lion returned its attention to Astria. Unhindered by the snow or snowshoes, the lion gave chase, beat her to the exit, and crouched, leaving her no escape.

With her flint knife in front of her, Astria bared her teeth and growled. When the lion pounced, its claws straight out in front, she sidestepped and slashed. Her blade bit deep into the lion's chest and side, but its momentum carried her back against the side of the ravine. Her head struck a rock, and the world filled with stars and blackness.

***

The outer door of the Manor House opened, bringing heads around to grunt at the cold draft and snow that blew inside. Ice fell from Astria's boots, soaked a dark brown from the wet snow, as she dropped a pile of pelts at their feet and a sack by the counter.

Her thick fur coat came off first, followed by leggings and boots. Reduced to one-third of her bulk, the goggles and parka came off, exposing Astria's face.

Although a Rogue and not a Rider, she was no stranger here, and a tacit acceptance of Astria and Zephyr grew. Alone of all the partners who flew together, the clans called them Swallow because they sang.

Kendrick smiled as she approached the counter. "How fares your dragon?"

"Well, sir, but tired and wet. We've been out for a fortnight."

"You need oil for those boots and grease for your face."

"Aye," she said as she stomped her feet to warm them. "And jerky. And arrows."

Kendrick took out a tube filled with arrows, some new and some used, and laid it on the counter. "Find some straw to line your boots."

Taking an arrow, Astria sighted down the shaft, laid it aside, and then examined two dozen more. "These will do." As she reached to take them, he put his hand on them.

"Sorry. What've you got to trade?"

"The hide and pelts there. And there's meat here from a stag and a mountain lion."

His nose twitched. "Hmm . . . cat. People don't like cat."

"It tried to kill me."

He smiled at her with what might be esteem. "And still tastes like cat. Is the fur to trade?"

"Of course," she said but failed to mention the long gash.

"I'll take the rabbit pelts," called a man from the fire.

"Take what bread and cheese you need," Kendrick said. "And jerky."

"And a mead."

He took the teapot instead. "Next year."

"I'm Rogue, sir. What does my age matter?"

He winked. "I'll bring you something better."

"Oh . . . and some of Philina's balm, the one with tarragon and thyme."

He studied her. "Are you all right? Should I call Philina?"

Squinting to hold back a tear, she smiled. "No. But thank you for asking."

She took the small pouch of balm and sat in her usual dark but warm corner. Removing her boots, she rubbed her toes to ease the tingle and stiffness. She grimaced as she peeled the shirt from her shoulders, exposing the claw scratches. With a dab of balm on her fingers, she tried to reach around to her back but was too sore to tend her wounds. Covering her shoulders again, she looked into the fire and shook her head.

Right outside this door, it's as cold and snowy as it is in the Wild. But here they have stored food from the harvest and a century-old building to shelter in. They have food to eat and time to rest because they can rely on one another.

I have nothing . . . but Zephyr.

She turned away from the others, not wanting them to witness her despair. Hungry and exhausted, she could not go home to her mother with visible injuries.

How long can I stay before they kick me out? I'm sixteen, for Olim's sake. Is this all I have to look forward to?

Kendrick's voice came from behind her. "Here."

She wiped her eyes before turning. On the table, he placed a thick sandwich and a cup of amber liquid. The alcohol and fruit scent filled her nose as she brought the warm cup to her lips to taste his special brew of jenalei and plum brandy.

"This is mine," he said. "The Council has no say in this."

"Thank you," she said and put a hand on his.

The first sip burned her throat but warmed her, and she reached for the sandwich.

As Kendrick returned to the counter, the door opened, and snow whooshed in. Yana, dressed as a novice Rider in a long cloak and sleek, brown leathers, entered to a hurrah of welcome from the men at the fireplace. She surveyed the trading post and waved to Astria.

"Aye, stranger," Yana called, removing her gear. Grabbing a tankard of mead, she joined Astria at her table. "How have you been, girl?"

"Busy earning my dinner."

After scanning the room, Yana hugged her. "I've missed you so much."

Astria winced at the hug and gave her friend the pouch of balm. "Can you help me?" she said and turned around to expose the claw scratches and purple bruises on her neck.

"Damn," Yana said. "How'd you get these?"

"From the mountain lion whose skin sits by the fire," Astria said and pulled out her flint knife. "And it was your gift that killed him."

Yana frowned, put her hands on Astria's shoulders, and then laid her cheek on Astria's back. "I'm sorry."

"I'll heal. Just don't tell my mother."

Yana leaned over and lowered her voice. "Be on the lookout for Fynn."

"Why?"

"He visited Skye."

Astria stiffened. "About what?"

"I think he's working up to ask for your hand."

Astria frowned, and the ache in her heart returned that he still had not visited her in the Wild. "But he's seeing Furnia."

"She doesn't know."

"I'll bet she suspects," Astria said and shook her head. "He negotiates for my hand behind her back, but he can't come to visit me?"

"I'm sure if—"

Astria waved her to silence. "No. I've heard enough." She checked the room and whispered, "I can't let the Council pick for me. If I refuse, they'll think I'm defying them and exile me for sure. And don't tell Fynn you told me, or I'll lose a friend." She leaned back again. "But who else would want me, anyway?" With a finger, she pointed to her white eyes surrounded by wind-burned cheeks.

"Nothing a good bath and a day's rest wouldn't fix."

Astria uncoiled a lock of her oily and matted hair.

"Then again . . ."

As Astria finished buttoning her shirt, the door swung open, and Fynn walked in. At the sight of Astria and Yana, he blushed, grabbed his own tankard of mead, and walked over.

Astria winced at his hug but closed her eyes and held him.

"It's wonderful to see you, kid," he said. "How have you been?"

Kid? Starving, in pain, exhausted all the time, worried about my next meal and the wolves and the graxes, missing you and Yana and my mother, and I want to come home . . .

"Fine," she said, and they sat again.

"The pass to Andeir is closed by an avalanche," he said, but lost in her thoughts, Astria did not hear him.

He wants me. He'll have a place here and a full larder and a warm bed that would welcome me.

No. Zephyr would have no place, and I'd never be a Rider.

And he's never come to visit me.

Astria took both of their hands. "I'm so glad to see you both. I'm lonely out there, and I miss you so much. Please tell my mother when you'll be off duty so I can join you. And please always be my friends. Nothing more. Nothing less. I need you."

Yana smiled and hugged her, but Fynn frowned.

From across the room, a Farmer she had seen with Britta called out. "Haven't you completed your trading by now, Rogue?"

Astria rose to leave, and Yana rose with her.

"My duty starts soon," Yana said. "I'll walk you out."

Astria turned to Fynn, who stood for a hug. "Safe flight, Rider," she said and left with Yana.

As she walked out the door, Astria glanced back as Fynn threw his tankard into the fire.

At the clearing, Astria bid Yana good night and then returned to the Manor House. But as she passed the window, she saw Fynn slouching in his chair, brooding at the fireplace.

If I go to him, I could come home again and be safe. She sighed.

But he never came to visit.

Astria could not go back inside to Fynn and could not visit her mother while wounded, but she was not invited anywhere else.

And as she gazed into the window, Furnia came to Fynn and kissed him.

There's no place for me here anymore.

The door opened, but she turned away from the safety and the warmth into the frigid night.

Chapter 8
Pennant

With saddlebags over her shoulder, Astria threw open the flap to her lean-to and stepped over the trench that directed the spring snow melt.

"You know, I'd eat a lot better if you didn't scare away the mountain goats," she said, but Zephyr only blinked.

She had gained back the weight she lost during the winter, and the clothing that saw her through the worst of it chafed: too tight around her shoulders and thighs from the new muscle and too tight around her hips and breasts for her blossoming womanhood.

Outside, she dropped the saddlebags and turned the spit where a rabbit roasted over a fire. From a line strung between trees, she took the drying pelts of badger and wolverine, rolled them up, and stuffed them into the saddlebags. She had enough now and planned to stop in Invernell to trade.

From a cold pit, she retrieved the meat and game that would spoil without the layers of snow. Half she put in a bag and hung it in the icy creek that carried the glacier melt down to the Blois River. The rest she put in another bag with a jar of mashed roots to bring home to her mother.

A sniff reminded her of the cooking rabbit, and she removed it from the fire. With her knife, she tore strips from it, blew to cool it, and ate it with the table manners of a bear.

With a rabbit leg in her mouth, she made another notch on the tree marking her 250th day in the Wild and chatted to Zephyr.

"Summer's coming, and we're likely to be here for at least another year. So where will we go? East to the ocean? It's maybe a two-day journey, but we can scout our way first." She glanced at Zephyr, who merely blinked. "Or west and the Source? Would the dragons get mad if I visited?"

Zephyr blinked again.

Astria took another slice of meat. "North?"

He peered at her, and she gritted her teeth.

Winter's end had brought good hunting and left time for her to explore. At each opportunity, she searched for signs of her father, and each day found her farther from home. But now, a day's ride presented the same barrier to her explorations as valley walls once had. The constraint sparked arguments with her mother and gave her more reasons not to return home on her biweekly visits.

"I know, I know. That's where the caravan was attacked, and Mama doesn't want us to go there. But I'm betting that's where Papa went, and—"

Bells on strings jingled to alert her to predators. Without thinking, she grabbed her bow, nocked an arrow, and spun to the sound. Mud sucked on her moccasins as she crept forward.

There at the trip line, the doe with a shredded ear had just given birth to a fawn that lay at her side, glistening with snowmelt and afterbirth. Astria eased the tension from the bow and squatted to watch as the doe licked the fawn dry.

The fawn rose on his hind legs with his forelegs still folded and shuddered. Then he looked to the doe as if to say, "I'm ready," and the doe gave him a nudge in the rump. He fell with his legs splayed to his sides and rested with his head on the ground. A minute later, the fawn rose onto his hind legs again, straightened one foreleg and then the other, and wobbled to his mother.

In the clearing to the side, the buck grazed unconcerned. But behind Astria, Zephyr watched the fawn with sparkling eyes as though recognizing the miracle they witnessed.

"I'm ready too," she said with a nod to the fawn, and mounted Zephyr for the ride home.

***

That night, Astria pushed her empty plate away and leaned the chair back against the wall. The little cottage where she had spent most of her life felt even smaller after a winter in the Wild.

"Please, Mama," Astria said. "I've searched everywhere else."

"Not north," Skye said. "Not alone."

"Only for the week."

Skye took their plates to the washtub and turned with her hand on her hip. "It's too dangerous up north alone."

"Your Council voted me Rogue, Mama. They can't command me."

"It's not *my* Council, and I voted against them. This is my voice now, not theirs."

Astria pursed her lips.

Returning to the table, her mother sat opposite and folded her hands in front of her. "Fynn stopped by again. I think he wants me to give my permission for you two—"

Astria narrowed her eyes and raised her palms. "Don't finish, Mama," she said and pushed her chair from the table.

"Why? You like him."

"He's a friend." *Or was.*

"Members of the Council asked me to—"

Astria rolled her eyes. "Gods, not *them* again." She stood, too annoyed to sit.

"Fynn is wild and getting into fights. They think you can tame him."

"I'm Rogue. They can't force me to marry now." She crossed her arms and glanced at her mother sideways. "Is this a bribe?"

Skye shrugged. "They might be more generous if you are engaged."

Astria leaned over the table. "Generous? Will they let me be a Rider?" she asked, but a crease formed in her brow. *And would I marry Fynn for the chance?*

"They wouldn't promise."

"That means no."

"He'll be a Rider when his training is over."

That stung. "And not me? Is his life so much more valuable that I should abandon my dreams for his? Was this deal your idea?" Astria asked and turned away.

"No. Lothen and Britta are pushing this. I'm against it unless that's what you want."

"And what about Furnia? Does she know?"

"No. And neither does Kendrick." Skye reached out and held Astria's hand. "I worry for you so out there."

"I don't love him."

"This is an opportunity to come home and be safe even if you're not a Rider."

Astria gazed out the window of their little cottage and sighed. "He never came to see me, Mama. Throughout the winter, through the worst of it, he never visited."

"I'm sorry, dear."

Astria stiffened. "I'm Rogue, and that's all the answer they need," she said and shook her head. "Enough of this. And what of you?"

Skye blushed. "I think Efrin wants to declare his intentions." She twirled a lock of hair around her finger.

Astria put a hand on her mother's shoulder. "Are they pressuring you again?"

"No."

"Then you're thinking about it?"

"You like him."

"He's been a wonderful friend." Astria narrowed her eyes. "But tell him you are spoken for."

Skye chuckled. "Didn't you once ask me to marry him so you could ride?"

"I was afraid of exile." *And even more so now.*

"It's been six years. More than enough for tradition to—"

Without thinking, Astria clenched her fist. "I don't care about tradition. Papa is alive. I'm sure of it."

"We searched for him for years, and—"

"You gave up. I won't."

Pain crossed Skye's face. "That's not fair. I don't ride and they denied my appeals. You need a father, hon."

"Not anymore."

"Maybe now more than ever, especially since you have a dragon partner." Skye went to the mantel and touched Astria's sketch of her husband. "I've been true to your father. I've always loved him . . . and I still do." She lowered her head. "But sometimes it's hard."

Astria went to her mother and hugged her from behind.

"He loves me," Skye said. "And I think of how safe and loved I'd feel in his arms . . ."

Astria held her breath, waiting for the next words.

"But each time I have those thoughts, I see your father's face. I couldn't do that to either of them, or you."

Out of her mother's sight, Astria smiled. "I can help search, Mama."

Skye broke the hug and sat with tears glistening in the corners of her eyes. "It's not safe that far north."

"Please, Mama. Zephyr will be there to protect me."

"Like he protected you from the mountain lion?"

"How do you know about—"

"If you go, bring Yana."

"She's on duty, Mama. Please."

"No."

Astria pursed her lips and turned away. "Did your friends at the Clanough say they'd accept me as a citizen in the other valleys? If they don't want me here, I want somewhere else to go."

Skye dropped her gaze. "They've not committed yet."

"Tell them to hurry," Astria said and stormed out the door.

"You'll stay the night?" Skye called after her.

"Sure."

Astria's anger simmered, but on her way to meet Zephyr, it broke into a boil.

Fynn is my friend, yet he plays a double game. One of us, maybe all of us, will get hurt. I will not be put in the middle of this as a prize to be won or an object to be bargained for.

As she passed the Manor House, Fynn lounged against the tavern door, talking with other novice Riders. Astria pushed them aside and wrinkled her nose at the stench of drink on his breath and body.

"We need to talk," she said, and took Fynn by the collar, dragging him around the corner of the building, where she pushed him up against the wall. "My mother told me you are bargaining with some Elders for my hand."

He blinked with red eyes and a sloppy smile. "Yes, I missed you, too, and—"

"Stop this. You are with Furnia and need to focus on her."

His smile melted as her words registered. "But . . . I love you."

She pushed him into the shutters and poked a finger into his shoulder. "You love me? Everyone we know who went into the Wild was injured or killed. Yet in the months I've been there, you haven't come to visit me."

"Efrin gave us your status."

"And 'status' is enough for someone you 'love?'"

"You're resilient, and I knew . . ."

Resilient. It was a slap in the face and diminished her ordeal into a mere challenge. "You knew what? That I'd give up and come home?"

Fynn turned away, and she leaned with her back against the shutters as tears glistened in her eyes. "Then you really don't know me at all."

"Asti, I—"

"You are my friend. But when I was sick, where were you? Was it too hard to come visit me when you knew I was struggling to survive? You are my friend and couldn't visit? Not once?"

"Training is hard, Asti, and took most—"

"Not once?"

"You don't understand," he said and turned to leave.

She grabbed his sleeve. "Were you too afraid to risk the Council if you came to visit? Are you too soft and happy with your new girlfriend?"

Fynn spun to face her with his shoulders squared. "You're not being fair. You have no idea what this has been like for me!"

"For *you?*"

"I've wanted you since we first met, and you pushed me off, and—"

She dropped her gaze. "I asked you to wait. And because I wouldn't lie down with you as a woman, you couldn't visit me as a friend?"

He winced as her words struck.

She dropped her arms to her sides and lowered her voice. "All those months in the cold when you didn't come, I . . . If you loved me, you'd have found a way."

"Then tell me there's a chance."

"You showed me what you care about," she said. "Furnia waits for you. And I will not betray her the way you have."

At the clearing, Zephyr waited, and without so much as a hello, Astria mounted him and took off.

Zephyr carried her along the core of the Spine to the highest peak with the best view of the sunset. To the west, tall clouds warned a hard rain would come tomorrow. So for now, she would take her mother's advice not to venture so far alone. But when the storm passed, she would explore.

After two gentle kicks, Zephyr rolled and dove a thousand feet to a prominent ridge with a clear view west. There, they jostled with other dragons for position as they hummed and honked. When the sun approached the horizon, a long absent friend rushed past.

Fluttering before the group, Vandrare honked and then dashed north pursued by the other dragons. Zephyr glanced back at Astria, but she shook her head. When the old dragon returned a minute later, he made it clear he wanted Swallow not the others, and she followed.

Vandrare sped to the northeast, high above the Blois River. That was where Astria wanted to explore, where her father might have gone. But that way lay danger. Even if she turned back now, she would still be late.

I had to go, mama. Vandrare clearly wanted us to follow him. Someone may have been injured or needed help. Or maybe he knew something about Papa. Mama will understand.

And if she doesn't, well . . .

One by one, the other dragons landed to enjoy the sunset until Swallow followed the old one alone.

Hours later, they flew over the northern brink of the Spine, far beyond where the Riders patrolled. Here, where the Blois River spilled onto the Derryh foothills, no borders marked the land, only ragged lines on maps showed where passage south could be fatal.

This is where Papa might have gone.

Zephyr carried her past the falls and over rows of tents and flickering campfires. Beyond, they flew over a plain where men slept in the open. In the dim, red light of the smallest moon, Fures, they glided toward a dark funnel meandering across the field. But her dragon braked and stalled when they hit a wall of flies that choked and blinded them. He fluttered to a landing and snorted to clear his nose.

As the funnel approached, she recognized it as a tornado of crows circling beneath a cloud of vultures. Spears stuck in the ground glinted, and curious, she dismounted and walked toward them, taking a pennant that fluttered from one and stuffing it in her pocket. As she did, a gust of wind swept past, and the stench of rotting meat assaulted her.

Out of her control, she bent over and retched.

When she rose again, the cloud passed, and Fures lit a field of men and horses, from horizon to horizon, dead but unburied. The moon also reflected from red-eyed beasts that lifted their bloody muzzles from torn flesh and growled at her.

Wild dogs!

Astria ran and jumped on Zephyr's back as he clawed at the beasts and took off.

On a bluff overlooking the camp, they rejoined Vandrare. After leaving behind what remained in her stomach, Astria crawled to the edge of the cliff to observe. She could not make out the dark shapes moving in the gloom and scattered clouds, so she waited for another moon to rise.

When Lon's gentle moonlight flooded the scene below, she gasped. Thousands of armed men camped there at the foothills of the Blois River, the same river that passed through her home. And into the canyons of that river trailed scores of wagons. The smells of barbecued meats and garlic drifting from the camp carried an unfamiliar tang, and moonlight glinted off what might be metal weapons or armor in the distance.

Are these the Northmen? Or are they rotting on the battlefield?

Astria turned to the old dragon and knit her brows.

"Why the urgency? We're many leagues from home and not in immediate danger. Why bring us here?"

No answer came, and she prepared to mount and return home when a piercing shriek shook her to the bones, and she fell to her knees. She set her hand on Zephyr's muzzle to stop him from crying out in response and waited.

The brightest moon, Elein, rose above the horizon and disclosed the source of the cry. Below them, a dragon lay bound in heavy chains. He was the same size as Klokbror, her father's dragon, but at this distance, she could not identify him.

Vandrare turned to her and cocked his head.

She shook her head at the old one. "What can I do? I'm not a fighter. What could even a squadron of Riders do against an army? There's nothing I can do."

Hearing it from her own mouth sounded cold and heartless. *I promised,* she thought and turned back to the chained dragon. *But what can I do?*

"No one knows I'm here. There will be no rescue if I'm captured and no help if I'm injured."

I promised, but did I promise this?

Vandrare gave her no excuse, and she burned with questions she had carried for years.

The enormous camp surrounded the dragon, but the west side appeared to be near a dry gulley. In the light of the moons, she memorized the terrain and landmarks, decided on her path, and took a bota of water from the saddle.

Out of sight from the camp, she crawled backward off the hilltop. Zephyr took a step to follow but stopped when she raised her hand. At the base of the hill, she rubbed dirt on her exposed skin and hair to reduce the shine and then slipped into the gulley.

A cold mist enveloped her, and she shivered, but the fog also helped to hide her. Creeping low, she followed the gulley toward the noise and lights. In the dark, she stumbled on a bramble and scolded herself to be more careful: any injury might be fatal if it stopped her from returning home.

Blood pounded in her ears to the rhythm of the drums as she neared the camp. When torchlight threatened to expose her, she hid in shadows below the undercut bank. Here, the fruity liquor smells of mead and jenalei flowed over the bank, mixed with the scents of unwashed men and spices that tickled her nose.

Bright torches lit colorful tents when she peered over the edge. Around tables, rough men in red or green tunics and leather armor sat with tankards in their hands. Most had beards and tied their long hair in ponytails or top knots. Nearby, scantily clad women danced to the beat of drums and tambourine and the tune of a panpipe. At one table, men threw what might be bones or stones and cheered.

Gambling. A brothel. Camp followers to satisfy men's basest needs lest they turn on each other.

The bones rolled again, and one gambler attacked another. The music stopped, and other men shouted. They spoke in a strange dialect, but some words sounded familiar: "cheat," "liar," "kill," and "mother." She ducked below the overhang again and slunk away, but noises from the fight followed her. On the opposite bank, shadows battled as the fight above progressed from fists to weapons.

Those above cheered as a man fell to the stones at her feet. With her heart in her throat, she froze against the bank, stifling a gasp with a hand over her mouth.

But he lay still, his neck bent at an unnatural angle. Moonlight glimmered from metal script tooled into the heels of his riding boots, and blood spilled from a slash across his belly, sliced open like the caravan leader before the grax attack the year prior. And like the men in her vision the day her father disappeared, furs draped his shoulders.

She held her breath as his mates leaned over the edge, and she scurried away when they leaned back. But they did not come, and when the music resumed, they shuffled back to the brothel and abandoned the body.

Astria hurried to the other side of the gulley, then crawled up and out of the mist that hid her. Exposed now, she slunk from tree to bush. Horses neighed, and she crept to the picket line to quiet them. These were smaller than the horses of the Spine, almost ponies, with broad chests and coarse hair. They were well cared for, all of them fit with hay in front of each and a light blanket in the cool evening. At the end of the picket line, a soldier brushed one down.

Near the horses lay a line of saddles like she had never seen before with the rider wedged between a high back like a dragon saddle and two high pommels in front. The stirrups also lay higher than on saddles of the mountains.

Next to the picket line lay a field of wooden machines as wide as the Manor House and three times as tall. Some flung boulders that disappeared into the dark. Others were being disassembled and loaded onto wagons heading up the river valley toward her home.

Weapons of war? Why else would an army have them?

Hiding in the shadows behind a row of small tents, she snuck toward the captive dragon. In gaps between tents, a torchlit path appeared that ran parallel to hers. Along it strode rough men in leather armor or metal breastplates. Others sat and sharpened curved swords longer than those carried by Riders.

The mud-and-fire smell of a blacksmith reached her before the ring of a hammer on anvil. In front of the smithy's forge stood racks of spears tipped with four grooved metal blades. Next to them, pikes long enough to frighten horses stood bound in a bundle.

The line of tents ended at a low corral, typical of holding pens for pigs or sheep. With no shelter for many yards beyond, she approached in a crouch. Instead of animals, she found sleeping humans—some huddled together, others shivering alone. The same dirty, gray tunic dressed each: too thin to protect them from the chilly night or weather. A common chain ran through their shackles and rattled when they moved. With shaved heads, Astria could not tell male from female, but some were small children.

Slaves, held like animals to be used and abused. Or killed. Were my ancestors treated this badly in the Imperium?

Unable to resist, she ducked below the rails and entered the corral to check each filthy and bruised face, and each one broke her heart.

In the arms of a gaunt woman huddled a small boy with a dirty face, and Astria placed her hand on his cheek. The child looked up at her with a weary smile, and when she traded smiles, the child went back to sleep.

How could anyone do this? she thought and bit her lip to stop her tears.

On a separate chain lay a druim, with a necklace of blocks cut with runes. Drugged rather than sleeping, she blinked and purple glinted from the corner of her eyes in the moonlight. Long whip scabs marred her arms, and the chalky clay flaked from her face and beaded hair.

What's a druim doing in the north? An emissary? A missionary?

Just outside the corral, a man kneeled, his hands held above his head by straps tied to a post. Long, red welts crisscrossed his back, and he bled from open cuts. *A whip. Another slave. And within view of the pen as a lesson.*

With his head bowed, she could not tell whether he was alive or dead. Afraid of whom it might be, she set her jaw, raised his head, and then sighed. *All slaves, and Papa is not among them.*

A man shouted, and Astria huddled next to a fence post. Nearby, a tent flap opened, and through it, a girl in a ripped tunic stumbled and fell into the mud. A ray of light from the tent exposed Astria, and she froze.

For a moment, the girl stared with her mouth open, but then rose and returned to close the flap. Placing a shoulder yoke with water buckets on her neck, she made her way to Astria.

In front of Astria, the girl dropped the yoke and put her finger to her bloody lip. She grabbed Astria's arm, trying to drag her away. But Astria shook her head and pointed to the dragon. The girl lowered the shoulder of her tunic to expose a brand and more bruises. Astria understood the warning and nodded.

I could be her if I'm caught. But I made a promise. Unable to explain, Astria pointed to the dragon again.

The girl raised the hem of her tunic, but Astria stopped her. *The brand might be the least painful of her injuries. What more abuse could they heap upon her?*

Astria drew her knife and handed it to the slave, hilt first, but the girl shook her head and ran her thumb across her neck.

They'll kill her if they find her with a weapon.

The slave went to the corral, pulled a stained tunic from a pile, and gave it to Astria. After sheathing the knife, Astria slipped the tunic over her riding leathers. The girl then raised Astria's hood to hide her hair and, on her shoulders, put the yoke and buckets. They stood to leave, but Astria gave her the bota of water and pointed to the man secured to the post. The girl nodded and went to him.

With the water buckets on her shoulders, Astria went to the dragon. A thick, bronze muzzle restrained his jaws, and chains fettered each leg to stakes in the ground. Nets of thick cable weighted with boulders covered both wings, and from putrid-smelling wounds seeped an iridescent purple.

How could they be so cruel? Yet she sighed with relief that the dragon was not Klokbror.

When the guards turned away, she approached the dragon and set the buckets near his head. Sitting by his cheek, she stroked his brow ridge, but he did not move. When she placed a ladle of water under his nose, he lifted his eyelid a bit, but his eye remained dull and unfocused. With her free hand, she lifted his upper lip, and her tears joined the water she poured between his teeth.

Once she emptied the bucket, she checked the chains on the dragon's legs and found no latches to pry open. With her head low and the water bucket as a ruse, she worked her way to a rack of spears. When unobserved, she took two and brought them back to the chained dragon.

She inserted the spears in the master link, but she was not strong enough to lever it open. The spear also could not pry the chain from the stakes. And a spear point dug into the hard dirt around a stake did not dislodge it.

When the blisters on her hands burst and bled, she quit to work on the nets that hobbled his wings. The cables were too thick for her knife to sever. And each of the weights that held the net down was too heavy for her to lift. Sweating and exhausted, she fell to her knees by the dragon's head and stroked his cheek.

"I'm sorry. I'm not strong enough, or clever enough, or . . ." she said. Tears streaked her dirty face, knowing even if she could free him, he might be too weak to fly away.

The scuff of boots announced approaching soldiers, and she scurried under a wing. Drunk, judging by their stench, they poked the enormous dragon with their spears and laughed at his weakness.

He did not rise to protest but twitched and shuddered with every jab. With each insult, Astria's rage grew, and unable to hold it back, she rose from under his wing.

"Stop!" she cried and threw an empty bucket at the tormentors. But as she threw the bucket, the hood fell, exposing her unshaved head.

One soldier shouted an alarm as they moved in with spears now pointed at her. Too startled to run, she backed up into the helpless dragon.

A muffled roar stopped the soldiers in their tracks. Behind her, the dragon rose on shaky legs and pulled one stake from the dirt, the one she worked so hard to loosen. With the free paw, he tore off his muzzle and roared so loud she covered her ears, and the soldiers dropped their spears.

"I am Turmordare, the Bull Slayer!" she heard in his roar, and in another roar, "Run!"

This time, she ran past the astonished soldiers who fixed their eyes on the dragon looming above them.

With a shake, Turmordare lifted his wings and tore the weighted nets from the ground. A single flutter sent the nets flying: one landed on the machines, the other collapsed a section of tents.

He lunged and bit down on his captors, cut them in half, and spit the bloody pieces into a gathering crowd of soldiers. Struggling to free his last leg, he stumbled, and his tail sliced through them like a scythe in a wheat field, shattering the wooden machines.

Astria turned at the crash as splinters and broken men fell around her, and she froze. She had not seen the power of a dragon before, to turn the most powerful works of men to ruin. If freed, he could destroy them all, and she shuddered. For a moment, fear of him overcame her fear of the soldiers, and with them, she stood riveted watching the mayhem that one dragon wrought.

She backed up as another swipe of his tail shattered the post securing the slaves' common chain. The slaves bolted for freedom, and she ran toward them, hoping to lose herself. But more soldiers came to recapture them, and she could not hide her hair if they rounded her up with the others.

Soldiers hurried to restrain Turmordare, and more armed men arrived to chase her. She ran to the gulley, but before she reached it, men blocked her escape with swords and spears. She stopped, and the men surrounded her. A nightmare of her life as a slave girl flashed before her as the spear tips closed in, and she bared her teeth.

Never!

She drew her knife and slashed the first warrior to come near, cutting deep into his leather vambrace. But the rest only laughed at her. As she shouted her battle cry, Turmordare roared again, stopping the warriors' attack. Before they recovered, claws yanked on Astria's leathers, lifting her above her pursuers and away. A wingbeat later, something struck Zephyr's saddle, and he screeched.

He dropped Astria on the hillock where Vandrare waited and landed in a crouch, preparing to return to the melee. Grabbing his reins to restrain him, Zephyr lifted her off the ground, but the old one honked and fluttered in front of them until her dragon calmed.

In the camp below, scores of men threw more chains and nets around the exhausted Turmordare. When he stumbled and fell, they tied his wings with chains and fixed his legs with new shackles.

As the big dragon struggled, tears ran down Astria's cheeks. Although sick and mortally wounded, the captive dragon used the last of his energy to help her escape. *And I may have hastened his death in my attempt to free him.*

She turned to Vandrare. "You brought us here to witness—not to die, not to save him," she said, but he only stared back at her.

Below the hillock, men followed the gulley toward them. After a deafening honk from the captive dragon, Zephyr turned away, kneeled, and lowered his head. As she mounted, she found a shaft embedded in the saddle and stuck it in her boot. She bid Vandrare goodbye and took the reins.

On the flight home, images of Turmordare's mayhem dispelled the horror of the field of slain men. Dragons would never again be just gentle neighbors and friends. The Farmers were right to fear them, for dragons were giants who could turn their power against humans and destroy them.

If there's a war with the dragons, humans started it.

***

Deep in the night after the moons set, Swallow landed in Invernell. Exhausted, Astria jumped from Zephyr's back and ran through the fog to the fire bell that hung in the square across from the Manor House. When she rang it, villagers in nightshirts gathered at the alarm, waiting for instructions from the Elders. Among the first to arrive was Fynn, who lost his smile at her grim expression.

Elder Philina arrived in her nightshirt. "What's the emergency?"

Astria raised her hand. "Warriors march south into our river valley!"

The crowd grumbled.

Philina frowned and narrowed her eyes. "What nonsense is this?"

Before Astria could reply, Elder Radlig joined them.

"Who calls us, Philina?" he asked.

"Our little Rogue says we're being invaded." Philina rolled her eyes and waved her hand over the valley. "I don't see anyone."

Astria glared at her. "Not here. A three-hour flight northeast."

"That's impossible, child," Philina said. "Next you'll be telling us you've seen Aeterna."

"Let's hear the girl out," Radlig said.

Skye ran up to join them, and Philina turned to her. "Your child tells us an incredible story."

Skye put her arm around her daughter's shoulder. And after Kendrick joined them, Astria repeated her story.

He nodded. "A three-hour ride? That's about two hundred miles through the teeth of the Spine, so they'll not be here by dawn. Go home, everyone." He brushed his hands to shoo them away. "We'll sort this out tomorrow. Back to bed with you."

With a wave, he led the Council into the Manor House. Once inside, Elders hovered around the long table but did not sit. Astria stood in front of them with her friends to each side while anxious villagers filed in behind.

Skye spoke first. "We must confirm this. The three moons—"

"Why are we losing sleep over the ramblings of a Rogue?" Britta asked with a scowl.

Terach leaned over the table. "Britta's right. Astria doesn't belong with us now, and we're not obliged to believe her stories."

Astria crossed her arms and cocked her head. *I bring news of your destruction, and all you can think of is I'm Rogue?*

"Go see for yourself," Astria said.

Lothen spoke over Astria's head to those gathered. "That would take a Rider from their other vital duties, and—"

Vinga raised her voice. "This is important enough to check. A herald can fly now and return as soon as the sun rises."

"Astria, how can you be sure of this?" Britta asked.

Withdrawing the arrow from her boot, she raised it over her head to show them. The short, wooden shaft had a thin sheet of metal hammered around a conical point that shimmered in the torchlight, just like her father's souvenir on the mantel at home.

She handed the object to her mother, who squinted and cocked her head but passed it on without remark. While the rest of them inspected the object, Astria told them what brought her to the site.

"Where was this?" Kendrick asked.

Taking a char from the brazier, she drew a map on the floor, showing the peaks between Invernell and Derryh. Then she scratched an *X* where the Blois River exited the mountains. But a memory of the field brought with it the stench of death, and her nausea returned.

Radlig shook his head. "If they got that far, it's only a matter of time before they reach us."

The object passed to Elder Urquil, who stood and cleared his throat. "Crossbow bolt," the old man said in a croak too loud for his frail body. "Quarajii."

Philina gasped. "The Hordes!"

Skye placed a hand over her mouth and sat hard. She glanced at Urquil and then Astria.

Her face ashen, Astria ran to the door, and Skye rushed to her side.

"What is it, dear?" her mother asked.

Astria bent over, trying to forget. "There was a field with many dead." She took the pennant from her jacket and gave it to Skye. "Show them this."

Efrin pushed his way through the crowd and kneeled by the X Astria had drawn. "The Northmen hold Derryh here and west."

Skye unfurled the pennant. "Astria described a battlefield."

"That's a standard of the Army of the North," Urquil said. "Where did you find that?"

"With the dead," Astria called from the door.

"Then the Northmen lost."

Astria raised her hand. "They hold slaves in the camp."

Skye turned to her daughter with wide eyes. "How did you—"

"The Northmen don't keep slaves," Urquil said.

Kendrick sat on the edge of the table and crossed his arms. "Derryh has fallen."

"Then the Quarajii have access to the mountains," Skye said.

The Seer raised her hand to her mouth. "The Darkness comes!"

"There's more," Astria said, but the anxious talk smothered her words. She repeated it louder, but still they ignored her. Exasperated, she whistled between her fingers the way she would call Zephyr.

"They're killing a dragon!" she shouted, stunning the Council to silence. "In the moonlight, I saw a dragon in chains . . . dying."

The scraping of claws on the roof and whining interrupted as Zephyr tried to answer Astria's whistle.

"Why would they do this?" Philina said. "We are poor and hundreds of miles from their home."

"Thank the gods the Spine protects us, or we'd be slaves already," Radlig said.

"Or dead!" someone called from the back.

Kendrick raised his hands. "Now, hold on. We don't know enough yet, and it's late. Flight Leader Lothen, arrange for a herald. Everyone, bring your ideas to the Council tomorrow morning after the herald returns. You're invited, too, Astria."

Astria nodded and squeezed Skye's hand.

Above them on the roof, the scrabbling and whining blended with the flutter of wings. "And tell your dragon to get off the roof," Kendrick said. "Please."

On the way home, Astria stopped. "What did you see in the crossbow bolt?"

Skye stopped as well but said nothing.

"When Urquil said it was Quarajii, you gasped."

Skye sat on a nearby bench and patted the space beside her. "About a month after your father went missing, a Rider found his kit but not . . . him. Stuck in it was the metal tip."

Astria joined her on the bench. "The object on the mantel at home?"

Skye gripped Astria's hand. "I thought your father found it."

"And Quarajii scouts roam the Spine?"

"North of the Tops, yes."

"Where Papa disappeared?"

Skye nodded. "But not to the west or south. The dragons won't let them."

Astria crossed her arms and shook her head. "And the man wounded by a blade during the grax attack last spring?"

Skye lowered her chin. "Kendrick thinks the attackers wounded him to bait the graxes and disguise the raid on the caravan."

"And he who wielded that blade?"

"A thief, or a Qu scout, perhaps. Whoever he was, he meant the graxes to destroy the evidence, but La'a arrived first."

"And you didn't tell me any of this," Astria said.

They sat in silence while Astria gazed into the night.

"Asti?" Skye said and took her hand.

Astria dropped her mother's hand and stood. "This is a lot to take in, Mama. That the Qu walk the Spine and may have Papa." She turned to face her. "And you think me so childish that tonight is the first I hear of it."

She sighed and walked away, leaving her mother alone on the bench.

***

"Hurry!" called a voice as Astria raced through the field of rotting corpses. A bell tolled, and she ran toward it. But she tripped on a dead horse, landing with her face inches from worms crawling from a dead soldier's mouth.

"Hurry!"

Dripping with sweat, Astria jerked up in her bed, and hugged her mother.

"When you're ready, dear," Skye said. "They want us at Council."

Astria threw on her clothing and grabbed a slice of bread and a peach. Then she left their house with her mother and ran through raindrops over the cobblestone path to the Manor House.

The meeting had already begun. Near the front stood a tall, female Rider in worn leathers bleached by the sun to shades of tan, her eyes sharp as a hawk's with semaphores to match: Yana. Next to her stood Jenks, the new herald who now addressed the Council.

"What of . . . oh, welcome, Skye," Kendrick said as Astria and her mother entered. "You were right, girl. Jenks confirmed your sighting."

Uh huh. Astria glanced at Philina who fixed her eyes on Kendrick. "And what of the captive dragon? How does he fare?"

"Dead," Jenks said. "Or at least, it struggles no more."

Astria stopped at the door and knitted her brow. *He exhausted his strength to help me escape.*

Philina's brow furrowed. "Why would they hold a dragon?"

Radlig scoffed. "Perhaps they want to tame him," he said, and laughter filled the room.

Urquil banged his cane on the floor. "The Qu fear dragons and destroy what they fear. The Sul also pay dearly for aphrodisiacs and fertility potions made from the organs and bones."

Astria covered her ears, unable to listen to any more of the horror. But she could not dispel the image of Turmordare being butchered.

"They don't need an army to hunt dragons," Efrin said. "Did the Sul hire them for this?"

Radlig spoke up. "They imagine we are rich. What more reason does a thief need to steal?"

"I believe they force a way south," Urquil said. "Their lands are poor, and shamans fill their heads with legends of paradise where horses run free and ambrosia spills from heaven. They're trapped by the Northmen and the Sulerians to the west and by the ocean to the east. They want to go south, and we are on their path."

"There are wagons stacked with timber heading up the river," Jenks said.

Astria raised her hand. "I saw them assembled, lofting large rocks long distances."

"Catapults," Urquil said, and the crowd gasped.

"We don't have a defense against that kind of power," Radlig said.

"More scouts will take months to get here unless they have a means to fly," Skye said. "Maybe two years before they get here in force." The others mumbled agreement.

Kendrick rose for attention. "We must prepare. We need the passes closed again, and that requires help from the Northmen."

Philina raised her hand. "We don't have the strength to resist the Qu. If we're in the way, then why not get out of the way?"

Astria gasped, and her jaw dropped.

Radlig shook his head. "They're warriors and conquerors, Phil."

"But their culture is simply different from ours," Philina said. "Can we ask the Sulerians for help?"

Kendrick frowned. "Philina, the Qu and the Sul both believe those who don't recognize their right to rule deserve death or slavery. If they enter Invernell, our freedom ends. Our people once died to escape the Imperator's bondage. Will we submit to it now?"

"And what of our dragons?" Astria asked.

Philina persisted. "Is there nothing we can give them that'll make them pass us by?"

Radlig spat. "Only sheep sacrifice other sheep, and by doing so, you invite more wolves to dinner."

And they would be near our dragons to hunt them and butcher them.

Astria glared at Philina. "You'd let dragon slayers into our valley?"

Philina blushed.

"No, no," Kendrick said with a raised hand.

Skye stared at him and tipped her head toward her daughter. "We will need Couriers."

Kendrick nodded and turned to Astria. "Will you volunteer?"

Astria glanced to both sides, not sure whom he referred to.

"Yes, you, Astria. Do you volunteer?"

She blushed, surprised. *This could be an invitation back to the clan.* Her eyes narrowed, and everyone seemed frozen in place as she scanned their faces. *But this is the Council, and they aren't my friends. Are they throwing me a bone? Do I take it? At what cost? But this is Kendrick's invitation . . .*

Astria glanced at Skye, who nodded at her slowly.

And Mama's. I need this clear. "Am I to remain Rogue?"

Kendrick shook his head. "You are invited back to Invernell."

Before Astria replied, Lothen stood and scowled.

"We chose Couriers from the Riders," Lothen said. "And she's not trained for—"

Efrin stood. "I'll vouch for her skill."

Lothen fumed. "We can't have a Rogue—"

"This isn't the Riders' choice, Lothen. The Council selects its Couriers."

"If this is a Council decision, then I want a show of hands. Who favors Astria as a Courier?"

Astria glanced among the faces of Lothen, Britta, Kendrick, and her mother, their jaws set and their eyes fixed on her. *And what consequence will I face if Mama wins this fight?*

Skye glared at Lothen and raised her hand. Vinga and Radlig joined her and, to Astria's surprise, Philina. With timid glances to Lothen, three others concurred, making Kendrick's vote unnecessary.

"I accept," Astria said.

Lothen returned to his seat and mirrored Skye's glare. To his side, Britta sulked, and the Farmers grumbled.

Efrin broke the tense silence. "She'll need to go with someone more experienced."

Yana raised her fist. "Yana will ride," she said, and then took Astria's arm and led her to the door.

"Settled," Kendrick said and then addressed Lothen. "Flight Leader, gather your captains and meet here at dusk. We need to plan our defense. And Jenks, let's alert our neighbors."

Yana led her outside, but Astria paused.

"Wait a moment," she said, leaving to find Vinga.

"What is it, dear?" Vinga asked.

"Last year, I asked the difference between our Council and slavery if we have limited choice," Astria said.

"I remember."

Images came to Astria of the abused and starving children in the barbarian camp. "There is a big difference."

Vinga nodded and took her hands. "Everyone has limited choices. It's—"

"It's who decides," Astria said.

Vinga nodded again. "And to what purpose."

"I'm glad it's you and my mother who help us," she said and hugged her.

Vinga raised her eyebrows and smiled. "Thank you."

Astria rejoined Yana and found her with a broad smile.

"Our Riders are the best and the bravest fighters in the mountains," Yana said.

"Yes, they're brave and the best in the Spine, but they haven't been challenged for centuries."

"You escaped the barbarians. How fierce could they be?"

Astria frowned and twisted her mouth at Yana's downplaying her peril. "I had three dragons to help me," she said. But she could never tell her friend the whole story because of her guilt for leaving Turmordare. It did not matter that Vandrare stopped them from intervening: Turmordare died, and she lived.

"You can't be worried."

"I've seen the barbarians up close, and they aren't like us. Our Riders may not be skilled enough or plentiful enough." An image came of the slave girl in the barbarian camp, and she gripped Yana's arm.

"Do you remember when you teased us with the fantasy of being the captive of a barbarian?"

Yana grinned. "Yes. It was fun to—"

"Never hope for that. Ever."

***

While Yana coached Astria, Skye left the Manor House with Efrin.

"Well, Rider, it appears my daughter will become our first emissary to the Northmen in generations."

He turned to her. "That was your doing?"

Skye smiled.

"You mean to keep her from harm," he said.

"I do."

"This trouble is too big to shield anyone."

Skye's jaw tightened. "Then she'll make friends and have a place to go . . . and not die here."

"Don't speak of losing yet."

"You imagine Woodcarvers and Farmers winning a war against warriors?"

"We're not helpless," Efrin said. "The mountains will delay them and give us time to prepare. Our terrain is a formidable ally, and the barbarians are unlikely to defeat us both."

A few yards from them, Astria and Yana sat near their dragons, chatting over a map of the North. When her daughter turned back to her and frowned, Skye shrugged off Efrin's arm.

"My little girl's childhood is over," Skye said.

"She left her childhood in the Wild," Efrin said.

Chapter 9
Northmen

High above the Blois River near the Derryh battlefield two days later, Yana pointed to a dust cloud rising in the west, and Trunghanger dove for a look. Close behind, Astria and Zephyr followed the squadron of Quarajii cavalry ten miles west to another sprawling but smaller encampment segmented by primary colors, this one surrounded by a ditch. Another twenty miles west, they circled a camp laid out in a grid of geometric precision. Swooping low, they spotted pennants that flew like the one she found on the battlefield. A short walk from the camp, they landed.

Sweeping her cloak to the side, Astria strapped the sword hilt to her waist and a quiver of arrows to her shoulder.

Yana raised an eyebrow. "Kendrick said to be unthreatening."

"How can we be sure Lothen didn't send us to die just to be rid of us?"

Yana glanced away for a second. "Kendrick and your mother are behind our mission."

Astria pursed her lips. "I'm bringing the staff," she said and left her other weapons strapped to the saddle.

"I'll take my knife."

A short hike from the foothills, a sentry threatened them with a spear. His words weren't clear, but the spear tip was, and Astria dropped the staff and raised her hands.

"We are Couriers from the mountain clans," Yana said.

The soldier frowned and said something they did not understand.

Yana pointed south. "We live in the high mountains of the Spine."

He frowned again, pointed toward the camp, and, with the spear, coaxed them toward a tall pole where an ornate flag waved.

The flag stood in front of a large tent that faced an expansive field where soldiers trained. When they arrived, the soldier stopped and lowered his hand. "Sit," he said, the first word they understood. They sat as the soldier spoke to another who ran to the tent.

While they waited, Astria and Yana studied the soldiers in the field.

"This appears to be a single camp and not the many camps of the barbarians," Astria said to Yana. "And the soldiers drill as a team."

"Perhaps military camps look different in the sunlight," Yana replied.

"I think it's a difference in leadership."

A well-dressed soldier approached and tipped his head. "Hello. My name is Lieutenant Denys. And who do I have the pleasure of meeting?"

Yana stood and swept her cloak to the side and put a hand on her hip revealing her comely shape in the tight-fitting riding leathers. "Are you from the Army of the North?"

Denys stared, stammering at the sight of her. "Why . . . yes."

"We are Couriers from the mountain clans with a message for your commander."

"Really?" he said. "We've not had contact for decades. And what is this message?"

"That's for your commander's ears only."

"I see. If you'll wait here, I will inform General Xander." He turned to the sentry. "Please bring refreshments, Corporal. And find them a comfortable spot in the shade."

He left, and the soldier led them to a lean-to, where they waited.

A private returned with mugs of cold lemon tea, and they waited further.

But as the sun approached the horizon, General Xander had yet to appear.

At sunset, Denys returned. "Apologies, but the general is unavailable. Perhaps you can return another time."

Astria frowned. "We just flew hundreds of miles to find him."

Unseen by Denys, Yana winked at Astria and patted the spot next to her. When Denys sat, she slid over to be closer to him.

"Perhaps we can brief you," Yana said with an engaging smile and flip of her ponytail.

***

In Invernell, Lothen paced in front of the Council table and listened to Yana and Astria's report. All wore frowns or furrowed brows except for Skye, who smiled at Astria.

"Well, sir," Yana said. "The spoken language of the Northmen is similar, with the same structure, but a few different nouns and verbs. Their translator has been working with us. And we know their ranks. The aides wouldn't share any tactics or formations. But their weapons are traditional bronze sword, shield, spear, and cavalry. No heavy weapons or machines."

"But in three weeks, you've not been able to speak to the commander?" Kendrick asked.

"No," Yana said. "We briefed General Xander's aides, but they made it clear he has no time for us."

"We need this alliance. The barbarians are a mutual enemy. The more we can learn of Qu combat behavior, the better we can prepare to defend against it. And the more the Northmen can harass them in Derryh, the less bother the Qu will be to us here."

"I suspect our age is the reason," Yana said. "Perhaps if someone—"

Astria jumped to her feet and raised her hand in front of Yana.

"Yes, Astria?" Kendrick said.

"We heard of a shakeup in command, sir. A young colonel, Richard Stewart from Cherbourne, will take command this week." She glanced at Yana. "We expect he'll be more open to our message and—"

Lothen nodded. "The chaos in their officer corps would explain the defeat in Derryh."

"Can you visit more often to increase your opportunities for conversation?" Vinga asked. "It's within your range, no?"

"Yes, ma'am," Yana said. "But we found no berries nearby, and our dragons must return to the Spine to find some before returning us home."

"You say they know you both now?" Lothen said.

"Yes, sir," the girls said in unison.

Lothen turned to the Council. "I suggest we alternate visits."

Skye frowned. "And they'll fly alone?"

Astria answered with a lie. "Our dragons can protect us."

"Zephyr is younger and fit," Lothen said. "Astria will fly first. Agreed?"

After the Council agreed and rose to leave, Skye came to hug Astria and Yana. "Come for dinner?"

"A word, Astria," Lothen said.

Uh-oh. She nodded. "Yes, sir."

Skye gave Lothen a side-eye and smiled at Astria. "I'll see you at home," she said and left with Yana.

As the Council room emptied, Lothen stood with his arms folded across his chest.

"Yana alluded to the need for a more seasoned Courier. Is that your assessment?"

Oh crap. "No, sir," Astria replied. "I think Yana is more than competent . . ."

"And you?"

"Yes, sir. We know the dialect well enough to speak without translation or embarrassing ourselves." *That's a stretch.*

"Good. Because Yana will have a place as a Rider if we need to replace the two of you. But without an alliance with the Northmen, the Council will have no use for you. Understood?"

"Yes, sir."

***

Sweat glistened on Astria's forehead as she faced the most frightening challenge after her discovery of the barbarian Horde, and she would face it alone. It was an honor, but any misstep would return her to Rogue status and end her chance to become a Rider.

A week after Lothen's warning, Astria visited the Northmen, hoping she would have more success at forging an agreement. Richard Stewart had just assumed command of the Army of the North and agreed to meet with her.

But Astria found Richard was late to a reception in his honor held by the prior commander. While waiting, Richard's wife, Lady Katheryn, roped Astria into attending as one of the few young women in the area other than the camp followers. To Katheryn, this was a treat for a welcome guest, but to Astria, it was another opportunity to fail.

So, instead of a meeting, Astria sat on the cushioned stool of a small vanity, overdressed in a formal gown. Even in the depths of winter, she would never wear so many layers of clothing at a single time.

Behind her, Lady Katheryn fixed her hair with a pin. And while adding a crown of baby's breath, she coached Astria in Northern etiquette.

Astria fidgeted in the tight dress. "Katheryn, if you introduce me as someone from the mountains, shouldn't I wear my normal clothing?"

"We don't want to scare them, dear," Katheryn said with a broad smile. "You're much too fierce for these boys. Your dragon is safely away?"

Safely away? For whom? "Yes, he's having lunch."

Astria glanced at her knife that lay with her flying leathers on a stool and frowned. She felt naked without the knife at her belt, and thought to strap it to her thigh, but reconsidered.

If I use a knife, it might break any possibility of alliance. And it might get me killed. Even drawing it at a party would show I don't trust them.

And they might take it as an assassination attempt.

Katheryn tightened the bindings of her dress, and Astria squirmed to loosen them. "But it's too—"

"Don't fuss now," Katheryn said, leaning back to admire her work. "Perfect!"

Astria frowned. "I'm afraid these fine clothes won't make this pig's ear into a lady."

Katheryn raised an eyebrow. "Clearly Invernell has few mirrors."

How could she know? "What do you mean?" Astria asked, but Katheryn only smiled.

Astria liked Katheryn from the moment she approached Zephyr without fear. She was the most beautiful woman Astria had ever met and carried herself with grace and authority. A frayed anklet and a long scar on her cheek were Katheryn's only imperfections, and Astria feared her own plain looks would shame her hosts.

The small dressing room was a simple arrangement of canvas and tapestries, one room of many in a larger complex built for her husband.

"What will I say?" Astria asked.

Katheryn readjusted one of Astria's new curls. "Say little and smile often. That's always worked for me."

"Will Colonel Richard be there?"

"I'm not sure, dear. It's a new command," Katheryn said. "But he answered your questions about Quarajii captives."

Papa, she thought. "Thank you."

"He said to tell you the Qu prefer to kill rather than capture soldiers."

Would they regard Papa as a soldier? "And civilians?"

"They sell them to the Sulerians, who take them north for obedience training. The strongest are sent to the galleys." Katheryn tipped her head. "Are you concerned for someone in particular?"

"Not really," Astria said, smiling to change the subject. She glanced at Katheryn's heeled shoes and then at her own shiny but flat-heeled footwear. "What about my shoes?"

"I've tortured you enough for this affair. Now let's introduce you." She took Astria's hand and led her through the halls of tapestries to the reception. At the entrance, Astria hesitated.

The noon sun lit the large, central room through thin canvas and the opening in the crown. Eight tall poles held up the canopy, and from them hung colorful lanterns. Scents of spices and sweets rose from a table where a bowl of punch sat beside plates of what might be cakes or small sandwiches. Opposite, men sat on a dais holding odd musical instruments.

Scattered throughout the room, three-score uniformed men and well-dressed women stood in groups apart. The women wore dresses of the same style as hers, although fancier and all strange compared with the simple style of her home.

Many of the dresses had hoops that kept the men at a respectable distance. All the dresses, including hers, had frills and lace or puffy shoulders that to her served no purpose. But rather than the bright prints and patterns of the mountain styles, these dresses were in single pastel hues. And thankfully, the dress Katheryn picked for her was more modest than the plumped bosoms of the older women. But the dresses were the most beautiful things about them, and without the finery, they would appear as plain as the Farmers of Invernell.

In the middle of the room, surrounded by senior officers, a portly man she guessed to be General Xander held court. His raised chin and arrogant sneer reminded her of many Riders.

Does Colonel Richard have the same temperament?

A tug from Katheryn's arm pulled her into the room, and she blushed as everyone turned and stared.

"Smile, girl," Katheryn said. "They don't bite." She scanned the room with impatience and then waved above the dancers to a lanky junior officer. As he walked toward them, the musicians began to play. Around her, couples bowed, took each other's hands, and moved to the middle of the floor. Unlike dancers at home who stepped to music strong in rhythm, here they twirled like eddies in a river to melodies that ebbed and flowed.

When the young man joined them, he snapped his heels and saluted to Katheryn. "At your service, Milady."

"Astria Sannfjaer, I'd like you to meet Ensign Gustalvo Cervies," Katheryn said. "Gustalvo, Astria."

Gustalvo blushed and offered his hand to Astria. "Ahh . . . pleased to meet you Miss Sann . . . Sannfi—"

"Sannfjaer. It means 'Truefeather.' Just Asti is fine, Gustalvo."

Katheryn glanced at both of them and smiled. "Gustalvo, please entertain our guest while I find your commander." She patted Astria's hand. "Dear, I leave you in the hands of one of the North's finest."

"W-w-wait! I . . . ." Astria stammered, but Katheryn turned and melted into the crowd.

Gustalvo fidgeted and ran a finger inside his shirt collar. "Sannfjaer is an unusual name, miss. Where are you from?"

Astria smiled politely as her ear adjusted to a new accent from the North. "I'm from the high mountains to the southeast. A village called Invernell."

"So far away. And how did you get here?"

Wanting to fit in, Astria was reluctant to tell him of Zephyr but did not want to lie. She leaned forward.

"A dragon," she whispered and grinned playfully, "with wings as wide as this room."

He smiled and played along. "Fearsome and deadly?"

"Indeed! With fangs as long as your arm. And claws," she said, curling her index finger and swishing an arc in front of her, "that could slice you in half."

Gustalvo laughed. "What an imagination you have," he said, not pursuing the topic further.

The music resumed, and as before, couples moved to the middle of the room and bowed to each other. When the dance began, dresses whirled and billowed, reminding her of pinwheels spun by a gust at the spring faire.

Gustalvo bowed and offered his arm. "May I have this dance?"

She blushed. "I'm sorry. I don't know your dances."

"It's really quite simple," he said with a broad smile. "I'll show you. Just follow me."

He took her arm abruptly and put a hand behind her back. "Now, mirror me. One . . ."

She immediately stepped on his foot. Twice. Embarrassed, she stepped away from him.

"I'm sorry, Gustalvo. Perhaps you can tell me about your home instead." She took his hand and led him off the dance floor to stand near a group of senior officers.

"Well, I'm from the far west, a port called Royan. I was visiting my cousins in Beirn when the recruiters caught me up." He sat straight, his eyes wide with excitement. "I thought this to be a grand adventure."

An image of corpses rotting on the battlefield came, but Astria did not have the heart to tell him his adventure could cost him his life.

How can an officer be so naïve?

During the awkward silences and the breaks in the music, she overheard the senior officers who stood behind her.

"This will be my last tour," a gruff voice said. "The kids are getting older now, and it's time they see their papa before the Hordes grind him up."

"Now, now," said another voice. "Sounds like you're giving up on this fight."

"We're still using fixed formations of infantry, and their ponies can outflank us and run over our cohorts.

We don't have enough men to counter that. I aim to take the wife north to see her folks in Auxiere and ride this out."

"North of Cherbourne? They won't get that far."

"If they run over us, there's nothing between here and Wikkert to stop them. Beirn has better natural defenses—"

A third voice interrupted. "Bah. You'd run on the eve of victory? Richard has command now and has brought his cavalry from Cherbourne. His horses can outrun the barbarian ponies. And he went straight to the Northern States individually to gather men. Says they're marching here now."

Scoffing, the first voice went on. "He's untested in a large conflict. Each state has its own tactical formations, and they've never fought together with any success. And now I hear we're to help fight for the mountain folks? It'll be at least a few years before the barbarians reach a populated valley in force. They have time to run."

Astria flushed. She wanted to spin and confront him but pursed her lips instead.

"Colonel Richard says it's containment. If they win in the mountains, they will have a base to hide and attack us. Derryh and Cherbourne are much more fertile and would give them better land for their slaves. That's their goal."

As she listened, she scanned the room for Katheryn, but her gaze rested on a handsome, young ensign. A few years older than she, he held himself like Efrin, with square shoulders and a calm presence. Standing with his hands behind his back, he was the one man here whose uniform did not seem to be a costume.

When he smiled at her, she realized she was staring and blushed but returned the smile.

A tall lieutenant stepped between them and intercepted the exchange. His was not the open face of the ensign, but narrow eyes above an over-groomed mustache. He winked at her and grinned, but she frowned at his misunderstanding and turned back to her escort.

A moment later, the narrow-eyed lieutenant spoke. "I'm embarrassed for you, Gustalvo." Four other junior officers joined him, none as well-groomed as his mustache. "A beautiful maiden stands here at your side without refreshment. We must be gentlemen and fetch her something to drink, now, mustn't we?"

"Yes, we must," the others said.

Taking Gustalvo by the arms, two of them lifted him off the floor and carried him away. Startled, Astria wanted to call out, but hesitated, not wishing to disgrace Katheryn.

"You must be the exotic we've heard rumored. Your name is?"

"Astria Sannfjaer, sir," she said and looked for a path to escape.

"My, so formal. I am Lieutenant Etheridge." He leaned over to her. "But I prefer Soren. My companions and I are seasoned veterans of the conflict here."

"You will be part of Richard's force?" she asked, trying to step to the side, but one of Soren's companions blocked her.

Contempt flashed across Soren's face before he recovered his charm.

"Perhaps. We are the professional army and battle-hardened heroes." He glanced at his friends. "Richard will need to offer us promotions to get us to join him, aye?"

With a conspiratorial leer, he leaned over to her. "I expect to be a major this time next year."

"He's younger than we are and has no—" began a companion, but Soren glared at him.

"Tut. We'll see." Soren returned his gaze to Astria. "You fascinate me, young lady. Tell me all about yourself."

She tried to look past him for Gustalvo, but Soren leaned into her line of sight. "I'm a Courier from the Council of Invernell."

"Ah, an exotic with a job. How charming. Tell me about your people, your dress, your... entertainments."

As he spoke, his eyes followed the two companions who carried off Gustalvo. When they left the room, his expression shifted to a feral sneer.

"Might I offer you some air, young lady?" he asked and took her hand.

Astria pulled away, but his grip tightened. "I'm sorry, but Gustalvo is my escort, and—" She backed away but bumped into Soren's companions.

"Not to fret. We're all chivalrous and up to the task. Now, while Gustalvo fetches your refreshments, step this way, please."

He pulled her hand and took her arm, which left her little choice. She resisted, but the others shouldered her until she had to step forward or lose her balance.

Once outside, Soren kept her arm in his, and his friends blocked the doorway behind her.

"We would like to beguile you with epic tales of our bravery, but this place is much too stiff. Ah, isn't this a beautiful day for a ride?"

"But Lady Katheryn—"

"Lady Katheryn won't miss us for a few moments."

A carriage approached, driven by the two men who had left with Gustalvo.

Astria prepared to whistle for Zephyr but hesitated. If he attacked humans, even in her defense, he would terrorize those at the party. Eyeing Soren's throat, she found a target for her knuckles but stopped. Like the knife she left in Katheryn's quarters, either defense could end the alliance before it began, and the Council might declare her Rogue again.

"I won't go with you," she said and made a fist.

"We'll see about—"

At that moment, the ensign who smiled at her earlier approached. "Hold, sir. The lady has me on her dance card."

The charming Soren turned icy cold. "Buzz off, Lance. This is none of your affair."

Lance ignored him and addressed Astria. "Miss, do you wish to go with these men?"

"No, sir. I wish to remain inside the party and wait for Lady Katheryn."

Soren glared at the ensign. "I said to butt out."

"Lady Katheryn will not take kindly to officers waylaying her guests," Lance said.

"She's a peasant. A mountain girl." The lieutenant sneered again. "And we'd like a taste. Perhaps you, too?" He gave Astria's arm to his companion but kept an eye on Lance. "Leave. That's an order."

"An order you cannot give and I cannot follow."

"She's the reason my fellows are here, and we won't be disappointed. Leave, or I'll report you to your captain."

"And I'll report you to Colonel Richard."

The two companions took Astria and moved sideways, but Lance blocked their path. She jerked to free herself and kicked out, but her slippers did no damage. The men were too tall for a headbutt, and with her hands tightly held, she could not escape. She prepared to scream, but Soren acted first.

"If you live," Soren growled and spun on Lance with a fist.

Lance parried the punch and stepped back with his hands raised, palms facing Soren. "A score of senior officers wait inside. Colonel Richard may court-martial us if we fight at his party. We don't want to hear about the next battle from inside the stockade, now, do we?"

Soren's friends from the carriage stalked over, and one of Astria's captors joined them. Her remaining captor held her by the wrist and the waist but kept his eyes on Soren and Lance. Sensing his distraction, she rotated her captive forearm and drove her free hand under his thumb. That locked his wrist, and with a twist, she drove him to his knees. But before she slammed a knuckle into his throat, Lance whistled.

Men pushed their way out the door, and Astria released her prey.

"What's the ruckus?" a captain asked.

"Nothing, sir," Lance replied. "A simple misunderstanding regarding the young lady's intentions."

Soren glared at Lance. "We'll deal with you later." He gathered his companions and stomped away.

Lance offered his arm to her. "May I escort you back inside?"

Astria's hand shook as she took his arm, her blood still hot from the conflict. It had been close. Her punch could have been deadly, ruining any chance of her becoming a Rider. She might even have made an alliance with the Northmen impossible.

Leaning over, Lance whispered in her ear, "Breathe."

He pressed her hand until she nodded. With a pat on her hand, he led her back to the party.

As they entered, the eyes of everyone in the room seemed to follow her and accuse her with the merest glimpse or frown. After all, she had left the party with one man and returned with another after an altercation. Astria fought to suppress her tears and wanted to run away and hide to collect herself.

When she could speak, she asked, "Whom should I thank for the assistance?"

"Ensign Lance Early of Lehrain, at your service. And you are?"

His smile warmed her, and she blushed. "Astria Sannfjaer."

Once near the appetizer table, Lance offered her a glass of punch. But as she reached for it, her hand shook again, and he held it.

He replaced the glass of punch with a smaller glass of bright yellow liquid. With the inviting smell of burned sugar and flavors she had never tasted before, it warmed her throat without the hard bite of Kendrick's brandy.

"A uniform is no guarantee of chivalry, milady," he said and smiled.

Milady, she thought and frowned at the compliment. She had spent the last year sleeping on the ground and tearing meat from the bone with her teeth, but he addressed her as he would Lady Katheryn. It was the kindest thing anyone ever said to her and so at odds with her self-image that she stared in disbelief.

"Did I say something wrong?" he asked, but she bit her lip. "Perhaps that dance?"

"I'm sorry, sir, but I seem too clumsy for your dances."

"Do you dance at home?"

"Yes."

"Here," he said. He put her left hand on his shoulder and took her right hand in his left. "Close your eyes."

He put his right hand on her upper back. "Just back and forth, now."

His was not Gustalvo's jerky precision, but the gentle sway of a bough in a summer breeze.

"That's right. Feel the rhythm," he said.

As the music flowed around them, the room lost its hostility, and the intimidating strangers warmed to her. And though Lance was an arm's length away, all Astria felt was him.

"Ah, there you are," Katheryn said.

Astria opened her eyes, blushed, and stepped to Lance's side but kept her hand in his. "Yes, milady," she said and curtsied.

"I found Gustalvo stumbling about and came to find you," Katheryn said, frowning at the missing crown of flowers and a lock of hair out of place. "You are well?"

"Yes. I was . . . diverted, and Lance escorted me back inside."

Katheryn gave Lance a narrow gaze. "Lance?"

He bowed. "Ensign Early, milady. At your service."

"Hmm. Well, I've found Richard, and he has a few minutes. Astria, if you would join me, please."

"Thank you again," Astria said to Lance with a smile. But Katheryn gave him another glare as she led Astria away.

At the end of the labyrinth of halls, they approached an armed guard, who pulled aside a tapestry to reveal a room with three walls. The fourth side opened to horses hitched to a picket line, and Astria's nose twitched at the camp smells of men and manure that rose from the plains beyond.

In the field below, uniformed men marched in tight units—formations suited the open spaces, not the mountains the Riders protected. This was the Army of the North, not the Riders who possessed neither their discipline nor their numbers.

Each has weapons and tactics suited to their terrain. How would our Riders fare here in the open fields of Derryh? And how would this army fare against Riders in the mountains of the Spine?

From the picket line, a man entered and removed his wide-brimmed hat and duster. He was nothing like General Xander: more Farmer than colonel, with a day's growth of beard and deep-blue eyes. Add a smile and remove the beard, and he might appear as the handsome junior officer she had just met. Close behind him followed Denys who traded nods with Astria.

"Ah, Katie, this is Astria?" Richard asked. Without waiting for a response, he shook her hand. "Sit, please. Stay, Katie." He sat on the corner of his desk and faced Astria. "You are well?"

She smiled. "Yes, sir."

He scanned the letters, pulled out the one Astria delivered that day from the Council, and handed it to his adjutant.

"Have this translated, Denys," he said and turned back to Astria. "We have only a sketch on your situation in the mountains. General Xander was not so forthcoming about the briefings you and Miss Yana provided to his staff. You are here alone this visit?"

"Yes, sir," she said. "Yana and I will alternate."

"I'm told your leaders are the Council of Twelve. Is that right?"

"Yes, sir."

"Any issues?" He tapped another letter on his leg and set it aside.

"Only that I hope this dress will not be required of me in the future."

"Not by me, but in that domain, you are Katheryn's protégé. Katie?"

"No," Katheryn said, then frowned. "But you might have a conversation with your young officers about chivalry."

A glance passed between her and her husband, and he nodded.

Astria stood straight. "Sir, we have limited forces and only a few score Riders. But the Council aims to call a meeting of the Clanough and unite the valleys. Invernell is first on their path, but the way up the river has so far been impossible."

As she spoke, a corporal brought a tea set, and Katheryn served.

"You have an advantage in scouting from the air?" Richard asked.

"Yes, sir," Astria said and sipped her tea.

"Can your dragons fight?"

"Unknown, sir. They're not guards or weapons and have minds of their own. They are big targets for crossbows and have difficulty maneuvering within the narrow canyons."

"What about here on the plains?"

"Dragons need to stay near the Spine, sir, and Derryh is beyond where most can fly."

Richard paced with his hands behind his back. "We're in transition here. Progress has been slow and costly." He unrolled a map of the Derryh foothills including the Blois River exit from the Spine. "We stopped them twenty miles east of here."

Astria closed her eyes and envisioned the terrain and distances from memory to orient herself. Then, she pointed to a spot on the map. "We saw an encampment there at the edge of a forest."

He smiled at Katheryn. "The capitol in Wikkert feels safe a thousand miles northwest. But Cherbourne is closer and the threat more tangible, so we've taken it upon ourselves to ... provide a more aggressive deterrent."

"One of your officers said you think the barbarians aim to conquer Derryh and Cherbourne."

He sat at the edge of the desk and crossed his arms. "And your Elders?"

"Our Council believes their aim is the South, where their myths tell them paradise lies. The river valleys like the Blois and Pelsuk are their means to get there. Habitable communities like Invernell are in their way."

Richard raised his eyebrows. "I think our fertile plains here are a valuable target."

She smiled. "You have not seen Invernell or the South."

"Aye, but it will take years to reach you through the passes—"

"There are no passes south, sir. Only the river valleys and seasonal footpaths."

"Making infantry vulnerable to ambush. Then Derryh remains the apple under their nose."

"An apple isn't the paradise they seek."

He glanced at Katheryn, who raised her eyebrows. "I see."

Astria continued. "Another of your officers thought little of your chances to succeed here. And another was angry your offensive appears to protect us in the mountains. My Council will want to know your priorities."

Katheryn pursed her lips and eyed Richard.

He narrowed his gaze. "How old are you, Astria?"

"Sixteen summers, sir."

"You and Yana are young to be emissaries."

"We are mere Couriers, sir. The distance is too far for our Elders to fly."

He smiled. "I didn't challenge your competence, only your age."

Outside, a horse galloped up, and the rider soldier off before it stopped. Unlike mountain saddles, his had no stirrups, making it easy to dismount. The pommel also had two horns that she guessed lodged the thighs for stability when shooting or fighting. After hitching his mount to a post, he marched to the open side and saluted.

Richard held his hand up, and the horseman stood at ease. "Give us a few minutes, Sergeant." He turned back to Astria. "I assure you if my priorities change from denying the Hordes access to the valleys, west or south, I'll tell you."

He sat again. "We will have more candid conversations like this. Some will include strategy and tactics that cannot fall into enemy hands."

"Yes, sir."

He handed her a sealed letter. "This is for your Council. I won't write everything I intend to convey, so I expect you to relay our discussions verbatim." He waved to the sergeant, who entered and placed an envelope on the table.

"Sir, scouts found this on a barbarian," the sergeant said.

Richard opened the envelope and emptied two crow feathers onto his desk. "His affiliation?"

"Crimson Horde, sir."

"Crimson?" Astria said. "How was that denoted?"

"By a red belt," the sergeant said.

"What is your interest, Astria?" Richard asked.

"From the air, the barbarian camps are separated and laid out by color: green, gold, red, and blue are largest."

"Ah, four tribes under separate chiefs. And what do the feathers mean?"

The sergeant relaxed. "Sir, a single crow feather is a squadron of cavalry."

"Not infantry?"

"That would be a hawk feather for a company."

"Then they mean to raid our rear. Is the supply line protected?"

"Only lightly. Infantry hold the west side of the forest."

"Well, we can't stay if they steal our dinner. Advise Major Thompson to muster the cavalry." Richard nodded to the sergeant. "Thank you, Sam. Anything else?"

"Sir, what of the Qu infantry?"

"Their army cannot exit the forest unseen. This should be a cavalry skirmish only."

Astria raised her hand. "Sir, the Qu have swords with curved blades that may be more effective than your short swords."

"We've heard of them."

"And they have catapults you may not see until too late."

Richard frowned. "You've seen these?"

"Yes, sir."

"Identified from the air, of course, at a distance?"

Astria noted his skepticism. "No, sir. From the ground."

"You were there?"

"Yes, sir," she said. From the pocket of her gown, she took the pennant she found on the battlefield and handed it to him.

Katheryn gasped, and Richard stared at Astria, making her wonder if she violated another sacred custom.

He stood, came to her, and took the pennant. "You found this in the Blois River Valley?"

She nodded, and he continued. "This battalion standard was retired after they died to a man protecting Xander's retreat. When our victory here is assured, I will hang this in the halls of Wikkert to remind the politicians what bravery and honor mean."

Richard handed the pennant to the sergeant, who saluted and put the pennant under his arm.

"Hang this in the chapel for now," Richard ordered and turned back to Astria. "We owe you a debt, Rider."

"I'm not a Rider yet," she said.

"You saw catapults?"

"Yes, sir. They transport them in pieces by wagon."

"Quarajii don't have such devices."

Astria opened her mouth to protest, but he raised his hand.

"Or didn't until recently," he said. "And they didn't have engineers who could tackle the mountains." He glanced at Katheryn. "The Qu are getting help from Suleria."

Richard studied Astria. "That will change our tactics. Thank you."

"Shall I advise General Xander?" the adjutant asked.

"No. I will lead. But ask him for a moment of his time."

"Aye, sir," the sergeant said and left with the pennant.

Richard regarded Astria under a furrowed brow. "You have freedom to fly where you will?"

"Yes, sir."

"Then I request you never fly near barbarian-held lands again."

"I'll need to scout their progress up the Blois."

"Engage another observer. You and Yana must never risk yourselves or the information we will discuss by flying near the enemy. The Sulerians have spies everywhere, and we cannot risk your capture. You understand?"

She flinched at the image of the branded and beaten slaves shivering in the cold. "Yes, sir," she said, dismayed by what that meant: no more searching for her father.

He studied her and folded his hands on the desk. "When have your people last defended your lands?"

"Hundreds of years, sir."

"Then war is new to you. It's not a job or a duty. War is where men die. Women die. Children die. Villages burn to ash, and countries are lost forever. You are a part of this now to prevent the worst from happening to your people. We need you and you need to take your role seriously: life and death seriously."

Astria paused. "Yes, sir."

He nodded. "See that either you or Yana stop by at least once a week. And on your next visit, please tell us more about their camp." His eyes softened, and he smiled as Efrin would.

"Katheryn implied an incident earlier. Do you have a complaint?"

"No, sir."

He studied her. "Who helped you?"

"He called himself Lance Early, sir."

"While you are here, you and Yana are considered part of my staff and afforded all the courtesies and protections of your status." He stood and offered his hand. "Thank you for your visit and your candor."

"Thank you, sir. Your help in dealing with the barbarians is important to the Council."

"As your help is to us here. Will you stay for the party?"

She glanced at Katheryn. "Excuse me, sir, but I'll need to start home before it gets too cold."

"Godspeed, then."

"Thank you, sir," Astria said, but the scrolls on his table had already stolen his attention, and Katheryn pulled her away.

Outside Richard's office, Katheryn turned and hugged her tight. "Returning the pennant means a great deal to us here. We all had friends in that unit, and they disappeared like ghosts in the night. Their families will remember you."

Katheryn hugged Astria again, smiling, and took her arm. "And now to free you from your bondage."

Back in her dressing room, Katheryn helped loosen the laces on Astria's dress, and she drew a deep breath.

"Well, I think you hit it off with Richard," Katheryn said. "He only speaks so candidly with a few senior officers."

"I'm honored, milady, and thank you." Astria shed the layers of clothing and slipped into her flying leathers. "Milady, is there a small plot of ground I might use for an experiment?"

"Yes. Why?"

"Dragons need a berry to fly that grows only in the mountains. It'd help if Zephyr and Trunghanger could rely on a source nearby and not have to fly back to the Spine to find it."

"Of course. Let me know if you need help, and I'll recruit the idle soldiers. Oh, and tell Yana I have more comfortable dresses for you two if you wish."

"Thank you, milady."

"Sit with me for a moment," Katheryn said, patting the chair next to her. And when Astria sat, Katheryn took her hands.

"Richard and I have been at war with the Sul for much of our lives, from slavers to invaders to smugglers, and have seen . . . our loved ones fall. Unlike General Xander, Richard does not think of his soldiers as replaceable parts and thus expendable. His concern is for you and every soldier that fights at his side. You and Yana are brave, or you would not be here, and you need to prove nothing to Richard or to us in the North. Do not risk your life unnecessarily."

Astria nodded slowly, and Katheryn smiled and stood. "You mentioned Lance's chivalry. May I invite him to tea the next time you come?"

"That would be nice, milady," she said, but a mirror exposed the blush and twinkle in her eyes.

As the sun approached late afternoon, Astria mounted Zephyr for the ride home. Circling the compound once, a young officer on horseback waved up at her.

She remembered Lance's smile, his quiet competence, and how she warmed at his glance. He had none of Fynn's edgy impatience, but a strength that calmed her.

On the long flight, the cold did not interrupt her thoughts of him. And when her wishing star came within sight, she prayed for her father and added a wish for Lance.

***

In Katheryn's parlor two weeks later, Astria sat with Lance and a coterie of young officers and ladies as camouflage for their meeting. Her dress was not as stiff as the ball gown, but not by much, and she fidgeted in the dead air over a cup of bland tea.

Around her, the conversation meandered between dress styles and courtesies, leaving Astria to smile politely while her thoughts ran through the lifesaving disciplines she'd learned in the Wild: her snares, the fire, her inventory of arrows, and the work to be done to keep her alive. When she finished her checklist, her head bobbed, and she excused herself to breathe the open air on the porch.

"They're all like this," Lance said as he joined her. "Tea parties and soirees and balls."

"How can they sit in a camp full of soldiers within a few days of battle and think of their dresses?"

"We've held Derryh for decades, and they know nothing of conflict." He frowned. "I'm afraid Lady Katheryn arranged this for you and you're disappointed."

"No longer," she said and smiled. "It's just that the dress and formalities are uncomfortable."

"You'll learn."

"I'm not sure I want to. Other than troop deployment and tactics, what I learn isn't useful when I return home."

"Why did you accept?"

Astria turned her head to hide her blush. *Because I wanted to spend more time with you.* "Because I wanted to thank you for helping me last week at the ball."

Lance bowed. "Your presence is thanks enough."

"How charming," she said but lost her smile.

"Perhaps if you're uncomfortable, you should wear your own clothing."

"Lady Katheryn said it might be . . . inappropriate in the company of dresses and uniforms."

"I don't see how. Come, now. I'll start." He removed his jacket and threw it over his shoulder. "If we're to be friends, let's be honest."

She was taking a chance, but she could not endure months of these stiff clothes. *Maybe here I can be myself, where women like Katheryn have a prominent place and they aren't afraid of me. A place where I can be free.*

She smiled again and went to Katheryn's dressing room to change. Expecting her riding leathers would entertain him, she practiced her explanations for why her pragmatic clothing took the shape it did.

But when she found Lance, he lost his smile and blushed. Her summer leathers were tight-fitting breeches and a matching top, shiny with tanning and weatherproofing oil that caught the angles of the sun at every curve and crease of her body. In the sheath at her side was her hunting knife.

"I understand why Lady Katheryn advised you not to wear your riding gear."

"You're offended?"

"No. But the style is more . . . revealing than the ladies here would be comfortable wearing. And the men might not take you seriously." He put his jacket back on. "Perhaps we should return to the party."

She put a fist on her hip and glared at him. "I didn't mean to put you off, sir, if I appear too . . . primitive."

"No, of course not. I'll wait here."

Astria marched back to the dressing room but passed it to head to the bluff overlooking the training grounds. She picked up a branch and slapped it against a tree.

I'm being asked to act like an adult woman, and I don't know how to do that in a strange country. And with every mistake, I either offend them or embarrass myself. The constraints of style and custom echoed the Council and angered her even more.

"To Hel with them," she mumbled and threw the branch over the cliff.

A twig snapped behind her, and she spun as a man walked toward her with his hands up, palms forward.

"Well, well," he said. "Here you are without your pretty disguise." He wore sergeant's stripes on fatigues, and at first, Astria did not recognize him. When she did, her heart raced.

Soren.

"What're you doing here?" she asked.

"I saw you from the parade ground below and came to ask your forgiveness for my ungentlemanly conduct at our last meeting." He kneeled and opened his arms.

Another twig snapped to her left, and she turned as a soldier from Soren's squad flanked her. When she looked back, Soren was on his feet, closing the distance between them. Another of his men approached from her right. With her back to the bluff, retreat was impossible.

I might break a leg, but they'll never have me.

When she faced forward again, Soren stood in front of her and grabbed her wrist before she jumped.

"Remove your hand or I'll break it," she said. "Katheryn isn't here to stop me."

"Neither is your savior." He hardened his grip, and his men moved in. She had only seconds now.

She took a step to her left, grabbed the back of his hand with her free hand, and rotated her wrist over his. With his hand trapped on hers, she pushed down to break his wrist. But he kneeled to avoid injury and grabbed for her legs. Before he could knock her off her feet, she repeatedly kneed him in the face until his grip relaxed. His head bobbed, and she held him to keep him from falling.

His men moved in, and she drew her knife.

"What're you going to do with that, little girl?" one asked.

"I gutted a mountain lion with this blade, and your friend is about the same size."

He moved on her, and she put the blade to Soren's throat. "Touch me, and I'll kill him."

The soldiers backed off. "We're the witnesses now," one said. "We merely defended ourselves from a mad savage who tried to murder us."

"There's another witness," Lance said from the edge of the clearing and drew his sword.

The soldier drew his blade and took a step toward Lance.

"I'd advise against that," Lance said. "Attacking a superior officer will mean a hanging."

The men backed off when Lance approached, and Astria released Soren.

"Find a different unit by tomorrow, and I won't report this," Lance said as they dragged Soren away.

Still flushed with battle fever, Astria asked, "Why did you let him go?"

"He's a good soldier in the field, and we need all we can get. But if you wish to press charges, I'll be your witness."

Astria slowed her breathing. "Thank you for returning for me."

"Perhaps I should change my duty to be your bodyguard," he said with a charming smile.

Astria crossed her arms and frowned. "Excuse me, sir. I don't need protection from a thug like him."

"Apologies, milady. I thought at the party—"

"At the party, I held back to not embarrass Lady Katheryn. I am grateful you came to my aid, sir, but don't think I need your protection."

He frowned and stood at attention. "Apologies, milady. If I'm of no further help, then let me escort you back to Lady Katheryn, and I'll take my leave."

She put a hand on her hip. "Is that how you see me? A simpering maiden to be rescued? And because I don't depend on your protection, I am of no interest as a person?"

"Then who are you?" he asked without expression.

She shook her head and furrowed her brow. *He's earnest but condescending, protective but patronizing. And how in Hel do I answer that?*

"Someone like you've never met," she said and walked away.

Without stopping to say goodbye to Katheryn, Astria found Zephyr and flew south. Before reaching the mountains, she stopped on a peak overlooking Derryh. From her saddlebag, she took a bota of tea and a biscuit and sat next to her dragon to let her passions cool.

"I don't understand them, Zephyr, any more than my own people. They judge me by how I look and the rumors that swirl around me. Will anyone ever know who I am?"

He blinked and his eyes sparkled.

She leaned into his shoulder. "Well, maybe you."

***

Two weeks after her argument with Lance, Zephyr dropped Astria near Richard's compound.

As she walked to Katheryn's quarters, Astria stretched and rubbed her neck, stiff from lying forward on Zephyr's back for the long flight from Invernell.

In the courtyard, two soldiers in masks sparred with swords of different shapes and filled the air with the *bangs* and *clacks* of impact and the *whomp* on the padded armor. It appeared to be practice, as every few moves, one stopped to show a new stance or grip. After a parry, the attacker struck the other with an elbow in the mask. The defender tripped him and aimed the wooden sword, but he found only dirt as the other jumped up and put his sword at the other's throat.

When Astria approached, the attacker bowed to the opponent and walked over.

"Welcome, dear," Katheryn said after removing her mask. "We're trying out a new sword for the cavalry to match the Quarajii scimitar." She made a few strokes. "It's curved for slashing but can still kill with a thrust. The master of swords calls it a saber."

Astria raised her eyebrows and took the offered sword, much longer than hers and curved without added weight. *And better on horseback? Or dragonback?* "I have news for Richard."

"Come, then." Katheryn took Astria's arm and led her to her dressing room. "Richard is in the field today but will be back tomorrow," Katheryn said as she changed into a linen peasant dress with ornate, purple embroidery. "You can stay here with me tonight if you like."

"Zephyr will like that."

"My vacation with Richard is over, and I'll return to Cherbourne next week. My little girl, Diana, will run her maid into the ground if I'm not back soon."

"How old is she?"

"Seven summers and a handful. The quarters next to mine will remain for you and Yana. Are you settled in?"

"Yes, milady."

"Ensign Early came to see me and wants to apologize to you. May I ask for what?"

Uh-oh. "It's unimportant, milady. An argument about nothing."

Katheryn studied her. "Did the argument have anything to do with Sergeant Soren?"

"I meant him no permanent harm."

"I hear he volunteered for a unit at the front."

"The argument with Lance . . . Ensign Early was after."

"I see," Katheryn said. "Did Ensign Early act in any way inappropriate or unchivalrous?"

"No, milady. Perhaps too chivalrous, and it angered me. I'm a Rider—or will be."

Katheryn's face softened. "I don't mean to belittle your position or skill, Astria, but you are still a young woman and unable to disguise it. Men naturally want to protect you. It's their nature, dear, and not a flaw."

"Yes, milady."

"And what of Ensign Early's invitation?"

"I don't think I'm . . . Tell him no."

"He's right outside, dear. Tell him yourself."

Astria pursed her lips. "I won't change into your dresses, milady."

Katheryn smiled. "Your choice. Now scoot."

Time to grow up and not hide behind Katheryn.

Astria startled Lance when she stepped onto the porch, and he dropped his padding and wooden sword. She blushed at his bare chest, and he put on his officer's jacket.

"Milady, I wanted to apologize for our last meeting," he said and bowed.

"That's unnecessary, sir," she said, which came out colder than she meant.

"I'm not sure what—"

"Really. There's nothing to apologize for. Just a difference of cultures. If you will excuse me now," she said and turned to leave.

"If I may, I've arranged a picnic."

"I'm sorry, but—"

"You'll need to eat lunch after your long flight."

Her stomach betrayed her with a growl, and she surveyed the area. *Let's get this over with.* "Well, then, where is it?"

"If you'll follow me," he said and went to two horses tied to a hitching post.

"No."

"You have nothing to fear from me, milady. On your dragon, then?"

She nodded and whistled for Zephyr as Lance mounted his horse.

After a brief ride, Lance stopped on a hillock with a view of the Derryh plain and dismounted. There, Zephyr dropped Astria off before returning to the mountains. On the ground lay a spread with dishes and glasses and cushions.

"This is your doing?" she asked, and he tipped his head. "Lance, I—"

"Please, let's just enjoy the meal in silence and not risk stumbling on the differences in our cultures."

She opened her mouth to speak, but he raised his hand to silence her, and they began their lunch without words.

As he handed her a sandwich with the crust cut from the bread. She noticed the bruised knuckles and calloused palms from sword practice. He offered wine, but she drank only a sip. On a small plate, he gave her a slice of cake that, once bitten, dissolved into raspberry and sugar in her mouth. After dessert, he lay on his back with his hands behind his head as the clouds drifted past.

"The pastry was a treat," she said. "Thank you. Perhaps I should be the one to apologize for our argument."

"How so?" he asked but concentrated on the clouds.

"We have our own tyranny in the mountains. I mistook your chivalry as a trap I needed to escape."

"Tyranny?"

"Our Council of Twelve prescribes our duties and meddles in everything, including who we can marry. It's our ancient governance from when we were a seafaring folk, before we escaped from the Imperator's slave pens."

Lance turned to lie on his side and faced her. "I don't think of chivalry as tyranny."

She narrowed her eyes. "What do the women think?"

"They're bound by the same code: to honor and protect the vulnerable, not to humble them. Some women hold office in Wikkert and don't want those protections. Others are soldiers and serve with me in the militias."

"Swords are heavy to swing all day."

"My captain is a woman, and she can spear a melon swinging on a string at a gallop."

"Women are Riders and fight alongside men."

He nodded. "Most civilians here can't defend themselves as well as you can. We have large open spaces where brigands and slavers roam. The roads are filled with ruffians exiled from their villages."

"Exile . . . exile from our valley often means death."

"That's rough justice."

"It's to teach us compliance," she said and sighed. "But I didn't learn that lesson."

"If I may ask," he said, "I only know of your dragon and Yana's. Are there any . . . do they all look similar?"

Astria glanced at him with a glint in her eye. "You mean frightening and ugly? Without horns or claws or feral eyes?"

Lance blushed. "Well . . . yes. Are there any pretty ones?

"Are you insulting our dragons?"

"No, really, I meant no offense."

She laughed. "No. There are no pretty ones. But among them, Trunghanger and Zephyr aren't so bad." She turned to Lance. "Is Lady Katheryn a good student with the sword?"

He laughed. "Oh, she's not learning. She's our trainer." He glanced away. Then he frowned and faced her. "Milady, it was not chivalry that drove me to your aid. I thought you needed my help. Nothing in your demeanor led me to believe you didn't need it."

Astria smiled. "Then I am a good actress. It seems we've both jumped to conclusions. Apology accepted."

"Let's start again." He rose and bowed. "Good afternoon, milady. I am En—"

"If we're to be friends, then drop the formality. My name is Astria, and yours is Lance. Now let's talk of real things." She took the wine and sipped what she still could not drink at home. "Come," she said to break his silence. "What's on your mind?"

He smiled and sat again. "Why did Katheryn invite me to tea?"

She blushed. "I wanted to see you again."

"Why?"

"Because you don't treat me like a child."

"You don't act like one."

Astria glanced at the hills. "I haven't been a child for a long time."

"Is there someone at home you care about?"

She blushed and picked a daisy to weave into a bracelet. "You mean a boyfriend?"

He nodded.

"No."

"Never?"

"Once, there might have been, but he cared more about becoming a Rider than he cared about me," she said and added another daisy to the chain. "And you? Surely the dashing, young officer must have many young ladies."

"Not since I joined. Soldiering leaves me little time for romance, and the camp girls..." Lance's brow furrowed for a moment. "If I had not trained under Richard, I might have become like Soren." He gazed at her directly. "Would you have killed him?"

She put the daisies in her lap. "Soren?"

"Yes."

"I meant to scare them. But yes, I would if it came to that." Her face hardened. "I will next time."

"I've spent years of my life in the militia with his like, men more skilled at war than peace." He rolled his sleeve up to expose a long scar on his forearm. "This is from a Sulerian child slaver near Beirn."

Astria unbuttoned her shirt to the breast and rolled down the shoulders that hid the claw scars. "These are from a mountain lion's claws," she said and drew her knife, "that fell to mine."

Lance winced. "You're right. I've never met anyone like you."

She frowned, shamed by her rough past and afraid she put him off. "But not so frightening?"

"No longer," he said with a smile and put his hand on hers.

His nearness stirred her heart. *But how can we care for each other when we're so different?*

From the trees, she caught a glimmer of Zephyr's sparkling eyes, and she understood. She turned her hand over to hold his and then looked away to hide her blush.

***

A week later, on the beach of Lake Norven, Efrin struggled with Agnarr.

"Hold him, I said!" Efrin shouted to Jenks as Fynn buckled the leather armor on Agnarr's chest. Efrin's dragon would have none of it and hunched his shoulders to thicken his neck. He bit the section of armor and shook it like a grax with a snake. With a whip of his neck, he flung the leather slab into the trees.

Belastad refused to fly with the armor and bucked off Huld when he tried to mount. The dragon took off and jerked until the straps broke, and the armor fell free. Zephyr caught the torn pieces and tossed them to the other dragons, who played with them until shredded, all the while chuffing and honking.

The onlookers laughed, and the Riders, sweaty from the day's effort, joined them.

"Their wings are the biggest target," Efrin said and handed a bottle to Yana.

"And we can't armor them," Astria said.

He nodded. "Then we'll have to stay out of crossbow range."

"If the Sul are helping the Qu as Richard thinks, then they may have other weapons as well."

Efrin nodded again. "Urquil mentioned ballistae that can loft heavy spears."

"And if the Sul are helping them with grain, then they'll have almost infinite resources. It's not the Qu at all. It's Suleria using the Hordes." He stood and left the bottle with Yana. "I need to talk to the Council."

When Efrin was out of earshot, Yana leaned over to Astria. "I hear you have a new friend in the North. A young ensign? Dashing, I hear, and almost as pretty as my Jenks."

"Just a friend," Astria said with a blush. "And maybe not that yet. I'm simple and odd and don't know how to act."

"We're only there because we're useful," Yana said and patted her hand. "And that's why you aren't still a Rogue."

"Because I am useful to those who cower in fear that I might be this Speaker person."

Yana lost her smile. "Remember, he's a soldier in a foreign army."

"They're allies."

"All alliances are temporary." She glanced at Jenks. "Only love is eternal."

"He can teach me about the North. Maybe I can learn where my father went."

"The Council may think your loyalty is split."

"That damn Council again."

"Just keep it quiet."

Chapter 10
The Great Divide

Over the next year, Astria and Lance became close. She stayed with Katheryn during his brief leaves every two months; too rare and short, leaving them hungry for more time. Zephyr was always close by, and in a clearing near Richard's compound the following spring, the dragon kneeled to offer Lance a ride.

"You're very special, you know," Astria said, helping him into the saddle. "Dragons rarely offer rides to grounders. It means he trusts you."

He buckled the riding belt over his duster as Astria secured him with tethers. "I think he knows I like you."

She blushed. "He's a lot faster than your horse, so don't lean back in the saddle."

"Where are the stirrups?" he asked.

"There aren't any, and you don't need them," Astria said and tied another tether to his belt. "Once you're airborne, lean forward in the shadow of his crest, or the wind will push you back and you'll stay that way until you land." As she spoke, she ran her hand under the edge of the saddle searching for wrinkles in the blanket.

Zephyr turned a sparkling eye to Lance, who leaned forward to rub the dragon's forehead.

"You're not pretty, big fellow, but you are charming," Lance said. "Where are the reins? How do I guide him?"

"He's not a horse, and you can't command him."

"How do they follow instructions?"

"They don't, really. You might call it a mutual interest." She put a fist on her hip. "Don't think of them like horses or pets. People keep putting human motives and behavior on them and they don't behave that way. Just be grateful he offers you a ride."

"How will I tell him where to go?"

"You don't and you shouldn't. You don't know how to navigate from the air. He'll take care of you today. Just don't nudge him in the side, or you may be riding upside down for a while."

"Come with me."

"I told you, he can't carry two adults."

"Does he understand verbal instructions?"

She put goggles on him and tied them behind his head. "No. And you can't speak in the wind, anyway." From her pocket, she took a small pouch and tucked it in his shirt. "This is ginger and peppermint if you feel nauseous."

With a smile, she jumped from Zephyr's shoulder. "Ready now? Lie forward. Just pat him on the sides of his neck when you want to come down." She waved to Zephyr, who jumped into the air and sped away.

Zephyr's flight was smooth, with gentle banks and even glides, without the exuberant dives and flips of her first ride. A minute later, he became a speck. And when they disappeared into the darkening clouds, Astria ate lunch from her saddlebag and nodded off in the afternoon sun.

An hour later, a raindrop wet her cheek, and Astria rose as Zephyr and Lance spiraled down into the clearing.

"You never told him to come back," she said as she unharnessed him.

With shaky legs, wet hair, and soaked pants, he dismounted. "No."

"How was it?"

"Wait," Lance said with a big smile. He took a few steps, flung his duster open wide, and fell on his back in the grass. She sat by his side as he gazed up through the drizzle.

"I never imagined anything so exhilarating," he said. "So close to the clouds. I reached out to touch them, but they dissolved as we flew through them." He waved his hand over his head. "I saw all of our troop deployments to the north and the peaks of the Spine to the south."

He shivered. "It's so cold up there."

She held his wrist and felt a racing pulse, unsure if it was his or her own. "How's your stomach?"

"A little queasy, but I'll be fine."

She lay next to him with her head on her hand. "Now all dragons will know you."

"How? Do they read each other's thoughts? Can they read ours?"

"No. They just chat a lot with one another."

He raised his eyebrows. "That's a lot of chatting."

"It's easier for them. My father thought they talk in pictures and color."

"I don't understand."

"Well, we speak words in a sequence of sounds, one after another. Dragons do all that at once with many pitches at the same time. It's like painting with many colors that combine into a picture. They do that with sound, I think. That honk you heard, I think that's your name in dragon speech."

"What does it mean?"

She blushed. "Astria's . . . friend."

He smiled and turned to her. "If you can't understand them, how do you know?"

She shrugged. "It's a guess. He only makes that sound when you're near." The rain fell steady, and she sat up. "We'll need to find shelter."

"Wait," he said. "The rain feels good."

Zephyr fidgeted restlessly, and Astria waved him away to find shelter.

When the rain fell in earnest, the trees provided no cover, and they mounted Lance's horse with Astria holding on to Lance's waist. A chill breeze came as they raced through the rain with Astria shielded by Lance's duster. By the time he found a barn by the road, the rain fell in sheets.

Inside, they dismounted, and Lance removed the horse's tack. He wiped it down with his shirt and then put his duster on the horse's back to warm it. All the while, Lance shivered.

"You need to take off those wet clothes," she said. "Don't be shy, or you'll get sick."

He removed his trousers, wrung them out, and laid them over a stall gate. She put her waterproof cloak around him, but he still shivered. Opening the cloak, she put her arms around him and felt the shape of his body. When she laid her cheek on his chest, he drew the cloak around her and held her close.

In time, his shivering stopped, but he kept the embrace, and she did not let him go. She was safe, and the Council and war dispersed into the fog. All she smelled was him, and all that mattered was the moment.

Lance put a finger under Astria's chin and peered into her eyes, and with a kiss, swept her away like the rising river and over the falls to dissolve in the mist. An eon later, she opened her eyes to his soft-brown ones and gentle smile.

When he pulled her toward the hay, she shook her head. Instead, she returned the kiss, led him to the door of the barn, and sat. He put the cloak around her again and his arm around her.

"My home up north is like Derryh," he said. "With wide-open plains and good farmland. That was the last place I was truly happy. Until I met you."

She leaned into him. "What brought you here?"

"When my mother died, my father was distraught and left me with too much time alone, and I . . . got into mischief. He said the militias would season me and teach me discipline. And the constable gave me no choice."

"And the war found you."

"Yes. I was fortunate to be with Richard and not Xander."

"The Seers seem to think the Quarajii threaten the dragons and bring the Darkness."

"What's that?"

"The End Times, the end of the world."

"We have no such myth. But if Derryh falls, civilization here falls with it. The Sulerians bring slavery, and that's as dark a future as I can imagine." He brushed her palm with his fingertips. "And you? How did the war find you?"

"I guess I found it. I was a Rogue then."

"What's that?"

"It's like an exile who's only allowed into the valley to trade."

"Who has the power to do that?"

"The Elders on the Council of Twelve. It seems my entire life has been a battle with them. They only value me for what I can do for them. But I can't live like that. My value isn't simply what others place on me, but my value to myself."

He nodded.

"As a Rogue, I lived on my own with Zephyr. I hunted and trapped my food and traded furs and meat. I made my shelters in the snow and rain and slept on the dirt. And I was hungry all the time."

"Could Zephyr not hunt for you?"

She shook her head. "Dragons don't share," she said and closed her eyes. "I was away from my mother and friends and could only see them for a few hours a month. I was so . . . so lonely."

He took her hand and held her close. "And what of your friends?"

"They did their best and tried to help when they could, but they were not there when I needed them most. And I couldn't tell them because they could do nothing about it. I . . . I can't go through that again. Now, as a Courier, I can ride Zephyr and be with my friends and family in my own home." She took his hand and held it to her cheek. "And I can see you."

With nothing more to say, they listened to the rain until Astria drifted off to sleep in his arms.

Across the Derryh battlefield she trudged, her feet mired in gore with carrion birds and dogs on her heels. But the gore bogged her down until her feet could not move, and she swooned at the stench of death and rot. The wild dogs leaped for her with their bloody maws open, and she screamed.

Astria woke with a pounding heart and jumped to her feet, poised to run.

"There, there, now," Lance said and stood next to her.

She scanned the gloom, and the scavengers were gone. Zephyr lay curled up in the stable, gazing at her.

Lance put his arm around her. "Nothing here can harm you."

"Stay with me," she said.

"Forever," he whispered.

After a few minutes, she sighed and sat again, staring into the murk.

"In your sleep, you mentioned a pennant," he said.

"That was the night I found the pennant for Richard," she said and told him of her discovery of the battlefield and the torture of Turmordare. Lance was the first she told the horrors of that night, and other than Richard, he was the only other person she thought would understand.

He hugged her closer. "Most of us don't see the horror until it's upon us, and then it's too late. Do the memories come often?"

"Only in dreams now. But the closer the barbarians come to my home, the worse they get."

"Perhaps if you remember Zephyr rescued you . . ."

"What do you mean?"

"Before you sleep, remember he swooped you out of danger. Then maybe you'll be at peace dreaming your dragon saved you."

She hugged him.

"Or maybe a gallant and handsome, young cavalry officer whose only concern is your happiness."

"Maybe," she whispered and drifted off again in his arms. This time when the barbarians came for her, Lance rode up on his horse and cut them down. Grasping her forearm, he lifted her to sit behind his saddle, and they galloped away.

In her sleep, she smiled.

But the enemy they ran from followed close behind.

Chapter 11
Elementals

Lance filled Astria's thoughts on the flight home. Though tired and hungry, she would not stop to rest, bubbling over to tell Yana and troubled about what to say to her mother.

Halfway home, Zephyr landed at a pond above a waterfall, where dragons basked in the sun. Astria pulled his reins, but he did not move.

"Let's go, big guy," she said, pointing to storm clouds building to the west. "I'm tired, and we only have a few hours before the storm." But he would not budge. "Why stop here?"

She dismounted and walked to the inlet, where a pile of cobbles diverted water from the river into a pond before it fell into the gorge below. It resembled the pond she and her friends had spotted from the Tops, this one filled with fish.

At the outlet of the pond, another pile of cobbles let some water flow through, but large fish could not pass. *Men didn't make this. Then who?*

From the east, a flock of dragons flew low and dropped red salmon into the pond, where basking dragons fished with their claws in the water.

She returned to Zephyr and stroked his eye ridges. "Too lazy to fly yourselves?" she asked. He nudged her with his snout, forcing her to higher ground. With a squawk, he took off, and other dragons followed.

The flock picked up large cobbles, flew over the pond, and dropped them on the pond outlet until it collapsed, spilling the water. Before the fish escaped, they picked up new stones and repaired the outlet.

Zephyr landed by Astria and the others behind him, and they all stared at her.

"Really? You built it, and you can destroy it as well. Why?"

He cocked his head and gazed at her for a moment and then kneeled with the offer to ride.

Instead of continuing home, Zephyr flew alongside other dragons to the Blois River Canyon a few miles north of Invernell, and the spear tip of the Quarajii invasion. Below them at a turn on the river, Sulerian engineers built a wooden bridge to bypass a rocky cliff, and upon the bridge, the dragons dropped their cobbles.

The first pass set the workers scrambling. Then larger dragons followed with small boulders and shattered the wooden beams that fell into the river and floated downstream.

The dragons chuffed and honked at Astria as Zephyr banked to fly her home.

On their return to Invernell, lightning arced over the glaciers, and the wild dragons headed for shelter from the rain. At the valley's south entrance, a long caravan parked inside the fortified gate. Near it stood the finished bivouac for Riders and infantry who joined the fight.

Zephyr dropped Astria off close to the village center where smithies and bowyers made new weapons. As she passed, they eyed the clouds and closed their shutters against the coming rain.

At the Manor House, Astria weaved through Seers and acolytes to enter. Inside, she found Efrin with her friends integrating a new squadron of volunteer Riders from Andeir. Fynn glanced at her with a frown, but raised his mug to her. She nodded to him and waved to Efrin and Yana, who joined her.

"Reporting, sir," Astria said.

Efrin nodded. "The Council is meeting now in closed session."

"Why are the Seers out front?"

"The Seers pray for Olim to bring help."

"That'd be fun, huh?" Yana said. "To watch the Einerkel and Berserkers ride from Kriegheim and join the fight."

Efrin smiled. "Some families are moving south with the caravans. To visit, they say, but are bringing their things."

"We may have other help," Astria said. "I watched dragons destroy a Quarajii bridge by dropping rocks on it."

Efrin narrowed an eye. "How'd you get them to do that?"

"I didn't. They showed me." *And no, I'm not the Speaker,* she wanted to say.

"That will help us stay out of range of the crossbows."

"And we won't have to dive into the canyons to get at them," Yana said.

"Let's tell Lothen and Kendrick at the Council meeting," Efrin said. "And Jenks and Fynn can experiment on how much they can carry and how accurate they can be."

"Why did they show you first?" Yana asked.

"I'm not sure," Astria said. "Maybe to check if they were doing the right thing." *But why show me?*

"If they can help to slow the Qu advance, we'll have more time to prepare," Efrin said. "And maybe we can make their invasion too costly to continue."

Edgy laughter erupted from the new volunteers from Andeir at the bar, and they turned.

"The brutes were dumbfounded," a young Rider said and used his hands to imitate his dragon's flight. "I broke formation and swooped down on their position. Daraktig grabbed the pike right out of the warrior's hands."

The Andeir Riders listened with awe, but the Invernell Riders frowned.

"When I flew away, all he could do was shake his fist at me," the Rider said.

Efrin interrupted their laughter. "That was too dangerous, Tegbert."

"Bah. Barbarians are too stupid to threaten us and have nothing to match our skill.

Efrin turned to the Flight Leader of the volunteers. "I'll not be telling you how to lead your Riders. But if you can't discipline them, I'll ask you to take them home. We don't need dead Riders."

Rain beat on the Manor House as a Rider from Andeir put his arm around Tegbert's shoulders.

"The storm is making us antsy, pay no mind to—" the Rider said.

"Those 'stupid barbarians' defeated the Army of the North," Astria said.

Tegbert shrugged off his mate's arm and faced Astria. "Posh, little girl, you'd deny us our sport?"

The volunteers laughed and raised their mugs, but Efrin frowned. "This is war, Rider, not an opportunity to flaunt your daring. If they capture you, then we're obliged to rescue you."

"You worry too much. Dragons are elementals and invulnerable. With them, we are invincible."

"No, they're not," Astria said. "And neither are we."

Tegbert's semaphores resembled scorpions as he sneered at her. "Then perhaps you *couriers* need lessons in bravery to match my dragon."

Thunder cracked outside just as Astria's fist smashed Tegbert's nose, and he stumbled backward. Blood flowed over his lips, and he scowled, tearing open his shirt to show grax scars. "I was the first to meet the Quarajii scouts on the Northern Pass."

"But you weren't the first to fight back," said the Flight Leader from Winterthur and pointed to Astria. "She was."

Tegbert lunged at her, but Fynn stopped him, and the two flights of Riders started swinging.

Efrin came to stand by her side, and they watched the fight. "Well, that didn't go as I'd hoped. Isn't he the kid you helped to patch up years ago?"

Astria nodded. "He'll get them killed."

"Come," he said.

Astria and Yana followed Efrin to the Council chamber where he knocked on the door. Kendrick opened it and waved them in. At the table, Skye smiled at Astria, and they traded subtle waves. Kendrick raised his hand, and Efrin stopped and closed the door.

"Continue Britta," Kendrick said.

"I've been working with the other Farmers at the Clannough," Britta said. "And we have wagons scheduled from the southern valleys"

Kendrick glanced at Skye who nodded.

"Each valley all the way from Vernier will send wagons to the next valley north," Britta said. "And the excess of all will be sent here. We expect an extra wagon of grain and salted meat every three days. That will match the number of riders expected to bivouac in Invernell."

"And the riders to protect the caravans?" Lothen asked.

"Those who will stay with us are included in the tally. The other valleys will protect their caravans and feed their Riders."

"Excellent," Lothen said, and Britta sat.

Kendrick waved to Efrin. "Any change in the status of forces?"

"The Northmen have pushed the Quarajii back to the Blois River and secured Derryh," Yana said.

"Have they closed the path to the river canyon?" Lothen asked.

"No. The path east of the river and south is open."

"When do they expect to close it?"

Yana turned to Astria with raised eyebrows.

"The path is on the east side of the river," Astria said. "And closing it will require the Northmen to cross the Bois. The Quarajii have their forces and the Sulerian engines of war there. The river will be their next major action."

Efrin raised his hand. "Astria has discovered that the dragons are motivated to target the Qu from the air with cobbles. I'll have a squadron try to repeat this on a larger scale."

"Excellent," Lothen said and stood. "I'll meet with the Riders with you." He turned to Yana. "You say The Quarajii are still progressing up the Blois River Valley. If that's the case, I think this Council should reconsider our alliance with the Northmen."

Astria stiffened. *Without that alliance, I have no role and no excuse to visit Lance.*

"What do you mean?" Kendrick asked as lightning flashed and thunder rattled the shutters.

"Some have suggested the Northmen are funneling the Qu up our valley to keep them from advancing in Derryh."

"Who specifically?" Kendrick asked.

"I'm not at liberty to say."

"Are these speculations or facts?"

"Hard to say, Chairman."

Britta stood. "The Northmen may fight hard, but if their fighting only makes our struggle worse, then the alliance is not working to our advantage."

"Excuse me," Astria said. "I saw thousands of dead Northmen at the Blois River battlefield on my first encounter. I doubt they'd sacrifice an army just to divert the Qu toward us."

Lothen frowned and glared down at her. "It isn't your station to speak for the Northmen or—"

As they spoke, Skye set her jaw and focused on Lothen and Britta like a cat ready to pounce. Kendrick glanced at her, the palm of his hand an inch above the table.

"Actually, it is," Kendrick said. "Perhaps if you request Richard confirm his commitments to us again in writing what he has committed to many times before. I am sure Astria or Yana would deliver that message."

As Kendrick defended her, Lothen's semaphores wrinkled at the temples, and in his eyes lay a threat to everything she wanted.

"If you wish," Astria said. "I could politely ask Richard to confirm his intent without exposing tactical information."

Lothen narrowed his gaze and eyed each of them. "Yes, thank you. That's all I have then," Lothen said and sat with a smile that never got as far as his eyes.

"That concludes our meeting then," Kendrick said, "And Yana, Astria, good to see you."

Skye took Astria's arm and led her outside. "You're grumpy today."

"I'm tired, Mama. Maybe it's the weather. Do you know why Fynn's in a bad mood?"

"Sit dear," Skye said, and Astria joined her on a bench beneath the broad eves of the Manor House. "He and Furnia fought."

"About what?"

"I suspect it's because he wants more than she's willing to give before marriage. He mentioned you to Lothen again."

Astria took a deep breath. *It's now or never.*

"What if I'm spoken for?"

Skye smiled but lost it in a moment. "Is this hypothetical?"

Astria shrugged.

"This mysterious stranger, what's he like?"

"Well, he's tall like Efrin and fit. Too polite sometimes."

Skye took her hands. "How did you . . . how will you meet?"

"He came to my rescue to protect me."

"How chivalrous. How old will he be?"

"Just a little older."

"How little?"

"Maybe nineteen, Mama. But he doesn't act like the boys here. He doesn't treat me like a child or an object or a prize the way they do here."

Skye nodded slowly and gazed at her softly in a way she never had before.

"He took me on a picnic," Astria said and blushed at the memory.

Skye caught the blush and narrowed her gaze.

"Zephyr let him ride," Astria said to distract her.

Her mother smiled gently. "Your dragon trusts him," she said, and her voice softened. "Do you love this boy?"

Astria dropped her gaze. "I don't know."

"Could you?"

"Maybe."

"Then bring him to dinner," Skye said as a light rain began dripping from the eaves.

Uh-oh. "He's too far away, and Zephyr can't carry us both."

Skye let her breath out. "He's not a Rider, then. Distance is hard on a relationship. If he doesn't ride, then you won't come home to visit."

"I haven't thought that far, Mama, and it may not work out."

"What does he do?"

"He's an officer in Richard's cavalry."

Skye tightened her grip on Astria's hands. "If you hope to be a Rider, then keep this to yourself."

"Why?" she asked but already knew.

"They judged you Rogue because of your rebelliousness. They wouldn't trust you. And a dragon under the influence of outsiders is dangerous."

"I'd never do anything to hurt our valley."

"This is about perceptions, hon."

Astria stood and struck back. "Perceptions? Like I'm the Speaker person? Or defiant? Will I ever be free of these rumors?" She pulled her hands away. "Will you tell the Council?"

"Of course not. But find a man in the Spine."

"They're all boring, and none are likely to let me travel to find Papa."

"But they're not soldiers. Soldiers die, hon." She turned away. "And I won't be there to mourn his death with you."

"I'm not even in love, and you've declared him dead? Fynn's a Rider and in as much in danger as I am."

"I hoped that—"

A crack of thunder interrupted and echoed within the valley.

"You hoped what?" Astria asked.

Skye looked away.

"You don't approve?"

Her mother shook her head.

"Could you sway the Council?"

"I won't try."

Astria raised her hands. "Why did I bother to tell you if you can't support me?"

Skye leaned forward and whispered, "If I do, they'll exile you for good, and I'll never see you again."

A dragon honked, and Astria cringed at a sharp pain in her chest.

"Something's happening, Mama!" she cried and rushed to the Riders' bivouac.

The storm broke, and a steady rain fell as the dragons returned from a foray over the Blois River Canyon. Out of formation, a dragon with a ridged frill, Daraktig, faltered, and the Rider on his back wobbled in the saddle like a rag doll.

Zephyr and the other dragons squawked and wheeled to follow, and near Lake Norven, Daraktig fell on the beach. Zephyr and Omattlig landed, and Astria and Fynn rushed to the injured Rider and dragon.

It was Tegbert from Andeir, pierced by crossbow bolts. The rain washed his blood over the saddle and onto the dragon, whose eyes were closed tight with blue tears. Daraktig's wings trembled, and he drew them close to his body, exposing the ballista bolt that ran through his chest and into the Rider.

"They're erecting nets to keep the dragons away," Fynn said. "We warned him to fly higher, but he wouldn't listen and flew underneath to taunt them. Daraktig loved him and would do anything he asked."

Philina came and examined the young Rider. She shook her head, and his fellows took him away. Then she kneeled to examine Daraktig and lowered her head. Riders came to pull the bolt from his chest, but the midwife raised her hand.

"Leave him," Philina said. "The bolt staunches the bleeding. If you try to remove it, it will cause great pain, and he will bleed out."

"He can't live with that in him," Jenks said.

"And he won't live with it removed." Philina held the dragon for a moment, kissed him, and backed away. With her eyes glistening, she raised her head to the dragons gathering above. "Leave him to his friends."

"There must be something you can do," Astria said.

Philina shook her head again.

As people backed away, dragons landed to fill the space near Daraktig.

"They are our first to fall," Jenks said. "We've been able to fly high above without danger."

"Tegbert believed he was invincible and our dragons beyond death," Fynn said.

Astria stared at the horizon. "And so did we. This is how it will be now. And it will get worse. This is what the Northmen see every day. They on the ground know death firsthand. They—"

Lightning flashed and thundered almost simultaneously, and Daraktig moaned.

Astria screamed, fell to her knees, and covered her ears.

"What is it?" Fynn asked and kneeled beside her.

Daraktig moaned again and his pain consumed her. The spear in his chest and the broken ribs that tore his flesh with every breath and beat of his heart, and the agony of losing his Rider, were all hers. She gasped and fought for breath.

"No!" Astria moaned and gripped her chest. "No more!"

Zephyr honked, and the dragons roared and turned to her, but Astria ran away into the rain, lost in Daraktig's pain.

After sunset, the storm passed, and a light mist fell as Angelica and the Seer found Astria at the valley rim.

The Seer lowered her hood "Yana and Fynn search for you. Do you need more time?"

Astria shook her head.

"I'll tell the others you are here," the Seer said and left Angelica to sit next to Astria.

The blind girl was silent until a flock of dragons lifted Daraktig into the sky and flew west.

"Daraktig leaves us," Angelica said.

Lon and Fures broke through the clouds, bringing the mountains that ringed their valley into relief. The blind girl seemed to sense the light and raised her chin.

"I felt his pain," Astria said and gripped Angelica's hand. "I promised to help them, but all I can do is die with them. And more will die."

Angelica laid her other hand on Astria's. "Did you know they have a name for you?"

Astria paused. "Do you talk to them?"

"No. Only Kari, the goddess of the wind, can do that. But like you, in the quiet moments, they whisper to me. They call you Singer. When you sing, they know your heart."

"What does that mean?"

Wispy clouds veiled the moons again, and faint thunder echoed as the storm moved east.

"You care about what they care about, and they care about you," Angelica said. "Perhaps neither of you know why, but you do. Dragons show you what's in their hearts, and in your own." She frowned and her voice hardened. "That makes you dangerous."

Astria shook her head. "Why?"

"They care about you," Angelica said. "And that changes them."

"I don't want to change them."

"It isn't your choice but theirs. But if your heart is poisoned, you will poison them."

"I can't herd them like sheep or command them like soldiers," Astria said.

"Dragons can't be led like the gullible who live by the word. But they are naïve, and their hearts are like ours: we go where our passions lead us and live and die as our hearts will. But they can be influenced as they influence you. That's what makes you dangerous."

"If we care for one another, why is that dangerous?"

"Dragons are elementals, like lightning and blizzards, the claws of Fairma. Do you realize what it means to rouse the tempest? You have a grave responsibility, Astria. Temper your feelings—all of them—or dragons will magnify them."

Astria jumped to her feet and crossed her arms. "This Speaker nonsense again? Can I not escape this damned prophesy?"

"The prophesy is not yours to escape. The Druims fear the barbarians bring the Darkness and threaten Aeterna and the dragons. They fear the end of the world unless the Speaker leads the dragons to Aeterna's defense. Unlike the Seers, the Druims pray for the Speaker to rise, and the Farmers fear the dragons cannot be controlled."

"They must know I'm not the Speaker."

"It's not who you are now, but who you might *become*. They watch, and wait, and pray to the gods."

"Is that to be my destiny then?"

"Perhaps, if your will is weak and your spirit too timid to choose another path." The Seer smiled and searched for Astria's hand. "The gods celebrate those most who defy them to forge their own destinies."

Astria took Angelica's hand and sat again until bright Elein rose and set shadows of the clouds adrift over the valley.

"The day my father left, a vision came during Klokbror's song, of armies of men in furs fighting in the glaciers near the Source. Were they barbarians who hunt dragons?"

"I don't know," Angelica said. "Perhaps it was a different battle in the past or the future. But the dragons are afraid, and they make you afraid."

"You speak differently than the old Seer," Astria said.

"I still live in this world rather than the next." She gripped Astria's hand again. "And I listen."

Astria gazed at the moons and remembered the havoc wreaked by Turmordare, a single dragon. "If I follow my heart, will I lead them astray?"

Angelica raised her chin as if to view the moons but said nothing.

Chapter 12
Indravay

In the fall of the year of Tegbert's death, Astria passed the signaling and coordinated flight tests to qualify to be a novice Rider. Uncoordinated with the other novices, Astria took part alone. Now, on an overcast day, she approached the end of the first physical challenge of the all-day initiation: a rim-run around the valley and a swim. Exhaustion tainted her mood, and her body told her to quit.

"If Huld did this, I can," she had said to Efrin.

But Efrin replied, "He's gained a hundred pounds since he passed."

She changed to the breaststroke to conserve energy near the end of her half-mile swim across Lake Norven. And on the sandy beach, La'a met her and handed her a towel.

With purple lips, Astria shivered as she opened her mouth to speak, but La'a shook her head.

"Now's the time to listen," the Rider said and led her into a shack built against a cliff face. Inside, a single candle lit the runes painted on the three walls of wood. On the stone wall were carved symbols around a hole that would fit a large man's arm. In front of it stood a stool.

"Sit," La'a said and took Astria's hands. "These are the hands that hold the reins of a dragon, the most powerful creatures on Juro. The Riders must trust that you can manage that power.

"All the Riders you know passed this test. No one speaks the names of those who failed. There are no grave markers or memorials. This was the bargain you made when you chose to be a Rider."

"What is this test?"

"Later, I will ask you one question, and if you answer correctly, you will pass."

"What's the question?"

"Can you control your dragon?"

Astria thought of all the times Zephyr flew her to where she wanted, stayed with her, and helped protect her. *Yes, of course I can.* But when she opened her mouth to answer, La'a raised her hand.

"I'll ask that question later. Do you wish to take this test and accept the consequences of failure?"

Exile or death? "Yes."

"Inside the hole and vertical to it runs a leather rein, the same as on your dragon. Place your arm in the hole and hold the rein. If you let go and the rein slips between your fingers, we will know you cannot manage a dragon."

Astria reached her hand into the hole in the stone and gripped the leather rein. Immediately, she felt it pull downward and firmed her grip. Within a minute, her entire arm burned to support the muscles of her hand and wrist. It seemed like the strap became heavier, and it slipped slightly before she gripped it tighter.

If they keep increasing the weight, I'll eventually fail.

Ignoring the burn, she twisted her wrist and wrapped the strap around her hand. Now either the strap or her wrist would break.

Sunlight flashed, men shouted, and drums banged to distract her, but she held on. The weight increased until her wrist bent, and her forearm pressed against the jagged bottom of the hole in the stone.

Pain was her enemy now, not weakness. But still she held the strap.

I have no future except as a Rider.

The bound strap would not slip, and she felt the tendons of her wrist stretch as her hand bent backward and the bones of her forearm pressed hard against the stone. The strap did not break but stretched, squeezing the bones of her hand together. She gritted her teeth at the pain as tears ran down her cheeks.

"Do you wish to quit?" a voice asked.

"No," she whispered. *I can ride with one hand. But can I fight as well?*

The weight increased, and the fingers of her hand lost strength. Despite her will, one by one, her fingers gave out, and her future slipped from her grasp.

How could Yana do this, and I can't?

"Argh!" she screamed in frustration as her last finger opened, and the rein slipped from her hands.

She pulled her hand out, rubbed her wrist, and licked the blood from the wound where the bone had scraped against the jagged stone.

I failed. What's left for me now? Exile again?

La'a came and led her back to the beach. There they sat cross-legged as La'a bandaged Astria's wrist and applied a cold compress.

"What's to become of me?" Astria asked. "All I wanted was to be a Rider."

"You failed to hold the reins," La'a said with a hint of sympathy.

Astria pursed her lips in anger. "You kept increasing the weight."

La'a smiled gently. "The weight is nothing compared with the power of a dragon."

"What's the purpose of a test if I am meant to fail?"

La'a paused and looked into Astria's eyes. "The test is a lesson. Your strength is not enough. Your tolerance for pain is not enough. Your passion, your virtue, your desire are not enough. The test is for you to remember that you are human, not dragon.

"You and your partner travel the same path together, but you are separate. His strength belongs only to him, not to you. He is neither sword nor servant. The scars on your wrist remain to remind you."

La'a eyes bored into Astria's. "I ask now: Can you control your dragon?"

Astria dropped her gaze to her hands. "No."

"Correct," La'a said, standing. She offered her hand. "Come. Your Indravay awaits."

Through a drizzle, La'a led Astria along the valley rim to a tent of sheepskin over a domed frame.

"Bring your questions and you may find answers in the Indravay," La'a said, opening the flap from which sweet smoke drifted. "And meditate on an animal to guide your journey."

As Astria entered, she thought of the most majestic animals who might guide her: eagles and hawks, even the mountain lion she had killed. But her thoughts returned to her commitments to Zephyr and the dragons.

Inside in the stifling heat, she sat between a pair of Riders from Andier. Across the pit of coals, Angelica swayed with the rhythm of the Seer's chants and a Druim's finger drums.

What questions will I ask? Is my promise to the dragons a trade for my life? Is my destiny to be the Speaker they fear?

Angelica passed a pipe to Astria, from which she took a drag. Closing her eyes, the smoke swept her up.

The Seer's chants came to her as visions, and she swayed with the wheat in a fall breeze. Around her came the animals of the Wild, the rabbits, the deer, the bear, and all those she had hunted but were at peace with her. The graxes were there too and sat with their jaws on their forepaws watching her. Into the middle of their circle, the swallows brought fire and light but frightened none of the animals. Among them she sat, belonging there with them all. At peace, she asked no questions, and no answers were needed.

As reality drifted in and out, the Druim abducted the chant. Astria felt welcomed and smiled. The breeze carried her into the air, where she found scores of wild dragons in formation. She took the lead as they soared above the Spine like a ribbon in the wind. Below them, barbarians camped, and she dove to inspect them. But the dragons following her attacked the camp. She hovered, confused, as blood and gore splashed on her wings, and she honked in distress.

"No!" someone shouted, and Astria opened her eyes as Angelica beat the Druim with her cane.

"You can't wish that on someone you care for!" Angelica shouted. "Begone and plague us no more with your superstitions."

When she had driven the Druim from the lodge, the blind girl sat again and faced Astria as if she looked into her soul.

***

A small fire danced within a copse of oaks as a chill wind swept the fog up from Lake Norven. At the edge of the fire boiled a small pot of water.

"Tea, sir?" the Farmer asked.

"Something stronger," Lothen said, and the Farmer passed him a flask. After a drink, the Rider inhaled through his teeth and handed it back. "And how long am I to wait here in the cold?"

"No longer," Britta said and entered the firelight with two more Farmers. "The Council has not confirmed her choice to be a Rider, Flight Leader. But your consent to initiate her puts her on that path."

"I had no option, or the Riders would revolt. She's been in our service for a year."

"Her influence grows over both Riders and dragons, even as just a Courier. We can't let this continue."

"It grows because of her value to us, Britta. And you should see that as a benefit."

Britta shook her head. "She's too dangerous. You saw how the dragons reacted to her."

"You're referring to the dragons' distress when Daraktig died?"

"And Astria's response."

Lothen raised an eyebrow. "That was an emotional moment among the dragons. Daraktig was the first to fall in this conflict."

A Farmer shook his head. "You saw it. They reacted to Astria like no other."

Lothen scoffed. "So now you understand the dragons? Then tell them to come when I call so I can be home for dinner."

"The Speaker appears in our midst, and you do nothing?" the Farmer said.

Lothen shook his head. "This Speaker nonsense? The Druims' myth is only real in your nightmares. She's no more the Speaker than I am."

Britta smirked. "But they don't sing to you."

He scowled. "Come now. Everything she's done has helped us."

"Really? She's defied us at every step, first to grow the berries after we forbade it and then to feed it to her crippled dragon—"

"Crippled no more," Lothen said.

"And defied us to ride him. Now she's back and with loyal friends."

"And familiar with a foreign army," said another Farmer.

"Would she defy us again with a private alliance with the Army of the North?" Britta proposed, and the Farmers grumbled.

"Bah," Lothen said.

A Farmer stood and paced behind Britta. "I thought the Wild would rid us of this threat."

"We meant her punishment to be severe," Lothen said. "An example to others. Not deadly."

Britta scoffed. "Pretend that if you must if it helps you sleep at night, but you knew her odds of survival were low, even with a dragon."

Lothen stared at the fire.

"She showed the dragons how to drop stones as weapons," said a Farmer.

"They showed her," Lothen said.

Britta waved a hand. "So she says. And what else will they teach each other? It's too dangerous. If we elevate her to Rider, she'll bring more dragons under her spell. You must cast her out before she enchants the others."

"No. She's too useful now," Lothen said.

"Then before it's too late, and the world falls to Darkness," said a Farmer.

Lothen shook his head. "The barbarians are a few minutes flight from the Tops now, and if it's Darkness you fear, it may come sooner without her."

"We need to act now," Britta said, and the Farmers mumbled their agreement.

"No, Britta. We're at war."

Britta narrowed her gaze and curled her lip. "Your Riders are big eaters, *Flight Leader—*"

"And your fields need lots of Riders to protect them, *Farmer.*"

"It would be a shame to reduce their rations."

Lothen glared at her. "If we lose, you'll have nothing to ration. Cut them? If it's death by starvation or death in battle, I choose battle."

"If you think I can't—"

He raised his hand. "Enough. What do you propose?"

"To give her what she wants most."

He gave Britta a side-eye. "And other than her choice, you know what that is?"

As Britta outlined her plan, Lothen studied her cold eyes and the Farmers' set jaws.

"Take no action at Council until this conflict is over," he said and stood. "And leave me out of it."

"As you wish," Britta said with a smirk.

"Take heed, Britta," he said. "Her desires are much stronger than your fears."

When Lothen left, she turned to a Farmer. "Come. Let's have a talk with Skye."

"And if Astria refuses your offer?" the Farmer asked.

Britta smirked again. "She can't."

Chapter 13
The Tops

A week after the initiation, Yana returned from her mission north and found Astria on the Tops overlooking the valley. During the two years since Astria had first discovered the barbarians, the Sulerian engineers defeated all the rugged terrain of the Blois River: from rapids to deep water, from unsteady rubble slopes to sheer cliffs, all except their last natural defense—the Tops. If the barbarians controlled the Tops, nothing could stop them from engulfing Astria's and Yana's home.

Yana sat by her friend's side and traced the tattoo on Astria's temple that outlined her new semaphores.

"Will that be a butterfly when the Seers finish?" Yana asked.

Astria's blush made her eyes shimmer. "The tail of a swallow," she said and turned Yana's wrist over to see the scars from her initiation. "I didn't notice them before."

"What does Lance think?"

"He's seen your semaphores, so he expects mine."

"And you think the Riders will let you finish them if you are with Lance?"

"No. But I'll be eighteen soon and can choose my mate for myself without their interference."

Yana shook her head. "If they know, the Council won't just sit by."

"I've followed their rules this time."

"The Farmers will argue otherwise. And your mother won't be able to stop them." Sunlight glinted from Yana's eyes. "Are you sure your motives are pure?"

"What do you mean?"

"Zephyr is your means to become a Rider, and Lance is your way out, away from Invernell. They're your means to snub your nose at the Council, and . . ."

Astria smirked at the idea of defying them, and she chafed at the chains of love and obligation with which they bound her.

"All of this for what *you* want," Yana said.

Astria frowned. *Is that the only reason I love him? Have I been using him?*

"I want to be free like my father. You know the feeling: to fly free, to see the wide world, all of it beyond this tiny valley, to see how other people face the problems we face, and to—"

"Jorie was not free but bound to our people."

"And so am I," Astria said as she studied her hands.

"You didn't have to come back from the Wild. And yet you did. You didn't have to sacrifice the freedom you treasure to be a Courier. And yet you did."

Astria nodded.

Yana took Astria's hand. "Like your father, you're bound by what you love, and it is us. All of us, and the dragons. Do you want to be free of that?"

Astria recalled her times alone with Lance in Derryh and that afternoon in the rain. And she smiled at Zephyr's happiness when they were together.

"No," Astria said. "But how can I make it all work out?"

"It may not."

Yana led Astria to the southern edge of the Tops where sunbeams shone through the clouds and glimmered from Lake Norven. The nearby cornfields were bare, and the clans busied themselves with the wheat harvest. Along the valley rim, elm trees glowed yellow between live oaks, and scattered within the village, maple trees blazed red. Amid the rolling plains of Derryh and the high mountain lakes of the Spine, this was the most beautiful place they had ever been.

"We could lose all this," Yana said. "The future Jenks and I planned for could all be gone soon."

"Can you imagine a life without him?"

Yana shook her head. "Not a happy one."

"Would you stay if it meant slavery?" Astria asked.

Yana paused and sighed. "No. They wouldn't let me stay with Jenks, and I have no future without him. We'd have to leave."

"If you can."

When they reached the Tops and the defenders, a woman's shout interrupted. There, Furnia, red-faced and hands on her hips, argued with Fynn. She spun and ran past with tears on her cheeks toward the trailhead leading to the valley floor. Fynn threw his hands in the air and walked toward them.

"What's that about?" Yana asked.

"Kendrick found out that I asked for Astria's hand last year, and he told Furnia."

Astria scowled. "And you haven't told her yet?"

Fynn shook his head.

Astria poked him in the shoulder with her finger. "You are so stupid! If you have a brain in your skull, chase after her and tell her how much you love her and that it was a silly mistake. If you don't, you'll lose her forever."

He backed up. "I'll meet her on the bottom with Omattlig."

"No, on foot. She wants you, the man—not the Rider."

Fynn took a step to chase after Furnia, but Huld called.

"Whoa, Fynn!" Huld said and pointed to the break in the clouds. "The rain's stopped for a spell, and I think the barbarians need some troubles. Let's find Jenks and our lazy dragons."

The men excused themselves. But before mounting Omattlig, Fynn glanced back at Astria and nodded.

When they took off, Yana and Astria walked to the north side of the Tops to report.

Efrin and Lothen stood at the edge of the Tops where the waterfall fell hundreds of feet to the canyons below. At the bottom, eddies of mist and smoke swirled like wraiths to obscure the work camp. And there, Astria peered into the fog for some hint of their plans as Lothen turned to her.

Astria looked up. "Couriers reporting, sir."

"The Notch holds them," Efrin said.

Lothen nodded. "The winter ice has not stopped them, and the spring floods didn't flush them out. The Spine hasn't broken them."

"But it has slowed them." Efrin pointed to the archers lining the edge of the cliff. "Fifty bowmen defend each of the Tops. We can hold here."

"Is that enough?"

"There are swordsmen to match and reserves camped just below," Efrin replied.

"What else?"

"They're widening the trails along the canyon wall. Wider than they need for men and supplies."

"Why?" Lothen asked.

"I don't know. The wagons are backed up to the last bend behind the excavation."

The mist cleared below them, exposing wooden platforms that spanned the river.

"Now, what on Juro are those for?" Lothen asked.

Astria shuddered and asked, "What do the wagons look like?"

"Long," Efrin said. "Stacked with beams. Some are filled with barrels."

"I know what the platforms are for," she said. "Catapults. The wagons bring them in pieces. Below are the firing platforms."

Lothen's jaw dropped. "Come all the way from Derryh?"

Efrin nodded. "They knew how hard this would be."

"Catapults can loft missiles over the Tops and into the valley," Lothen said. "And there'll be nothing left worth fighting for."

On the platform below, a man drew a large ring in chalk.

"What's he doing?" Lothen asked.

"A training circle, perhaps," Efrin said.

One barbarian placed weapons—sword, spear, flail, and battleaxe—on opposite sides of the circle. Around the circumference barbarians gathered, laughing and shouting. Two shirtless men entered the ring halfway between the weapons: one with a red belt and a much larger man with a blue armband. The smaller of the men threw something shiny into the middle, and the crowd roared. A horn blared, and the two men raced to grab swords and stalked each other.

"Those don't look like training weapons," Lothen said.

Using techniques unknown in the valleys, the combatants moved with a skill and grace the village folk had never witnessed. Riders could never match these men in hand-to-hand combat.

Astria studied the fighters, twisting her body to mimic their moves on the platform below. She waved to Fynn when he landed. "Come. Watch them train."

The large man slashed the other's side with a curved sword, and the smaller man countered by raking the larger man's legs with a flail. Red blood smeared both of their bodies.

Yana leaned away, her eyes wide. "This isn't training."

Efrin shook his head. "This demonstration is meant for us—to intimidate us."

"It's working," Yana said.

In the contest ring, the smaller man choked his opponent with a forearm. With a hip in the big man's back, he dragged him on the rain-slick platform to keep him off his feet. After a roar, he raised one arm in the air, dropped the big man gasping to the floor, and then strutted across the circle with his hands held high.

Recovering quickly, the large man scooped up a sword. The smaller man limped and feinted to the left, appearing exhausted and vulnerable. But when his opponent committed his thrust, the smaller man dropped to one knee, parried, and slashed the man across the stomach. Turning away from his foe, he raised his sword in triumph.

As a pool of blood grew around him, the big man fell to his knees and lowered his head, which the winner hacked off. Holding the head at arm's length, he faced each group of warriors who saluted with bowed heads and a fist clasped in a palm. From the severed head, the winner cut an ear and threw the head into the audience to roars of approval. Then he turned to the Riders on the Tops, raised a fist, and jeered.

"Seems they just selected a new leader," Lothen said. "What are his plans for us?"

Efrin nodded. "And what are our plans for him?"

The light rain cleared, Lothen and Efrin took off. A minute later, they appeared again with a trio of dragons that carried a boulder in a sling. At the sight of them, the barbarians ran for shelter. The sling fell away, and the boulder slammed onto the platform with a crash and splintering of wood. Men streamed from under it like bugs from a rotten log only to be struck down by a deadly rain of cobbles. Dragons honked and defenders cheered as barbarians fell injured.

When the rain picked up again, the Riders returned.

"Their weapons have improved," Jenks said. "We flew at two hundred feet, and they nearly reached us. And they volley fire."

"If they're willing to waste bolts, they needn't be accurate," Efrin said. "And if they get past the Notch, they'll roll us up like a tarp."

"Crossbows would be less of a threat if we could convince our dragons to wear armor," Jenks said.

Yana stifled a giggle at the memory. "And the nets?"

"Still deployed," Jenks said. "But we never fly that low."

Lothen nodded. "Send regular sorties to bombard them whenever they mass together. And at vulnerable points on the trail. No schedule so they cannot predict us."

"Yes sir," Efrin said.

After a glance west, Lothen frowned. "Snow will fall soon."

"Aye. The Hordes can't remain below the Notch when the snow closes their new trails. We need to cut their supply lines from Suleria and starve a final push."

"That means help from the Northmen," Lothen said and turned to Astria. "Does Richard still lead them?"

"Yes," Astria said. "He's merged the state militias under a common command."

"Tell him they must deny access to the river valley within two weeks, or we are lost."

"Aye, sir," she said and smiled to herself at the chance to visit Lance again.

Astria stopped at home for her gear and found Skye packing her lunch.

"When will you be back?"

"Day after tomorrow, Mama."

"Will you see your soldier?"

"I hope to."

"Britta came to me with an offer you might want to hear."

Astria slammed the meal into her saddlebag. "Let me guess: Fynn again."

Skye shook her head. "She said it's what you want most."

Astria stood straight with her eyes wide. "Do they know about Lance?"

"No. And if they did, they'd exile you immediately."

Astria put a hand on her hip. "So what's the offer?"

"To support you as a permanent Courier and invite you back to Invernell."

"But I'm already a Courier and a novice."

"The Council did not accept your offer to serve then as a Rider," Skye said. "And they can remove your position as a Courier at any time. Think about it. You'll be able to ride Zephyr and be back at home safe in Invernell with me and your friends."

"That's good news. What's the catch?"

"If you accept, you must renounce your offer and remain a Courier, but never be a Rider."

Astria paced the little cottage. "That means Britta thinks the Council will accept my choice of Rider over the Farmers' objections."

Skye shook her head. "I wouldn't count on the Council."

"Britta thinks safety is my goal," Astria said. "And will deny me my choice. Then no."

"Don't be stubborn, dear. If you hold out, you may get nothing. Whether we lose the valley or win it, the Council will have no further need of you, and they may end your position."

"And declare me Rogue again and kick me out?"

Skye nodded.

"Another threat. Gods, Mama, what did I do to deserve this?"

Tears glistened in Skye's eyes. "Nothing," she said and hugged her.

Astria set her jaw. "The Council taught me fear, not compliance."

Skye peered into her daughter's eyes. "What will you do?"

Chapter 14
In Derryh

Early that afternoon, Swallow landed in a grassy paddock forty miles west of the Blois River with an unobstructed view of the Derryh plains. This was Richard's new bivouac as the army advanced.

In the plains below, soldiers tore down tents, and wagon trains of men and supplies lined up to the east, evidence of the army's redeployment to the front. And from the field, the shouts and bustle of an army preparing for battle reached her.

But from the east came carts where men with bandaged legs sat on the tailgates. On each side of the carts marched lines of men on crutches or with bandaged arms or heads. At the end of the column passed carts with beds covered by sheets.

Her heart skipped a beat. *Where's Lance?*

Caught up in thoughts of him, Astria did not notice Katheryn until she took her arm.

"Oh Lady Katheryn. I didn't expect you to be here today."

"I'm just here for a visit, dear."

"What of the little one?"

"Diana is well. She seems to have a talent for shepherding, and I can't keep her indoors."

"Good for her," Astria said but glanced at the passing wagons.

Once inside Richard's tent, Katheryn poured tea for the two of them. Next to the tray lay a tiny, woven bracelet like the one Katheryn wore on her ankle.

"This will be for Diana," Katheryn said with a gentle smile.

Astria reached out her hand. "May I?"

Katheryn handed her the bracelet. "Women from Nordes weave these to keep their families close. There are clan patterns with family variations and different colors for family members."

"It's the same as the one you wear," Astria said. "But with a golden cord added to the purple. What does that mean?"

"Purple is a declaration of royalty. Gold is for the crown, which is my family's birthright."

"Your family are royals?"

"Only in a tiny country a long time ago," she said, leaning over with a conspiratorial smile. "Northerners tend to kill their kings. Now, what news for Richard, dear?"

"Not good. If the Hordes are resupplied from Suleria, we will lose the valley. Richard must deny access to the river valley at the foothills within a fortnight."

"Is it that desperate?" Katheryn asked, and Astria nodded. "Richard will return this afternoon."

Astria did not respond and gazed out the tent flap as a new column of wounded passed.

"You worry for him?" Katheryn asked.

"He's all I can think of and what might happen to him."

"You love a soldier," Katheryn said and matched Astria's gaze. "As do I."

"But war is new to us. Is that what we face at home? Losing those we love? That the best of us may die?"

Katheryn nodded. "We fight for our children, that they not bear the yoke of slavery. You're a soldier, too. What do you fight for?"

"My family and friends, and a future with Lance and Zephyr," Astria said and peered out to the passing column. *But what if he's . . . No! Don't even think that!* "And you worry for Richard."

"Every moment he's away."

Astria sighed. "I've not met Lance's folks yet."

"They live far north near Wikkert, and traveling here is difficult."

"They won't approve of me if they see me. Will I have to disguise my semaphores? Do they make me look too savage?"

"Lance doesn't seem to be bothered, and he's the one who counts."

Astria blushed. "I have other scars as well."

Katheryn laid her hand on Astria's and spoke softly. "As do I."

"Do you ever cover your scar to please people?"

"This one? She pointed to her cheek and Astria nodded. "No. Richard doesn't care." She scowled "When I growl, I frighten my enemies, and," she smiled and her entire face glowed, "and when I smile no one notices."

Astria nodded. *She's right.* But Katheryn's encouragement did not quell her fears.

"How will I fit in? I look nothing like Northern girls."

Katheryn grinned. "You'll always be different, dear."

When Astria frowned, Katheryn patted her hand.

"You ride a dragon," Katheryn said "And when you land with Zephyr, no one will notice your semaphores."

Astria returned Katheryn's smile but dropped it quickly. *I might not be able to bring Zephyr when I meet them.*

"Relax, dear."

After a sip of tea, Astria sighed and smiled. "Oh! I have something for you."

She set the cup down and removed a package from her Courier satchel. Within lay a small, burlwood box with pearlescent white inlay, the twin to her father's that sat on her mantel at home. When Katheryn held it up to the sun, it resembled Zephyr's eyes when they sparkled.

Katheryn hugged Astria. "It's exquisite. Thank you," she said, mesmerized by the shimmering box. "What's the inlay?"

"Dragon fang. They fall out every few years, so we have plenty. And the dragons don't seem to mind that we use them."

"What's the occasion?"

"It's to thank you," Astria said. "Without you, I would never have met him or known what to say or what to wear."

"You don't know how little I did. You have charm enough for—"

Astria held Katheryn's hand. "Just . . . thank you, milady."

Horses snorted, and Katheryn smiled. "That must be Richard."

Astria rose and followed Katheryn to Richard's office and mentally rehearsed how to deliver the Council's requests.

"Two weeks to close the passes," Richard said after Astria relayed the message.

"Aye, sir."

"It will be done. But tell your Council if we split their forces at the foothills, their fighters will be bottled up in the canyons. And if we block their return north, they will come your way." There was no reservation in his voice, no fear, and none of Lance's youthful optimism, only a veteran's counseled confidence.

"It's Yana's turn next, yes? If we don't see you before the battles, then good luck." He extended his hand, and she shook it.

"Thank you, sir."

"Godspeed, Astria, and send word as soon as your situation has . . . stabilized."

Stabilized? She bit her lip. *In victory or defeat. And if in defeat, the alliance will not matter.*

"Yes, sir."

And would there be a home for Lance and me here? she thought but could not ask.

As she waited for Zephyr, the remains of the Northern militias assembled on the plains below. Cavalry units galloped past men in long columns and supply wagons. Up the hill from those plains galloped Lance on his chestnut mare. At the sight of him, she smiled.

"How's my girl?" he asked and dismounted. Not caring if they were observed, she kissed him hard on the lips, then hugged him with her head on his chest and eyes closed.

"I'm not yours yet, Lieutenant. The Council has not granted their permission." *And they won't,* but she would not tell him that. "But I'll be eighteen soon and can then act for myself."

"You'd marry without their blessing?"

"If need be," she said with cold eyes.

"Never fear. I'll petition them myself. How could they refuse an epic alliance between the mountain clans and the Northmen? It would be historic. I'll make our case in person—"

Astria smiled with hope. "It'd take less than a day if Zephyr flies you there."

"When this deployment is finished." He dropped his voice. "I've missed you. When will you have more than a few hours to spend with me?"

"We'll have all the time in the world soon," she said, but could not tell him of Lothen's threat.

He faced her and took her arms. "Don't despair, sweetheart," he said and then lowered his voice. "We're off to the front today to relieve General Malveaux."

Astria pursed her lips and gazed into his eyes. *He'll be in danger.* But a trumpet sounded the call to assembly before she could say what was in her heart.

"Duty calls us both, darling. Fear not. We will defeat the Hordes, and I'll visit your mother. Together we'll convince her and the Council."

"And if we cannot?"

"I was waiting for the right time for this." He reached into his pocket to retrieve a tiny box and kneeled.

Astria pulled him back to his feet. "Let's wait a few weeks until the future of the Valley is decided," she said. "If we win, then—"

"*If?* You're not thinking the barbarians will succeed."

She raised an eyebrow. "And you've not considered it? If we win, I want the Council to declare me a Rider. That'll give me standing in the other valleys and more choice of where I can go, like my father."

"And you can't do that if we're together?"

She turned away.

"Why wait?" he asked. "We can spend the next weeks together regardless of what happens."

Astria's heart skipped a beat, and she gasped. *Isn't this what I truly want, to be together without the forces that pull us apart?*

She knew what his offer meant: if they eloped before the last battle, they would live their future together, without Council, or valley, or Northmen. But her world was not his, and they would live in his.

As if she asked directly, *would they desert*, Lance looked down with pain in his face for the choice they faced: being together meant dishonor. And it was her choice as well.

If he chose to be with her and desert his unit, he would live his life in shame. All she had to do was ask.

And if she did, they would leave their people behind and be together. They would spend every day as one and love each other completely.

And every day we're together, I'll know you dishonored yourself to please me, to be with me. And even if you don't blame me, you will know it was because of me. She blinked and a tear fell.

"I don't need proof you love me," she said. "Let's wait." *But must I give up my promise to the dragons as well?*

"Katheryn told me your people live far to the North, beyond where Zephyr can fly," she said softly

She hugged him and laid her cheek to his chest to hide her reaction to her next question. "Would we have a place with you?"

He hugged her tight. "Always, wherever we are, whatever I do, I will never separate you from your dragon."

He held her at arm's length and faced her squarely. "Darling, I don't have solutions to all our problems, but

I love you and will not live without you. We can figure this all out together."

She nodded and kissed him. "We wait."

He leaned over and whispered in her ear. "Fear not, my love. We'll find a way to keep your promises and find your father. And we'll live happily together the rest of our lives."

He smiled. "And when I get back, we'll have a picnic with strawberries and chocolate."

She smiled at his earnest face. "What's chocolate?"

"You'll love it."

He kissed her hard, and she melted into it. With his hands on her cheeks, he kissed the tears from her eyes. A minute later, he released her with another kiss and walked to his mount.

"And no more thoughts of losing this war," he said, swinging onto the saddle. "The future belongs to us, and no barbarian will ever keep us apart."

With lips still tingling from his kiss, she waved as Lance rode into the dust plume of the thousands who marched off to war.

The sun set over Astria's right shoulder as she flew home with Zephyr, warm and happy despite the long ride. Too full of energy to sit still in the saddle, she stopped to stretch.

In a clearing halfway home, she danced under the sky with Lance's face in every star, wishing he were there to hold her. With her eyes closed, she hummed a melody of the Northmen and swayed with her arms around him remembering the rainy afternoon in the barn.

She twirled and stumbled, and when she opened her eyes, Zephyr played above her, rolling and diving. And during the rest of the journey home, he flew with spurts of energy matching her joy.

"Thank you," Astria said to her wishing star, and then to Zephyr, for without him, she would never have met Lance.

***

The season's first storm clouds hid the moons as Swallow landed near the Manor House that night. The owls and loons cowered in the dark as Astria, exhausted and famished, pushed through Riders with grim faces and dirty clothes to find a place by the fire.

Inside, Efrin addressed the Council.

"They hold," Efrin said. "Archers keep the barbarians beyond the falls and the ballistae out of range."

Kendrick leaned over the table. "It'll be a war of attrition, and we can't win such a war."

"How can you say that?" Philina asked. "We've been able to keep them back for nearly two years and have lost only a few Riders, rest their dear souls."

"We've only slowed them," Lothen said. "Our casualties are light because we keep our distance. But whatever obstacles we and the mountains have thrown at them hasn't been enough. And the Qu seem in no mood to go back home."

Kendrick sat and scratched the stubble on his chin. "More defenders mean fewer Farmers, Philina. We've exhausted our grain reserves and burden the other valleys, while Suleria can supply the barbarians for many years."

"Astria, what of Richard and the passes?"

Lost in thoughts of Lance, Astria put her fingers to her lips where he had kissed her.

"Astria?"

"Sorry," she said and stepped forward. "Richard promised to close the river valley in a fortnight or less."

Lothen relaxed. "Good. Then it's on us to hold the Notch."

"Sir, storm clouds form above the glaciers," Astria said.

That was bad news. The Hordes might rush their assault if they feared snow threatened their supply lines.

"We may not have two weeks," Kendrick said.

Exhausted from the long ride, Astria collapsed into the nearest chair. But before she fell asleep, Kendrick's voice caught her ear.

"Prepare the clans to evacuate," he said. "And make sure Furnia is with them."

"It's that precarious?" Radlig asked.

Kendrick put a hand on his shoulder. "Quietly."

Chapter 15
Crimson Dawn

On a wooded ridge above the Blois River, Lieutenant Lance Early peered into the predawn gloom. Through the morning fog in the plain below, he observed Field Marshal Richard Stewart array the Army of the North for the coming battle.

"Steady, girl," he said as his mare snorted and pawed the dirt.

A half-mile south to his right, the river fell hundreds of feet from the Spine. Beside it, wagons piled high with food and supplies entered the mountains. Behind them followed the last of the Sulerian war machines designed to crush Invernell on their way south. Three had turned back, and men rushed to assemble them in time to defend the Quarajii deployment. To the north, the Blois River cut a path through the thick forest shielding Quarajii horsemen who had crossed the river in secret the night before.

And though the battle was near, thoughts of Astria fought for his attention.

A week is too long to be without her, he thought and held the ring on his necklace—the ring meant for their wedding. *But what will become of us? Could we live in the foothills of Cherbourne so Zephyr would still be near the berries? Will our neighbors even let a dragon near?* He smiled. *Will she teach me to ride?*

He inhaled deeply and slowed his breathing. *Clear your mind.*

His sergeant rode up to his right and pointed east where the rising sun lit the clouds blood red. "The gods show us what to expect today."

"Aye," Lance said and returned his attention to the battlefield. "It's like home in Lehrain there."

"We only need a picnic basket and a few maidens to make a day of it by the river there. But first, we'll need to sweep the rabble from the woods to have some peace."

"What is it, Sergeant?"

"Sir, our deployment worries Ensign Nowak, and he wishes a word," the sergeant said and waved the rider forward. The guidon rode up to his left with a frown and the squadron banner at a tilt. Lance nodded, and the sergeant backed his horse to his post at the right of the squadron.

"What troubles you, Ensign?" Lance asked, but the young man pursed his lips. "Be candid, Nowak. Whatever worries have possessed you will be resolved in a few hours."

"The barbarians outnumber us, sir," Nowak said. "They have as many men on each side of the river as we have on one and outnumber our cavalry. I worry for our safety."

"Is safety the reason you joined our corps?"

"No, sir."

"Good. For if we lose today, nowhere south of Wikkert will be safe."

The ensign stared at the field below. "We lost the last battle just north of here."

"General Xander lost," Lance said. "Richard will not lose."

"Why not?"

"Because he has us," Lance said and pointed to the pennants behind the center formation. "That's him there with the main force." *Nowak is a soldier, and that isn't what he needs to hear.* "I am only a lieutenant, Nowak, and they don't confide their battle strategies in me. What do you know of tactics?

"I just graduated from officer training, sir," Nowak said.

"Then I'll be blunt. Richard has arrayed the phalanxes from the forest below us to the river's edge. There's no gap to either side, and the enemy can neither fight from the river nor charge through the forest."

"Why are they slanted toward the river?"

"To prevent the Quarajii horsemen from charging straight at them. The slant will divert them toward the river, where they will bog down in the muddy bank. That removes the advantage from their skilled horsemen."

Who am I comforting with my assessments? Lance thought. *Him or me?*

"Then our victory is assured by our deployment."

"There will be plenty of opportunities for victory or defeat, regardless of how Richard arranges our forces."

"Still, we're vastly outnumbered," the ensign said. "Did Richard make a mistake in letting them cross at night unimpeded?"

Lance shook his head. "In their eagerness to meet us in battle, the Qu split their forces and met us on our side of the river. We have supply lines extending back to Cherbourne, while the Qu reinforcements can't cross the river in a reasonable time."

"And what of the dragons?"

"They're the ones who warned us. This is our land, Ensign. Do you expect the dragons to fight our battles for us as well?"

"No, sir." Nowak pointed to the thick formation below them at the forest's edge. "I can see our strongest units on the left flank."

"Correct. And if the flank falls, Richard must withdraw. He mustn't get trapped between the Qu and the river."

Battle cries came from the forest to their left, and the horses neighed and snorted with impatience.

"Keep them still, Sergeant," Lance said. "Soon, now."

Amid the shouts, a flight of arrows arced toward the middle of Richard's formation.

"The turtle," Nowak said as the phalanxes formed close ranks shield to shield above their heads without a gap for an arrow to slip through.

"Yes. And here comes the cavalry," he said as horsemen with blue armbands charged from the forest. In response, the middle square joined with its neighbors to form a wall with three rows of pikes and spears.

"The porcupine," Nowak said as the horsemen crashed against the wall, pushed by those behind them.

Lance narrowed his eyes. *There, horses throw their riders under the hooves to avoid the pikes, and men die from sword and spear.*

But the wall held, and the ponies retreated, leaving behind scores of bodies mired in blood-stained mud.

"It's a great honor to lead the first attack," Lance said. "But not the most important."

A second flight of arrows aimed for the right flank, and a charge of Quarajii cavalry followed, these wearing green britches. As Lance predicted, the wall deflected the frightened ponies into the river and trapped the Qu in the mud where the right flank slaughtered them.

And more men die.

"Those were feints?" Nowak asked in a hush, as if the lives of the thousands of dead strewn in the field below finally struck him.

Lance nodded. "They test if the left flank will break to support the middle. But Richard has trained us well, and they hold."

The sergeant rode up again. "Sir, we stand here idle while the battle rages."

"We're the reserve, Sergeant."

"Reserve for what?" Nowak asked.

"For the unexpected. Ready the men, Sergeant."

A third flight of arrows flew from the forest, followed at once by three groups of horsemen that charged Richard's line, one to the middle and two to the left flank.

"This is the battle now," Lance said. "They attack the left flank."

The flank faltered. Twice the wall broke and twice it healed. But to heal it, the soldiers shifted right and left a widening gap between them and the forest.

Nowak smiled. "They hold."

"We will see," Lance said and pointed to horsemen at the edge of the woods to their left. A horn sounded, and the horsemen charged for the widening gap. These were fresh horses with red ribbons braided in their mains. "That's where we win or lose the day. Sergeant! Signal Richard that horsemen will overwhelm our flank."

From behind Lance, signal flags waved and popped, but from the middle of the fight, Richard did not respond.

"Has Richard fallen?" Nowak asked.

"Wait. If they break the flank and circle back on the center, they will overwhelm Richard, and Derryh will fall." *As will Invernell and Asti.*

Who am I fighting for? Invernell or the North? Until this moment, they were the same, and his honor remained intact.

Infantry from the center moved to bolster the flank, but another squadron of horsemen galloped from the woods, these with bright-red banners.

The sergeant frowned. "The reinforcements won't arrive soon enough."

"Why isn't Richard signaling?" Nowak asked.

Lance wheeled his horse to face his squadron.

"If the flank fails, Richard falls!" Lance shouted. "We all have a purpose in this war, and this is ours. To me!" he ordered and spurred his mare down the hill to the field of battle.

The ride to the battlefield was short, with time slowed by the battle fever. As soon as Lance's squadron had assembled at the edge of the forest, they charged. Within seconds, they crashed into the Qu ponies to close the gap, and saber clashed on scimitar.

A Qu thrust a spear into his horse's shoulder, and she bucked him off. Lance fell hard on his left shoulder, and a pain shot through his chest like lightning. He had fallen from his horse before but knew at once that this was different. Without refuge on a battlefield, Lance struggled to his knees, holding his left arm to his chest.

"To me!" Lance ordered, and Nowak ran to him, waving the unit pennant.

His squadron surrounded him and plugged the gap. A second later, a pony and rider slammed into the formation, knocking Lance off his feet again and trampling Nowak. Lance rose to his knees and with one hand tried to help the ensign to his feet, but Nowak did not move. After a brief frown, Lance crushed the thoughts of Nowak's injuries and his own, grabbed the unit pennant, and raised it to rally his men.

A Quarajii warrior with a red-and-blue sash and a belt of ears jumped from the pony and fought his way to Lance. With a two-handed grip, the warrior cut down the pennant and with the backstroke sliced Lance's leg. But Lance parried the next lunge and countered with a slash to the barbarian's arm.

Lance was a better swordsman but wounded. After a furious exchange of thrusts and parries, the warrior stepped within the arc of Lance's saber and elbowed him in the ribs. His sight flashed white as pain raced through his body, and he staggered backward. He tripped over a fallen soldier, and before he could rise on his wounded leg, the warrior put a foot on Lance's sword arm.

Though a dirk on his belt was in reach of his left hand, Lance could not overcome the pain to draw it. The warrior drew the dirk, but a glint from the ring on Lance's necklace caught the warrior's eye, and he tore it from Lance's neck.

Reinforcements from Richard arrived to close the gap, and the barbarian fought them with Lance's dirk before he turned and retreated. As the Army of the North rushed past to engage the Quarajii, cheers of victory reached Lance.

He had been in combat before and knew he would die here without help, but he did not have the strength to rise. While he remained still, the pain drifted into a distant memory, and the battlefield smells of shit and vomit lost its dominion as his mind drifted to more pleasant thoughts.

He smiled. *Father will be proud. But my duty is done, and he doesn't matter. Only Asti matters now, and my death would hurt her too much. I'll stay for her.*

He lifted his right arm to signal for help, but no one came. In time his arm tired, and he passed out.

Just before nightfall, as the search for the wounded came to an end, a faint light broke through Lance's delirium.

"Oh dear God!" Nowak cried and pulled Lance from the mud and gore. "Here!" he called and waved his lantern to the stretcher bearers.

"Sir, can you hear me? Sir?" he asked, but Lance could not reply.

Chapter 16
Night Falls

Astria slouched in a chair near the hearth in the Riders' barracks, groggy after another long scouting mission. Two nights ago, she had discovered invaders crowding below the Tops, a few yards out of crossbow range. Just after, Zephyr squawked in distress and headed north before she reined him back, and he fidgeted nervously since. Now, as she waited for her turn to visit the Northmen, she struggled to understand her dragon's behavior and navigate the promises and passions that entangled her.

How can I be a Rider and be with a foreign soldier? Does being a Rider mean more than being with him, or does he mean more than riding with Zephyr? And how can I meet my promise to the dragons if I am with him in the North?

A plan jelled that knit the jumbled pieces of her desires together: to be with them both, she only needed to give up one thing.

She could not wait to tell Lance. But Zephyr was tired, and she would have to wait.

Yana entered, removed her goggles from her windburned face, and rubbed her arms. "Letter for you," she said, biting her lip. "It's from Lance."

Astria rose and splashed her face with cold water from a basin by the door. She took the letter, and for a moment, she forgot the war. Then she sighed and broke the seal.

> *My darling Asti,*
> *Good news! I may visit earlier than we planned. I cannot tell you all that has transpired at the front in the last weeks. However, your wishes regarding the new trails have been fulfilled. Your friends here invite you to visit soon for a celebration.*
> *Please don't worry, but I might be out of the fighting for good, and I will need that dragon ride after all.*
> *I've also written to my parents about you, and they hope to meet you soon. Zephyr is unlikely to fly so far north, so they have offered to meet us in Cherbourne.*
> *Your dreams will be answered soon.*
>
> *Yours forever,*
> *Captain Lance Early*

Astria leaned with her back against the wall and slowly slid until she sat with her knees at her chest, staring ahead at nothing.

Yana kneeled. "What does it say?"

Astria looked up at her friend, but her presence did not register. "He's been promoted."

"That's wonderful," Yana replied but kept her worried smile. "Isn't it?"

Astria stared at the letter in her hands. "Did you see him?"

"No. Why?"

"This isn't his handwriting," she said and held up the letter. "He's trying not to worry me. I think he lost his horse, and he'd never leave her injured. Maybe he was hurt, too."

"Sorry, I didn't see him. Lady Katheryn asked me to deliver the letter as soon as I could."

Astria took another deep breath. "Did she mention progress at the front?"

"Only that it would be clear in the letter."

"Well, let's go tell them."

"Tell them what?"

"The Northmen closed access to the river valley."

"What wonderful news!" Yana said with a big smile. "You're not pleased?"

The horror of the battlefield in Derryh came to her, and she shuddered to think Lance had endured such brutality. "I fear it was costly," she said.

She rose and dressed quickly, brushing her hair back into a ponytail before hurrying to the Council chamber with her friend.

In the Council Room of the Manor House, Britta frowned and squinted. "The Quarajii at our throats won't know for nearly a week by horseback about their loss in Derryh."

"Or in a day by pigeon, and—" Radlig added.

Kendrick shook his head. "When the Qu find out we cut their supply line, they will become cornered boar, unable to retreat."

"They won't need to retreat if they take the valley," Skye said.

Radlig slapped his hand on the table. "Then we stop them here."

"Call in the reserves from the other valleys," Kendrick said. "Riders and fighters both."

Skye ignored Britta's glare and stood. "I'll go."

"Thank you," Kendrick said and signaled a Rider. "Telek, the councils all know Skye. Let her take Dalmogare, if he's so inclined. Skye, tell our neighbors if we stop the Qu here, they may not trouble the other valleys. But if we lose, they're next. Tell them here is where we stand."

Telek left to call his dragon, and Skye went to Astria.

"I'll be back in a few days, dear. It will be a dangerous time now. Don't be reckless."

Astria dropped her gaze. "Yes, Mama."

"Something's troubling you."

"I'll be fine. I'm just worried about Lance. Go, now."

Skye bit her lip. "Hon, about Lance. I have—"

Astria could not bear another lecture on the impossibility of being with her love and deflected her mother with a hug and a kiss.

"Please, hon," Skye said. "Stop home before you—"

Astria smiled. "Go. Everything will be fine."

Skye nodded and waved as she backed away.

The moment after her mother left, Astria rushed to Efrin. "Sir, I need to fly north."

"No, Astria. We need you here."

She lowered her voice. "Please, sir. A friend may be injured, and I must see him. For me, please. Just this once."

He raised an eyebrow and took her arm. "I'm sorry, girl, we need your eyes in the air." He leaned over and whispered. "And I want you close by me."

Astria frowned and turned to leave.

"Wait," he called. "Report to the West Top. We're short a scout."

***

Over the next two days, Astria worried about Lance, off-duty and on. When unable to sleep, she flew extra patrol missions. And when her wishing star rose, she prayed to Olim and Fairma for Lance's health and safety.

In the early afternoon, Astria and Zephyr glided below darkening clouds to the northwest of the Notch. There, they inspected the small trails up the West Top to make sure barbarians had not found them. The clouds warned of a coming storm, and the dragons were reluctant to fly, so Swallow patrolled alone. But thoughts of Lance interrupted again.

Lance's cryptic letter frightened her and forced her decision: life was too short, and she must be with him. She had her plan, and they would make it work. She banked Zephyr and flew back to Invernell.

"Sir, I need to fly north to see Richard," she said to Efrin.

He shook his head. "Your turn is at week's end, and Zephyr is tired from scouting."

"I need to see him ... I need to . . . see if . . ."

"Your friend? I'm sorry, girl. Truly I am. But we cannot spare you." He took her arm, but she brushed off his hand and glanced at the door.

Efrin shook his head. "It's too dangerous now, and I need you here."

Astria narrowed her eyes. "Why?"

He paused as if to say something more, but then turned to go.

When Efrin left, Astria searched for Yana.

"Please, Yana. I need to see Lance. Can you take my shift?"

"Zephyr's tired."

"He'll understand. Please. I know Lance is hurt, and—"

"You can't be sure of that."

Astria frowned. "I need to see him. You can tell Efrin that Zephyr is sick and you're covering for me.

"He's smarter than that."

Astria set her jaw. "I'm going, Yana."

Yana hugged her friend. "Go, hon. I'll think of something. Go."

Astria threw her kit together and called Zephyr. When he landed, Yana met them in the clearing.

"I may not see you so often," Astria said and hugged her friend.

Yana's jaw dropped and her eyes widened. "What're you planning, hon?"

Astria looked into Yana's eyes. *I have to tell her.* "I won't be a Rider."

"Don't give up. I'm sure if you—"

Astria shook her head. "I can't. To be with Zephyr and Lance and keep my promises means I must give up being a Rider."

"We dreamed of that our whole lives. What about the purpose you spoke of?"

"It's what I always wanted. But I'll give it up."

"And the path of your father?"

"I choose another."

"And the dignity of being a Rider you strove so hard for?"

"I have value beyond my usefulness to the Council and by my choice."

"But—"

"I'll return, and when they exile me, I'll have Zephyr and Lance and my freedom. I can live no other life, but I can live it only if I break the chains of the Council."

Astria hugged her friend and mounted her dragon.

"I'll give up everything for them," she said and took off.

And with her choice and by her declaration, she was free.

Chapter 17
Day Comes No More

As gray clouds stole the sunset, Zephyr circled above Richard's camp. The vast grid of tents had disappeared, replaced by a checkerboard of dead grass and large tents that housed the wounded. Nearby, haggard veterans of the fighting sat around small fires. The shouts and cheers of an army preparing for battle had left behind a solemn hush.

When Astria dismounted near the command tent, Zephyr honked and took off. At the entrance to her quarters, Katheryn did not smile as she took Astria's arm. Astria said nothing, afraid to ask what she wanted to know, afraid to make her fears real.

"Come inside," Katheryn said, her eyes red and hair mussed. "The rain will come soon, and the day grows chilly."

Drowning under the torrent of her fears, Astria heard nothing as they entered Richard's tent.

"I came to see Lance," Astria said as she took off her leathers and flying coat. "How is he?"

"Not well," Katheryn said. "The doctors don't know what to do." She dropped her gaze. "He calls for you."

"Can I see him?"

Katheryn held out her hand. "Come," she said as raindrops beat upon the canvas canopy that led to the infirmary.

Alcohol and willow bark tickled Astria's nose as the doctor pulled the tapestry aside. Next to the bed, a nurse stood and offered her a chair. Astria sat and crossed her arms over her chest at the sight: Lance lay there with a towel over his eyes, sweating with fever and white as bone.

"I smell a dragon," Lance said and held out his hand. "Is that you, Asti?"

She took Lance's icy hand in hers and put her other on his burning forehead. "Yes, my love."

At the door, Katheryn put her hand over her mouth.

"I longed to see you," he said. "Only with you am I at peace. Only you make me weep with joy."

She put his icy hand to her cheek, and her tears came.

"There's so much I've waited to tell you," he said.

"We will have all the time in the world."

He gripped her hand tighter. "And that time begins now. Before I met you, I sought death and my father's affection. He would be proud now."

"Your father would be here to speed your recovery and bring you cheer."

"How is it that my search for death brought me to life? To you. I want to live my life completely now—" He coughed, and blood frothed at the corner of his mouth.

"And we will," she said and wiped his mouth.

"I understand now. There's no life without love, and I was not living until you." He squeezed her hand with the weak grip of a child. "Let's not wait to elope as we planned. Let's marry now. To Hel with your Council. We can make a life here. Richard will surely let me go now, and we can hire a wagon until I am well."

Astria bit her lip. "Yes, darling. Anywhere. As long as we're together."

"We can go wherever you want. I have no future without you. We can live in the foothills where Zephyr can still find the berries. You can paint and ride and sing."

Astria's tears reached the hand on her cheek.

"Is that a tear? Why do you cry when our future lies before us?"

"Because I love you so much," she said.

Lance's breathing became labored, and the nurse placed a new towel over his eyes and forehead. He kept his grip on Astria's hand, but his hold weakened.

Katheryn stepped toward her, but he gasped, and she stopped.

"I stayed for you," Lance said. "To see you again."

"You need your rest, Captain," the doctor said.

"You will be here when I wake, Astria?" Lance asked.

"Of course, my love."

"Then I'll wait for you."

With her hands on his cheeks, she kissed his forehead and pressed her cheek against his lips.

Astria stumbled to the anteroom and collapsed into a chair by the firepit. She hugged herself and trembled, indifferent to the hard rain that drummed on the tent and the cold draft from the smoke hole.

From a cart, Katheryn poured a small goblet of whiskey and handed it to her. After downing it, Astria rocked and stared at the tapestry separating the rooms from the infirmary as though it were glass, watching Lance slip away.

Katheryn sat by her side and took her hand. "I'm sorry. We were sure he'd get better, and he didn't want to worry you during the conflict."

"I might have spent the week with him."

"Lance secured our victory at the battle to deny access to the Blois River Valley. He earned the Star of the North for his valor."

"I care nothing for medals and honors. What can I do?"

Katheryn turned away and shook her head. "The gods and the doctors will decide."

The doctor entered the room and kneeled by Astria's side. "If he makes it through the night, he may have a chance."

If? May? . . . No! Don't even think that!

When the tears ebbed, Astria drank from a fresh cup of tea and downed another shot of whiskey.

"You'll stay tonight?" Katheryn asked.

Astria nodded. "Until I know he's out of danger. Zephyr will return when the rain stops."

"Our fight has ended here. Yours is just beginning."

"I can't leave with him ill."

"You'd desert your valley?"

"They care nothing for me. Would you leave if Richard lay there instead?"

"Like Richard, I am bound by duty."

Astria gazed at her folded hands. "My duty has gotten me nothing."

Katheryn squeezed Astria's hands. "Then I'll stay with you. Tell me more of Lance."

And for the rest of the evening, Astria told Katheryn of Lance as if her words kept him alive. In time, exhausted from the long flight, she slept in her chair.

Torch in hand, Astria trudged through a battlefield strewn with men and horses, dead and dying. Her neighbors and friends lay there with them, and she was responsible for it all. She turned over a broken body and held the flame near the scarred and bloody face of Captain Lance Early.

"No, no . . ." she murmured, and her eyes popped open. At a cough, she jerked upright and rushed to Lance's room.

"Lance!"

"There you are, my dear," he said, reaching out his hand again. She took it and put her other hand to his cheek and his unchecked fever.

He patted his blanket. "Where is it? Ah, there," he said and gave her a small envelope. "I meant it for our wedding. The twin was stolen from me. I'm sorry."

She opened the envelope to find an intricately cut white-and-yellow gold band. "Rest now, my love," she said, closing her hand around the ring.

His breath rattled. "I'm sorry I cannot stay."

Astria gasped and turned to the doctor and then Katheryn. "Can you marry us now?"

Katheryn waved to a nurse. "Fetch the chaplain. Hurry, now."

"Tell me of our life after I leave this bed."

Astria bit her lip. "After we are married, you will build us a fine home in the foothills of the Spine near Derryh. I will hunt with Zephyr, and you will farm. And we will picnic with strawberries and chocolate." She closed her eyes and rocked with his hand to her cheek.

"Our children will grow strong there. I will teach them the stars and the seasons, and you will teach them to farm."

His hand went slack, and she cringed but did not stop.

"When they are grown, we will train them to ride the dragons and horses, and in the afternoons, we will go together to the ridge to watch the sunsets."

Lance's chest stilled, and the nurse rushed to help him, but the doctor held her back and shook his head.

With his fingers, the doctor traced the shape of an arrow across his heart. Katheryn and the nurse copied him.

"And we will love each other forever," Astria said and laid her head on Lance's chest and wept. "Because the future belongs to us, and no barbarian can ever keep us apart."

As the chaplain entered, Katheryn sat by Astria's side, hugged her, and wept with her.

***

That night, Astria helped Katheryn dress Lance in his uniform and then wrapped him in cloth in the way of the North. Around her neck, she wore Lance's ring on a necklace Katheryn had given her.

When the rain stopped after sunrise, Astria went outside and stared at the clouds drifting east.

On a hillock nearby, men stacked logs for the funeral pyre and, under it, kindling. Alongside, Katheryn's maid and bodyguards placed Lance's possessions and valuable objects gifted by Katheryn and the soldiers. Next to it, Ensign Nowak and a sergeant planted a pennant with the unit citation they had earned at the battle. To avoid thinking, Astria offered to help.

"He saved my life," Nowak said, and traced the sign of an arrow across his chest. "You are Astria?"

She nodded and added wood to the pyre.

"He spoke of you. I'm sorry for your loss."

"And I, yours. What does the gesture mean when you cross your chest?"

"It's an arrow, the sign of the bear. Bears can always find water, and it's a prayer that the gods will help us, and him, find our path."

She nodded. "Is there fighting still?" she asked mechanically, barely aware she said it.

"No. The Sulerian engineers and Quarajii drift back east into Sinefora."

"And no more supplies are headed south up the pass?"

Nowak shook his head. "No. But many soldiers fled that way."

"The Qu gather at our doorstep, and we fear their desperation. Winter will be here soon."

"Derryh is safe now. At least until the Qu hunger for land again. But have we only made things worse for you?"

"We will see."

As the sun set, Ensign Nowak and an honor guard lifted Lance's body upon the pyre. Astria did not hear the chaplain bless him. She did not feel the chill in the air or the cold of the shroud as she laid her head on Lance's chest. And only to him, she sang softly.

> *"The rainfall comes and goes,*
> *And true love ebbs and flows.*
> *But you're the one I prayed*
> *Would never leave.*
>
> *"Our stars still share the night.*
> *But hide above the clouds,*
> *Someday those stars will shine,*
> *But not for thee.*
>
> *"In the rain you loved me.*
> *In the rain you leave me.*
> *Someday the sun will shine,*
> *But not for me."*

"May the Valkyr take you swiftly to heaven," she whispered, crossing her heart in the sign of an arrow. "And wait for me there with strawberries and chocolate, for I may join you soon."

When she stepped away, Katheryn put an arm around her.

After a short fanfare of bugle and drums, the soldiers lit the pyre. And in the plains below, scores more pyres burned for the dead that extended to the horizon.

And in a pillar of smoke he leaves me.

"What life is there for me without him?" she said, leaning into Katheryn as the flames roared to the treetops.

As if sensing her need, Zephyr returned and joined her. He lifted her hand with his nose, and she put her arm around him.

"You knew he was hurt, didn't you?" she said, buried her head in Zephyr's neck, and cried. And while her tears fell, he whined softly until the fire burned down to embers.

Late that night, Astria dressed in her riding coat, hugged Katheryn, and made her way to Zephyr. As she passed her lover's funeral pyre, she ran her fingers across her cheeks, dipped her tear-moistened fingers into the warm ash, and ran them across her temples, transforming her unfinished semaphores into the eyes of a raven: the bird of death and lost souls.

***

From a table by the fire in the Manor House, a Farmer went to the window. "The snows begin," he said and smiled.

His companions breathed sighs of relief. "Winter will make it impossible for the Qu to succeed in their assault," said one and returned to his cards.

But a night's snowfall was not a winter, and the snow was not a sign the attack would end, but a signal for it to begin.

Chapter 18
Hel

Dawn broke in Invernell with the clang of the fire bell and blood on fresh snow.

Jenks burst into the Manor House and an emergency session of the Council.

"We've lost the West Top!" he shouted. "The Qu have put crossbowmen there."

Kendrick jumped to his feet. "How?"

"Unknown, sir," Jenks said. "Patrols declined because of the snow. The Qu must have found a route alongside the falls."

Kendrick paced with his hands behind his back. "If they hold either of the Tops, the Qu can spot for the catapults."

"Can we just fly higher?"

"Higher means less accurate. If they mount ballistae there, the dragons will always be in range and make counterattack impossible," Lothen said with a deep crease between his eyes. "If they cross to the East Top, we'll lose the valley."

"Then let's rain Hel on them from the air before they dig in," Yana said.

Efrin shook his head. "It won't be enough. We need to control it, and that means fighters on the West Top."

"How about the lighter teams harass and distract them?" Fynn suggested.

"Agreed," Lothen said. "And archers will take the ridge trail."

"Sir, scouts saw a long train of infantry marching up the canyon." Jenks said.

"How far?"

"A day's march."

"That's the remnants from the battle of Derryh," Kendrick said. "They'll overwhelm us if they reach the Tops."

Lothen nodded. "Let's arrange a rockslide to stop the reinforcements."

The Flight Leaders agreed. As they headed to their squadrons, Efrin went to Yana who stood with Vinga.

"Any word from Astria?" Efrin asked.

"No, sir. I'm—" Yana began, but he waved his hand to quiet her.

"Wait for her here. You, too, Fynn. That's an order," he said, softening his voice. "Remember, you and Astria are Couriers. She may . . ." A furrow etched his forehead, and he put a hand on her shoulder. "Keep her out of the fight, and make sure you stay out, too."

"Yes, sir," Yana said.

Efrin glanced at Vinga, and when she nodded, he left to call Agnarr.

***

Near home, Zephyr dodged a ballistae bolt that whizzed past as they flew high above the Blois River Canyon. There, catapults had made their way around the river bend and appeared on the rebuilt platforms. Below the cascades, barbarians crowded, and on the West Top, men fought.

Astria landed near the Manor House and dismounted to stare at the crowd of anxious villagers milling about. At the edges of the square, some kneeled in prayer and others laid offerings on shrines to Olim and Fairma,

Why did I return? They don't care for me here and want me gone.

From the crowd, Yana ran to her and hugged her, but Astria did not return the hug.

"How's Lance?" Yana asked. She peered into Astria's red eyes made fierce by the ash on her temples and reached out to touch them.

"I saw fighting on the Tops," Astria said as she brushed Yana's hand away. "What's happening?"

"Quarajii found the trails on the canyon side and took the West Top."

Astria gasped and put her hand to her mouth. "That was my area to scout, and I wasn't there."

"You can't blame yourself for this, hon. Efrin is leading a counterattack now."

Astria took her friend's hand. "It's all my fault," she said as the Riders took off.

"What is?" Yana asked.

"The war. And Lance. And now this."

"Don't be silly, girl. You're not respon—"

"I'm the one who found the invaders. Turmordare died to help me escape—"

"Who's Turmordare?" Yana asked.

"I'm the one who alerted the Northmen. If I'd stayed near home and not—"

"Now you're crazy. None of this is your—"

Astria took both of Yana's hands in hers. "I could have stopped him. We would have been married. I only had to stay with Katheryn."

"Lance? He proposed?"

Astria faced the Notch as the first squadron dove toward the West Top. "He wanted to elope. He said he'd . . . I tried, but . . ." Her breath quickened, and she put a hand to the ring that hung from her neck.

"What about Lance and your plans? How is he?"

"He's . . . dead," she said, tipping her head as if struggling to understand a story from long ago.

"Oh Asti," Yana said and hugged her tight. "What happened?"

But Astria did not hear, focusing on the dragons as they dove to battle. She gasped.

After their first dive, the dragons did not pull up. Two teams fell from the sky, another faltered, and the remaining squadrons veered away. In only a few seconds, the counterattack failed, and the best of their Riders had fallen.

The nearby dragons took flight and honked, and above all their voices, Zephyr honked loudest of all.

Astria whispered, "Efrin." And without a thought for the pain, she bit her lip until she tasted blood.

From the first squadron, only one pair out of eight returned: Huld and Belastad. The dragon landed but stumbled and threw the Rider to the ground. Above them, dragons flew in erratic circles and honked in distress.

Astria fought her way through the crowd to find Belastad unable to stand and breathing hard. With the tip of a stick, Philina touched a purplish ooze surrounding a hole in the dragon's wing and smelled it. Then she wiped the tip in the grass and the grass withered as the purple seeped into the ground.

Astria helped Huld to stand, and they ran back to his dragon.

"What is it?" he asked.

"Bring fire," Philina said and turned to Huld. "I don't know, but whatever it touches is cursed."

Huld stroked Belastad's eye ridges. "Will he live?"

"I think so," Philina said. "Just don't let him fly."

Beside them, Astria staggered. "He's not in pain. He's dizzy."

A boy brought a firebrand and Philina touched it to the withered grass. The grass flashed white, and the purple ground turned black.

Kendrick pushed his way to the front of the crowd. "What did you learn?"

"They're raising ballistae and men by rope to the West Top," Huld said. "The archers on the East Top can't stop them."

"We're losing it all," Kendrick said.

Astria gripped Huld's arm. "Efrin and Agnarr. What of Efrin?"

"I'm sorry. He tried to warn us away but took a bolt to the chest, and Agnarr took two. Lothen fell next—"

Efrin. She covered her ears with her hands and staggered backward. At the edge of the crowd, she turned and ran.

In the village, she leaned against a house to catch a breath that never came and cooled the fire of her thoughts with a handful of fresh snow on her face.

Efrin. The man who trained her and loved her. The man who wanted to be her father, was gone with Lance.

And I should have been there to fight by their side.

A blazing star crashed into the workshop next to her and exploded, throwing her to the ground and raining burning splinters on her as the entire row burst into flames. From a burning house ran a family, with the father carrying a child. Richard's words came to her:

War is where children die, villages burn to ash, and countries are lost forever.

The catapults are finished.

That will be the end of our valley, with nowhere to rest, nowhere to hide. And what Efrin and Lance died for will disappear forever.

Amid the flames with arms outstretched, Astria raised her head to the sky.

"Damn you, Olim! Why have you forsaken us?" she shouted and pointed to the Tops. "Those are the dragon slayers. Those are the killers who bathe in our blood."

She dropped her arm. "We are the faithful who prayed for your help."

As missiles roared above her and crashed into the village, Astria ran through the flames and smoke to the picnic ground where she last saw her father. She fell to her knees and watched as the village burned. But instead of tears, the fires set her blood to boil.

"I will not forsake what was bequeathed to me," she said, forming her hands into fists. She stood with her back straight, narrowed her eyes, and marched back to the Council.

"Olim, we can wait no longer for your answer!"

Villagers waiting for guidance and comfort gathered in the Manor House as Astria elbowed her way in. She listened as the Council made plans to protect the evacuees, but not to defeat the invaders.

"No!" Astria shouted. But no one heard her, and she ran to the Riders who gathered around Huld and the injured Belastad.

Yana took her arm to lead her away. "We have to leave."

Astria shook off the hand. "No. We're the guardians of—"

"No longer," Huld said. "We're beaten, Astria. There's no choice but to—"

"We can't."

Fynn faced Astria with his back to the others. "It's not too late," he whispered. "We can evacuate with the villagers and still live free."

"That's not freedom," she said.

"Then we'll just *live*, and—"

She shook her head. "Take Furnia and run if you must. But how can you live knowing you ran from this?"

A deafening crash interrupted as a corner of the Manor House tore away and exploded in flames. Some in the crowd ran to douse the fires, while others panicked and ran toward the southern gate.

As smoke from centuries of craftwork swirled around her, Astria pushed Fynn away and turned to the Riders nearby.

"We can't quit!" she shouted. "This land was entrusted to us by our ancestors. Will we abandon it so easily?"

"It's suicide," Huld said by Belastad's side.

"Instead, you choose slavery?" Astria asked as she pushed through the crowd, climbed a wagon, and stood on the bed.

"Riders, hear me!" Astria shouted, her visage fierce with the raven-winged ash on her temples. "A young captain and thousands of Northmen went to battle to help us. They never met you, but still they answered our call for help. Those brave soldiers died to give us a chance." She raised her fist and called, "Astria will fly!"

"We aren't enough to stop an army," Huld said, and the crowd murmured agreement.

Astria kept her fist up and shouted over the grumbling, "We're enough to keep them off the Tops! If we don't try now, if we don't resist them here, then those who fell died for nothing—all the Northmen, our Riders, and the dragons died for nothing."

"Better not to die at all!" called one from the back.

As those in the Manor House joined the crowd, a squadron of volunteer Riders landed nearby, laughing and slapping one another on the back.

"We stopped the reinforcements!" the Flight Leader shouted as he ran up to them. "The landslide closed the canyon pass."

"We aren't done!" Astria shouted above the cheers. "Two years, two *years*, we've held them back with only a few of those here. Will we quit now when we have the chance to stop them forever? Astria will fly!"

Fynn turned to the crowd where Furnia nodded to him. He put his hand on his heart, turned his palm to her, and raised it in a fist. "Fynn will fly!"

"I didn't sign up to die here!" shouted a Rider from the back.

"You signed up to do your *duty*!" Astria shouted. "And this is it. *This* is why they feed you, *this* is why they let you fly free, *this* is why they love you. To do your duty and protect them *today . . . right now.*"

"We have no future at all if we leave!" Jenks shouted and raised his fist. "Jenks will fly." Beside him, Yana put her arm around his and raised her fist.

"The refugees need our protection," said a rider from Andeir.

Astria smiled. "They need no help to flee." With her unraised arm, she pointed toward the Tops. "The danger is in the other direction."

She laughed, and others laughed with her. "And if you flee with the clan, what duty will you have then? If the barbarians win here, your valleys are next. Will you leave them as well when the threat visits them?"

"Where's your courage, mates?" another asked and raised his fist.

Astria's voice calmed and deepened. "If you flee now, you leave your courage and your freedom here, and you will never get them back. Where you run for safety, you will find only shame. And the barbarians you hide from will piss on the graves of those brave friends who died to save you."

She stood taller and put a hand on her hip. "And who's saying we can't beat them? Who speaks for the Nembs who know our fate? Maybe Olim needs to see our bravery before he picks a side, and we only need to get his attention. Aye?"

"Aye! The Berserker speaks!" a Rider shouted, and more fists rose.

She smiled again and raised her voice. "And if we die today, let the barbarians say we died with courage and shudder in terror before facing our kind again. Astria will fly!"

Cheers rose from the crowd.

"She's not a Rider yet!" shouted one, and the Riders grumbled.

The Flight Leader from Winterthur laughed. "She was the first to find them and fight them while you slept safe in bed." He raised his fist. "Winterthur will fly!"

Vernier's Flight Leader with thick gray braids shouted from the back. "I'm itching to attack. But do you have a plan where some of us will live to tell the tale?"

Astria leaned forward. "Out of range above, the largest dragons will harass the barbarians on the Tops. While they're distracted, the nimblest dragons will fly up the side of the Tops out of sight and dead stall on top of them. The surprise will overwhelm them. Foot soldiers will take the valley trails up and meet us."

"And what of you?"

"I will lead those willing to fly up the sides to attack." The Flight Leader studied Astria and nodded slowly. "Vernier will follow you," she said and raised her fist. "Gunnhild will fly!" Behind her, all the Vernier Riders raised their fists, and the crowd cheered again.

Astria pointed to the Notch. "And if you are the last man standing on the Tops, you don't fight alone. You bring all of us with you: those who came before you, those who loved you, and those who fell by your side are all with you." She raised her fist again and shouted, "The clans will ride!"

As the crowd cheered, Astria jumped down from the wagon and tucked her necklace and ring under the collar of her leathers. The Riders followed her to form their squadrons, and Astria walked to Fynn who stood with Vinga.

"Where's our squadron?" Astria asked Fynn.

"Wait," Vinga said quietly. "Efrin told you three not to fight."

"Why?" Astria asked.

"Because you two are Couriers and—"

"Efrin's dead."

Yana rested her hand on Astria's shoulder. "Please, you're still grieving and shouldn't ride yet."

But the Berserker had possessed Astria. "I'm fine," she said and brushed off her best friend's hand.

"No, girl, you're not." Yana took her arm and stepped between her and Zephyr. "You're dangerous."

"You're damn right I'm dangerous, so get outta my way!" Astria pushed Yana away and marched to her dragon with Fynn close behind.

Anguish etched Vinga's face. "Yana, Jenks, stop her! She's going to kill herself."

"No," Jenks said as he tightened his leather armor.

Vinga grabbed his arm. "She could take you with her."

"We need her," Jenks said and followed Fynn with Yana close behind.

In the fore, Astria walked without thought of herself or of her dragon, without calculation of their odds of success. She was without caution, only commitment—a weapon with only one purpose: victory, with the highest count of dead barbarians.

As Riders ran to their dragons, fireballs arced over their heads, crashed into buildings, and plowed eight-foot furrows through their village. Everything they touched burst into flames. Centuries of artistry fell to ruin in the blink of an eye.

Astria found Zephyr pacing at the edge of the crowd, and she mounted. Jittery and with his muscles twitching, he jumped into the air, and she reined him to circle the Manor house.

As she waited for the Winterthur squadron to join her, two squadrons of unfamiliar Riders landed with Dalmogare in the fore, and Astria smiled. From his back, Skye dismounted, and Vinga rushed to her.

A moment later, her mother collapsed, but Astria could not stop to comfort her. And when her team joined, she raced to the Tops while her clan evacuated Invernell Valley to the south.

On their flight to the West Top, Astria's squadron dodged fireballs and boulders aimed at their valley. Behind them, projectiles raked the pristine white of fresh snow and made it bleed with flame.

While the Invernell infantry climbed the valley side of the West Top, the biggest dragons led the attack from high above, dropping rocks to damage the ballistae, allowing dragons to fly lower and harass the catapultiers. One bombing run caused a tar-covered fireball to fall from the bucket prematurely, which rolled across the firing platform, spilled the barrels of tar, and set the entire structure ablaze.

Another rock fell on a net designed to keep the dragons away. The falling net entangled a catapult that flung its missile on a low trajectory, brushing a squad of Qu spotters off the West Top as if they were flies.

Below the valley rim, out of sight from the Tops, Astria and her squadron circled. There, they waited for the signal that the infantry was poised to attack. When the fire arrow arced, Zephyr skimmed the treetops and zoomed up the Notch past the infantry. At the crown, he stopped, and Astria let fly with arrows while the barbarians faced the valley. One by one, her squadron appeared to each side, loosed a volley, and jumped off their dragons with drawn swords.

Shouting, "For home and clan!" the infantry ran up the trail and swarmed the Top.

In the first minutes, the defenders pushed the barbarians to the brink, and the infantry closed the small trails up from the canyons to stop any Qu reinforcements.

Astria smiled at her plan's success until a shout reached her from the East Top, and she turned. There, amid a score of bodies, a few survivors defended themselves from Qu who had scaled the cliffs unseen.

"To the east!" she yelled, but those on the West Top did not hear her over the clamor of battle. Turning at the sound of her voice, Fynn sat up in his saddle, but a crossbow bolt struck him in the shoulder, and he fell. Yana dismounted to help him, and Kendrick defended her.

With her team unable to help, Astria whistled for her dragon and mounted, and Swallow raced to the East Top alone.

When she landed, only ten defending archers remained to face twenty Quarajii. Zephyr made one pass to force them to discharge their crossbows and then dove to engage them. Before the Qu reloaded, Swallow was upon them with claws and spear, driving a half dozen off the edge. Zephyr landed for Astria to dismount, and she waved him away to keep him out of danger.

The terrain was familiar to her, the places where she could hide or shoot with some protection well known. But she could not leave her dragon exposed to take all the fire, and so she remained in the open.

As she nocked an arrow, she was at peace, and the songs of her ancestors came to her.

> *I am vengeance for the crimes committed against me . . .*

Her first arrow hit a thigh, and the barbarian fell over the edge.

> *I am retribution for the crimes against my people.*

Her second arrow lodged in a leather breastplate, and the man charged her.

> *I am the arm of Fairma, protector of our home.*

The next arrow exploited the weakness in his armor, driving into his chest, and he collapsed.

Ullir, guide my arrows . . .

She aimed next for a chest, but her target moved, and the arrow struck his throat. He dropped his sword and grabbed his neck, falling to his knees and gasping for air as blood spurted through his fingers.

Astria had not engaged men in combat before, having always flown high above her targets. But this was a man, not a rabbit—a man drowning in his own blood who stared at her with an outstretched hand, a man who might be a neighbor or a friend of Lance's.

Lance.

The image of her lover's chalk-white face on his deathbed stopped her cold.

Still holding his throat, the dying man fell forward, kicked by another behind him. Wearing leather armor and a bloody red bandage on his arm, the warrior bared his teeth. This was the man of her nightmares, the man who had won the brutal contest for leadership in the circle.

The warrior sneered and raised his crossbow, but she dodged, and the bolt grazed her leather jacket. She let fly but missed him and, instead, sliced his comrade's ear. Before she drew the next arrow, a screech like Turmordare's and a pain in her heart stunned her, the same as had begun this horror years earlier, and she spun.

Behind her, Zephyr stumbled with a hole in his wing while a barbarian stood with raised sword ready to butcher him.

"No!" she shouted, swung her bow to the new threat, and struck the swordsman in the chest with an arrow, driving him off the edge.

In that moment of inattention, the Qu crossbowman reloaded and fired. But the crossbow bolt with a purple tip that grazed her leg did not distract her aim as she shot an arrow into the warrior's side.

Zephyr squealed again, and Astria stiffened as his pain shot through every nerve in her body. When she screamed, dragons stopped in midair and rallied to her call.

Astria saw the barbarian watching the dragons, but she could not turn her head. Each heartbeat pushed the toxins deeper into her body, and the next shaft slipped from her fingers. She glanced down as the bow dropped from her hand, and she fell to her knees.

The barbarian limped to her and drew his sword, but a glint from her necklace caught his eye. He grinned and removed a cord from his leather jerkin that held another: an intricate white-and-yellow gold band—the mate to hers.

He raised his sword, but before he sliced off her head to free the ring, an arrow pierced his right shoulder. The blade dropped from his hand, and he roared. A second arrow pierced his thigh, and he fell to one knee and roared again. With his left hand, he drew a knife to cut the ring from her necklace. But the man with the bloody ear pulled him off.

"Bring her!" the warrior shouted, but his men dragged him cursing from the Tops.

Just before disappearing over the edge, he threw a shiny object that rolled to her and spun to a stop at her knees. As if in a dream, two serpents entwined at the tail unwound from the medallion and slithered to her.

A smile crossed her lips that she would follow her love on his way to heaven, and she relaxed as death took her. She fell on her face, hearing the crack as her nose broke on the stone but feeling nothing.

As Astria lay on her cheek on the cold rock, a goddess appeared. With sword drawn, she jumped from the back of a dragon—a woman who might have been her mother except for her feral grimace. Two crossbow bolts pierced the woman's leather armor but did not slow her. Instead, she growled.

A Valkyr joins the battle. Has Mama died and been reborn?

Astria closed her eyes and smiled, unaware her wounded dragon had picked her up. Expecting heaven, she opened her eyes again, but instead viewed the bloodshed from the sky and her village burning to the ground.

This isn't Kriegheim.
This is Hel.

Chapter 19
The World's End

That evening, with her leg bandaged and her face swollen a blotchy purple from the broken nose, Astria sat with Zephyr near the peach grove.

Her dragon lay unable to move, breathing in wheezing pants, his big eyes gazing at Astria as she sang by his side. When he groaned, she could not close her ears. His pain was hers, along with his confusion and delirium, and she would not miss a moment of it.

She placed her arm around his head and rested her purple cheek upon his while, overhead, dragons carried their dead brothers to the Source.

Wavering between rage and agony, Astria swayed and moaned, gripping the ring and the reins until her knuckles turned white, fearing if she let go, her loved ones would be gone forever. Her broken fingernails pierced her palms, and the blood fell to stain the pristine snow. In the middle of the night after Lon rose, they pried her fists open, and she stared at her bleeding hands as if they belonged to someone else.

When a light snow fell, the villagers built a lean-to to shield them, but Astria screamed if anything blocked their view of the sky. They covered Astria and Zephyr with blankets, but as the snow piled up in drifts against them, she cried out.

They made a fire for her, but in the sparks that flew from it, Astria saw dragons fall to their death and fireballs destroy her valley, and she whimpered.

And all the while, the ghostlike Valkyr hovered at Astria's side.

"I've done all I can for them," said the healer from Briey. "She will live; he may not."

"She just sits there and moans," the Valkyr said, and her wings fluttered.

"It's delirium. She took a small dose of whatever is killing the dragon."

"Is there nothing more we can do?"

"Yes. Be grateful. Other Riders died with their partners. She's lucky to be alive."

The Valkyr shook her head, and a tear fell. "She would disagree."

A goddess cries for me. Did I disappoint her so?

***

Days later, a village girl ran to the healer as he performed his rounds.

"Please, come quickly! Astria stopped singing," the girl said.

The healer followed her to the peach grove, where Astria lay unconscious by Zephyr's side.

"Hurry," the Valkyr said as they carried Astria to the field hospital near the Manor House.

***

Late that night, the crushing weight of Zephyr's agony was gone from Astria's chest, leaving only the dull ache in her thigh and her delirium. As she trudged with the dead through her dreams, whispers interrupted their moans.

"The child was lost," a soft voice said, and Astria opened her eyes as a gauzy figure walked away.

Was that Olim? Has he come for me?

"Kriegheim," she mumbled and jerked bolt upright, her eyes wild. Gazing down, she found her bandaged palm in the hands of the blind girl, Angelica, who shimmered within a silver glow.

"I broke my promise," Astria croaked.

"To whom?" Angelica asked.

"The dragons. Is he here? Zephyr."

"No, dear."

Astria took the girl's hand and rested it on her cheek. "I will wait," she said and gazed at her with a crooked smile. "He spoke to me."

"What did he say?"

"He said, 'Let go.' I need to ask him what he meant."

While Angelica wept for her, the dragons flew Zephyr to the Source, and Astria collapsed back on the pillow.

Chapter 20
Crucible

Weeks after the battle on the Tops, dirges and laments drifted to Astria through the field hospital's canvas walls. But the words came like a puzzle to be reassembled, followed by more words before she solved the last.

Next to her, the Valkyr spoke with the healer. Astria, thin and frail, rocked and rubbed her palm as the healer removed the bandage from her thigh. Through the mottled purple, the thin, red gash still seeped an iridescent indigo.

And their words meant she was not in heaven.

"This wound was made by a bladed tip," the Valkyr said.

The same as the spearheads I found in the Quarajii war camp. Had she been there, too?

The healer nodded. "Meant to cause massive bleeding. Meant for a dragon."

But it barely touched me.

He pressed the purple area and then the red wound, but Astria did not flinch.

"She has no feeling."

"But it cripples her still," the goddess said. "The hallucinations and dizziness haven't improved in weeks, and she can't walk without help. Her wound still seeps, and her head won't clear."

The healer rubbed his chin. "It's the curse. It's still in her system."

"There must be something you can do."

"I recommend exercise, fresh vegetables, sleep . . . and time. I'm sorry I don't have more to offer."

"That's all you can do?"

"We know little about their curses, but it must have found a place to hide in her body. If it's not replenished, her symptoms may diminish in time."

"How much time?"

"Hard to say. Those with similar conditions found clarity after wasting away until near death. We found another coherent after wandering in the Wild for years."

"And the others?" the Valkyr asked but received no answer.

***

Astria spent her 18th birthday in a cloud of hallucinations. Why the sun still rose every day, and the tears still fell, confused her when the world had ended, and the dead walked with her in twilight. She could not take part in the celebration and would not tell them why—for today she had planned to marry Lance, without permission from her mother or the Council.

With little feeling, she lived as if wrapped in gauze. And from her cot, she could not tell if she lay with scores of injured or viewed herself reflected many times in a double mirror. Milk was water, solid food was the chalks she once drew with, and the only time she smelled anything was the stench of the battlefield in her dreams.

Children cared for her. It was a simple task because she could not walk far before dizziness forced her to sit. And they cut her hair because she could no longer care for it.

After years in the Wild and the open air, she fought to be outside to sleep in sight of her wishing star. And though her dragon had gone to the Source, still he perched at the ridge of the mountains and called to her in the wind.

Instead of sleep, the nightmares of the battlefield in Derryh came. Zephyr and Lance were not here to rescue her now, and just as the scavengers leaped for her neck, a terrible beast came to carry her away—a dream dragon that smelled of rotting flesh.

Beyond her control, the phantasms entrapped her: Efrin with the fallen Riders and dragons; the barbarian she killed who had reached out for her; Zephyr; and Lance, always Lance.

In what once was a wheat field, her minders led her past a sea of small wooden memorials. She could not focus to read the names or make out the runes upon them, so she did not know whom to cry for. But from the graves, the dead moaned, and the fallen cried out to her.

"Our deaths are your fault!" they shouted. "*You* brought this upon us. Without you, the barbarians would never have found us. *You* taunted them with your dragons and forced them to attack or starve. Without you, we would have lived our lives in peace!"

She had no argument for the voices because it was all true.

She rarely spoke, the words still too hard to form and thoughts too muddled to order. And she listened only to the goddess who had judged her on the Tops:

the winged Valkyr with her mother's face who came to her.

Mama, Astria yearned to say, *show me you are real.*

But she could not ask, too sick to pierce the bubble of her delirium and too afraid her mother had died with all the others.

The goddess opened her wings to enfold her, and she spoke. But the words jumbled up in Astria's head as she struggled to make sense of it.

"The battles are fought elsewhere," the Valkyr said. "And I can wait for you no longer. I leave you with the best healers in the Spine, safe within the walls of your valley." The goddess folded her wings and turned.

When the words had reassembled in a way Astria could understand, she whispered, "Will you return for me?"

But the Valkyr had left with her fallen friends to a new battle.

Dragons visited no more, and she had no one to sing with. The world was cold and white, with forms sliding from one shape to another. Ghosts of her friends hovered briefly and came no more.

And Astria reverted to an animal with only the basest of needs.

***

On a dull midwinter morning, Astria growled as she swept her empty bowl of porridge off the table, then stumbled and fell. When her minders set her back at the table, she grabbed the bowl from her neighbor and ate without asking.

This was not chalky porridge or watery milk, but thick chicken broth and celery and carrots.

Astria looked up at the others at her table who stared at her. "What?" she asked and stood. But woozy, she flushed and sat back down as the blood roared in her ears.

Nausea gripped her, and she threw up to the side of the table. She closed her eyes as the fever rose. As her body warred with itself, she laid her head on her arms, moaning, and lost consciousness.

Astria woke two hours later wrapped in a blanket with a cold cloth on her forehead and Philina at her side. Sitting up, her reflection appeared in a bowl of water, and she recognized a shadow of herself with ragged hair and feral eyes. For the first time in months, Astria glanced at her hands, remembered who she was, and gasped. She pulled back in shock.

Lance would despair to see me like this. And Zephyr . . .

Zephyr. Where is he?

Astria turned to Philina who sat by her side and gripped her wrist. "How long have I been in this stupor?"

"Oh my," Philina said. "You can talk!"

"How long?"

"Four months, dear," Philina said. "We didn't think—"

Months! "Did the healer say to improve my diet?"

"Yes, these are the freshest—"

"What was different in what I just ate?"

Philina raised her eyebrows and scolded. "It made you sick, dear."

"But it cleared my head. Please, make a list of all the fruits, vegetables, grains, and fish we have access to here in Invernell. Start with my last meal."

"Why, dear?"

"I want you to repeat the method I used to find the fertilizer for daemonberries. Hurry, before my head clouds again!"

Philina waved to the minders and instructed them to search the stores and make a list. "Then what?"

Astria closed her eyes to concentrate. "Once you've made the list, make a meal like I just had. For the next meal, replace one of the ingredients with another on the list and make a meal of that as concentrated as you can. After each meal, keep track of my symptoms." She opened her eyes, and the world spun, forcing her to close them again. "When we've gone through the list, make meals of combinations and track my symptoms with each combination. And include plants from the Wild. Each time, choose the ingredients that improve my symptoms the most."

"That'll take a long time, dear."

"Time is all I have left." She took Philina's hand. "Did I mention him? Lance?"

"Yes, dear. You cried out for him many times."

The world spun again, and she took Philina's hand. "Where's Zephyr?"

Astria did not hear the answer, but watched Philina's lips move as the delirium seized her again.

***

Over the next weeks, none of the single ingredients eased Astria's symptoms, and some combinations made her sicker. But a few eased her symptoms. And from those, Philina excluded the harmful and included the most beneficial: raw fish, wild fruits and vegetables, edible flowers, and herbs.

When Astria could walk again without help, she took her staff and hiked through the deep snow. Driven by the same impulse as her need to fly, she hiked with no future beyond her next step. For a time, she searched for the dragons, but they had left with the Valkyr.

In her wanderings, she found herself at the palisade at the valley entrance. As she approached, her minders rang a small bell. A guard descended the tower and stopped her at the gate.

"You're getting stronger, girl," he said with a smile. "Out for a stroll?"

She nodded and took a step through the open gate.

"Aye," the guard said and took her arm. "Far enough. Where are you aiming?"

She pointed through the gate to the Wild.

"Sorry. Not for you."

"I once lived there."

He shook his head. "No longer. Where in the valley can I take you?"

"To the Tops, then."

After an hour, they stopped at the lowest ledge where she had often come with Zephyr. The guard excused himself, and her minders built a fire to warm her. But she sat apart as she had with Zephyr in the Wild.

As the Spine to the west devoured the remains of the sun, she kneeled in the snow and held the gold ring around her neck, memorizing its shape with her fingers: the engraved inside, the smooth edges, and the knurled surface cut to sparkle in the light.

The barbarian who had aimed to kill her, lusted for the ring to sate his vengeance for his defeat in Derryh. And in the moment he took to gloat, the Valkyr had stopped him.

Lance's ring and the goddess had saved her life. But that realization did not ease her pain, and the tears fell again.

Another sword thrust into her heart. And she gripped her chest and moaned.

Lance's death was my fault.

It wasn't the beautiful valley he cared for and gave his life for. It wasn't my friends or my family or the freedom of my people.

It was me.

He died because of me.

There was no recourse for this pain, nothing to erase her part in his death, and she rocked back and forth and groaned.

Is he there now with Zephyr? Will I see them again? Maybe soon. She rose on shaky legs to find them but sat again. *These legs won't carry me now. But when they can . . .*

***

In late afternoon, Angelica and the Seer came to sit by her side at the valley rim.

The blind girl sniffed the air. "A storm will come soon."

Astria sat quiet and gazed west as the sun cast the clouds in shades of orange.

"You don't sing anymore," Angelica said.

"Zephyr is gone."

"You once sang to them all."

"And they've all gone."

"You once sang for the love of it," Angelica said.

"What is there to sing for? I live my life with one foot in the grave, a prisoner now, unable to live or die, given no choice by gods or men. They keep me as a pet and steal from the living to feed me. I claw through the mud to think and can barely feel the ground under my feet. I am the undead, and my life is Hel."

The Seer shook her head. "No, no, dear. This isn't Hel."

"But the Valkyr didn't take me. I didn't die in battle and cannot go to heaven."

"You misunderstand the gods," Angelica said. "The wound that may kill you was received in battle. If you waste away and die from the curse, the Valkyr will come again. But Fairma will welcome you to heaven if Olim does not."

"If I will reach either heaven, why don't I die now?"

"Now is not your time."

"Am I to live my entire life a cripple?"

"That is not for us to say. But Olim needs you here, or you would be dead already. Be at peace with that."

Astria gazed west to the glaciers. "They would take him there, you know, alive or dead."

"Where, dear?"

"The Source," Astria said. "If he lives, he's sick like me and likely worse."

"How could the dragons help him?" Angelica asked. "They know nothing of medicines or curses. Even the simple foods that help you are foreign to them."

Astria could hold back no longer. "Angel, did I betray them? Did my madness lead our dragons to their death?"

Angelica turned to her. "Zephyr?"

With a nod, Astria's tears flowed again.

"And your lover?"

Astria gasped, unable to take a full breath.

Angelica straightened her back. "Really? You believe *your* dragon and *your* soldier would have fled with you to safety? That they would follow your commands like servants or pets?"

"No, I—"

"Zephyr would be insulted, and so would your soldier."

"I'm sorry. I meant it as my . . . my friends."

"Your friends have free will. Would you grant the dragons less? And would you belittle their bravery and that of Efrin and Agnarr as if they did your bidding like puppets?"

Astria flushed in silence and shame.

Angelica's tone softened. "You misunderstand, dear. This is the dragons' war, and *they* invited *you*."

When the sun set, the Seer led Angelica away. As they left, Astria rubbed the dead flesh on her thigh and stared at the dark clouds that swallowed the glaciers.

The war is over for them and for Invernell. But my war is yet to be won.

Chapter 21
Nemesis

In early spring, after the last snows, parchments fluttered on the Council table as Radlig opened the Manor House door and reached for his dagger.

There, Urquil and Vinga sat with Britta. Across the table stood a Quarajii warrior in furs and full leather armor surrounded by three guards.

A tight ponytail bound his hair, and an earring held together two parts of his torn ear. The silver inlay on his boot heels gleamed, and other than a day's beard, his appearance was neat. On his red belt hung a dagger, the hilt tied to the sheath with a gold cord to declare it could not be used. And though straps secured his wrists and ankles, he leaned forward as if ready to pounce.

"And who is this now?" Radlig asked.

A guard spoke. "This lot came to the traders' pass. Says he has a means to save the valley."

Radlig sat on the edge of the table. "It's already saved. Who is he?"

The barbarian shrugged off the guards' hands. "I am Nogrexx of the Crimson Horde. Chief Senekx Kurak has declared a blood feud to cleanse his honor. You have the circle of serpents and know this."

From the desk, Radlig picked up the medallion Senekx threw to Astria on the Tops. "This?"

Nogrexx nodded.

"We're unfamiliar with your customs. How does this affect us?"

"The Maid from the Tops must surrender to him alive, or you must defend her in the circle. If you decline, anyone who aids her risks slavery."

Radlig frowned and looked to the others. "What maid is this?"

"The girl with the ring who rides a dragon."

"Astria? What's her offense other than victory?"

"She did not cower in the presence of my chief but defended herself. That she didn't beg for mercy is an insult. You must surrender her alive or defend her. Chief Senekx offers a gift to help you decide."

Urquil stood and leaned over the table. "We won't bargain for our own!"

Nogrexx sneered. "See first, then decide. The gift waits at the guarded gate."

Vinga whispered to Britta and Radlig, "You can't trust him."

"Let's see what he offers," Britta said.

Radlig approached the barbarian. "It'll be awhile."

Nogrexx grinned. "I will wait."

"Philina, please bring our guest something to eat," Radlig said.

She brought a cold lunch from the larder and set it on the table, but the barbarian's hands were bound, and his guard made no move to untie him.

Without a word, Nogrexx slipped his bindings, looped them around the guard's neck, bent him backward, and dropped him to his knees. When the other guards drew their swords, he smirked, released the guard, and raised his hands.

A guard reached for Nogrexx's dagger.

Nogrexx glared at him. "If you touch that, I am honor-bound to kill you," he said, and the guard backed away.

The warrior sat. Though he ate with his fingers, he used the napkin to wipe them.

A few minutes later, a guard returned with a trader from a neighboring village, his face bruised, and his jacket torn.

"Speak, slave," Nogrexx said.

"I am Osman from Andeir. They're holding my family but say they will return them if you do what they want."

Radlig turned to Nogrexx. "That's extortion,"

Nogrexx waved a hand. "They're already slaves and belong to us. We offer the entire family as a gift to speed your decision."

"Extortion still."

He scowled. "A matter of honor and our law."

"The valleys don't abide by your law."

"The sword enforces the law. Are your words stronger than our swords?" He glanced at the guards and scoffed. "I think not. Your Riders are away defending Vernier, and your defenses are flimsy."

Radlig waved a hand to dismiss the threat. "You're too weak to attack, or you wouldn't be talking."

"We need not attack. You cannot protect your supply lines."

"The traders? And if we don't honor your grudge?"

"Then we will sell one of your people into slavery every week until the girl is ours."

Vinga shook a finger at him. "How dare you threaten us! We will not trade our own. And especially not her."

Nogrexx gave her a side-eye and turned to Radlig. "She speaks for you?"

"We speak as a group," Radlig said.

"Hmm. Then you might listen to the trader."

"Please, sir," Osman begged. "They hold my four children."

"And more Osmans will beg you in the coming weeks," Nogrexx said.

"I will offer myself for her," Urquil said.

"His vendetta isn't against you, old man, but the Maid."

"What if she escapes?" Philina asked.

The barbarian shook his head. "You cannot evade vendetta. Surrender her alive or defend her. There is no third way."

Nogrexx scoffed at the guards. "Do you plan to challenge with men such as these? If your champion loses, you forfeit her anyway."

A guard raised his sword. "Why, you—"

"At ease, Sethel," Radlig said and turned back to Nogrexx. "Tell your chief we'll get back to him."

"Three days. Remember, the token does not age. And our friends the Sulerians have spies far and wide." He walked to the door. When Sethel grabbed his arm, Nogrexx pushed him away and left.

"Rest now, Osman," Radlig said. "We won't abandon your family. Philina, please treat his wounds."

Taking the hint, Philina led Osman to the field hospital.

When Osman was out of earshot, Vinga shook her head. "We cannot even consider this."

"Astria brought this on us," Britta said. "What obligation do we have to her?"

"You dolt!" Vinga said. "She saved us all from what Osman now faces."

Britta scowled. "Not for long."

Radlig raised his hand. "Stop. We must speak with one voice. Let's find it."

"Typically, one or more dead bodies will satisfy a vendetta," Urquil croaked. "If they want her alive, it's a ruse. She knows the secret ways into the valley."

Radlig folded his arms. "They could kidnap any of our citizens to divulge those trails."

Urquil shook his head. "He'd need an honorable justification for kidnap and torture."

"They might have come to us sooner with this ultimatum," Radlig said.

Urquil nodded. "I suspect it took this long to learn to survive the Wild and then come up with an excuse consistent with their honor code."

"Perhaps they're more civilized than we believed," Britta said.

"No, they're not," Vinga said, "They aim to enslave a girl and force us to help them. We can't allow this."

Radlig paced. "I fear our resolve will fail once they fulfill their promise to enslave the hostages. How many will it take before we relent? Just Osman's family? Five more families? *Your* family?"

"We can warn the valleys not to trade with us," Britta said.

"It will be another week before a Courier arrives by air."

"They hope to settle this before we can get the word out," Urquil said.

"If we wait, Osman will lose his family."

Britta narrowed her eyes and sneered, "But we'll survive."

"And our home would become a prison where we stew in our guilt."

"How can we trust any deal we make with them?" Vinga asked.

"We can't," Radlig said. "But they're outside the gate and unlikely to break in without an army."

"But how do we free the hostages?" Britta asked. "And how do we prevent more?"

Vinga frowned. "And what of Astria?"

***

Against a tree in the peach grove, Astria rested to let another spell of dizziness pass. Through the bare trees, the village and Manor House appeared as they once did, with snow hiding the fire damage and filling the furrows of the catapult missiles. The snow would soon be gone and the damage painfully clear. But soon after, the trees would hide it again under thick leaves and pink blossoms.

Leaning heavily on his cane, Urquil limped to her. "Ah, there you are," he said and turned to Astria's minders. "Give us a moment, please."

When the children left to play, he sat beside her.

"I'm sorry to bring you this news, but I owe you honesty for your sacrifice. The love that drove your heroism has—"

She glared at him with eyes hard as granite. "The dead are the heroes, Elder, and love did not drive me."

"I come as a friend, Astria, not as an Elder. And by doing so, I defy the Council."

She softened her voice. "You've never lied to me or been unfair. What is it?"

"The warrior you shamed at the Tops is a chief. He has claimed your life and will not rest until he enslaves you, along with anyone who protects you."

"Enslaves me?" A memory came of the battle of the Tops and Zephyr's cry, and she shuddered. "A blood feud. Why?" she asked and held her hands to stop them from shaking.

"Those were his men and his battle. He lost because of you, and so the barbarians lost the war. If he doesn't pursue you, it will show weakness, and his men will kill him."

"Why me? I was not alone."

"You were first, and you are female." Urquil scratched his beard. "He said you didn't cower or plead for mercy. While you live free, he suffers humiliation."

"How can he fulfill that threat? We defeated them."

"They hold hostages." He softened his tone. "You aren't safe here. Nor is anyone you care for."

"Can't the Riders defend us?"

"They are fighting elsewhere, and by the time they arrive, it will be too late for the hostages."

"How can I end this . . . this vendetta?"

"By their law, you must surrender or defeat him in the circle."

"When I was at my physical best and possessed by the Berserker rage, still I couldn't save myself or my dragon. How could I defeat him now?"

"You might choose a champion in your stead."

"Then I condemn them to their death. No, enough people have died for me." She looked directly at him. "But you know this."

Urquil looked away.

"Can I invite one of the Qu to be my champion?"

"I asked. It's within the rules, but they won't challenge their commander."

"And if I comply and surrender?"

"Then you'll also give them the valley. He would have you lead him by the secret paths and overwhelm us."

And if I take my own life, the Valkyr will abandon me and keep me from my loved ones in heaven. His victory would be complete, but others would live free.

"Will my dead body satisfy him?" she asked, her voice tinged with bitterness.

He shook his head.

And if I defy the Council again, they'll exile me.

The warm familiarity left the valley, and the cold seeped through her jacket. The snow that hid the damage also buried her hope, and she turned away, unable to comprehend what was happening.

"How thinks the Council?" She crossed her fingers, hoping to learn of her mother but afraid to ask.

"The Elders are honorable and will not abandon you or send you away," he said. "Their loyalty to you endangers everyone here. Do you understand?"

"Yes. But you aren't telling me everything."

"I told you what the barbarians offer."

"But not what you imply. Who will give me up?"

Urquil stared at the dirt.

"You are only here because the Council cannot decide," she said. "Who wants me to surrender?"

"Britta and the Farmers."

With blank eyes, she faced him and shuddered at a chill gust that blew from the Wild. "Still."

He sighed. "I know you can make your own decisions. I will help you in any way I can and will support any decision you make. But those who care for you are in danger if you stay."

"What can I do?"

"Direct them elsewhere."

"To where?"

"Anywhere but here. The barbarians will follow you."

She gasped, unaware she had been holding her breath. "Exile?"

Urquil turned away.

Delirium swept her up, and the world spun. *Is this just another nightmare that will vanish with the morning fog?*

"He thinks he has tied us in a knot impossible to untangle. Your escape will stymie him."

She shook her head to clear it. "But if I escape, the Quarajii remain and will lay siege."

"We are many against a few. We will survive here. You won us our freedom, and it's our responsibility to keep it."

"The family will remain slaves—"

"You're not responsible for the wickedness of others," Urquil said.

"No. Only my response to it. The lands of the dragons aren't safe while the slayers linger."

"You call the Spine the dragons' land, not ours?"

Astria nodded as her delirium brought the dead to life to walk the grove. Overwhelmed by bitterness and loss, a tear fell.

"Is this what victory looks like, Elder? Please explain this to me. I am young and still new to this life. They killed my betrothed and my friends. They left my dragon and me to die. And now . . . now because they threaten again, I must leave?"

The old man's hand shook, and his eyes glistened. "I and many others would take your place, but he wants you alive, not us dead."

"If I leave, where can I go to get my life back?"

"You might ask instead where to build a new one."

"I understand," she said with a weary smile. She patted his hand to absolve him, and he hobbled away.

She was lost now, unable to stay but too weak to leave. If the hostages died because of her decision to stay, she would be responsible. The Council was split, and if she told them she planned to escape, some would stop her to give her up, and others would stop her to protect her. And the threat to them and the dragons would never pass.

Any decision she or the Council could make benefited the beast who had stolen her future, and her loved ones would never have justice. No good choice was left, and her mind was too cloudy to puzzle it out.

She tightened her fists until the scars on her palms ached while struggling to clear the dead from her sight.

At sunset, the old Seer came to her with Angelica in tow and sat by her side.

"You heard?" Astria asked.

Angelica nodded. "You worry about your path now?"

"Yes."

"I hear life calling you. Like dragons once did."

"I hear death," Astria replied.

"You believe exile means death?"

"Yes."

"You've survived before."

"Only because I could visit and trade. And I had a dragon to frighten the graxes and mountain lions away, and friends, and . . ." She gritted her teeth. "And still, I nearly starved to death."

"You think to stay? Look around. This is not the place that nurtured you."

"But it's safe."

"Not for long," Angelica said. "Not for you."

"I promised to help the dragons."

"You can't help them here."

"Then tell me. How am I to escape without escaping and putting the valley at risk? How can I surrender without surrendering the valley?"

Angelica was silent.

Astria dropped her gaze. "If you have no answers for me, why did you come?"

The Seer spoke. "I had a vision. The Quarajii have cursed you. It has corrupted you and will not leave. You need a new body."

"How's that possible?"

"You must strip off the body you have, sear it, and shed the corruption with the husk. Only then can you be free."

"How am I to do that?"

"That was not in my dream. But the journey will be difficult." Into Astria's scarred palm, the crone slipped a note and closed her hand over it. "There are others in the South. Find the Singers. The dragons remember the way."

Astria opened the note and found a crude map of the mountains. To the west and below them, appeared a symbol with a line through concentric circles like the pin Merythe wore.

The College that Merythe searched for? In the Provinces! Astria's despair was complete.

"Why?"

"You'll need to eat, and they will teach you a trade. And they may know what you seek to learn."

She glared at the Seer. "How to defeat the dragon slayers?"

"Perhaps. But vengeance is a small thing. Do not forget what you seek."

The Seer rose and took Angelica's hand. But Astria gripped her sleeve. "Was I fated not to ride? I cursed Olim. Is this punishment for defying the gods?"

The Seer studied her. "Are we Nembs to know your fate? Only the gods know but do not tell us so we will strive for the loftiest heights."

"The Valkyr tests my fortitude again," Astria said. *And I may yet be redeemed.*

When the Seer left with Angelica, the sun disappeared over the horizon and Brother Moon rose. With a dark sky and Invernell in shadow, the glaciers to the west gleamed red in Fures's light.

I'm ill and need the Valley to live, but they may trade me for their safety.

Where on Juro am I safe? With Richard and Katheryn? They'd find me there and threaten them and little Diana. Where else?

She gazed west where the Spine blocked the stars, and the words came.

The dragons.

"I'll only be safe where men cannot go."

I can't live or die, captive of gods and men, with only the choice of captors. Do I surrender my honor and freedom because of my dependence on them?

No!

Then I'll defy them all!

She turned to her minders, her jaw set, and eyes narrowed. "Bring Britta here to me.

***

Fog swirled around the hem of Britta's cape as she entered the circle of firelight.

"You want to end this siege?" Astria asked.

The Farmer nodded.

"I understand the Council balks at handing me over."

"How do you . . ." Britta frowned. "I'm sorry. No one wants to, but we've not imagined another way to save the captive family or remove the threat. It's unfortunate that—"

Astria scowled at the evasion. "Where are they camped?"

"Near the entrance gate, just beyond a ridge."

"Bring the Qu here to me at the peach grove tomorrow morning when the sun shines on the Tops. Tell no one else."

"I hope for a different outcome but have—"

The world spun again, and Astria raised her hand. "Leave, please. The curse overwhelms me. Just bring him tomorrow. And tell no one."

That night while her minders slept, Astria took her quiver and slipped through the fog to a cabinet maker's shop and the inviting smells of sawdust and glue. After drilling holes crosswise through a walnut, she drove the arrow through it to make a child's toy that whistled in flight. When completed, she made a second and returned to the field hospital.

***

The next morning, Astria's minders helped her dress in leather armor, armed her with sword and bow, and added charcoal to complete her semaphores. Over them, she wore a white cape and cowl. With her staff and their support, she found the grove before sunlight struck the Tops.

Her minders brought a stool and set it against a tree. From a peg in the tree, they hung her fur coat to drape over the stool, converting it into a throne. On it, Astria sat and waited.

With two guards at his side and an archer trailing behind, Britta brought Nogrexx unbound, his dagger still tied with the gold cord.

At the sight of him, Astria gasped, and her body ached to run.

He was there.

A vision came of the monster standing beside him, smirking and dangling Lance's ring in front of her, his sword dripping with Lance's blood. Behind them, a funeral pyre burned, into which her friends marched single file, their wounds still seeping.

Blood pounded in her ears, and she turned away, but an echo came of Zephyr's cries and his days of agony.

Lance's words echoed in her ears: *No barbarian can ever keep us apart.*

Yet here they are.

She glanced up as Nogrexx eyed her necklace, and she covered the ring with her hand.

How can I even sit here with one who killed all that I loved?

Britta touched her arm and broke the spell. "Dear, join us, please."

Astria peered at the snow at his feet, then raised her head under the cowl. "You were there at the Tops," she whispered.

He nodded. "I am Nogrexx."

She opened her mouth, but words did not come. *Where's my courage? Must I sit here like a child and cower in his presence?*

In answer, the Valkyr appeared by her side and put her hand on Astria's shoulder.

"Where's your dragon, Rider?" he asked.

Zephyr's cries clawed at her heart. "I'm not a Rider."

"Then what are you?"

"Something else."

Save your grief, girl, the Valkyr said. *They respect strength. Give him nothing but scorn.*

Nogrexx sat on a log and faced her at eye level. "And your dragon?"

"He grows fat feeding on your dead comrades," Astria said and raised a hand to silence Britta.

The warrior leaned forward, and the archer nocked an arrow.

"I see your ear refuses to heal," she said of his torn ear. "But then, your woman won't notice in the dark."

His lip twitched and his eyes narrowed. "Your archer can't protect you," he whispered. "If I wish, I can kill you before he raises his bow."

Astria rotated her wrist to let the tip of a hidden dagger glimmer in the sun. "They're here to protect Britta, not me." She turned to the archer and the guards. "You swore to silence?" she asked, and they nodded. "Thank you for coming. If you please, stand at the edge of the clearing so we can talk in private."

The guards nodded again and backed away.

"You don't fear me?" he asked.

"My life means little to me," Astria replied.

He raised an eyebrow and grinned. "Then come with me now."

"And you will leave in peace and never return?"

Nogrexx raised his hands and smiled. "When you satisfy the vendetta, we have no reason to stay."

"That isn't enough. Who will protect them when I'm gone?"

"My chief is an honorable man and will keep his promise."

The dizziness came, and Astria swayed and gripped the staff.

"I see the Sulerian curse still afflicts you," he said with a smirk.

"If your chief breaks his word, do we risk the circle again? I need a vow that when my dragon and I aren't here to defend the valley, you will leave and not return."

He leaned back and squinted. "Suicide won't protect your village."

"I had not considered it," she said and turned away.

"If anyone helps you escape, the agreement is broken, and his revenge will be swift. I need your promise to meet the challenge or surrender to—"

She spun back on him, and her voice firmed. "Your threats are nothing to what I face. I've met your slaves and seen how you treat them."

Nogrexx straightened his back. "How do you know this?"

"I was in your camp the night you killed a dragon."

"That was you?"

She nodded.

He laughed. "You are no end of trouble."

"That's what he wants, yes?" she asked. "To parade the victor as his slave?"

"Your Council has offered—"

"The Council has no role in this. I speak for myself."

Beside her, the Valkyr patted her shoulder with approval.

"Then you promise to surrender? Say it."

Astria sat straight and raised her chin. "I, Astria Sannfjaer, promise to present myself at your camp so you can enslave me. How many ways can I say that? Agreed?"

Britta put her hand over her mouth.

"Elder Britta is my witness," Astria said. "Are we agreed?"

Nogrexx nodded. "Agreed."

"And you will release the family you hold hostage and never threaten travelers again?"

"We will release them when you present yourself."

"I was told your chief offered them as a gift, not a trade. You mean to deceive us."

He scowled and stood. "Yes, yes, they're a gift. We are done. Come with me now."

He held out his hand, and across the lifeline on his palm appeared a white scar within a purple stain, a wound like that on her thigh.

She took his hand and held it but did not rise. Instead, she pulled him closer and peered into his eyes.

"You have a potion for the curse," she said.

He turned away and gritted his teeth.

"I want that cure."

"When you are his slave, he will cure you."

"Now."

He shook his head. "No. Not before. You are still his enemy."

"Another incentive for surrender?"

His eyes softened. "I know what it is to be haunted by the dead. Surely, you don't plan to continue living this way."

She dropped her gaze. "No."

Access to a cure changed her scheme. *I could walk again without stumbling and be free of these nightmares. What would I give? Or give up?*

Is that the limit of your dreams? the Valkyr asked.

But she had no time to change plans.

"I need the day for farewells," Astria said. "Tomorrow, after the sun leaves the Tops, and I see the hostages safe within the valley, only then will I present myself to him."

"No," Nogrexx said. "I will only release the hosta . . . the gifts after you present yourself."

Astria rubbed her thigh, dropped her gaze, and sighed. Then she crossed her arms and pursed her lips. After a few moments, she waved the archer over, and from his quiver, removed the whistling arrow and held it out to Nogrexx.

"Have your chief shoot this arrow toward the pass when they have me secured in your camp. When you hear the whistle, you can release the hostages. We will have no part in that, and you will control both sides of the exchange."

Nogrexx squinted and studied her. Then he took the arrow and nodded. "Tomorrow at dusk, then. And be sure to bring the ring, or we will have to come get it," he said and took a step to leave.

Not yet! the Valkyr said and gripped Astria's shoulder, but a spell of dizziness came before she could stop Nogrexx.

After a quick glance at Astria, Britta took his arm. "How do your people record such a promise?"

He scowled. "With a token."

"We'll need such a token."

"I'll have to get one from my chief."

Astria smiled. "Did you not expect to keep this promise?"

The barbarian sneered. "We are honorable men, and—"

"Honorable men who enslave children and keep them chained in pigpens. Spare me such hollow words."

He scowled, reached into a pouch, and retrieved a small wooden carving of a grax. "This is my family's honor and commits them to uphold this agreement."

Astria held out her hand. "I accept. For them."

He sneered and closed his fist around the token. "I will exchange this with the gifts *after* I hear my chief confirm your surrender." Instead of the token, he gave her half of a hawk feather. "We will come tomorrow."

Britta tried to speak, but again Astria silenced her with a glare.

Nogrexx smirked. "When my dead comrades visit your dreams, give them my regards," he said and left with the guards.

Astria's hand shook as Nogrexx disappeared over the ridge, and she turned to Britta. "Tell no one else of our agreement until the hostages are safe. Say only that

Nogrexx has accepted food as a tribute. If you speak a word of this conversation to anyone, we will all die. Understand?"

The Farmer nodded and bowed. "You have given us another gift."

Astria stood and leaned on her staff with both hands. "This is not for you or the Council. When this is done, tell them I am not an object to pity or a flower to protect. This is my gift because of who I am, not what you want me to be. I earned my freedom, and it's not for you to give or take.

"And tell the Farmers I saw the Darkness you fear up close. It came to me first, and it's not about the Speaker or the dragons. You have nothing to fear from the dragons. They watch with pity as we slaughter each other. And the Speaker can do no worse than we do to one another."

"The barbarians who—"

Astria shook her head. "*You* brought the Darkness long before the barbarians came, and you used it against a child. Me."

Britta winced, then backed up and turned away. And when she left the grove, Astria collapsed.

When the moons were high, Astria packed as much bread and dried meat as she could carry. Beside it, she added a parchment sack of her diet of fresh fruits and vegetables. Then she wrapped it along with her weapons, snowshoes, twine, and supplies in the mottled white-and-brown fur coat and leggings she had made while Rogue. By the secret passage to the Wild, she buried the bundle in the snow and returned to the field hospital.

The next afternoon, as shadows crawled up the Tops, Astria hid with the Valkyr behind sheets of falling water in the undercut exit of the secret way. A few feet on the other side, barbarians led the hostages to the Invernell gate.

After they passed, she climbed high up the ridge with a clear view of both the barbarian camp and the entrance gate. The Qu would take hours to find her here, and by then, it would be dark.

In the camp below is the cure for my crippling illness, and all I need to do is walk down there. My agony will be over, and the dead will no longer haunt me. But cured or not, I could never leave, and if Zephyr still lives, he would languish and die.

The barbarians stopped at the gate waiting for the signal of Astria's surrender. But instead of a whistling arrow from their camp, Astria shot the copy she had made.

Thinking it was from Chief Senekx, Nogrexx turned over the hostages to the Invernell guards and gave his token to Britta. After the Invernell gate closed, Astria waved her arms and shouted to the Quarajii warriors in the camp.

"I am Astria Sannfjaer, presenting myself to Chief Senekx!"

From a large tent, Chief Senekx appeared and joined the archer with the signal arrow. Her legs trembled as she stared at the monster.

Courage, the Valkyr said at her side.

"Come, Chief. Tame me if you dare!"

She could not run, and with her heavy kit, fell on her first step. But the way was west.

This was her world: the Wild, the world of the Rogue, without the Council, without fear or regret.

Free again but marked by vendetta and pursued by warriors.

Free again to walk amid the thousands who died in my wake.

"The barbarians will follow you," Urquil had said.

Both the living and the dead.

"This is my world," she declared. "If they follow, they will die."

Chapter 22
Exile

Through that night and the next day, she walked, dragging branches to sweep her trail of tracks through melting snow and mud. With each sound, her muscles tensed at the memory of threats that lurked behind every tree and within every shadow.

There was no trail to the Source, only west and higher. But it mattered not; Zephyr's destination would be her journey's end, regardless of where it was or how long it took.

The Source is the dragons' sanctuary, and it will be mine. But will they let me in?

The dragons that once filled her life had deserted her, unable to lead her or protect her. Like the wind and the sky, they had always been within a touch, within a glance. But now they were gone.

She had no time to hunt, but at the right shape of a leaf or a flower, she stopped to dig up an edible root or a tuber and took care to fill and cover the hole. She ate while she walked, slowing when hallucinations or dizziness beset her. Only in the morning of the second day, after leaving her trackers far behind, did she dare cook over a fire and sleep, knowing the midday sun would slice through the trees to wake her.

At sunset, she climbed a ridge, turned back east, and sat on her haunches. As she munched a wild carrot, she squinted into the distance to see smoke filtering through the trees. At their rate of pursuit, they would catch her before she reached the glaciers where her snow gear would camouflage her.

Doubling back east, Astria headed for the campfire that winked between the trees. And along her path, the forest woke with the hoots of owls and the chirps of graxes that stalked her.

Sniffing the sharp tang of grax spoor, she held her nose, spread it on her boots and pants, and crept within sight of the camp. There, a score of warriors sat eating dinner around the fire, unconcerned with the graxes or the attention their dinner might bring. And one was Nogrexx.

Unseen, Astria set bits of her food at the edges of the camp. She left more food as she backed away but paused at a chirp from behind her; the carnivores circled her instead of the camp. In one move, she grabbed her food, dropped the pack, and climbed a tree above where the graxes could jump. As they snapped at her, she dropped bits of food until they fought for the tiniest scraps.

Once the hungry graxes had gathered, Astria threw the food toward the Qu. Then she put food on an arrow, let the graxes smell it, and shot it toward the edge of the camp. The graxes raced for it, and when they reached the camp edges, they fought over the bits she had left earlier. They smelled the camp now and aimed their attention to the meat on the spit.

The Qu jumped to defend themselves as forty graxes rushed for the spit and anything edible in range of their teeth. But the little beasts were faster than the sword strokes and dragged one screaming Qu from his bedroll, his neck gushing blood. Others snapped at ankles as they dragged packs away into the night.

One grax dragged a stolen pack under the tree where Astria hid, and she froze. A Qu arrow found the grax that dropped the pack and limped away into the dark. But the Qu did not retrieve the pack.

When the warriors retreated to their camp and the night sounds of owl and racoon returned, Astria descended. She searched the pack to find a week's rations of hardtack, jerky, and smoked fish, along with a rope and battleaxe. Closing the pack, she checked the stars and headed west again to the glacier where the Qu would not risk following.

On her way, she set a false trail, leaving tracks and broken branches for the Qu to find.

The next day, the stenifer and pine thinned, leaving deeper snow to melt in the sun. From her pack, she mixed a sunscreen from beeswax, balm, and tree resins, and applied it to her face. Over them, she added the goggles.

She tossed away the branches that had swept her trail and replaced them with her cloak dragging from her waist. On her boots, she tied the snowshoes to keep her on the surface of the snow. As dinnertime came, she skipped her diet and snacked from the Quarajii pack.

At sunset, a cracking and thumping reached her from the glaciers ahead. With each step it grew louder, as if the earth were splitting apart and falling away into the night. And near dawn when she slept, the Worm of the World filled her dreams as it gnawed the land and swallowed her whole.

A crash woke Astria at noon, and an hour's trek later, she came to the Pinnacles, the hundred-foot-tall spires of blue ice that split from the glacier foot. Too dangerous to navigate, she headed up the snow-covered slope to the mountains that constrained the glacier flow.

Just before sunset, Astria noticed shapes at the Pinnacles and narrowed her eyes: the graxes had not stopped Nogrexx. Trekking the mountains would be too dangerous at night, and they would close more of the gap if she did not slow them.

When she passed a hollow in the slope with an icy rock wall to reflect a fire's heat and a snow-covered ridge to protect it from the wind, she stopped. *This will be his campsite.*

After setting a false trail forward, she left her pack and staff, and climbed the ridge to wait.

As the sun set, Astria peered over the ridge where Nogrexx and his men set up camp in the hollow and set game to roast on a spit.

They've time to hunt, but their food won't last long at this rate. They must expect to catch me soon.

Nogrexx and a half dozen men and women sat at the fire, and another half dozen slept behind them. Three at the fire had bandages on their arms or legs, and two others had kerchiefs tied around their eyes.

Snowblind and useless. Like I would be without goggles.

Safe on her perch, she rolled two large snowballs until they were half her height and pushed them near the edge. Then she kneeled to slow her breathing and calm her pounding heart.

Out of view from the firelight below, she shouted, "You should give up!"

"Is that you, Rider? We are honor-bound to retrieve you," Nogrexx said and signaled his men to pursue her. "Alive or dead."

"I'm not a Rider. Has he left my village alone?"

Other men took their bows and aimed arrows at the ridge. They could not see her, their eyes accustomed to the bright firelight. But she could see them.

"Yes, the token protects them."

Without ice axes and special gear, they could not scale the ice wall and ran to the sides to find her path above.

"Your warriors are injured," she said. "It would be wise to treat their wounds back at camp rather than drag them further into danger."

He turned and sneered as grumbles rose from the bandaged warriors. "That was clever of you to bait the graxes," he said.

"They are part of the Wild like me."

She felt a hand on her shoulder as the Valkyr kneeled at her side.

Nogrexx opened his arms to the open snow field. "What's your plan, woman? You can't defeat us and have nowhere to run."

"And you have nowhere to hide."

"We don't need to hide. All I see is ice and snow."

"Then you are blind."

He put his hands on his hips. "You hold the high ground and have us at a disadvantage. Why don't you shoot me?" he asked, arms wide, unafraid.

"I don't have to. The spirits of the Spine will kill you."

She was talking to his men, not him, and they grumbled, uneasy with her invocation of the supernatural.

"You are the enemy here, not the mountains," Nogrexx said, staring straight at her.

Can he see the Valkyr, too?

"Your death is not my goal," she said. "I have another mission, and your pursuit slows me. I only mean to help you avoid disaster and death. You know you can't succeed."

"And why not? You lead the way over open ground and are easy to follow. And you can't outrun the curse."

"My goal is to survive, but yours is to capture me and return my body."

He laughed. "There are more of us, and we are stronger."

"The Wild does not care about such things."

"We will conquer the Spine like we will conquer your people."

"You cannot conquer the Wild. You must become it."

"Ha! The curse speaks through you now."

He's right.

Nogrexx whistled, and a moment later, whistles replied from her left and right. *They're near.*

The Valkyr put a hand on her shoulder. *Steady, now.*

"This is my last warning," Astria said. "Leave, or you will not escape."

"You don't speak for the mountains. We will follow until you are ours."

Every moment she stayed in conversation, his men got closer to finding her, but she was ready.

"Then you will die."

She pushed one snowball over the ridge onto a sleeping warrior and grabbed her bow. Her targets were well lit by the fire, and she let fly. But hidden in the shadow of the ledge, their arrows missed her.

Hearing the crunch of feet on snow, she pushed the other snowball off the edge to douse the fire and then jumped off into the snow, grabbed a pack, and trudged away.

With their eyes accustomed to the bright firelight, Astria was hidden by the night, and their arrows whizzed past. One ran after her but fell into a snowdrift, and without snowshoes, the warriors could not catch her.

***

The next afternoon, Astria squinted through the glare back along her trail to a mirage of dark shapes that wavered on the eastern horizon. She shook her head and pursed her lips.

Nogrexx persists. They haven't heeded my warnings, and I can't win a fight.

Her path ahead had no place to hide in the featureless white expanse, no place to set a false trail. Then she gazed north across the desolate glacier she judged too dangerous to traverse and gritted her teeth.

Unlike at the foot of the glacier, this was not the impassable field of shattered ice like broken glass, but an unbroken, chalk-white field, dusted with snow that drifted across it in waves. Beneath the snow lay crevasses and mills, traps for anyone who dared to cross. But if she did not know where the dangers lay, at least she knew they existed.

It will be more dangerous for them.

Conserving her food and diet, she skipped dinner and headed on to the glacier.

The long shadows of the afternoon sun amplified the glacier's contours as her staff tested the surface along her path. After the sun set, the three moons emerged and carried the faces of her loved ones across the sky to remind her of her part in their deaths. Brother Moon, Fures, rose first and bore Fynn's face, still an angry red, and the rumbling of the glacier spoke for him. Following him, Sister Moon appeared with Yana's unhappy face, lonely for Jenks. Mother Moon, Lon, rose last with Skye's gentle smile, bathing the glacier in a soft glow.

When the moons set, the stars blazed. The constellation Nidhogg flew through the heavens and condensed into Zephyr dragging her parents' stars behind him. She reached for her wishing star, and once she touched it, the stars fell from the sky as snow.

On her next step, her staff sunk deep, and she tightened her grip before it disappeared in the dark. She backed up, carefully stepping into her snowshoe prints.

The far edge of the ice field appeared in the stars as shadows of the surrounding peaks: too far to go and too dangerous at night. She slept there in the open, but every moment she delayed, the Qu narrowed her lead.

At dawn the next morning, she surveyed the wide crack in the glacier. Where she had stopped the night before, eves of melting snow collapsed with the familiar thump, exposing the translucent aquamarine walls of a crevasse. From the bottom came the rush of melt water undercutting the glaciers, which miles to the east fed the Blois River.

A hundred feet deep with sheer ice walls, she could never escape without help, ropes, and special gear. If she survived the fall, she would freeze to death. Every crevasse was a death trap, and between her and freedom lay scores more. This wasn't escape; it was a killing field.

To the east, five brown dots quivered below the rising sun, close enough to catch her before she could find an alternate route: Nogrexx again.

Probing the snow with her staff before each step, she walked parallel to the crack, found the end, and turned west. At the next crevasse, she looked back. Knowing her route, the Qu did not need to test the surface and closed the gap. But she could not quicken her pace, and like a horse in a burning barn, she could not do what she wanted most—to run.

With blood pounding in her ears, she tested each step along the cut.

At a narrow ice bridge, an arrow fell by her side. She was in range and had no choice now: it was capture or the crevasse, but only one offered freedom, and she headed for the bridge.

Halfway across, where the ice was thinnest, an arrow hit her shoulder and spun her. She fell face down in the snow, and her goggles fell over the edge. Holding her staff close, the bridge vibrated and crackled.

Hoping to spread her weight over a wider base, she crawled as more arrows fell around her. Across the bridge, on the other side of the crevasse, she rose and quickened her pace.

Three hundred yards past, a crack and a thump came from behind her, followed by panicked yells, and she spun.

Nogrexx and the Qu warriors had disappeared.

She walked back to the crevasse and peered over the edge. Only three warriors remained huddled on a ledge, Nogrexx among them.

"I warned you," Astria said. "The spirits of the Spine have punished you for your arrogance."

"I am bound by my honor," Nogrexx said.

"Your honor will kill you."

"Curse you, Rider!"

"Not here. I am blessed by the Wild. You are not. The world and your family will hear from you no more. No one will know of your bravery on the Tops against the dragons. No one will hear of your trek across this treacherous land to pursue me for 'your honor.' Your legend will be lost like a snowflake in spring."

"Have you no mercy that you leave men to die, Rider!" he shouted.

"I'm not a Rider," she said, turning away from their curses.

Dumping the Qu pack on the snow, she transferred the rations to her pack. With the battleaxe, she chopped a slot in the ice two feet deep and parallel to the crevasse. She stuck the head of the axe into it and tied one end of the rope to the handle. Then she went to the edge of the fissure.

"Remember me," she said and threw the rope over the edge.

Turning back west, she squinted into the sun reflecting from the glacier, testing the snow in front of her with her staff.

The battle fever ebbed a half-mile from the bridge, and the pain in her shoulder throbbed. With the Qu out of sight, she stopped and removed her coat to find her shirt sleeve soaked with blood and the broken tip of the crossbow bolt that had knocked her down.

After removing her shirt, she washed the wound with snow, applied Philina's balm and a bandage, and dressed again. From her pack, she took a strap of leather, cut two small slits in it, and tied it around her head to replace the lost goggles. Deciding the ice was too dangerous, she made her way to the north peaks that bounded the glacier as the sun set.

That night, she finished the rest of the Qu rations and prepared to eat her diet. But there would not be enough for Zephyr if she reached him, and she returned it to her pack. Exhausted, she slept.

The next morning, the fog on her senses returned, and with it, the hallucinations in which Lance walked beside her and Zephyr soared above the crest of the next peak. But when she turned, those she loved dissolved into a drift of snow or a flicker of sunlight. The specters were wishes but knowing did not help to dispel them.

Joining them were the spirits of her enemies who surrounded her and smothered her. Unable to see her path, she collapsed to her knees.

"Begone!" she said and waved her hands. "And worry me no more. Haunt those who care for you and will listen to your moans and gripes, for I tire of you. Plague your own house. You chose this war, and I care not for your motive."

And with a last wave of her hand, she fell forward and slept.

Dreams and delusions blended in her sleep. In one, after the battlefield, she rode the dream dragon, soaring in the clouds and watching the sunsets. She gripped the reins but wanted to stretch out her arms as she had as a child.

"Let go," Lance said, but she did not trust the dragon.

She could not see what she rode, unable to confront something terrible. She could not stop, could not land, and could not look down. And when she tried to see its face, she could not, for in its eyes were the horrors of the battlefields where Lance and everyone she loved had died.

Long hours became endless days as Astria followed the setting sun west. In the quiet dawn before the sun woke the winds, she walked across the heavens, where cloud tops broke against the mountain ridge just below her feet. There, she walked on top of the blanket of white that stretched to the far horizon in all directions, all the way to heaven. One step off her path, though, and she would fall thousands of feet to her death.

The finch nests held no eggs, and her arrows lost trying to fell the rare bird. And as her food ran low, she ate less and less, and the delirium increased.

She hiked in drifting snow past crystal palaces whose spires pierced the clouds and crossed translucent bridges that spanned the glacier valleys.

Past the palaces, a frozen waterfall held men captive in blood-stained ice, some fallen with spears in their chests and others grappling with knives—an echo of her vision as a child.

One of them moved, a frightful beast that mimicked her. Covered in tattered fur, it was her size, with sunken cheeks below dark hollows. It grew larger as she approached until blue eyes shaped like hers shone clear.

That night, a blizzard struck and hid the sun, the moons, and the stars. Without them, Astria lost her sense of direction but did not stop for fear of freezing to death. Every muscle ached, every wound hurt, and the dead taunted her every step.

Stumbling through the snow for hours, with every tiny flake stinging her cheeks, she faltered. Exhausted and dizzy, she fell to her knees.

Her quest had failed.

As she wiped away the tears that froze on her cheeks, a warm hand took hers. She raised her eyes to Lance's face. Cupping her cheek in his palm, he kneeled beside her and embraced her.

"Nearly there, darling," he said.

Astria gazed into his eyes. "You said no barbarian could keep us apart."

"I am here now."

With a sigh, she leaned her head on his shoulder. "Don't leave me," she said, squeezing his hand. "Don't leave me, ever. You and Zephyr—stay. I don't want you to go. I don't care if you are a dream. You're all I have."

"I will always be with you." Keeping her hand, he rose and helped her to her feet. "Come. Not far now," he said, and she followed him through the storm.

When the snowfall ebbed, the dark outlines of barbarians approached. But as soon as they appeared, the phantasms vanished into the drifts. Still, she held Lance's hand and followed.

He led her back to Invernell engulfed in flame, where hundreds of years of exquisite craftworks burned even during the blizzard. And she gripped his hand tighter and followed.

Beyond her village lay a field where snow flurries muffled the sounds of battle and the cries of the wounded. In the center, Zephyr lay with Richard, his cavalry lying dead next to him.

Past the carnage, Lance found shelter for them within an ice palace whose walls glittered with its own light. Inside, the winds calmed, and a gentle snow drifted through gaps in the vaulted ceiling. At its center, the high dome pierced the clouds and gave her a sight of the stars. Around her shone fantastical constructions that could only be a dream.

Through the clear walls to the left, Astria viewed a field of open grasses and lakes even more beautiful than her home.

Heaven.

There lies Folkshome and Fairma's hall, Evanfall, where the virtuous rejoice for eternity.

Through a wall on the other side lay the high mountains and halls of Kriegheim where Olim ruled.

And here, Astria wanted only to rest in wonder and sleep while awaiting her judgment.

A blinding light beamed through the hole in the ceiling, and from within the light stepped the Valkyr. Astria kneeled before the goddess as the light burned away the guilt and regret and obligation.

"Take me," Astria said. "My life is spent, and I have nothing left."

"Your life has just begun," the Valkyr said and vanished with the light.

"That's not for you," Lance said and pulled her to her feet. "This way. Only a little farther."

Outside the shelter, the tempest peaked in fury again. Lance's hand slipped from hers, and she stared at her empty palm, knowing he was gone as well. Behind her, the crystal palaces disappeared, and her visions faded to white and gray in the blizzard.

Longing for his touch again, she kept walking until she stepped through a snow cornice. The cornice collapsed and followed her down the mountainside, tumbling and rolling until she stopped.

That night in her dreams, a small and colorful dragon came to her in a field of green and nuzzled her neck.

Aeterna? she thought and smiled.

Chapter 23
Songs to the Dead

A bright sun and a whiff of daemonberries woke Astria, and she opened her eyes to wisps of clouds drifting in a blue sky. Four-winged wheezits chittered their annoyance as she rose from a sea of green leaves stretching to the mountains on all sides. But for her growling stomach and aching muscles, this might be heaven.

Above the valley rim, the storm raged and hid everything beyond, making the ice palaces of the night before just another mirage. Below her steamed a field of hot springs that obscured much of the lower valley. From its center, lost in mist from the pools, loomed a volcano with a peak hidden in the clouds. Around the caldera circled dots she guessed were dragons soaring in the thermals.

At her feet, a rustle of leaves brought her attention to a pair of opalescent eyes glittering among the berries. When she rose, it disappeared and scurried through the field with only a colorful tail slicing through the bushes.

Astria followed through the field and tracked the occasional flash of color or blink of an eye behind a rock. Beyond the curve of the caldera, it led her to a field of black sand that steamed from the hot springs. Within lay rib bones of beasts taller than the Manor

House. Old and brittle, they turned to dust at her touch and disappeared into the mist surrounding them.

A shadow resolved in the fog, and she smiled at the first sight of a dragon in months. But her smile fell when he drew closer: it was not her Zephyr, and this was not Kriegheim.

An old dragon she had met a lifetime ago examined her semaphores and snuffed in her face. It was Vandrare, the dragon who had saved her from drowning; the same dragon who had led her and Zephyr to the barbarian camp with the captive Turmordare.

But he wasn't Zephyr.

Then why did I come? What is left for me? And what can I do here?

Whistling the way Zephyr once did, Vandrare led her out of the mist to the hot springs. He nudged her to stop, and with a paw, diverted a stream of snow melt from the valley rim into a shallow pit in the rocks. He lapped it up, diverted more, and peered at her.

As she leaned over to drink, the wrist and hand of an old woman appeared from her sleeve. Bony knuckles and pale skin blotched with red hung from her wrists, proof of the hunger she suppressed as part of her delusions. Dizziness beset her again, and she sat by the spring with her arms around her knees.

When the wooziness left, Vandrare was gone. In the pool, a familiar face with mottled brown-and-green fur and opalescent eyes appeared. *Another dream, but a welcome one.*

But she pursed her lips. The apparition had holes in his wings and purple scars like those on her leg, and she winced at the pain those wounds caused and her part in creating them.

The vision snuffed, and when the image in the pool wavered, she raised her head.

Zephyr.

She ran to hug him, and he trembled when she put her palm on his cheek. His pain was hers again, and she groaned. But when he hummed, her agony dissolved.

Images of their time together came with his feelings: of his happiness at their first meeting and the joy of their first ride together. A scene came of her and Lance and the rush of joy in Zephyr's heart to match hers. In his song came his panic for her at the Tops when he screeched to make himself the target. He echoed her suffering at his pain in the peach grove, and she realized the dragons had flown him to the Source to ease her suffering, not his.

The visions ended, and his eyes sparkled.

"I'm sorry," she said, still believing Zephyr would be healthy if he had not fought by her side at the Tops.

From her pack, she removed the parchment sack with the remains of the diet she carried all the way from Invernell to help him as it had helped her. But when she opened it, the putrid smell of rotting food made her gag, and she backed away. As she stared at her latest failure, her hope to end his suffering died.

"I have nothing for you," she said and stared at her empty hands and then at him.

He came to her and sat beside her with his nose under her arm. She hugged him, and her tears wet his fur.

Vandrare came, wrinkled his nose at the rotting pile of her diet, honked, and flew away with a dozen other dragons.

As she watched the dragons disappear over the rim, she leaned into Zephyr.

In the late afternoon, when Zephyr drifted off to sleep, she took off her coat and shirt. Untreated, the shoulder wound had turned an angry red and painful to the touch but not purple, and it would heal. She washed the wound, applied the last of Philina's salve, and bandaged it with fresh cloth. Then she lay next to Zephyr.

"Maybe Angelica was right, that it was your choice to fight in that last battle. But it wasn't that simple for me. You were the means to everything I wanted. You were the way to fulfill my purpose to the valley and the dragons. And to see Lance.

"We're free now, whether we ride or not—free from their control, free of the past, free to make our own future.

"But what will that future be with both of us crippled? How will we fare, unable to fly together? I can't stay: there's no food for me here. But can I make it out of the Spine without my diet?" She frowned. "Should I even try?"

She put her chin on his nose, smiled, and looked into his eyes. "Shall we spend our last days together, partner?"

Vandrare returned, and at her feet, dropped fresh fruits and vegetables from his claws. She offered some to Zephyr and then ate some herself. A few minutes later, other dragons came with raw fish, edible flowers, and herbs that matched her diet. After her first bite, they squawked and hopped from foot to foot. With a nod, she thanked them and ate with Zephyr by her side. And from the fog came another wounded dragon with purplish wounds like hers, who ate with them.

As they ate, she looked to Vandrare. "Did I keep my promise?"

He did not answer, but she knew instantly that was wrong. Like Angelica had said, her life was not over. Her promise was a responsibility, not a task.

And with that realization, the Oracle's story came to her. The Darkness that plagued her since the first time she had expressed her desire to ride. That dark world ended, and the dragons had brought back the light.

The grueling trek had depleted her body of excess fat, the reservoir for the Quarajii scourge, and the fresh food suppressed the rest. For the first time in months, Astria's hallucinations vanished, and her first clear thought was to honor those who had passed.

From the springs, Astria carried cobblestones to a ridge with a view of the valley and the sunset. Zephyr and the dragons mimicked her, and using the stones they brought, she built a cairn in memory of Lance. And with the wildflowers the dragons brought, she wove a betrothal wreath and laid it there.

As she worked, memories came of the party when they had first met and the barn where they sheltered from the rain—the day she fell in love. She crossed her heart in the sign of an arrow, and when she spoke, the dragons gathered.

"We'd be married now. And in the foothills of the Spine near Derryh, you would have built the house where we'd raise our children. I would hunt with Zephyr while you farm." She closed her eyes and held the ring on her necklace. "Our children would grow strong there. I would teach them the stars and the seasons, and you would teach them to farm."

Lance's voice came to her: *Let go*.

She struggled to forget Skye's opposition, that Lance led a dangerous life and would break her heart. She was certain her mother loved her and feared he would take her far away, but still her mother did not understand— she was in love. It hurt that her mother had been right, but Astria longed to hear her voice.

Let go, he said again.

From around her neck, she took the gold ring and chain and reached over to place them on the chaplet. But she hesitated, gripping them in her hand until her knuckles blanched.

Let go.

"No," she said aloud and wept. "You are everything sweet and bright and safe."

Instead of the ring, Astria left a tear on the stones and returned the ring to her necklace.

Near the cairn, she laid a memorial stone for Efrin and Agnarr, and said a prayer for them. Next to it, she placed smaller stones for the Riders and dragons who had fallen at the Tops.

She turned to Zephyr. "Should I have stones for mother and my friends?" *And for us?* "No, there's hope yet," she said and closed her eyes.

For thousands of years, old dragons had come here to die. But the dead still sang when the winds blew through their sun-bleached skulls. From those voices, Astria learned the dragons' name for the Source.

She began to sing, but her voice deserted her in the thin air. When she fell to her knees, and sobbed, Zephyr whined, and the dragons bleated in distress.

With her hands open and eyes closed, she began again. With deeper breaths, a weak song came: a song she had sung to Klokbror. And for the first time in years, she sang to the dragons.

"When winds come ashore
And ships land no more,
I will wait on the Isle of Gilmora . . ."

The song took her, and she stood and turned slowly.

"My lover is he,
And waiting I'll be
For his touch while . . ."

She stood, and with her face raised to the sky and her voice to the clouds, a vision came.

In her mind's eye, a field of eggs partially buried in the volcanic sands filled the valley. Steam from the hot springs drifted across them and up the valley rim to the peaks that ringed the Source. Towering over the glacier, white clouds rose from the volcano. At the foot of it lay a field of daemonberry sprouts.

But there were no dragons.

The images were as clear as a glacial lake: the sun rising over a vast ocean and setting through layers of clouds; gliding above the glacier flows east; soaring in an open sky to follow the moons west.

The vision brought elation that dissolved into anxiety. The base of the caldera filled with unbroken eggs that one by one faded to dust, and strange thoughts came with the images.

I was alone, and now we are many.
　　Once there were eggs, and now there are none.
River of White asks Young Sun of my fate,
　　And Moon asks Old Sun if I am the last,
But Sun does not answer our questions.

These were the questions of children. *But dragons are as old as the world.*

She opened her eyes and raised her head to the sky, where dragons circled with a colorful, little dragon in the lead. And right behind her flew Zephyr and Vandrare. And like the first day that Zephyr flew, Astria swayed with his movement, arms wide, delighting in every maneuver.

When the setting sun lit the bottoms of the clouds in yellow and orange, the dragons landed, and Vandrare kneeled to invite her to ride. It was what she wanted, to fly free without care, without a past, without a future, only the now.

But she shook her head. "I'm not your person," she said and turned to Zephyr. "I'm his."

Zephyr looked at her with sparkling eyes, and her doubt and regret evaporated.

Since that first day they met, all her decisions were made to be with Zephyr. Even her love for Lance was conditioned on being with her dragon. From the first day at the river, to growing the daemonberries, to risking her life in the Wild rather than abandoning him, to her troubled future with Lance. It was all because she had chosen Zephyr.

Her dragon kneeled.

Astria's heart skipped a beat, but unwilling to burden him with her needs, she shook her head. "You're not well enough to carry me."

But the Oracle's words came to her: *We know them by their actions, for actions do not lie.*

Blood pounded in her ears as the terror of their last ride overwhelmed her. She closed her eyes and slowed her breathing to quell the pain that had burrowed deep within her.

Zephyr's cold nose slipped under her hand, and before she could stop him, Vandrare put his nose under her leg and boosted her onto Zephyr's back.

"Stop! You'll kill yourself," she said, but Zephyr did not listen.

He stumbled on the takeoff but recovered, and once aloft, Vandrare flew below him. Zephyr trembled with effort as he rose to join the flock, but his struggles eased when he found the air patterns of those that flew in the V ahead. And when he faltered, Vandrare supported him from below.

The flock circled above the warm shelter of the Source, led by the little female. As one, they soared above the clouds that stormed around the rim to find the sun again and then turned east over the glaciers of the Spine.

She smiled. *Along the River of White, like the dragons' dream.*

When the clouds blushed, a banking turn dropped them a thousand feet and west to race the sun to the horizon.

And what will I ask Old Sun when I catch him?

The pain was gone. The past was gone, and with it, the loss and regret. The open sky and her dragon were all that remained.

"This is all I ever wanted," she said as the wind dried her tears. "And you gave it to me."

No, he said with sparkling eyes. *We gave this to each other.*

Appendix

Major Characters
(In Order of Appearance)

Astria Sannfjaer
>   Rider, Singer, spy. Daughter of Skye and Jorie. From Invernell.

Jorie Sannfjaer
>   Astria's father. Dragon Rider and Explorer from Invernell.

Skye Sannfjaer
>   Astria's mother. Elder on the Invernell Council of Twelve.

Efrin Danek
>   Flight Leader and Rider from Invernell.

Yana Mirim
>   Astria's friend who is one year older.

Fynn Selcast
>   Astria's childhood friend.

Angelica (Angel)
>Blind Seer and friend of Astria from Invernell.

Katheryn Stewart (Lady Katheryn of Cherbourne, Kate)
>Wife of Richard.

Captain Lance Early
>Officer of the Army of the North.

Richard Stewart (Richard of Cherbourne)
>Field Marshal of the Army of the North.

Senekx Kurak
>Quarajii war chief and prince; leader of the Crimson Horde. Youngest son of the Governor of SeAu and War Chief from Suleria.

The Dragons and Riders

Name	Meaning	Rider
Zephyr	Gentle Breeze	Astria
Vandrare	Wanderer	wild
Agnarr	Dust	Efrin
Belastad	Burden Carrier	Huld
Getmordare	Goat Killer	La'a
Klokbror	Wise Brother	Jorie
Turmordare	Bull Slayer	wild
Omattlig	Insatiable	Fynn
Trunghanger	Loyal Follower	Yana
Daraktig	Foolish	Tegbert
Dalmogare	Patient Warrior	Telek

Krigsmanen	Warrior	Kendrick
Orkvanin	Hurricane Wind	Jenks
Lusmiddag	Bright Noon	Skye
Aeterna	Mythical Mother of dragons	
Munte	Mythical Father of dragons	

The Three Moons

Three moons orbit Juro, each with various names depending on the culture.

Lon:
> Mother Moon. The largest of Juro's three moons, with the largest orbital period. Epitomizing fertility and abundance; aids in the preservation of the world.

Elein:
> Sister Moon. Smaller than Lon but brighter, with a slightly faster orbital period. Epitomizing community and civilization.

Fures:
> Brother Moon, the Demon Moon, or the War Moon. Smallest of the three moons, with a red cast. Epitomizing courage and strength.

Special Words and Terms

Clanough: Meeting of clans from different valleys.

daemonberry: A small bushy fruit that grows best in the winter. The fruit has a flavor of liquor and thyme due to the high concentration of alcohol. The concentration increases as it gets colder.

Dorin: Feast of Dorin held at the winter solstice, a time of celebration and gift giving. The feast follows a survey of the food reserves and announcement that they have enough to last until spring,

flitterbie: A winged four-legged flier, about the size of the hand. They are very colorful and omnivorous, with a diet mainly of wheezits, jenalei, and daemonberry.

grax: A four-legged, wingless raptor about half the length of a person.

Indravay: A guided spiritual meditation for those at great crossroads in their life.

jenalei: A small white plant with a high concentration of alcohol in the sap, that thrives in the cold and winter. The open leaves catch seeds drifting past and store them in a pod of neutral fluid that preserves them. It grows everywhere but the high glaciers and the lowlands of the South and North.

Juro: The World

Nidhogg: Constellation of the dragon.

semaphores: Unique tattoos around the eyes or on the temples that mark the wearer as a dragon Rider. Sometimes laced with iridescent pigments that glow with the Rider's emotions, they help to communicate with the dragons.

stenifer: Tree with high alcohol/alcohol sap and wide branches like a fir tree. Some change colors from the usual red to yellow, orange, and green in spring through summer.

vambrace: Armor to protect the forearms and wrists; padded leather for practice with weapons.

wheezit: Winged flier with six legs and four wings, about the size of a person's little finger; they serve to pollinate the native plants.

Religion of the Mountain Peoples

Each region of Juro has a different cosmology and pantheon appropriate to their respective cultures. The clans of the Spine worship warrior gods who inspired them to escape the slavery of the Imperium and resist both the Imperator's legions from the south and the Quarajii barbarians from the north.

Pantheon of the Mountain Clans

Name   *Position in the Pantheon*

Olim
> King of the gods; god of war and protector of the vulnerable.

Fairma
> Queen of the gods; goddess of fertility and the harvest.

Yemilgan
> Fallen brother of Olim.

Kriegheim
> Heaven for the bravest warriors, ruled by Olim.

Folkshome
> Heaven for the virtuous, ruled by Fairma.

Evanfall
    Fairma's hall in Folkshome.

Valkyr
    Winged goddess who guides fallen warriors to heaven.

Nembs
    The three fates:

    Jurdi: Goddess of *what once was* (the past).

    Jerdani: Goddess of *what is coming to be* (the here and now).

    Jeluuk: Goddess of *what is yet to come* (the future).

Einerkel
    Fallen warriors who wait in Kriegheim for the Final Battle.

Ullir
    God of winter and archery.

The Worm of the World
    The Worm that devours Juro, builds its features, and turns rock into soil.

The Oracle's Cosmology

Olim and his twin brother, Yemilgan, were born of the sun (Helios) and the stars that floated free in the heavens. Elein and Fures, children of the largest moon, Lon, created more gods and goddesses who chose Fairma as their queen. The marriage of Olim and Fairma united day with night and peace with war into one whole.

To order the universe and keep a watchful eye on their children, Helios and Lon created time with the cycles of the sun, the moons, and the seasons. Because the future is a consequence of the past, they also bore the three Nembs—past, present, and future.

Olim made Juro to play on, and from it spontaneously arose The Worm of the World, whose back-plates make the Spine and the Archipelago that dives into the Ocean of Daggers. At Fairma's touch, the Worm bore the dragons, beginning with Aeterna (love) and Munte (virtue), who tamed their father. Olim has no power over the dragons, who live in a state of grace with Juro and the gods—elementals at one with the rocks and the sky, and, like them, cannot lie.

Out of jealousy of Fairma's love for Olim, Yemilgan froze the Worm and brought the Darkness that devastated Juro. But Olim exiled Yemilgan before he destroyed the dragons.

Fairma loves the dragons and sent them to lift the Darkness and tame the lands. From the fertile soil, other creatures arose, and humans last of all. Seeing how smart dragons and humans were, Fairma gave them free will so that over time, they might learn from their mistakes and live virtuous lives.

After all life was created, Aeterna and Munte lay down to die, leaving their children to prosper. Fairma will resurrect Aeterna if the Darkness returns, and Aeterna will choose her mate and birth the new generation of dragons.

Dragons live at peace with all creatures except humans, because humans strive to rule. At Yemilgan's whisperings, the Speaker arose from the humans. The Speaker lied to the dragons and used them to enslave humans and bring the Chaos. Dragons have free will, and when the Speaker set some dragons on their brothers reluctant to join him, the dragons realized what they had become and killed the Speaker and his minions. But not before human culture was devastated.

To prevent the Speaker from rising again, Fairma took from humans the ability to understand and speak to the dragons. But humans are clever, and a Speaker may rise again.

With Juro in balance, humans survived the Chaos, and after the Wandering, the Imperium was formed. Humans now prosper alongside the dragons. But the Nembs warn that the Darkness and the Chaos can return if humans forget the paths of virtue and instead heed the whisperings of Yemilgan.

About the Author

Ray Strong is an award-winning author, recognized by Writer's Digest, Global eBook Awards, and Readers' Favorite International. His latest series, The Dragons' War, will launch beginning in the spring of 2025.

Ray's love for fantasy began when he first learned to read Orphan Annie comic books—mostly to keep up with his older sister. That love deepened after discovering Andre Norton's Witch World, sparking a lifelong passion for epic storytelling.

After early publications in Chicago newspapers, Ray took a detour to earn a graduate degree in engineering, leading to a global career that exposed him to diverse cultures and perspectives. Now writing full time, he crafts immersive worlds filled with adventure, mythology, and magic.

A Note of Thanks

Thank you for reading my book. If you enjoyed it, please take a moment to post a review at your favorite retailer. And follow me to learn about the latest news and releases about the Dragons' War series.

- ☐ Friend me: <u>Facebook</u>
- ☐ Follow me: <u>Twitter/X</u>
- ☐ Subscribe: <u>Impulse Fiction</u>

Ray Strong

The Wounded Sky
(From Book Two of the Dragons' War)

Chapter 1
Sanctuary

At twilight, with three moons at full, a dragon landed in a meadow in the Provinces for the first time in a thousand years, and from his back fell a dying girl.

She opened her eyes to two rough men in brown cassocks who spoke in words she did not understand. Through fangs tinted blood-red by the war moon, her dragon snarled a warning. Ignoring the pearlescent claws that could slice them in half, the men kneeled at her side.

Her eyes closed again, and visions of snow and crystal palaces swept her away.

***

Within green fields of daemonberry, Astria inhaled the hot springs' salty tang at the birthplace of the dragons. But the hoot of an owl and a whiff of manure hinted the Source was only a dream.

Women's voices interrupted, and shadows moved past her half-opened eyes.

"She might die with it," one said.

"But she'll surely die without it," said another.

Something pinched Astria's forearm, and the dream returned, of chasing the sunset past a volcano to the edge of the world.

***

A bright sun pried Astria's eyes open, and she woke in a bed with the smell of cut grass drifting past the curtains of an open window.

Where's my dragon?

For comfort, she reached for the engagement ring on her necklace, but both were gone.

She jerked upright and groaned at the stab of a headache. When the world spun, she lay back and closed her eyes until the pain became bearable.

When the dizziness eased, she opened her eyes again to find her necklace with the silver-gray rune coin on a table beside her bed, but her ring was missing.

Thieves?

Two empty beds sat on each side of hers, and opposite them stood cabinets with tiny bottles and jars on shelves behind glass doors. On the wall hung crutches and canes.

Vandrare, where are you?

A thousand miles from safety, the three Fates had driven her into the Wild to be hunted by men and beasts. And here in the South, where she knew nothing other than what she hoped it to be, her dragon, Vandrare, was protection and escape.

Lifting the blanket, she found herself in a long linen nightshirt. Raising the hem exposed her thigh where the iridescent purple halo of a barbarian curse surrounded the white scar, and she rubbed the senseless flesh until the feeling returned.

Purple tendrils from the scar snaked toward her hip as if it lived. The same tendrils appeared on dragons cursed like Zephyr, and when they reached the heart, they died.

How long do I have left?

She rose and walked on shaky legs to the door, and found it unlocked and unguarded. At the window opposite the door, Astria put a hand on the sill to stop the world from spinning again, but frowned at the pale skin and bony knuckles emerging from her sleeve.

Vandrare, Vandrare, where are you?

Outside lay a courtyard crossed by cobbled paths with a fountain in the middle. Another building stood across the courtyard and a similar one to her right to form a *U*, leaving an open side to a field of wheat and an orchard. No threats appeared, but Vandrare was not in sight, and she needed to know if he was being hunted.

On the table under a mirror sat a basin of water, and beside it a bowl of cold broth, a spoon, and a bun. Foregoing the spoon, Astria drank the broth and pocketed the bun in her jumper. From the basin, she splashed water on her face and the tattoos at her temples. She gasped at her hollow cheeks; the world spun again, and she gripped the table until the dizziness left.

The tattoos could expose her, so she found a cream in a cabinet to cover them. Over her undershirt, she threw on a linen blouse and brown-and-white jumper that hung from a hook on the door and put on the necklace.

A bell rang and footsteps passed in the hall. Outside the window, men in brown cassocks and women in jumpers like hers hurried toward her building.

Alarm? Are they coming for me?

Astria ducked out of sight at the edge of the window and watched them. None were armed or armored, and most were in their teens. Once the bustle in the hall passed, Astria slipped out, checking each doorway and corridor for threats. Descending the stairs, she caught a whiff of cooking bacon, and her stomach growled.

A bell to announce meals. Nothing more.

But she had no time to eat or chat and weaved her way upstream through cassocks and jumpers until she was past the courtyard.

Along the path north, she stopped on a hillock and scanned the sky. There, high above her, a silhouette resolved of a hunter soaring over the warming hills, a hunter the natives would not care enough to identify. But she cared and followed the shadow to a knoll where it disappeared in the tall grass.

As she searched in all directions, the hunter glided silently overhead close enough to ruffle her hair and dove into a thicket where an animal squealed. Pushing aside the underbrush, she came across his tail, and at the sight of him, she sighed.

At six times her length, Vandrare was larger than the average dragon, with fangs the length of her forearm. Mottled blue-green hair covered most of his body except the belly that matched the sky. Retractable claws armed each of his four paws. On his back were the tatters of the makeshift saddle and reins she had made from vines and foliage. And though big enough and armed enough to kill her, she smiled.

"There you are," Astria said. "Can you . . ."

Vandrare whipped his head around, and from his jaws, blood from the guts of a wild goat splashed on her face. When she wiped the gore from her eyes, Vandrare gazed at her with crimson eyes and grimaced with exposed fangs. With a flick of his tongue, he swallowed the innards and turned back to crunch on the bones.

Astria backed away and spit out the blood that dripped into her mouth. Near him was the safest place she could imagine, and as she watched the monster with a gentle smile, the morning's tension dissolved.

She did not care that blood dripped from her chin onto her clothes. And she did not care that he had threatened her or care that she had come within a few feet of an accidental death. She did not care because he had stayed close when she was ill, and she was just so happy to see him.

"I'll come back."

At a nearby creek, Astria washed the blood from her face and jumper, though stains remained on the linen sleeves and collar. When finished, she nibbled on the bun. Vandrare found her there and lay with his head next to her hand to invite a scratch.

Astria pointed to her lips, and Vandrare licked the last drops of blood from his own. When he placed his chin on her hand, she hugged him and left a tear on his forehead. And when she scratched his bumpy brow ridge, his green eyes sparkled.

"You're safe," she said, though he could not understand her words. *My only friend so far from home.* "Thank you for bringing me."

After finishing the bun, Astria lay back against Vandrare's big shoulder and told him of the infirmary and her morning, not because she thought he would understand, but just to sit with him awhile longer.

When done, she stood and laid her hand on his shoulder. "Now let's find out who here will kill us."